D1191637

Aila's Journal

Aila's Journal

A Tale of Southern Reconstruction

Charles M. Clemmons

Copyrighted Material

Aila's Journal: A Tale of Southern Reconstruction

Copyright © 2023 by Wiltonwood Productions LLC.
All Rights Reserved.

No part of this publication may be reproduced, stored in a retrieval system
or transmitted, in any form or by any means—electronic, mechanical,
photocopying, recording, or otherwise—without prior written permission
from the publisher, except for the inclusion of brief quotations in a review.

For information about this title or to order other books and/
or electronic media, contact the publisher:

Wiltonwood Productions LLC
www.wiltonwood.com
charles@wiltonwood.com

ISBNs:
979-8-9876349-0-5 (hardcover)
979-8-9876349-1-2 (softcover)
979-8-9876349-2-9 (eBook)

Printed in the United States of America

Cover and Interior Design: 1106 Design

Dedicated to the memory of my mother and father,
Nancy Verna Smith Clemmons & Moody Myzell Clemmons,
born and raised in Brunswick County, North Carolina.

Acknowledgement also is due other family members for
the contribution of oral history and cultural documentation
that inspired much of the storyline:

Gwendolyn Clemmons Causey
John Olton Smith
Cleo Smith Ganey
Juliette Smith Gales Kline
William Agnew (A. W.) Clemmons

And for her steadfast emotional support:
Lynn Howitt Poole

Chapter 1
THE RIVER
JUNE 1864

⌐⟍

THE PATH DOWN TO THE RIVER was as black as soot. Mud squeezed between her bare toes as she chose her steps carefully, trying to avoid sharp roots hidden in the muck.

Feels like puddin' but it don't smell like it. she thought. *More like hawg turds. I bes' be quiet passin' 'em stables colored folks stay in. No tellin' what 'em bucks might be up tuh.*

The sweltering heat and humidity sweat-soaked her shirt. She could still see the setting sun on the horizon through the bramble and majestic outstretched arms of live oaks ornamented with long strands of Spanish moss. Bullfrog croaks and tree frog chirps floated from the swampy delta made by Mott's Creek.

Waves of cicada choruses echoed around her, almost covering the hum of annoying mosquitoes around her head. She heard a small human musical chorus escaping the log cabin shacks in the distance that served as marginal shelter for the small assembly of slaves:

Go down Moses,
Way down in Egypt land.
Tell ol' Pharaoh
Tuh let mah peoples go!

1

Rev'rend Campbell was up at the Sanders' house this Sunday marnin' givin' us a preachin'. Miz Ginny played the pianer an' we all sung some hymns. I like that part more than anythin' else. She plays real sweet.

Preacher Campbell spent the bes' part of the afternoon learnin' 'em darkies the Bible. He come an' puts on a service at the Sanders' house on Sunday onest a month, I reckin. Miz Ginny makes me stay an listen, but I ain't understandin' 'em stories he tells. They talked funny back in 'em Bible days. She sez I oughta love Jesus so I kin go tuh Heaven an' live with 'im furever.

I ain't never met Jesus, but from what I heared, he died a long time back. An' I'm kind-ah skeered of livin' in Heaven furever with some dead man I ain't never met before. Well, maybe he ain't dead no more, I ain't knowin'. But what's a dead man come back alive look like . . . an' smell like?

I reckin 'em coloreds won't never git tuh Heaven noways. They ain't people folk like us, so I reckin they got the same chance as Mister James' hawgs.

"'em nigras . . . er whatever they's called . . . live like animals." she whispered to herself. "No wunder they git treated bad. Worse than me. They mus' deserve it."

She carefully watched her steps to avoid roots and occasional patties and turds left by free-range cattle and hogs that roamed the woods. She missed a buried cypress knee near swampy water and stepped squarely on it.

"Ow!" she suppressed a scream under her breath. "Maybe I'll wahr some shoes next time!"

Then she noticed something bright white among the bushes beside the path. Coming closer, she could see several cup-sized white flowers. Moving some bush branches, she could see an open area with a bush-sized tree covered with several of the flowers, brightly lit by rays of the setting sun.

"Well, I'll swanny!" she exclaimed quietly. "What purdy flahers!" Drawing closer, she sniffed one of the flowers.

What a nice smell! Looks like God jes' put 'em thur an' shined his light on 'em jes' fur me! God does make a purdy world. We jes' ain't seein' it sometimes.

She picked one of the smallest blooms and put it in her hair.

The river was in sight through branches of some milkweed bushes. Beyond, she knew her fallen bald cypress tree log pew, downed by a hurricane several years back, was waiting for her. Pushing the branches aside, she stepped into another open area.

She had a clear view of the river now, its normal blackish water glimmering in the reflection of the setting sun, scattered clouds floating above illuminated into brilliant red-yellow patterns by the sun's rays. She could see the back-lit silhouettes of boats floating on the water. She recalled similar scenes of moon-lit river vessels that reminded her of the "moonlight pianer tune" Miz Ginny played.

"Glory be!" she whispered under her breath, only lightly masking her excitement. Letting out a quiet sigh, she brushed another quartet of mosquitoes away from her face and ears.

"That thur is 'bout the purdiest thang I ever did see. God ain't in Heaven. He's right here."

Then she saw it. The intruder. The silhouette of a person about her own size and shape, sitting on her cypress log. It didn't move but seemed to be looking out over the river toward the sunset. Slowly, she approached.

"Who are yuh an' what yuh doin' down here?" she shouted.

Startled, the figure turned its head toward her to reveal the face of a Black girl. The girl stood facing her but said nothing. The girl looked to be her own age, but more petite and as skinny as a rail. She realized she had seen the girl before from a distance, living in the shacks with the other slaves and working in the farm fields. But their paths had never crossed until now.

"Don't yuh know . . . they gonna wear yuh out . . . if'n they find yuh here?" she stuttered to the Black girl. "This here's mah place. Yuh ain't belongin' down here!"

"Yessum, I knows dat." drawled the Black girl. "I seen yuh down here 'fo. But dis time, I ain't knowin' yuh wuz comin'. I come here wen I kin, but I neva wanted tuh come wen yuh come."

"Why's that?"

"On account o' I knows yuh might tell dem I wuz down here, an' I ain't s'posed tuh be. An' I ain't s'posed tuh be 'round White chillens 'less udda White peoples is 'round."

"Yuh tryin' tuh run away, ain't yuh?"

"Naw, ma'am! I ain't fo' sho! I knows wat dey do tuh me if'n I did dat."

"Then why do yuh come here?"

"Same reason yuh do, I reckins. It quiet an' purdy. Let me thank by mahself fo' a time."

"But yuh know that overseer Dunbar is gonna beat yuh if'n he finds out. He ain't got no left arm, but that right arm of hissin kin do the job jes' fine."

"I knows dat. But dis place's worth a beatin' onest in a w'ile. E'tha Dunbar er Massa Sanders is gwaine beat me anyways. No matter."

The White girl continued to look at the black face, then turned toward the sunset. She thought about sitting on her favorite log to watch the sun's grand finale. But that would be unfittingly relaxed for such a tense situation. And sitting next to the Black girl would be repulsive and even scary.

"Whur'd yuh git dat dere red hair, girl?" queried the Black girl. "An' dem freckles?"

"From mah daddy, I reckin. He had 'em. He said I got 'em when he got mad at me one day an' kicked me out in the rain . . . an' I rusted!"

The slave girl could not suppress a smile.

The red-haired girl said "Sun's jes' 'bout gone. Yuh know yuh ain't s'posed tuh look right at the sun when it's up, don't yuh? Miz Ginny done told me that."

"How come Miz Ginny so worried 'bout yuh? She ain't yo' mamma, an' yuh jes' a White servant tuh her . . . ain't much diff'rent from us slaves. Ain't she gwaine tell Massa James yuh down here? An' yuh knows Massa James gwaine whup yuh if'n he knowed yuh is down here."

"Mister James is off somewhur buyin' a mule, I reckin. One of hissin died the other day. She sez I kin come here when he's gone, long as I ain't tellin' nobody but her. Miz Ginny's kind-ah nice, not much like her husband."

The Black girl frowned. "One o' deese days she gwaine git ketched doin' wat he ain't wantin' her tuh do. Den she git a whuppin' too."

They stared at each other for a moment, then returned to their gaze at the sunset.

"It 'bout gone now, 'hind dem clouds." said the slave girl. As she spoke, the sky above the clouds slowly turned red-yellow with shades of violet, and sunrays gradually emerged through breaks in the clouds.

"Sure is purdy." observed the White girl again.

The slave girl shook her head slowly in agreement. "Whur'd yuh git dat flaher in yo' hair, ma'am? It real purdy too."

"Up the path thur a piece . . . on yer right-hand side 'hind some bushes. I never seen 'em thur before. They might be hard tuh see now that the light's 'bout gone."

"I might jes' pick me one. Mamma say I's thirteen tuhday . . . an' one o' dem flahers might suit me jes' fine on mah birthday."

She's the same age as me.

"Yuh better git back up tuh yer place before the path gits too dark." said the White girl.

The slave started walking back up toward the muddy path to the shacks.

"Next time yuh come down here, that'll be all right with me." the White girl called out as the slave departed. The smile she expected to see on the girl's black face did not materialize.

Chapter 2

MIZ GINNY & AILA

JUNE 1864

THE SLAVE GIRL'S PATH BACK from the river led directly to the slave shacks. The White girl's way to the farmhouse followed a different path. It passed the hay and work animal barn, the smokehouse, the family outhouse, the roofed hand-dug well, and the vegetable and flower gardens.

Virginia watched the White girl through the kitchen window as she emerged from the woods west of the farmhouse and crossed the farmyard toward the back door.

"Aila, I need you to bring me a bucket of water for the dishes." she called out to the girl.

Guilt flashed through Aila's gut.

Lord 'ave mercy! I furgot tuh warsh 'em supper dishes before I went down tuh the river.

She went straight to the well, lowered the well bucket down into the darkness with the counterbalanced well sweep, waited for it to fill, and let it rise back up again. Unhooking the bucket from the sweep, she carried it into the kitchen and set it on the shelf next to the sink. She didn't look up at Virginia.

"Don't you know you are our servant?" demanded Virginia. "That means you *serve* us! And you know your service means washing dishes after every meal. You helped me cook supper, but that's not enough. If he was here, I'm sure Mister Sanders would be glad to use his favorite whipping strap over there on the rack."

"I know, Miz Ginny." the girl said, her voice shaking. "I . . . I'm so sorry I furgot this time. I know I'm s'posed tuh do that. I feel bad I didn't he'p yuh like I'm s'posed tuh." Putting her hands to her face, she started to shake and cry.

Miz Ginny looked at the girl and shook her head. "You can never forget when James is around . . . you understand! I don't need any of his whippings in my condition. Now stop that sobbing and get on with those dishes. I need to sit a spell." She waddled over to her rocker and eased into the pillowed seat.

"Yes ma'am. I'll git right tuh it" was Aila's firm response, wiping her eyes with her hands.

While she waited for the stove to heat up the water for dish washing, she turned to Ginny.

"An' how yuh feelin' tuhday, Miz Ginny? I noticed yuh was movin' kind-ah slow when we was eatin' supper."

It was then that they heard screaming and shouting coming from the area of Dunbar's cabin.

"See what that's all about, Aila." Ginny ordered.

Through the kitchen window, Aila could see Dunbar threatening the slave girl with the cowhide lash. He yelled at her, then pushed and drug her across the farmyard. A lump rose in Aila's throat.

"Dunbar's 'bout tuh give that slave girl a beatin' looks like." *That could've been me*, she thought.

"That's his job!" pronounced Ginny. "He's a mean man, but that's what we need to keep those darkies in line."

Aila watched as Dunbar continued to force the girl up the hill toward his cabin. She had seen enough and turned away from the window.

"That don't seem right . . . he's pushin' an' draggin' her up tuh his cabin. He a'ways whups 'em right in front of everbody tuh make a example. I 'member las' time he stripped Sally down tuh her waist, tied her hands up tuh that peach tree branch, an' whupped her good. Won't nothin' she could do but scream an' kick her feet. Ever now an' then, he'd empty his pipe embers out on her fur good measure. So she could git back tuh work sooner, he poured buckets of salt water all over her wounds."

"No need to watch that." ordered Ginny. "He'll take care of it. It's a little dark inside the house right now, girl. You'd better light that lamp over there."

Aila pulled a large splinter from the wood pile next to the stove. Opening the cookstove fire door, she started the splinter with fire from the stove and lit the coal oil lamp on the table where Ginny was sitting.

"This baby's got me down." Ginny finally answered. "It's a lot of extra weight to carry around. I'm gonna be glad when I can push her out of this tired body and get on with raising her."

"Yuh know it's a girl?"

"Bad sickness in the morning. I sure had enough of that. Me craving sweets, James getting fatter along with me . . . me carrying high. Those are all signs that it's a girl. But then the real test is the ring on a string."

"What's the rang on a strang?"

"Tie a finger ring on a string and hold it up over your belly. If it moves in a circle, it's a girl. This is a girl, all right. All the signs point that way."

When the water was warm, Aila poured it from the pot into a larger wash pan and started washing dirty dishes, rinsing them in the rinse pan and drying them with a cotton drying cloth.

Ginny watched Aila move and work. "You're becoming a strong young woman, Aila." she said. "You've gone through so much with your daddy getting killed in the war and your mamma dying of yellow fever."

Aila looked away, melancholy sweeping over her. She sensed tears forming. *I need tuh cry right now, but I gotta stay strong.*

"I know the work here's hard, and James treats you bad. But I see you care about people, and you almost always seem happy. I saw you walking back from the river around sunset with a big smile on your face."

"That river's a special place fur me." Aila sniffed and rubbed tears away. "Thur's peace an' beauty thur." Her thoughts returned to the slave girl, their meeting at the river, and the overseer whipping her.

That could've been me.

She looked at Ginny. "An' I found a big bush with the purdiest flahers on it."

"I can see that. Some folks call them Sweet Bay, but I think they're Loblolly Bay. They look a lot alike."

Aila realized she was still wearing the flower. She snatched it from her hair and put it on Ginny's table.

"You don't need to take it off, Aila. It looked nice there. But now that you've done that, why don't you put it in some water?"

"I like the name 'Sweet Bay' better." Aila declared. "That's what I'm gonna call 'em."

She got a bowl from the pantry, poured water left over from the well bucket into the bowl, and placed the flower in it.

"Miz Ginny, yuh mind if'n I ask yuh a question?" Aila said. "I a'ways wundered why yuh don't talk like us 'round here."

"Well, I talk different 'cause I was born and grew up in Pennsylvania. My parents moved to Wilmington in 1858. I was their only child. My father had a store in Wilmington where he and Mister James met. Both my parents . . . and James' wife . . . died in the 1862 yellow fever epidemic. I was twenty and all by myself in this world. Soon after that, James and me got married."

"So you lost yer daddy an' mamma too." Aila reflected. "Did Mister James have children a'ready?"

"James had two sons. They both joined the army. John was killed somewhere up in Virginia, and we don't know what happened to James Jr. He could be dead . . . the army just lost track of him."

"So Mister James had a hard life." Aila said. "Maybe not as hard as that slave girl."

"Aila, you got to be careful with that girl. She can't just be running off like that on her own. Slaves are running away all up and down that river. I reckon they think they're free now that the Yankees took New Bern and Beaufort . . . and Lincoln made that proclamation last year."

"Yuh saw her go down tuh the river?"

"I knew you two would run into each other down there. But if James or Dunbar finds her doing that, she'll get another whipping. And you too. You aren't free either, you know."

"Yessum, I knowed that."

"You're indentured to us, and you can't be running around like that. James is a good man, but he can't let you and those slaves run free. If he finds out, he'll take it out on me if I don't tell him what you're doing."

"I knowed that, Miz Ginny. He kin't know what I'm doin'. I'll be careful that Dunbar don't see me, ne'ther."

"Did you tell that girl she shouldn't be wandering off by herself like that? Why was she down there anyway?"

"Yessum, she a'ready knowed that. She likes that river too, I reckin. An' we talked a little bit . . . made me wunder . . . how mah life an' her life was kind-ah the same . . . an' diff'rent at the same time."

"You just better be careful. You know you can't treat her like a White friend."

"Yessum. Yuh know what 'em nigras is like, a'ways stealin', lyin', an' cheatin'. An' she did cheat me . . . cheated me of mah peace an' quiet by mah river! I didn't say much tuh her. They're scary, scary animals, they are."

Chapter 3

WILSON DUNBAR

JUNE 1864

———

TRYING TO AVOID DETECTION BY DUNBAR, the slave girl crept back from the river up the slight incline to the log cabin slave shacks.

"Dat White girl seem a bit uppidy tuh me." she said to herself. "I ain't her slave an' she ain't nothin' but a servant tuh dem White folks anyways. Who she reckins she is?"

The girl knew her mother and the two male slaves would be looking for her. Except for the girl's father, who had been sold away from the farm several years before, the slaves had been together as a group for about ten years, and they knew each other well.

Two years earlier the slave Nat had tried to escape but was captured in a trap set by Confederates dressed as Yankee soldiers. He was severely whipped for his attempt. Even though the other male slaves, Aron, Tootsie, and Isaiah, and the mother and daughter, Sally and Mary Jane, had made no attempt to run away, they all were whipped as a signal to forego similar attempts.

As the slave girl took the last turn of the path from the river onto the farmyard, she gasped at the sight of Dunbar approaching with a cowhide lash clutched in his right hand. She knew what was coming.

"Mary Jane! Tryin' tuh run away, ain't yuh?" yelled Dunbar.

"Naw . . . Nawsuh!" Mary Jane shouted, shaking her head in denial. "I . . . I's jes' takin' a li'l walk down by de riva, suh!"

"Yuh lyin' nigger bitch!" yelled Dunbar. "Seems yuh need some punishment! Whada yuh reckin, girl?"

"I . . . I reckins so, Massa." she stammered, resolved to her fate.

"Then git yer li'l black ass tuh mah cabin up thur!"

"Yessuh . . . yessuh! But I won' runnin' 'way, suh. I jes' went down tuh see dat riva! Yuh ain't needin' tuh whup me—I ain't neva gwaine run 'way, suh!"

"Lyin' wench!" yelled Dunbar. "Now git goin'."

Dunbar grabbed her right arm, twisted it sharply behind her back, and jerked her around toward his cabin. She moved slowly at first, but he twisted her arm again more tightly and pushed her in front of him. She stumbled, her bare feet slipping in the mud, then regained balance, only to fall again and be dragged through the mud by her arm.

Now at the cabin door, she hesitated. "Yo' whuppin' need tuh be out here whur evabody can see, don' it Massa Dunbar?"

"Not this time! Now git in thur."

Dunbar kicked open the cabin door, pushed her through the threshold onto the black hard-dirt floor, and followed her in, slamming the door behind him.

"Now git dat dress off!" he ordered. "I need tuh see better how tuh whup yuh."

She turned away, pulled her dress over her head, covered her breasts with her arms, and said nothing. He pressed his body against hers from behind and grabbed her breasts with his right hand.

"Nice li'l teaties! Seems tuh me they need some squeezin'."

She jerked her body away from him, breaking his grasp for a moment.

"Tryin' tuh git away, are yuh?"

He jerked her back to his body. "Yuh know I kin choke yuh tuh death with one hand? I done it before tuh a man a lot bigger'n yuh. I kin sure do it aghen!"

Options for escape raced through her mind. Would kneeing him in his groin give her a chance to escape? That would only arouse anger and retaliation. Screaming louder might bring the Black men to attempt rescue, but that would bring retaliation on all the slaves. She could only resign herself to her fate.

"Wat yuh gwaine do, Massa? Yuh gwaine whup me er not?" she whimpered.

"Mighty nice!" he said, massaging her buttocks. "Yeah, I'm gonna whup yuh real good!"

The other slaves had seen Mary Jane and Dunbar go into the overseer's cabin and were now gathered outside their shacks. Sally paced back and forth in front of the shack that she and Mary Jane shared.

"Wat's dat devil doin' tuh mah baby?" she cried out.

Aron and Tootsie remained quiet. They thought the worst but could not speak it.

———

Dunbar finished and rolled off the cot where he had thrown Mary Jane.

"I reckins I oughta git back tuh mah mamma." Mary Jane mumbled, sitting up and starting to pull her dress back over her head.

"Yer ain't goin' nowhur yet!" he growled. "We still got that punishment tuh take care of." He picked up the lash.

"I thought yuh jes' did mah punishment. Ain't dat wat yuh said?"

"I ain't said nothin' like that! I ain't gonna tell Sanders I whupped yuh without 'im seein' lash marks on yer back."

The other slaves could hear familiar distant and muffled sounds of whip striking flesh and groans and cries from the girl. Mary Jane suddenly burst through the cabin door and ran toward them, sobbing. She flew into her mother's embrace as blood smeared from her back onto Sally's arms.

"Wat'd dat man do tuh yuh, Baby?" was all Sally could say, her voice trembling.

Mary Jane stood shaking, trembling, whimpering, and twisting her body from side to side as she tried to speak through her sobs. "He r-robbed me of mah virgin . . . an' he b-beat me wid dat cowhide! I ain't neva feels so dirdy."

"Dat son o' bitch!" growled Nat. "We gwaine do somethin' 'bout dis. We ain't gwaine let it pass dis time! Who wid me now?"

"I ain't killin' nobody." objected Aron. "Dat's a sin aghen de Lawd."

"I ain't got no problem killin' folks wid de Devil in dem!" Isaiah proclaimed. "But dat mean we all gotta leave dis place. Whur we gwaine go?"

"At de Meetin' Place, I heared tell dem Yankees done took New Bern an' Bowfo't, makin' safe places fo' runaways." said Nat. "Runaways from all ova de place makin' a town fo' demself in James City."

Tootsie shook his head and glared at Nat. "But we ain't even knowin' how tuh git dere er how fur it is. De Home Guard's gwaine be out dere lookin' fo' us in de woods 'tween here an' dere."

"Yuh's jes' skeered." countered Nat. "Ain't yuh wantin' yo' freedom?"

"Yeah, I's skeered." agreed Tootsie. "But if'n we stay, Massa Sandas ain't gwaine kill us. He need us tuh work dis here farm."

"He gwaine whup us fo' sho, but he don' treat us like some udda massas 'round here." argued Aron. "I done heared 'bout dat man Wilkins ova yonda beatin' his slaves wid a grubbin' hoe. Out dere, dem Home Guards might hang us fo' killin' Dunbar . . . er jes' fo' de fun o' it."

"I reckins we got better luck here, if'n yuh ax me." declared Sally.

"I's stayin' right here wid Sally fo' now." said Aron.

"Dere ain't no reason fo' yuh tuh stay here wid her!" countered Isaiah. "Yuh ain't married tuh her, an' Mary Jane ain't yo' chile!"

Aron frowned. "Now Isaiah, yuh knows as well as evabody dat mah place is here wid her!"

Isaiah scanned each face in the room, save Mary Jane. "Well den, I reckins it's me an' Nat dat take care o' Dunbar an' head fo' James City."

"I's wid yuh!" concurred Nat.

"Den we's all decided now!" proclaimed Isaiah.

Chapter 4

JAMES SANDERS & THE RECKONING

JUNE 1864

JAMES SANDERS ENTERED THE DARK FARMYARD on his horse, Susie, leading a large red mule. That day he had bought the mule, named Mary, from his neighbor, Reverend Jacob Campbell. He could see faint lamp light shining through the kitchen window of his farmhouse.

"Looks like she might still be up." he said out loud.

The moon was not full, but he had enough light to see the trail leading to his barn behind the farmhouse. The barn interior was also light enough to lead Mary into her stall and close the gate. After tossing a mound of hay into the mule stall, he did the same for Susie.

Entering the farmhouse kitchen, he saw his wife seated at the table, her head bowed as if she were napping. As he closed the door behind him, she twitched slightly and opened her eyes.

"Yuh waited up fur me, Ginny." he said. "Yuh didn't have tuh do that."

"I wanted to make sure you got home all right. It's late. I was worried. Did you get that mule?"

"Mary's in the barn now. We gonna need her if'n we ever turn this farm 'round. The markets jes' 'bout dried up alltuhgether on account of this damn wah. An' after all we done, I ain't sure we gonna come out on top. An' 'em Yankees done took New Bern an' Beaufort."

Ginny shook her head. "We still got our slaves and Dunbar to help, James. Lots of farms don't have that. And we got Aila too."

James looked at his wife and smiled knowingly. "Ginny, I jes' don't know what's gonna happen. I reckin this world's gonna change an' thur ain't nothin' we kin do 'bout it."

She smiled back. "I know. Maybe we will have to change with it. We'll get through it somehow."

He gazed at the floor. "Ginny, I reckin I need tuh hear that moonlight tune 'bout now."

She rose from her chair, sat at her piano, and began to play Beethoven's "Piano Sonata No. 14, 1st Movement, Adagio Sostenuto".

He leaned back in his chair and closed his eyes, transported to a place somewhere without uncertainty, turmoil, and hardship.

She finished playing, rose from the piano, and took a seat next to James, his eyes still closed.

"Real purdy. Yuh're a blessin' in mah life, Sweetheart." he said.

She took his hand, squeezed it, and smiled again. He opened his eyes and met her gaze. A tear trail descended the left side of his face.

"We been through a lot, you an' me." he reminisced. "When I first met yuh back in '63, I weren't sure a Yankee woman would be right fur me. But yuh was purdy an' I kind-ah felt sorry fur yuh, what with yuh losin' yer mamma an' daddy with that yeller fever. But yuh been a good wife."

"And you've been a good husband, James."

"I was real sad . . . losin' mah wife in '62 an' mah sons in the wah. Yuh he'ped me find mahself aghen."

She squeezed his hand. "We both needed each other."

"Now, I'm worryin' 'bout losin' this farm. Yuh know a lot of 'em slaves 'round here's been runnin' away up tuh New Bern whur 'em Yankees is in control. Nowadays I kin't let mine roam free a bit like they use tuh."

He then noticed the flower in the bowl on the table. "Whur'd that flaher come from?"

"Aila found it out yonder in the yard while she was feeding chickens." she lied. "I reckon that slave girl was down by the river, found it, and dropped it on the way back up here."

"What? Damn that nigger!" he declared, abandoning his somber mood. "She needs a beatin' fur that! 'Em slaves know they ain't free tuh roam off like that."

"I reckon Dunbar's already taken care of that. I heard a big commotion coming from down near the slave shacks earlier. Sounded like she already got her punishment."

"I'll talk tuh Dunbar in the marnin' 'bout that. Whur's Aila now?"

"She went to bed already. I reckon she's sleeping by now."

Aila was in bed, but she was not asleep. She could clearly hear their conversation.

———

Mary Jane lay on her corn-shuck tick bed and sobbed after the distant sounds of Ginny's piano died out. Sally moved into her daughter's bed and held her tightly, trying to console her as much as she could.

"Dis de worst feelin' I's eva had." whispered Mary Jane. "All dem whuppin's ain't nothin' like dis. De Lawd ain't done let dis happen tuh make me hate, but tuh make me strong. I knows dat now."

The faint melody and quiet chord progressions of Ginny's piano resumed in the distance. The music comforted her, eased her pain and fear, strengthened her resolve.

"I ain't neva gwaine be de same aghen!"

———

Crowing roosters awoke James at 5:00 a.m. He was eager to make sure Dunbar was up to start the slaves' collection of resin from the farm's longleaf pine taps and harvest of sweet corn, green beans, peanuts, and Irish potatoes.

He would need to awaken Aila to empty chamber pots and start making breakfast for Dunbar, Ginny, and himself. Dunbar would need to rouse the slaves to make their breakfast. Later, they would meet at the appointed place to receive orders for the day. He wanted the slaves to mend the split-rail and wire fences that protected the farm's garden from his cattle and hogs that roamed the woods. Tomorrow he would carry the early harvest by mule and cart to the market in Wilmington.

As he walked toward Dunbar's cabin across the farmyard, still muddied by a pre-dawn storm, he noticed the heavily overcast, almost black sky. Another morning storm was brewing. He was surprised not to see Dunbar already outside at the slave quarters.

He pushed open the door to Dunbar's cabin and gasped. "What the hell!"

Among turned-over chairs and table lay the form of Dunbar, the cowhide lash wrapped tightly around his neck and his disemboweled entrails scattered on the dirt floor around him. Still impaled in his chest was a packhaken timber hook, the obvious tool of his mortality.

James charged straight back to the farmhouse, cursing as he went. A loud clap of thunder echoed across the landscape as he approached the kitchen steps. Bounding up the steps and entering the kitchen door, he encountered Ginny sitting at the table while Aila cooked breakfast.

"'Em black bastards done kilt Dunbar!" he screamed. "His guts is scattered all over his cabin!"

In shock, Ginny and Aila said nothing. James marched through the kitchen to the hall closet, grabbed his double-barreled muzzle-loading 12-gauge shotgun and loaded it with black powder, wadding, buckshot, and percussion caps.

"You can't kill the slaves, James!" shouted Ginny. "How you gonna run this place without them!"

James slammed the screen door behind him. A sudden intense gust of wind swept through the farmyard as a lightning bolt cracked and flashed, striking one of the huge longleaf pines next to the farmhouse. A deafening clap of thunder seemed to shake the earth. The lightning strike kindled a small fire in the stricken pine, but he wasn't concerned about that now. The sky opened, dumping torrents of rain down on him.

He sloshed toward the shacks, struggling to see his path through the sheets of rain, across the now muddy yard.

"'Em black bastards gonna pay fur this!" he yelled.

His left foot lost traction, causing his leg to twist and slip out from under him. His body crashed into the mud.

"Awhhhh!" he screamed in pain as his body hit the ground with a thud, jolting the breath from his lungs. In agony and now nausea, he let the shotgun slip from his hands as he passed out.

His eyes opened to reveal large streams of storm water rushing down the incline of the farmyard. The rain had slowed to a drizzle.

He forced his body up on one elbow, questioning whether the intense nausea and lightheadedness would allow him to stand. He rested for several minutes, then retrieved his shotgun and used it as a support to lift him to his feet.

Now completely upright, he rested for several more minutes to regain his sense of balance as his nausea subsided.

"Lord a' mighty, what jes' happened?"

Out the corner of his eye, he saw that the lightning-stricken pine flames had been extinguished. Tolerating the intense pain in his left hip, he slowly resumed his attempt to reach the shacks.

Finally, he was there. He cocked both barrels of the shotgun, then forced in the door with his right shoulder, nearly knocking it off its rusty hinges.

"Who kilt Dunbar?" he demanded to Sally and Mary Jane, pointing the shotgun directly at Sally's head. "Didn't hardly leave 'im in one piece!"

"We ain't knowin' nothin', Massa." answered Sally, trying to awake herself. "He dead?"

"Git outside tuh the yard now!" he demanded. The three of them exited the shack into the yard.

James yelled out to the other shacks: "All of yuh, git yer black asses out here now!"

Aron and Tootsie pushed their shack door open and dragged themselves into the yard.

"Which of yuh kilt Dunbar?" James shouted. "An' whur the hell is Nat an' Isaiah?"

The slaves said nothing, all staring at the shotgun.

"Ain't none of us." Aron asserted. "Yuh knows we's all God-fearin' peoples, an' we knows killin's a sin aghen de Lawd's commandments."

Another lightning strike flashed through the yard, followed by an even louder thunderclap that caused them all to lurch.

"Whur's Nat an' Isaiah?" James demanded again.

"Ain't none o' us knows, Massa." Tootsie answered. "Dey wuz here las' night. Dey gone now?"

"Yuh know goddamn well they ain't here, yuh kin bet yer lyin' black asses on that!"

The sky opened again and a wall of rain flooded down on them.

"We jes' gwaine stand here in de rain, Massa?" asked Sally.

James, now being drenched again by the downpour and still overwhelmed by pain, nausea, and lightheadedness, momentarily staggered, then corrected himself.

"Y'all kin lie all yuh want. I know what happened here. But don't yuh thank yuh're gonna git away with this. Yuh know mah rules. Any of yuh run away, 'em remainin' gits the lash. Soon as this rain stops, each one of yuh gonna git yers."

He uncocked his shotgun, turned slowly, and began limping back toward the farmhouse.

"Don't do no damn good tuh shoot 'em monkeys!" James told himself. "They ain't gonna tell me nothin'."

Ginny and Aila stood on the kitchen porchway watching him limp toward the house.

"We thought you were gonna shoot somebody out there." said Ginny. "Now come on in here, change out of your wet, muddy clothes, and get some breakfast. What did they tell you?" Then she noticed his limp. "What's that limp all about? You hurt?"

"I lost mah footin' in all that mud an' twisted mah hip somehow. I'm fine now." he lied.

"What did they tell you?" repeated Ginny.

"Nothin' . . . nothin' atall." answered James as they sat down at the breakfast table. "But Nat an' Isaiah is gone, so what's that tell yuh? I gotta git some word tuh the sheriff er the Home Guard, I ain't sure which. This here wah has confused everthang. Nobody knows who's in charge no more."

"I'm sorry we lost another two slaves, James." said Ginny. "Seems like it's one thing after another."

"Well, 'em what's left knows what mah rule is. They all git beat fur the other two runnin' away."

"But Mister James, ain't it unfair tuh punish the ones that stayed?" asked Aila. "Ain't they jes' he'pin' yuh out by stayin'?"

"Unfair?" James yelled. "That's mah goddamn rule, an' they all know it! An' ever one of 'em lied through thur teeth 'bout whur Nat an' Isaiah run tuh! Now if'n yuh don't like it, I kin jes' include you in the whuppin' with 'em!"

Aila kept quiet.

It rained hard all the rest of that day and into the night, creating flooded areas scattered around the Sanders property. It was too wet to do any farming work, or much else. The Sanders couple and Aila stayed indoors, and Ginny tutored Aila with reading and writing.

What was left of Dunbar remained on his cabin floor. One thing was clear: The body would have to be buried soon.

The rain stopped and the sun came out the next morning, making conditions for Dunbar's burial the following day seem more likely. But first, the slaves would have to be punished for the Dunbar incident. Still suffering from his hip injury, James secretly felt too weak to execute the whippings. He sent Aila to fetch Reverend Jacob

Campbell, the closest neighbor, to ask that he return with his son Gideon to administer the punishment.

Aila rode Mary to the Campbell farm, returning within an hour with the Reverend and Gideon on their horses. Aila's shyness and anxiety over the slave whippings inhibited any conversation with the Campbells, even though Gideon tried several times to converse with her. On their arrival, they could see from across the farmyard that James already had the slaves lined up for the whippings at the peach tree near the slave shacks.

"Marnin' Jacob." James said as they approached. "I thank yuh fur comin' over tuh he'p out this marnin'."

"Glad tuh he'p." replied Reverend Campbell. "Yuh know thur ain't nothin' I like more than a good slave whuppin'! I kin pass the word 'bout the killin' an' the runaways on tuh the Guard an' tuh Sheriff Davis on mah way home."

"If'n yuh kin, I'm askin' if'n yuh kin come back here tuhmara an' lead a graveside service fur Dunbar."

"I'd be glad tuh send 'im on his way tuh the Lord." agreed Campbell. "Now, let's git this here punishment done."

Aila watched as Campbell and Gideon tied each slave's hands to the peach tree, but she had to turn away as the White men struck the blows with the cowhide cat-o'-nine-tails until blood ran down the slaves' backs. The bright morning sunshine seemingly yielded to incoming clouds with each crack of the straps on black flesh. The slaves remained stoically silent, but Aila winced and silently gasped with the sound of each blow.

By the time the beatings were over, clouds had darkened the sky, the temperature had dropped sharply, and a light rain had begun to fall. The slaves temporarily crowded into Sally and Mary Jane's shack for mutual emotional support and protection from the chilling drizzle. They wondered about the fate of Nat and Isaiah and whether they would make it to New Bern, Beaufort, or James City alive.

The weather had cleared by the next morning, and as expected, Sheriff Davis arrived to investigate Dunbar's death.

"Hit's clare tuh me what went on here." confirmed the sheriff. "Dunbar was murdered by 'em niggers what run away. Yuh might as well put 'im in the ground now. I need tuh let the Home Guard an' sheriffs north of here know 'bout this. Ain't no doubt 'em runaways is headed north somewhur."

James ordered Tootsie and Aron to remove the overseer's remains from the cabin and bury him after the sheriff had surveyed the apparent murder scene. Aron volunteered to craft a makeshift loblolly pine coffin from lumber James had stored in his barn.

Sally and Mary Jane watched from their shack as Aron and Tootsie entered Dunbar's cabin and later emerged carrying the body. They saw Dunbar had been disemboweled, his body drenched with blood. Mary Jane turned away from the grisly scene and sought comfort in her mother's arms.

"Mah Lawd!" exclaimed Sally. "Dat man's fallin' apart!"

Mary Jane suddenly broke from her mother's arms and ran across the yard to the body, screaming at the top of her lungs.

"Go tuh Hell!" she yelled, spitting in the dead man's face.

Sally caught up with her daughter and embraced the girl again. "Dat all right Baby . . . dat all right. He gone now, fo' sho right tuh Hell!"

James ordered Sally and Mary Jane to clean Dunbar's cabin, the last thing either of them wanted to do. Both were terrified of entering the structure. It was not only a reminder of Mary Jane's violent and traumatic attack, but also a gory mess. And they both knew that any murdering place had to be haunted.

Aron and Tootsie wrapped Dunbar's remains in burlap and carried it to a pre-dug grave in the edge of the woods. Tootsie stayed to protect it from buzzards, crows, and any other animals, wild or domesticated, that might pass by, while Tootsie helped Aron with the coffin construction. Reverend Campbell soon arrived for the graveside service, accompanied by Gideon.

Dunbar had no known relatives, so the graveside ritual only involved a prayer by Reverend Campbell, followed by a short sermon and a closing prayer. The Sanders slaves huddled some distance away, not too close to their White superiors.

James scooped a shovel of mud from the pile and emptied it into the grave. Reverend Campbell rendered the closing prayer:

"Fur out of the ground was thou taken . . . fur dust thou art, an' out of dust shalt thou return. We pray in the name of Jesus Christ, our Lord an' Save-yer. A-men."

"A-men." James whispered.

Aron and Tootsie filled the grave with mud taken from the grave cavity. James picked up a wooden cross that he had whittled from two pieces of longleaf pine fatwood, with the name "DUNBAR" carved into the crossarm.

"This here lite'ard cross is gonna las' a long time so folks'll know that Dunbar's lyin' here under this ground 'til Judgment Day."

Reverend Campbell drove the cross into the ground a foot from where the coffin head lay. "Thus is the end of Wilson Dunbar in this world. But he shall now be taken intuh the arms of the Lord intuh life everlastin'."

As James, Ginny, and Reverend Campbell departed the gravesite, Gideon approached Aila. They knew each other from his father's Sunday services at the Sanders farmhouse. Now, Aila shunned him because of his role in his father's whippings of the Sanders' slaves.

"Nice tuh see yuh aghen, Miss Aila." greeted Gideon. "Yer lookin' mighty fine . . . as ever. It's real sad 'bout Mister Dunbar, ain't it?"

"He was a mean man!" snapped Aila. "I'm sorry tuh say I ain't gonna miss 'im atall. If'n yer daddy's right 'bout Judgment Day, that man's gonna end up whur he ain't wantin' tuh be."

"From what I heared, he was a good man tuh oversee Mister Sanders' slaves." said Gideon. "Sometimes, yuh need a hard man tuh keep 'em niggers in line."

Aila stared at the grave and said nothing.

"Yuh know I'm going tuh join up an' go down tuh Fort Fisher this week." smiled Gideon, his face brightening. "We gonna drive 'em Yankees out from New Inlet so our tradin' ships kin git in an' out of Wilmin'ton."

"Yuh're gonna git kilt . . . that's what's gonna happen."

"Naw I ain't!" Gideon declared with confidence. "Yuh know Daddy's a hero? He wants me tuh be a hero, too, an' drive 'em Yankees back up north whur they come from!"

Aila could think only of the lash-on-flesh cracks delivered by Campbell and his son on the backs of the Sanders' slaves and her anger at the slave girl's least-deserving punishment. But she held her tongue. "How come yer daddy's a hero? He ain't in the army, is he?"

"He's a officer in the Home Guard, an' they're protectin' us on the home front while the army's away fightin' 'em Yankees."

"An' what 'bout yuh brother Robert? He gonna be a hero, too?"

"Yuh ain't heared? He left home las' year an' joined up with 'em Yankees! Mah daddy done disowned 'im!"

"Joined the Yankees? How's yer mamma feel 'bout that?"

"She ain't sayin' nothin' . . . but Daddy sez he ain't gonna let her see Robert ever aghen. He's a cow'rd an' traider in Daddy's eyes."

Aila fell silent and looked away.

"Anyways, nice tuh see yuh aghen. Daddy said we're havin' a service here on the second Sunday of the month an' talk 'bout buildin' the new church house. I'll see yuh aghen then, an' we kin talk some more."

Aila did not respond and continued looking away. Gideon started to walk away, then turned slightly to wave to Aila. "Bye now."

Aila did not reply as he continued to walk away.

Chapter 5

NOBODY KNOWS BUT JESUS?

AUGUST 1864

THREE MONTHS HAD PASSED since the death of Wilson Dunbar, and much had changed on the Sanders farm. The Home Guard and several county sheriffs continued the search for the Sanders runaway slaves. The slaves had a 10-hour lead on the bloodhounds and search party, and their trail had been lost in the vicinity of Bradly Creek. Both the sheriff and the local Home Guard basically gave up and alerted officials in Pender County, north of Wilmington.

Ginny Sanders had given birth to a daughter, Sarah, named for James' deceased sister. Aila loved the new baby, and caring for her made her life seem much brighter.

The war was not going well for the Confederates. Their defeat at Gettysburg and Lincoln's Emancipation Proclamation in 1863 had marked a major turning point. No longer could they hold on to hope that European nations would support their cause. It seemed to be only a matter of time before the Yankees would be at the doorsteps of Wilmington.

The trauma of the June murder had evolved into a sad, bitter memory that Aila felt would haunt her forever. She sought more escapes to her beloved river to ease her mind. Now, though, she would ask Mister Sanders for permission—and he would give it.

Aila set out for the river one late afternoon a half-hour before sunset. The path was less muddy now, the spring rains having long since passed, but the heat, humidity, and mosquitoes were still there in full force, as were new discomforts, pesky gnats, and sand flies.

As she approached the cypress log, a familiar sight came into view—the silhouette of the slave girl sitting on the log.

"Afternoon." Aila said in greeting.

"Aftanoon, ma'am. I's hopin' yuh don' mind me bein' here. Ain't yuh skeered Massa James gwaine whup yuh butt fo' dis?"

"I got his permission. Ain't yuh skeered he's gonna whup yuh aghen?"

"Naw, ma'am, too much wadda unda de bridge now. He know I ain't runnin' away. I had mah chance back wen dat devil Dunbar wuz kilt. Anyways, I ain't leavin' mah mamma, an' she ain't goin' nowhur."

Gazing out over the glistening river surface, the slave girl grew quiet. She finally spoke.

"Yuh knows dat Preacha Campbell say Jesus love all o' us. He say Jesus want us tuh love each udda. But I ain't seein' no love from no White folks fo' no cullud folks. Dey sees us as prop'ty. Most 'o dem hates us."

Aila struggled to understand what the girl was saying. She had never really thought much about people loving each other.

The girls were quiet for some time, pondering what to say next. Aila moved to the log and sat a few feet away from the slave girl.

"I ain't knowin' nothin' 'bout niggers, 'cept they got black skin an' smell like hawgs. Live like hawgs too."

"Yuh'd live an' smell like hawgs too, if'n dey treated yuh like dey treat us . . . make us sleep on corn shucks in dem shacks, pee an' poop in de woods, warsh in dat dirdy creek, sometime scramble fo' soup an' mush from no more dan a hawg trough, git a pass tuh go anywhur off de farm . . . an' all like dat. An' us girls an' womens is jes' dem White men's play thangs. Dey kin do anythang they want tuh us, an' we kin't complain. Yuh is a White girl. Yuh ain't needin' tuh do any o' dat. Yuh git tuh sleep up yonda in dat White man's house. His dawgs git treated better'n we do."

Aila stared at the slave in silence.

"Yuh knows we done been set free by Massa Lincoln las' year. We wuz so happy 'bout dat, but den we figger out no White peoples 'round here gwaine let us go free! Onlyest way fo' us tuh git free is tuh run away. Den de White ownas got dat Home Guard an' tuh ketch us, whup us wid dat cowhide, an' brang us back. We's lucky dey ain't jes' gwaine lynch us, if'n dey take a mind tuh it!

"An' it don' he'p wen y'all calls us names like coon an' buck . . . y'all thanks we some kind-ah animal? Den dere's *nigger*. Dat make us feel y'all reckins we is lazy, stupid, worthless nobodies . . . worse dan animals."

"But Miz Ginny sez she's heared y'all call yerself 'nigger'." Aila pointed out. "An' I thought 'Nigra' was yer fam'ly name."

"Wat we calls ourself is 'tween us . . . but we ain't wantin' no White folks callin' us 'nigger'! 'Nigra' a fam'ly name? Lawd 'ave mercy! Um-um-um! Yuh stupid er somethin'? I reckins we got a fam'ly name, but I ain't knowin' wat it is. It ain't dat fo' sho. Maybe it 'Sandas' . . . like Massa James. Dat de onlyest fam'ly name I knows."

Mary Jane then realized her outburst toward the White girl would not be tolerated by Massa James if he found out about it.

"I's sorry." she stepped backward. "I ain't meanin' tuh holler at yuh like dat." she lied. "It jes' hard bein' a po' slave."

"Well, I *do* got a fam'ly name." Aila bragged. "It's MacKenzie, like mah daddy. His first name was Calum. He told me his name means 'dove' in Scotland . . . his daddy an' mamma was from Scotland, somewhur 'cross the ocean. Mamma's name was Elizabeth . . . her fam'ly was from Scotland too. They all dead now. Mah first name's 'Aila'. That's a Scotland name too . . . means 'from a strong place'. Well, I ain't strong, fur sure. I ain't got no control over nothin'!"

"Bein' strong ain't all 'bout controllin' thangs." the slave countered. "Yuh jes' kin't control a lot o' thangs. Lot o' times, it jes' grittin' yuh teeth an' pushin' fo' wat's right, wid faith an' hope.

"Mamma call me Mary Jane." the slave continued. "I reckins dat de purdiest name I knows, 'cept maybe fo' mah mamma. Her name Sally."

The girls stared together toward the sunset again after the sun had sunk below the horizon. They were quiet for several minutes.

"I ain't knowin' if'n this talkin' tuh yuh is gonna git me in trouble." Aila said. "I ain't knowin' all the rules."

She paused. "The worse part is the rules 'bout what men kin do tuh girls an' women. Sometimes, Mister James acts like he's trainin' me tuh be a brood sow, jes' fur 'im. He's rubbin' up aghen mah body ever chance he gits. If'n I say somethin' er push 'im off, he lays that cowhide strop on mah behind like nobody's business. So I let 'im."

"Yuh lucky!" said Mary Jane. "Never mind rubbin'. Dat devil Dunbar a'ready done a lot mo' dan dat tuh me. Udda times, mah mamma too! Evabody know Mamma done birth Massa James' boo dat died las' year! Dem White mens thanks dey kin use us like dere playthangs any time dey wants, an' ain't nothin' we kin do 'bout it!"

Shocked at Mary Jane's disclosures, Aila changed the subject. "We're missin' the sunset. Come on . . . let's watch."

The color-saturated sky cast its reflection on the river. Neither girl spoke for some time.

Mary Jane finally broke the silence. "How come yuh here on dis farm?"

"Yankees kilt mah daddy three years back. Up at some place they told me was Ro'noke Island. They kilt 'mose everbody in Daddy's army. Mamma went crazy when she heared 'bout it. She couldn't keep the two of us up after he was kilt. She owed everbody money 'cause Daddy was away in the wah. She owed Mister James the mose.

"So Mister James, he went tuh that judge an' said I oughta be his servant . . . indentured servant . . . on account of Mamma not payin' 'im what she owed 'im. So that judge put me here. Fur how long I ain't knowin'. Maybe from now on 'til I'm dead."

"Whur yo' mamma now?"

"She died not too long after I come here, I reckin. They told me she was dead, but I ain't knowin' when she died er whur. I don't reckin they had a funeral er nothin'. Anyways, they didn't tell me nothin' 'cept she was dead from that yeller fever."

They were quiet again.

"An' how come yuh here, Mary Jane?"

Mary Jane lowered her voice. "Well, I oughta start from de beginnin' I reckins . . . de way Mamma told me. Time wuz, some White folks went way 'cross de ocean on a big boat tuh a place called Afriky an' paid money tuh somebody tuh take mah fam'ly tuh dat place dey calls Charleston.

"Dey make us slaves an' brung us tuh dis place. Dat mean we kin't go nowhur 'cept here, an' we kin't do nothin' but work fo' de White massa an' do wat he say."

Mary Jane's story had started with a whisper, but now it took over her body as she began to tremble.

"An' maybe de worst thang, he take our daddies an' mammas away from us if'n he wants an' sell dem tuh udda White massas. He took mah daddy away 'bout three years back. We ain't knowin' whur he is er if'n he still alive."

Mary Jane dropped her head in her hands and wept. "I miss Daddy somethin' terrible."

Stunned, Aila only stared at Mary Jane. She wanted to reach out and console her in some way, but she didn't know how. She waited for Mary Jane to stop crying. Then she reached out to grasp Mary Jane's hand.

"Yuh all right?" asked Aila.

"I's all right now, I reckins." sighed Mary Jane.

"I miss mah mamma an' daddy too." admitted Aila. "Sometimes . . . I pray tuh 'em like I'm prayin' tuh the Lord. I reckin they kin hear me jes' like He can."

Mary Jane smiled. "Ain't it 'bout time fur us tuh go back up yonder?"

Aila nodded *yes* and released Mary Jane's hand.

The two girls didn't speak while they ascended the path back toward their respective homes. Mary Jane took the left fork in the path, and Aila took the right.

Aila soon reached the edge of the farmyard and paused. She could hear music coming from the slave shacks.

Sounds like Aron an' Tootsie playin' fiddle an' banjer aghen. Real slow an' sweet like. The others hummin' 'long. I reckin that makes 'em feel better.

She walked slightly closer to the shacks to hear. The humming changed to words:

> *Nobody know de troubles I seen*
> *Nobody know but Jesus*
> *Nobody know de troubles I seen*
> *Glory, hallelujah!*

Does Jesus know thur troubles like they thank? I ain't no slave, but does Jesus know mah troubles?

Dusk had settled over the landscape, and hundreds of fireflies had emerged from their hiding places to consummate their nightly rituals, silently twinkling all around her. Aila looked up into the night sky.

All 'em twinkly stars up thur look so quiet an' peaceful. Feels like I could jes' reach out an' touch 'em sometimes. Rev'rend Campbell sez that's heaven whur God lives with Jesus at his side. They sure do got a purdy house.

She watched the hundreds of sparkling fireflies around her.

All 'em lightnin' bugs is kind-ah like heaven's done come down here tuh us in this world. Is the spirit of Jesus in 'em bugs somehow? Does he care 'bout our pain an' sufferin' like the preacher sez? Does he know mose of us is at the mercy of this place whur we live . . . a place we kin't change?

"That slave girl was back down at the river this evenin'." Aila said as she entered the kitchen where Ginny was nursing baby Sarah. "She got all upset when I told her I thought 'Nigra' was her fam'ly name."

Virginia looked up to face Aila but said nothing.

"She called me stupid! I might not know everthang, but I ain't stupid!"

After a pause, Ginny finally responded: "Do you know the name of that river, Aila?"

"No ma'am. I jes' know it's purdy, 'specially at sunset like tuhday."

"They call it the 'Cape Fear River'. Does that name scare you?"

"Well, I thank they could've come up with a better name fur a purdy river like that. I ain't seein' no 'fear' in it fur sure."

"It got that name because a lot of sailors ran into sandbars and bad storms where the river meets the ocean. A lot of sailors died, and others feared to go there. But they didn't fear the river . . . they feared the sandbars and storms.

"Some White people call Negro people all kinds of hateful names. Like the river, those names don't have much to do with what the Negroes really are. But White folks like to think they're better than colored people. So they call them hateful names, put them on the bottom, and try to keep them there."

"But how come they gotta be on the bottom, Miz Ginny? Why kin't we both be tuhgether? Me an' that colored girl seem purdy much alike, 'cept she's black an' talks funny . . . an' smells bad."

"Because they were brought here as slaves to serve us. Most White people want to keep it that way. That's mostly what this war is all about. We need slaves to help work our land, so we want to keep them below us. The Yankees want us to give up our slaves."

"Seems like crazy reasons tuh kill each other." said Aila. "But what's gonna happen if'n we lose this wah, Miz Ginny?"

"Nobody knows for sure what will happen if we lose the war. The slaves likely will be freed, and we'll have to work the farm without slaves. The Yankees will force us to do it, and you can bet we won't like that one bit."

"Then the colored people ain't gonna be below us no more after that?"

"I don't know, Aila. But I think they'll stay on the bottom for a very long time after the war. White folks could still be fighting this war in other ways for a long time after it's over."

Chapter 6

LOVE THY NEIGHBOR

EARLY DECEMBER 1864

꜡

Since the death of Dunbar and the escape of two of his slaves, James had questioned his strict restrictions on the movement of his remaining slaves. He reasoned that those who remained had decided it was in their best interest not to escape and could be trusted. That trust had softened his attitude toward Aila and Mary Jane's excursions, and the two girls had increased their walks to the river.

Instead of the sticky black mud that usually covered the path to the river, ice crystals now hardened the surface and covered the surrounding wetland, adding a dreamlike quality to the landscape. It was not a frigid cold, as the Carolina coast could sometimes be, but it was cold enough for Aila to wear the buckskin winter coat Ginny had made for her—and for Mary Jane to wear two wool sweaters she had knitted herself. The crystals crunched under their shoes as they carefully negotiated the path to avoid slipping on the ice.

"I's sho glad I put on extrie clothes tuhday on account of I's f–freezin'." Mary Jane shuddered.

"Me too." agreed Aila.

In the time since the summer tragedy, they had learned more about each other and had grown to like each other's company. Both were fully aware that White society around them scorned a relationship between a Negro and a White person. That didn't seem to matter in their small corner of the world. After all, didn't Jesus say, "Love thy neighbor"? He didn't say what color their skin should be.

Arriving at their favorite spot, they assumed their usual seats on the cypress log overlooking the river.

"Dis here log's like ice." Mary Jane said, her exhaled breath condensing into little clouds of puffy water vapor. "We gwaine freeze our butts off."

"They'll wahm up a bit in a while . . . I hope!" Aila laughed, shivering. "How're yuh feeling with that baby in yer belly?"

Mary Jane rubbed her hands together and placed them on either side of her face. "If'n yuh means 'sides mah icicle butt . . . I ain't feelin' too good. Marnin's de worse. Mamma say I be birthin' it come 'bout March. I gwaine be glad wen it all ova."

"Miz Ginny sez the hard part's still tuh come, so I kind-ah feel sorry fur yuh. Ain't yuh kind-ah skeered?"

"I'd be fibbin' if'n I said I ain't skeered. But Mamma say it be worth it wen de baby come. Dat be de happy part. Reckins I gwaine be glad tuh be a mamma. It'd be nice if'n somethin' good come out o' all dat Dunbar nightmare."

Aila shivered even more at the mention of Dunbar. She still had nightmares about the trauma of the previous summer.

"If'n it was me, I reckin I'd want a boy mahself, a boy tuh grow intuh a man like mah daddy. I loved mah daddy. I still miss 'im."

"I miss mah daddy too." Mary Jane lamented. "Maybe he a slave somewhur else. Maybe he be free now. I hope we all be free someday."

Mary Jane hesitated to imagine what freedom would be like. "I do longs fo' dat day. Mah daddy name 'Joshua'. But I ain't knowin' if'n he eva took a las' name. Maybe Sandas, I reckins."

They sat quietly and said nothing for some time. The landscape gradually grew darker as the sun sunk below the horizon, the river still radiant, reflecting the dimly lit sky.

It was then they noticed the silhouette of a large ship slowly drifting downstream near the river shore. It floated surprisingly low in the water and made hardly any sound. The girls had seen ships on the river before, but they were noisy, puffing black smoke and steam, and floated much higher in the water.

"That might be one of 'em blockade runners Mister James talks 'bout." Aila said. "They tryin' tuh sneak by a bunch of Yankee boats an' big cannons blockin' the mouth of the river."

"Why de Yankees blockin' de riva?"

"Mister James sez the Yankees ain't wantin' our boats tuh git in an' out of the river tuh brang food an' wah supplies tuh us an' take cotton tuh England. 'Em Yankees thank they kin win the wah if'n they kin stop the blockade runners. Mister James sez not many of our boats git in er out no more."

"Dat dere boat is gwaine tuh England?"

"I reckin' so. I ain't rightly knowin' whur England is, but Miz Ginny sez it's way 'cross the ocean. Might be somewhur near Scotland."

"Afriky's way 'cross de ocean too. Yuh reckins dey gwaine brang mo' cullud folks here wen dey come back?"

"I ain't knowin'. But I'm skeered on account of Mister James reckins we might git intuh a big fight with 'em Yankees down thur at Fort Fisher. Might spill over tuh this farm an' Wilmin'ton. We might be right in the middle of it."

"I ain't gwaine be skeered none if'n dem Yankees come an' sets us free. But right now it's gittin' mo' cold an' dark. We betta git back up yonda."

"I reckin it's time tuh go. Miz Ginny's gonna teach me some more readin' an' writin' tuhnight."

"Yuh reckins she might teach me sometime too?"

"I reckin she might. I kin ask her."

James didn't totally object to Ginny's teaching sessions with Aila, but he questioned the value of teaching a female.

"Ginny, if'n yuh want tuh waste yer time learnin' a girl, go right ahead." James had said. "Jes' make sure it ain't interferin' with yer work an' Aila's work 'round here. Mah mamma learned me tuh read an' write a li'l, but what li'l I learned was 'nuf. But females ain't got no business learnin'."

Ginny's answer had been the same as always: "If your mamma hadn't known how to read and write, how would you ever have learned?"

Aware of James' objection, Aila was reluctant to approach Ginny about teaching Mary Jane. She finally brought the subject up in her own learning session one evening.

"Miz Ginny, I thank yuh fur learnin' me readin' an' writin' like this. But kin yuh answer me one question?"

"Certainly, Aila. I will . . . if I can. But first, you need to understand the difference between 'teach' and 'learn'. I don't 'learn' you . . . I 'teach' you . . . and because of my teaching, you 'learn'. You understand?"

"I reckin so. I jes' gotta 'member."

"I'm gonna teach you now. And I hope you learn. Now, what is your question?"

"That girl Mary Jane wants real bad tuh learn tuh read an' write . . . an' I was wunderin' if'n yuh could . . . *teach* . . . her too. Kin yuh do that fur her . . . an' fur me?"

"Well, Aila, that is a real hard question. Mister James would be real mad if I did that. And you know that would be against the law for me . . . or anybody . . . to teach a slave?"

"No, ma'am, I ain't knowin' that." answered Aila. "What kind-ah law is that?"

"Aila, before I answer, you need to understand that 'I ain't knowin' that' isn't proper English. You should say, 'I didn't know that'. Do you understand?"

"I reckin so, Miz Ginny. I jes' gotta 'member that too."

"Anyway, that law against teaching slaves is the kind of law that keeps them from getting *uppidy*." continued Ginny. "You remember what I told you about Negro slaves being on the bottom and White folks wanting them to stay on the bottom? Well, that's the kind of law it is. A lot of White folks think the Negroes are happier if they are kept ignorant."

"Is that law goin' away if'n the Yankees win this here wah?"

"If it does go away and the White folks around here get their way, it very well might be replaced by another law that does the same thing. Now, I want to start with your lesson for tonight. But first, I want to show you something."

Ginny went to the cupboard, opened a false door in the rear of one of the shelves, and removed a large but relatively thin leather-bound book. She placed it on the table and opened it.

Aila noticed almost immediately that the book pages were handwritten, not printed. Several slips of paper were inserted among the pages, each with a sketch of a nature scene, a plant, an animal, or a person. "What kind-ah book is that?"

"This is my journal. This is where I keep my sketches and write down the things that interest me . . . the things I do, the things that happen to me, the people I know and the new people I meet, and how I feel about things. It's about my life."

"That sounds real int'restin'. When I learn tuh read, kin I read it?"

"It's real personal. It's mostly for me. But I'm showing it to you because it might be something you would want to do for yourself when you learn to read and write."

"I sure would, Miz Ginny! I kin't wait tuh *learn*."

It was early December. Weather had turned mild, not nearly cold enough for a hog killing. But it was time to start preparing for the slaughter. The hogs ran wild in the woods most of the year and had to be rounded up by the slaves and driven into a pen to be fattened with feed corn several weeks before the killing.

The fattening pens were made of interlocking logs to keep potential predators out. The pen was connected by a gated chute to the barn, leading to a stall where the hogs would be killed.

The day of the hog roundup, Aila stood on the kitchen walkway watching Mary Jane lean on the walls of her shack. She took a deep breath, descended the walkway steps, and walked across the yard toward Mary Jane.

"I sure' am glad I ain't no hawg 'round this time of year." Aila said as she approached Mary Jane.

"Me too, ma'am. But I'm kind-ah feelin' like a hawg with dis here baby in mah belly."

Aila pretended to watch the hog pen activities as she searched for the courage to speak.

"I talked tuh Miz Ginny 'bout her teachin' yuh readin' an' writin'. She didn't take too kindly tuh it on account of Mister James won't like it. She sez it's aghen the law fur somebody tuh teach a slave readin' an' writin'. I reckin that's a crazy law."

"Dat law's 'cause slaves ain't nothin' but prop'ty . . . dey jes' live-stock fo' White folks."

"Yuh ain't no livestock, Mary Jane. We're all God's children, jes' like Rev'rend Campbell sez."

"He jes' mean White folks is God's chillens. Black folks is live-stock. Yuh knows he own slaves? An' he ain't treatin' 'em like God's chillens! He treat 'em like livestock . . . animals he own!"

"How yuh know that?"

Mary Jane stared wide-eyed at Aila. "Yuh kin't tell nobody. Yuh ain't gwaine tell nobody, is yuh?"

"No. I got a lot of secrets I ain't tellin' nobody." assured Aila.

"All o' us meet sometimes ova at de Meetin' Place wid slaves from udda farms at night wen yuh White folks is sleepin'. Dere's a preacha dat come down from Wilmin'ton, an' he do a service fo' us now an' den. He learn us a little bit o' readin' an' writin' . . . but it ain't much. We tells each udda wat goin' on all ova dis county. Yuh White folks thanks we stupid. But we jes' gittin' ready."

"Gittin' ready fur what?" wondered Aila.

"Gittin' ready fo' us tuh be free, tuh be wat we wants without nobody tellin' us wat we is er wat we kin't be!"

"If'n Miz Ginny won't teach yuh tuh read an' write, then maybe I kin." Aila declared. "Maybe I kin add on tuh what yuh learn from that Wilmin'ton preacher. I *don't know* how tuh do it, but I reckin I kin jes' pass along what I git from Miz Ginny. That's the least I kin do fur a . . . fur a neighbor."

A 'neighbor'. Is that what I wanted tuh say?

Chapter 7

THE BOOM

LATE DECEMBER 1864

～

Hog killing long had been a Sanders family tradition involving James' paternal first cousin Nancy and her husband, Zechariah Price. The Prices, originally from Brunswick County, had crossed the Cape Fear River in 1862 to settle in Castle Hayne, north of Wilmington, about 20 miles from the Sanders farm.

The Prices had two teenage daughters and two teenage sons. Another daughter died of "the fever" in the spring of 1863. The teenage boys, David and Samuel, joined the Confederate infantry in 1861. David was killed at Gettysburg in 1863, and Samuel reportedly was taken prisoner. The Price family this year would only include the parents.

James' younger paternal first cousin, Alan Smith, along with his new wife, Rebecca, also would be joining them this year from Brunswick County across the river.

In 1863, Alan had been discharged from Confederate service after the Battle of Chancellorsville, having been struck by shell shrapnel that destroyed his left eye and shattered his scapula and cervical vertebrae. His injuries severely limited use of his left arm and his ability to turn his head. The shell fragments also ripped off his left ear, rendering him deaf in that ear, and disfiguring the left side of his face.

The hog killing was not only necessary to replenish the family's supply of meat for the entire year, but also had become a time for the family Christmas celebration. The killing process required cold weather to avoid meat spoilage, making timing of the activity crucial.

On the day of the Sanders' guests' scheduled arrival, the weather was too warm for the killing, and what temperatures would prevail was a guessing game. It was hard, dirty work, and its goriness repulsed Aila. But the good part for her was that the work could be enjoyed with Ginny and the slaves.

To reach the Sanders farm well before sunset on pothole-filled, muddy roads through marshes and swamps, the Smiths had to depart Brunswick County as soon as the road could be seen in the dawn light. The potentially hazardous early departure and the required oared-ferry crossings of the Brunswick and Cape Fear Rivers did not ease Rebecca's anxiety about the trip. But as a dutiful and obedient wife, she said nothing of her fears.

The Price family arrived about two o'clock in their mule-drawn wagon. As Zechariah tied the mule to the hitching post, the Sanderses exited to the front porch to greet the visitors.

"Well, it's that time of year aghen." said James, limping over to Zechariah to shake his hand. "I'm hopin' it's gonna git colder before the hog killin'."

"Good tuh see y'all aghen." Zechariah declared. "What yuh limpin' fur, James? Look like yuh kin't hardly git 'round."

"I twisted mah hip real bad back las' summer. Don't know what I did tuh it. Anyways, don't y'all worry 'bout me. Come on in the house whur it's wahmer."

"Whur's that new baby?" inquired Nancy. "I sure 'nuf wanna see the Lord's new gift tuh the fam'ly."

"Baby Sarah's right here inside." replied Ginny. "Y'all come on in."

Still continuing their family chatter, the men and boy followed the females into the house and took seats around the fireplace, while the women gathered around the cradle to view the infant newcomer and recite obligatory "oos" and "ahs."

Alan and Rebecca Smith arrived in their mule and cart about half past two, later than expected. Ginny went to the porch to greet them, then brought them to the front room to see the new baby and sit by the fire.

As they took their seats, Alan described their trip from Brunswick. "That's a hard trip . . . crossin' 'em two rivers . . . but we're happy as kin be tuh be here . . . an' still in one piece!"

"Well, it looks like one er two pieces didn't make it!" Zechariah joked, referring to Alan's lost eye and ear.

Shocked by Zechariah's brash insensitivity, everyone else remained quiet as he began his regular rant, now familiar to everyone.

"Ha! 'em Yankee bastards done kilt one of mah sons . . . sent the other off someplace, I ain't knowin' whur. He's likely sick an' starvin' tuh death up north somewhur . . . an' freezin' in that Yankeeland cold."

Zechariah's voice trailed off as he shook his head in disgust. "The Lord done made a special place in Hell fur all 'em Yankees, I do declare. What I hain't knowin' is why he's punishin' me by takin' mah sons."

"Damnit, Zechariah!" James exclaimed. "Y'all know good an' well I lost two sons in this damn wah, one of 'em dead somewhur an' one missin'. Yuh ain't the onlyest man what's made hard sacrifices fur the Cause! The Lawd ain't punishin' yuh no more than nobody else!"

"I knowed two men named Price in the 20th North Carolina Infantry." Alan interjected. "What unit was yer sons in, Mister Zechariah?"

"They both are . . . was in the 20th. I don't know whur they be now. David an' Samuel was thur names."

"I knowed 'em both, suh. We all joined up in Brunswick County in 1861. Fine men an' great wahiors. They was still in the 20th when I was discharged after Chancellorsville. What happened tuh 'em?"

"David was kilt at Gettysburg, an' they said Samuel likely got took tuh a prison somewhur . . . Maryland er New York."

"I'm so sorry tuh hear 'bout yer sons, suh." said Alan. "They was both brave men. I do hope Samuel will come home safe."

"Well, we're sure proud of the men like yuh, protectin' our home-land from 'em invaders." declared James. "I thank—"

"I reckin I'll take a chaw of mah tuhbaccer if'n y'all don't mind." interrupted Zechariah.

"Of course, we don't mind, cousin." lied Ginny. "Aila, go get that spittoon in the kitchen closet for Cousin Zechariah. Nancy, wouldn't you like a dip or two of your snuff as well?"

"Yes ma'am, I sure would." smiled Nancy. "I hain't had dip one since we left dis marnin'. That trip down here's sure a hard one. I was thankin' we was gonna sink in dat thur crossin' over Barnard's Creek."

"I ain't gonna mind if'n I have a dip too." Rebecca Smith declared.

Aila rose and walked to the kitchen to retrieve the brass spittoon. At least the single container would meet the needs of chewer and dipper alike.

Aila returned and awaited another set of orders.

"Would y'all like something' to drink?" offered Ginny.

"I sure 'nuf would!" said Zechariah. "Fact is, I brought me some of mah own drank here." He pulled a small bottle of moonshine from his pocket.

"Now, Zechariah, yuh know we are all Christians here, an' Ginny an' me been taught that hard licker's the Devil's handiwork. We'd sure appreciate yuh not drankin' that while yuh here in our home."

"Damn, James! Whur do the Bible say drankin' licker's a sin? The Lord Jesus an' the disciples dranked wine, didn't they?"

"Zechariah, wine ain't white licker. An' 'sides, that was fur the Lord's Easter supper."

"Now James, the onlyest reason they dranked wine was on account of thur won't no corn licker 'round back in 'em days!"

"I ain't gonna argue with yuh, Zechariah. Rev'rend Campbell sez drankin' corn licker is a sin, an' he's a man of the Lord."

"James, don't yuh know preachers is the worst hypocrites thur is? Campbell's been knowed tuh make licker *an'* blackberry wine on his place fur years."

"Kin't yuh jes' put away that bottle, Zechariah, an' hold yer peace!"

Zechariah refused to comply and took his first swig. The others asked for buttermilk, so without being asked, Aila departed to fetch glasses, then out to the well where the buttermilk and sweet milk glass jugs were stored. The jugs were tethered to the well sweep by a line of linked leather strips and kept cool just below water level.

Returning to the gathering, Aila could hear Zechariah's booming voice from a room away.

"We heared 'bout 'em murderin' niggers slaughterin' Dunbar las' summer!"

Aila felt a chill on hearing Dunbar's name.

"Why ain't they been ketched yet?" continued Zechariah, almost shouting. "Mah daddy told me 'bout that Nat Turner uprisin' back in 1831 up thur in Virginny. Before folks knowed it, slaves down here got all riled up too an' marched tuh Wilmin'ton, plannin' tuh kill White folks on the way. Daddy said they was two thousand of 'em joined up before it was over."

Zechariah's rant continued. "An' I jes' heared 'bout that Lumbee injun Lowry murderin' James Barns an' stealin' two hawgs of hissin over yonder in Robeson County. That was this week! 'Em injuns run off an' hid in the swamp with a gang of runaways, escaped Yankee prisoners, an' damn Confederate deserters. An' they was stockpilin' guns an' robbin' White folks' smokehouses.

"I'm tellin' yuh one thang, I hain't got none of 'em black asses 'round mah place. I work mah farm with mah fam'ly an' don't mess with 'em. That's why Nancy's gonna be birthin' more young'uns tuh add tuh mah brood, hain't that right Nancy?"

Nancy smiled tartly. Everyone else was quiet. Zechariah spit a stream of tobacco juice into the spittoon and continued talking.

"Be fruitful an' multiply . . . hain't that what the Bible sez? I ain't got no money tuh buy slaves noways. Yankees kin have all of 'em, if'n they want . . . jes' leave us by ourself. We got a right tuh be our own country, an' we don't need that jackass Lincoln tellin' us what tuh do an' how tuh do it.

"I wanted tuh ask yuh what's goin' on down at Fort Fisher, James." Zechariah said, changing the subject. "Talk is, 'em damn Yankees got

New Inlet all blocked up with ships. If'n they take the fort, they'll be goin' fur Wilmin'ton right through this farm, ain't they?"

"I been thankin' that might happen, but who knows what 'em Yankees might be up tuh?" James said. "If'n they come through here, I ain't sure what we gonna do."

~~~

Aila was awakened in the middle of the night by what she thought was a distant loud clap of thunder. She heard footsteps coming down the stairs but stayed in bed and listened quietly to hear what was going on.

"That hain't thunda, James." opined Zechariah. "Yuh reckin' it might be black powder blowin' up er cannon far?"

"That was a mother lode of black powder goin' off." declared Alan, descending the stairs. "I'd say 'bout eight er ten mile away. Likely down at Fort Fisher."

~~~

"Aila! Git yerself over here an' fix breakfas'!" James yelled, startling Aila awake. She rubbed her eyes open and stretched herself wide in her bed.

"Yessuh, Mister James!" she called out. *But first I need tuh go pee real bad, fur sure!* "I need tuh dress. I'm goin' right now, suh!" she said, throwing on her dress, shoes, and winter coat. Then she turned to see James standing in front of her.

"Well girl, yuh better git busy!" he admonished her.

"I gotta go collect some eggs first." she explained. She had collected eggs the afternoon before, but she needed an excuse to get out of the house. "Kin yuh please ask Miz Ginny if'n she kin start the biscuits?" she asked.

"She's busy feeding the baby an' cleanin' her up . . . she kin't do it. Now git goin'."

"Yessuh, yessuh." she replied, dashing out the door to the kitchen to grab the egg basket.

Gotta find a pee spot . . . outhouse too fur away! First thangs first.

She scurried behind the small patch of red-berried holly bushes next to the farmhouse, slipped down her cotton chemise and drawstring drawers to her knees, squatted, and relieved herself into the now frost-bitten weeds. She wiped herself with her left hand, pulled up her undergarments, and headed for the henhouse.

Once there, she dipped her left hand into the hen's water basin and rubbed it dry on the hen-nest pine straw before reaching under the hen, ignoring her frantic cackling and protective pecking, to grab the two warm eggs underneath. She gathered six other eggs in like manner, placed them carefully in her basket, and ran back to the kitchen to don her apron and start cooking breakfast.

Breakfast preparation took much longer than she, the Sanders, and the guests wanted. Now that everything was ready, Ginny, after having set dishes and utensils, helped put food and black coffee on the kitchen table. The six adults served themselves and took their seats at the table, after which Aila took her ration, sat in separate chairs in the corner, and used her lap as a table.

"Heads bowed, eyes closed fur the blessing." ordered James. "Good Lord, we are thankful fur these an' all others received from thy hand. We 'umbly pray in Jesus' name, A-men."

"A-men." pronounced the others.

"Hit's 'bout time yuh got breakfas' fixed." complained Zechariah as he cut into a slice of smoked ham and took a bite from a buttered biscuit. He poured black coffee from his cup into a saucer and slurped it while continuing to chew with his few remaining teeth.

"I'm worried 'bout that boom we heared las' night." said James. "I worry that 'em Yankees is movin' on Fort Fisher. Alan sez it was black powder, an' he should know 'bout thangs like that."

"It was our boys blowin' up 'em Yankee ships." declared Zechariah. "Now, we kin jes' git along with this here wah an' drive 'em back north . . . send 'em back in a pine box would be better."

"I thank we jes' don't know what's goin' on." said James. "If'n the Yankees is attackin' Fort Fisher, we oughta hear a lot more commotion.

Somebody needs tuh go down that way an' find out what's goin' on . . . so we kin move tuh a safer place if'n we need tuh. But mah hip's killin' me now. I kin't hardly walk er even ride a horse."

Without thinking, Aila spoke up. "I could ride down tuh Rev'rend Campbell's place an' ask 'im. He's in the Home Guard."

No one spoke, but all looked at Aila, dumbfounded at her gumption.

"What?" exclaimed Zechariah. "Yuh stupid girl. Yuh hain't smart 'nuf tuh know what they're talking 'bout. Naw, James would be crazy tuh let yuh—"

"Yuh wouldn't be safe goin' down thur by yerself." James interrupted. "A man oughta go."

"I ain't questionin' yuh, Mister James." Aila said. "But don't y'all men need tuh stay here an' start packin' up thangs we need tuh leave this place fas' if'n we have tuh?"

"Damn, James! Yuh gonna let her stand thur an' tell yuh' what tuh do?" shouted Zechariah.

"This is mah house yer in, an' I decide here." James shot back.

"Yuh gone plum crazy, James. Yuh ain't never gonna see her aghen, mark mah word!"

"She's had plenty of chances tuh run away before, if'n she wanted tuh. I reckin I kin trust her."

Aila felt a warm blush come over her when she heard James' words.

I never knowed he felt like that . . . after all 'em times he disrespected me, whupped me an' tried tuh feel mah body. Is he really gonna trust me? Kin I really trust 'im?

Alan spoke up. "If'n I may, suh, thur might be Yankee soldiers out thur she kin't deal with. I thank it bes' if'n I go along with her."

"I reckin that makes sense." said James. "Y'all go an' git Rev'rend Campbell tuh order the Home Guard tuh wahn us if'n we need tuh move someplace safer. It's bes' if'n we're packed an' ready tuh leave quick like."

Chapter 8

CHRISTMASTIME

DECEMBER 1864

⟞⟝

Early on Christmas Eve morning, Alan and Aila took Mary the Mule to ride to the Campbell farm. He sat in the saddle, and she sat on the Mary's rump, holding onto the back of the saddle. The temperature had dropped drastically since the previous day.

"Yuh too cold?" asked Alan as they crossed the narrow wooden bridge over Mott's Creek. "I figger less than a hour tuh git tuh the Campbell place. Mister James said it was 'bout three miles."

"Naw suh." answered Aila. "I kind-ah like cold weather. Seems a lot better than the hot, sweaty summer, with all 'em gnats, skeeters, an' sand flies tuh bother yuh. An' it's real nice when it snows. Everthang nice an' white, like a dream."

Aila finally got the gumption to ask the questions she had been wanting to ask. "What's the wah like, Mister Alan? How'd yuh git hurt?"

Alan did not respond immediately. He seemed lost in a trance as he stared at the trees beside the sandy, muddy dirt road, just wide enough for cart, wagon, or buggy to pass.

"It's hard tuh explain." he finally answered. "It ain't like nothin' I ever knowed before, er ever want tuh know aghen. Yer settin' 'round bored a lot, then yer fitein' fur yer life an' the lives of yer army brothers. An' yuh skeered tuh death 'mose all the time. Yuh kin't but hate 'em Yankees fur killin' yer friends an' trying tuh kill you. Yuh know they mus' feel the same way 'bout you.

48

"It's kill that man before he kills *you*, like a nightmare yuh kin't wake up from. I seen a lot of hawg killin' an' deer dressin' an' such, but when it's 'nother man gittin' shot er blowed up er cut tuh pieces with a sword er bayonet, it hits yuh real hard. An' after the battle, all yuh kin see is dead, dyin', moanin' soldiers piled on the ground 'mose as far as yuh kin see, so thick yuh in places yuh kin't hardly pass 'long."

Aila imagined the carnage for a moment before speaking. "Yer a brave man, Mister Alan. I sure ain't wantin' tuh go through all that, 'cept maybe tuh save mah own life."

"I ain't brave." replied Alan. "I jes' tried tuh keep mahself alive . . . an' save mah army brothers, if'n I could. Yuh ain't jes' skeered fur yerself . . . yuh skeered 'bout makin' a mistake an' gittin' yer brothers kilt."

Aila stared at the back of Alan's head and neck and the disfiguring scars and missing ear.

"Yuh mind me askin' how'd yuh git hurt like that?" she wondered out loud.

"I kin't recollect much. They told me a cannon shell blowed up right in the middle of us. I woke up an' thur was dead an' dyin' men all 'round me. The smell of black power smoke, blood, guts, an' burnt flesh was everwhur. It looked a lot like a hawg killin' . . . 'cept they was men, not hawgs. Shrapnel had hit the left side of mah head an' neck, knocked mah eyeball out, an' tore up mah neck bones.

"But I was lucky. A lot of other men was kilt. They told me later our boys captured that cannon an' turned it on the Yankees, so I reckin that was some payback."

Alan stopped speaking and gazed into the woods again.

"Three of mah good friends from Smithville was kilt." he almost whispered. "I could've got kilt 'long with 'em, easy. Sometimes, I wish I had been. Sometimes, I feel it's mah fault on account of they died an' I didn't.

"One good thang 'bout bein' in the wah is I got tuh see places I ain't never seen before. This here's the center of the world fur us. We ain't thankin' too much 'bout the world outside. Seein' the places I saw opened up mah eyes tuh that. Thur's a whole big world out thur mose folks don't know 'bout. We ain't a'ways seein' our world right here ne'ther. It's so close we don't even see how beautiful an' wunderful it is."

Alan paused. "I tell yuh, Aila, thur ain't nothin' I ever seen so grand an' beautiful as 'em Blue Ridge Mountains when we was up in northern Virginny."

The two didn't speak further until they reached Federal Point Road. Then she noticed the small clusters of shacks along the roadside that she had seen before on her trips to the Campbell farm.

'Em folks mus' be real poor. Look at all 'em children runnin' 'round in the yard with no winter coats jes' like it was summertime, playin' hide 'n' seek behind the trees an' under the house. I ain't seein' no outhouse nowhur. They jes' go in the woods?

"Was yer folks poor when yuh was growin' up?" she asked.

"I reckin so, but we didn't know we was. Mose folks nearby was jes' like we was. None of us thought much 'bout bein' poor er not. We could see that some other folks had bigger houses an' more thangs, but that didn't mean much tuh us."

"Fam'ly made us feel safe, an' fam'ly was 'bout all we had of any value. We knowed the Lord was watchin' over us. We reckined thangs was that way 'cause that was jes' the way they was. Didn't bother us much, 'cept when we didn't git 'nuf tuh eat. Daddy an' Mamma an' all us children worked hard an' raised what we could, an' we reckined that was normal.

"After I joined the army, I saw a lot more 'bout how other folks . . . richer folks . . . live. But none of that made me want it. It jes' made me miss mah home an' fam'ly even more."

⌒

Aila and Alan reached the Campbell farmhouse just before noon. Riding into the farmyard, Aila waved to the preacher and Martha, his wife. They recognized her right away but wondered who the man with her was. She slid off Mary's rear, and Alan dismounted.

"What brangs yuh down this here way, Aila?" Reverend Campbell asked, stroking his abundantly full beard. "An' who's this man with yuh?"

"This here is Mister Alan Smith. He's Mister James' cousin from Brunswick County."

"An' this here's Rev'rend Campbell." she said to Alan.

"Jes' call me Campbell." the preacher said, shaking Alan's hand. "Yuh was in the wah?" he asked, looking at the evidence of Alan's injuries.

"Chancellorsville, suh. North Carolina 20th Regiment. Served in Gen'ral Lee's Army of Northern Virginny."

Hearing of Alan's service, Martha Campbell bowed her head, then stared into the surrounding woods as if searching for someone.

"From 'em scars, I reckin yuh ain't no deserter." said Campbell. "We don't take too kindly tuh cow'rds like that 'round here. We got one too many cow'rd an' traider in our own fam'ly!"

"No, suh, I ain't. Medical discharge. I took a hit from shrapnel that messed me up fur sure. Kin't hear nothin' in mah left ear."

"I'm honored tuh make yer acquaintance, son." said Campbell.

"We all heared a big explosion in the middle of las' night." explained Alan. "Sounded like it come from Fort Fisher. Mister Sanders asked us tuh come see yuh an' find out if'n yuh know what's hap'nin' an' if'n we need tuh move someplace safer."

"I heared 'em Yankees blowed up one of thur own ships, tryin' tuh blow up the fort." replied Campbell. "They're so stupid, they blowed up that ship a mile away, nowhurs near the fort. Ain't no need tuh move out on account of that."

Campbell's explanation was suddenly interrupted by a series of loud booms from the direction of the fort. "That sounds like heavy cannon far too." he observed. "Kin't rightly tell if'n it's Yankee cannon er Confederate . . . er both."

"We need tuh run home now an' tell Mister James?" asked Aila excitedly as the explosions continued.

"Thur ain't no reason fur y'all tuh do nothin' right now." said Campbell. "That cannon far might go on fur days er weeks. Yankees ain't gonna take that fort noways. Mah boy Gideon's down thur with the army, an' thur ain't no way they gonna let 'em Yankees come up our way. Gen'ral Bragg's got a backup line of defense at Sugar Loaf, an' me an' the Home Guard's gonna back 'em up."

Aila looked at Alan for a response. Alan listened attentively to Campbell but remained silent.

"So y'all kin go back home an' tell James everthang's fine all the way tuh Fort Fisher." continued Campbell. "Ain't no need tuh worry. The Home Guard's gonna let yuh know what's goin' on."

Alan said "We will, suh. Thank yuh fur he'pin' us out."

Alan and Aila remounted Mary, waved to Campbell, and returned to the road toward the Sanders farm.

⁓

"He's right 'bout one thang." said Alan as they continued their return ride. "That cannon far's likely tuh go on fur days, maybe even longer. But 'em Yankees ain't gonna be stopped by our army . . . an' most certain . . . not by the Home Guard. It's jes' a matter of time before it's all over."

"Ain't they gonna jes' kill us all when they come through?" asked Aila. "I'm skeered. Ain't they gonna disrespect us women an' steal our food an' animals?"

"I 'spect mose of 'em Yankees is honorable as we are. Tuh be sure, thur's bad apples 'mong 'em, jes' like our army, but from what I seen, they try not tuh hurt civilians if they kin. Wah's dangerous, though, an' yuh kin't say what might happen."

Alan's comments did little to allay Aila's fears. Contemplating his observations and the events of the past two days would keep her silent for the remainder to the return trip to the Sanders farm.

⁓

Before the war, Christmastime had been a joyous occasion for both the celebrants in the Sanders home and the Sanders slaves. Not only was the religious significance of the day important for

Christians, both Black and White, but it also was viewed as a festive time to celebrate the coming new year and the ebb of winter's short days and long nights. Christmas 1864 was different, though, solemn and shrouded in uncertainty.

On Christmas Eve, Aron came out the woods carrying a small red cedar tree toward Sally, Mary Jane, and Tootsie, who had assembled outside Sally and Mary Jane's shack.

"Happy Christmas y'all!" he called out. "I's got de Christmas tree fo' Sally's house. Who gwaine he'p fancy it up?"

"Happy Christmas!" said the others.

Sally's shack had little room for the tree inside, so Aron dug a small hole and "planted" it outside, next to Sally's door. The others, who had gathered holly berries, painted pine cones and sweetgum balls, small wooden carvings of Mary, Joseph, and baby Jesus, hung them on the tree as they hummed, then sang with Aron:

> *Mary had a baby, oh, Lawd,*
> *Mary had a baby, oh mah Lawd,*
> *Mary had a baby, oh Lawd,*
> *Peoples keep a-comin' an' de train done gone.*

The decorating and singing finished, the group crowded into Sally's shack and sat on the cots to absorb some warmth from the fireplace.

"Christmas sure ain't wat it used tuh be. It 'mose a sad time now." declared Aron. "I's thankin' Massa Sandas ain't even givin' us presents dis year like he use tuh. Evabody still sad 'bout wat dat devil Dunbar done tuh our li'l Mary Jane here."

Mary Jane winced at the reminder of her rape.

"But I's thankin' everthang ain't gwaine be bad news, an' maybe de Lawd's jes' been waitin' fo' Christmastime tuh make good news happen."

"I ain't knowin' nothin' 'bout no good news right now!" said Tootsie. "Wat yuh talkin' 'bout?"

"Well, fo' one thang, Massa Sandas wuz tellin' me yesterdee he ain't gwaine mind us goin' ova tuh visit udda cullud folks on Christmas Day."

"He sho change his mind 'bout lettin' us go off de farm lately." observed Tootsie. "Why he lettin' us go . . . maybe he reckins dis here wah soon gwaine be ova, an' he worried 'bout wat happen wen we free."

"Maybe yuh right." Aron agreed. "Dat good news fo' sho. Now, Sally here got some mo' good news 'bout de two o' us!"

"Yessuh, dat ain't all dat surprisin' 'round here." said Sally. "I's a'ready told Mary Jane 'bout dis, an' she's agreein'. Ain't dat right, Mary Jane?"

Mary Jane nodded her approval. "Dis all 'bout Mamma marryin' Aron." she clarified to Tootsie. "I ain't standin' aghen it. But I ain't sho how it gwaine work out wen mah daddy come back."

"Yuh mean if'n he come back." said Sally. "Well, we jes' gwaine cross dat bridge wen we comes tuh it. We done talked tuh Massa Sandas dis marnin', an' he a'ready said it all right wid 'im. We jes' need tuh wait 'til afta hawg killin'."

"Now Aron, I knowed yuh wuz gwaine take dat purdy lady away from me someday!" joked Tootsie.

The men chuckled. Sally and Mary Jane smiled.

"Yuh a lucky man, Aron! But I ain't so sho 'bout Miz Sally's luck!" teased Tootsie.

"Yuh jes' messin' wid me now! I knows y'all happy fo' us." said Aron. "But y'all knows we kin't be married legal like White folks. Dat mean Massa Sandas kin still sell one o' us off tuh some udda farm if'n he want. But it do mean our babies ain't gwaine be bastards in de eyes o' de Lawd."

"Y'all ain't knowin' dis yet, but I's plannin' tuh git married too." Tootsie announced. "Yuh knows Hannah from ova yonda at de Meetin' Place? She want us tuh git married up jes' right."

"Well, dat mighty good news!" said Sally and Aron almost together.

"Dat tell me dere's hope fo' us all yet!" said Sally.

"Y'all knows joy, hope, an' celebration is part o' dis season fo' dem what is brothas an' sisters in Jesus." said Aron. "An' us here now got a lot tuh be happy 'bout. I reckins dis here wah is soon gwaine be ova, an' dis Christmas give us hope fo' freedom. I reckins God's gwaine finely deliva his chillens out o' slavery tuh de *Promise Land!* Not Christmas Day, maybe, but someday soon!"

"A-men!" they shouted together.

On Christmas Day, the sound of distant unrelenting shelling at Fort Fisher continued. Trying to ignore the continuous booms, the Sanders family and their guests gathered to decorate the red cedar Christmas tree that Alan had brought from the woods and set up a few feet from the fireplace.

Ginny and Aila decorated the tree with handmade ornaments and wax candles, to be lit only for short periods of time while guests are present. Hand-carved nativity figures and ornaments from James' family, as well as colorfully painted pine cones, spiky sweetgum balls and seashells made by Ginny and Aila soon danced and twirled on the tree, driven by fireplace heat currents.

A whitewashed wooden star of Bethlehem capped the cedar treetop. Running cedar and red-berried Christmas holly decorated doorways and, with paraffin wax candles, the fireplace mantel. The scent of evergreen pervaded the house. A Christmas wreath of running cedar and holly welcomingly hung on the exterior of the front door.

Ginny read the biblical account of the first Christmas from the Book of Luke:

"She brought forth her firstborn son, and wrapped him in swaddling clothes, and laid him in a manger, because there was no room for them in the inn."

As Ginny read the familiar story, Aila's mind wandered.

I reckin Jesus' fam'ly was 'bout as poor as 'em folks I see on the way tuh Rev'rend Campbell's place. Worse off than me.

Mary Jane oughta hear Miz Ginny read this story. Maybe she'd be thankin' her fam'ly ain't no worse off than Jesus' fam'ly. But I reckin that ain't so, on account of Jesus' fam'ly won't no black slaves.

Ginny continued:

> *"And, lo, the angel of the Lord came upon them, and the glory of the Lord shone round about them . . . and suddenly there was with the angel a multitude of the heavenly host praising God, and saying, Glory to God in the highest, and on earth peace, good will toward men."*

Peace an' good will. Is that God's wish fur us . . . er his command to us? E'ther way, it ain't workin' out too good nowadays.

The reading finished, Ginny sat at her piano and played as the assembly sang as best they could, "O Come All Ye Faithful" and "Joy to the World."

On the last note of the carols, James announced: "I see some presents thur under that tree. Reckin who they belong tuh?"

Everyone scrambled to the tree and pretended to jostle for position. Ginny served as the gift distributor, handing out socks, stems of dried raisins, apples, biscuits with honey, boiled salted peanuts, and homemade hard candy, all to be eaten after supper.

Everyone paused almost at once, realizing that the sound of shelling had stopped. After a long silence, James was the first to speak.

"It means one of two thangs. E'ther 'em Yankees' give up . . . er they done took the fort."

"They hain't took the fort . . . they done give up . . . that's mah thankin'!" declared Zechariah.

"It's hard tuh know." James said. "If'n the Yankees took the fort an' comin' up our way, thur ain't much we kin do 'bout it. Tryin' tuh move tuh a safer place ain't gonna work like I thought it might. Whur'd we go? An' what could we take with us? Maybe jes' the clothes on our back. If'n we leave here now, the hawg killin' won't git done, an' we won't git the meat we need tuh git through the year."

No one spoke. They realized that if the Yankees came, they would have few or no options.

"Y'all smell that good cookin'?" James exclaimed with a big smile Aila had never seen before. "Let's all take our place at the table and bow our heads while I ask the blessin' . . . so we kin eat!"

After everyone was seated, James prayed:

"Lord, we come before yuh this Christmas with 'umble an' thankful hearts. We trust in yuh tuh keep us safe from 'em Yankee invaders, Lord we pray. An' we ask yer blessin' on this food laid here fur the nourishment of our earthly bodies. We pray these thangs in the name of yer Son, Jesus Christ. A-men."

"A-men!" said the others in unison.

Group chatter erupted as everyone went about gathering servings for their supper plates: venison hash; lard-fried squirrel, boiled potatoes and onions; fatback-seasoned collards and black-eyed peas, insurance for health and happiness in the coming new year; baked sweet potatoes; butter beans; and lard biscuits with butter. Apple, pecan, pumpkin, and sweet potato pies completed the feast.

The sounds of conversation were replaced by chewing and the rustle and tinkle of cutlery. At least for the remainder of the evening, Peace on Earth was a reality in the Sanders home.

Chapter 9

WHAT WILL I BE?

DECEMBER 26, 1864

AFTER SUPPER, THE MEN SAT AROUND THE FIREPLACE and exchanged stories of times gone by and hopes for the future, while the women cleared the table and carried dishes to the kitchen to be washed. When the women's work was done, Rebecca and Nancy excused themselves to prepare for bed, leaving Ginny and Aila alone in the kitchen.

"Aila, I've been thinking about you and your future." Ginny revealed after a period of silence. "You're not always gonna be a servant. You're smart, and you pay attention to the people and the world around you. You've got a lot to learn, but you have the right attitude to learn. Have you thought about what kind of life you want for yourself . . . what will you record in your journal?"

"What will I be? It's hard tuh thank about, Miz Ginny. Thur's a lot I ain't knowin' 'bout this world an' the folks in it . . . er what the future is gonna bring. I ain't never even seen a city . . . not even Wilmin'ton. I reckin I want tuh get married an' have babies . . . ain't that what women is s'posed tuh do? I'd sure marry that Alan Smith fas' as the shake of a rabbit's tail!"

"Now, girl, don't you start thinking about something like that! The man's married already! Even thinking about that is a sin against God. You might as well put that silliness out of your mind for good!"

"Well, if'n it ain't 'im, somebody jes' like 'im."

"Being married and having babies is a noble calling, Aila. Mothers and grandmothers are the backbone of our society, even if men are in

58

charge. Mothers can shape what their sons—and their daughters—can be. But I've always felt a yearning to do more than just that. I just don't seem to have the strength of character to follow that path."

"Yuh 'bout the strongest woman I know. What's keepin' yuh from fallerin' that path?"

"It's hard . . . it's real hard to do something your husband doesn't want you to do, Honey. And people at church and neighbors think bad about you too."

"If'n yer husband an' 'em other folks won't in the way, what would yuh want tuh do?"

"I don't know. It's never seemed realistic to go that way, so I didn't think about it too much. Maybe I'd be an artist . . . draw pictures of the people and things around me . . . or maybe I'd write music . . . or books. You know, there are more women authors than you might think. I've read some of their books. You should do the same when you are reading better."

"Oh, I couldn't never write a book . . . er draw pictures e'ther, fur that matter."

"I have a little something for you." Ginny said to Aila as she walked to the cupboard, opened the false cupboard door, and withdrew a package of pencils, two leather-bound notebooks, and several slips of paper.

Handing the pencils and notebooks to Aila, she said, "These notebooks are for you. One is for you to use to practice your writing, and the other is for you to start your own journal when you're ready to write it. And you can practice your drawing on these paper sheets."

"Oh, Miz Ginny!" exclaimed Aila. "What nice presents! How kin I ever thank yuh 'nuf? This is mah bes' Christmas since I was a li'l girl!"

"You can thank me by continuing to read, write, and draw! And by keeping your memories, good and bad, for your children and your children's children. They need to know and understand your life to be able to make a better life for themselves . . . and a better world for everybody."

Chapter 10

THE HOG KILLING

December 27, 1864

~~~~

If the weather stayed cold, James' plan for the hog killing was to process five to six animals the first day, and if required, two or three on a second day. Five would be barrows, mature males castrated before the age of six months to avoid boar taint, a disflavoring of the meat brought on by puberty.

James and the workers arose before dawn and prepared for the slaughter. His injured hip disqualified him from physical tasks, but he would supervise the process. The men were assigned the demanding physical work, while the women were responsible for food preparation to feed the workers. Ginny helped the women as she could and attended to baby Sarah, swaddled warmly in her cradle next to the slaughtering tables.

James gave the honor of the hog kill to Aron, who entered the fattening pen, selected a hog, and with Tootsie's help, drove the selected animal through the open chute into the barn's hog stall where corn bait had been placed.

As the distracted animal ate the corn bait, Aron delivered a splitting axe blow to its skull, causing the barrow to slump to its knees and topple over. The hog now downed, twitching and convulsing, the three slaves dragged it from the pen to a space near a log scaffolding structure for the next step in the process.

With a butcher knife, Aron cut slits in the animal's hind legs at the tendon and the ankle joint. The men inserted the sharp ends of an iron hanging gambrel into the slits and hung the hog hind feet up, head down on wooden scaffolding. Aron sliced the animal's jugular vein, releasing a blood gush from the hog's throat that splashed into the collecting pan Tootsie held just below the animal's head. Most of the blood would be fed to James' hunting dogs, chained to the barn.

When the blood was completely drained, the hog was placed in a wooden trough filled with scalding hot water. Scalding allowed the women to scrape off the hog's hair with blacksmith-fashioned iron scrapers. Once the hair was removed, the men again hoisted the carcass up onto the scaffolding, sliced its belly and chest open to remove organs and intestines, and severed its head. The head would later be used to make hog head cheese, a traditional dish for Christmas and the new year.

As the gutting process continued, a lone rider approached the work area, dismounted, and tied his horse to a nearby sapling.

The man greeted James. "Good marnin', Mister Sanders an' Happy Christmas tuh y'all. Mah name's Jeremiah Wilkins, an' I'm with the Home Guard."

"Good marnin', Jeremiah, an' Happy Christmas tuh yuh." replied James. "What brangs yuh here so bright an' early tuhday, son?"

"I got news 'bout Fort Fisher." replied Jeremiah. "Rev'rend Campbell told me tuh come a' tell yuh Fort Fisher held! 'Em Yankees done withdrawed, suh. They ain't comin' up this way."

"Praise the Lord!" exclaimed Zechariah. "I told yuh our boys would hold the line! Hain't I a'ways said the Lord's on our side?"

"Well, thank yuh fur that good news, Jeremiah!" exclaimed James.

"I'm real glad tuh brang it tuh yuh." replied Jeremiah. "Now, if'n y'all will excuse me, I got some other visits tuh make this marnin'. Daddy wants me home by low tide tuh he'p 'im fish some oysters."

"Safe travels, Jeremiah." wished James. "Y'all eat some of 'em oysters fur us!"

"Good!" exclaimed James after Jeremiah had left. "A good reason to celebrate! Now we kin git 'bout the business of hawg killin'."

Gutting continued as the heart and liver were set aside to be cooked and served over the next few days. The small intestines would be used to stuff sausage, and the large intestines would be thoroughly washed to be cooked as "chitlins" by the slaves.

The hogs were hoisted one by one onto a wooden slab and butchered into various cuts of pork. Their skin would be fried into pork rinds, and skin with more fat attached would become fried "cracklins." The fatty layer under the skin of the back would become "fatback" bacon. The feet would become "pickled pigs' feet" and preserved in jars. The hogs' cheek would be smoked and cured to become "hawg jowl." The shank that connects the foot to the leg below the ham would be stewed and braised to become "ham hocks."

Leftover scraps, mostly fat, were cooked in cast iron pots to make lard and lye soap. The body parts not desired by the Whites were given to the slaves. Every part of the hog was used, either as food or for another purpose. Nothing was wasted.

Jeremiah rode toward Federal Point Road, wondering if he was right not to have told James about the rumor circulating among soldiers in the area. On Christmas Day, a telegraph message reportedly had informed local high-ranking officers that Atlanta had fallen on Christmas Eve.

"I reckin hit's bes' that folks don't know that right now, 'specially at Christmastime." Jeremiah said to himself. "This wah ain't lost yet. We all need tuh keep spirits up."

After the butchering, Aron and the other male slaves started the sausage making, meat salting, and smoking processes to preserve the meat for the Sanders' share. The shares allocated to Zechariah and Alan's families were wrapped in burlap to be transported with them back to their homes. The sausage, salting, and smoking processes would be completed there.

When the day became too dark to continue, the workers had completed processing of six hogs. Another day would be needed to complete the other three or perhaps four.

When the day's work was completed, Alan and Rebecca made a special effort to speak to the slaves. They had no slaves of their own but were interested in their lifestyle and wellbeing. They took a particular liking to Sally and Mary Jane.

"Ain't it hard tuh be a mamma an' daughter without no man in yer fam'ly?" Alan asked.

"Nawsuh." Sally answered. "We all here is fam'ly. Aron an' Tootsie, dey take care o' us jes' like we dere fam'ly. We all works tuhgetha tuh he'p each udda out."

"Kin I ask when yuh baby's due, Mary Jane?" Rebecca asked.

"Mah mamma say he be borned 'bout March, ma'am."

"So it's a boy chile, then?"

"Well, dat wat I be hopin' fo'."

"Where is yer daddy now? Why ain't he here with yuh an' yer mamma?"

"He got sold off tuh 'nudda massa sometime back. We ain't knowin' whur he is 'xactly. Someplace up north o' Wilmin'ton we reckins."

"Well, that's real sad, Mary Jane. I know yuh mus' miss 'im." Alan said, consolingly.

"Yessuh. I do. But mah mamma's gwaine marry Aron here sometime soon. Den I got a new daddy, I reckins."

Noticing from a distance that the Smiths were speaking with the slaves, Zechariah pulled James aside.

"James, they nigger lovers er somethin'?" Zechariah snarled.

"Maybe." James replied. "They ain't hurtin' nobody. Leave 'em be."

"Hit's clare tuh me that nigger girl's 'bout six months along." Zechariah declared. "She's so skinny hit's easy as hell tuh tell. Yuh been gittin' a li'l extrie on the side?"

"I seen that fur some time now." replied James. "Naw, it ain't me that caused it. Could be one of 'em black studs er maybe even

Dunbar. That wouldn't sa'prise me one bit. Whatever it is, it's gonna be mah property."

———

The hog killing continued into the second day to complete processing of the final four hogs. By December 29, the processing was completed. It was time for the Price and Smith families to return home and the Sanders to resume their normal winter routine. Early the following day, both guest families departed for home with their shares of hog products.

"Y'all come back, yuh hear?" James said as he, Ginny, and Aila watched the guests remount their mule carts.

"Come back and visit real soon." echoed Ginny. "Thanks for your help."

"We enjoyed seein' y'all aghen." said Alan as Rebecca waved goodbye.

"Maybe we kin all git tuhgether 'round Easter this year." suggested Zechariah. "I reckin by then our boys'll drive 'em Yankees back up north whur they belong an' we kin git along with our normal life aghen!"

———

Chapter 11

FORT FISHER & SUGAR LOAF

FEBRUARY 1865

⟿

THE UNION BOMBARDMENT and land operations to capture Fort Fisher that had failed on Christmas Day 1864 were resumed on January 13 with the support of a 60-vessel gunboat armada.

Two divisions of Union soldiers, including about 1,600 U.S. Colored Troops, one landing north of the fort and a second near the fort itself, spearheaded the land offensive. On January 15, Union land forces attacked, supported by fire from the gunboats. By evening the same day, Yankees had captured the fort. The Union victory closed the Confederacy's last port, eliminating the possibility of its recognition by European countries and any further trade with the rest of the world.

With the fall of Fort Fisher, the 30-mile path to Wilmington was opened all the way to the Confederate earthworks known as Sugar Loaf, about 13 miles south of Wilmington and six miles south of the Sanders farm. Between January 19 and February 11, Union forces launched several attacks on the Sugar Loaf defenses, but the Confederates held.

On February 12, Jeremiah Wilkins of the Home Guard stepped onto the Sanders' front porch, where he knocked on the door and was met by James, out of Ginny and Aila's earshot. It would be the last report the James family would hear from the Home Guard.

"Our boys is holdin' the line aghen 'em Yankees at Sugar Loaf!" James announced triumphantly as he returned to the front room. "They're keepin' the Yankees away fur now, but I ain't knowin' if'n they can hold on.

"We gonna need tuh watch out fur 'em, bar all the doors, an' hide upstairs if'n they come. I'll load mah shotgun an' we'll wait fur 'em upstairs in case they break in! I ain't gonna leave mah property!"

"What 'bout the slaves, Mister James?" Aila asked. "They ain't got no guns er nothin' tuh fight 'em Yankees! Don't they need tuh know the Yankees might be comin'?"

"I ain't worried none 'bout 'em slaves." James answered. "We'll jes' wait an' see what happens. I ain't sure 'bout nothin' right now."

〜

Early the next morning, Aila quietly left the farmhouse and headed to Mary Jane and Sally's shack. Mary Jane saw Aila coming and opened the door as she approached.

"Marnin' Miss Aila. How come yuh sneakin' ova here so early?" asked Mary Jane.

"Mister Sanders said y'all don't need tuh know, but I want tuh tell y'all somethin' y'all oughta know."

"Come on in now." said Mary Jane. "We got somethin' tuh tell yuh too."

Aila followed as Mary Jane reentered her home, the first time the White girl had seen the inside of the slave's shack. Sally, who had been seated on her bed, rose to greet her.

"Good marnin', Miss Aila. Welcome tuh our home!" said Sally. "So nice tuh have yuh visit. Come set down here by de fire."

Aila paused for a moment, looking around the sparse shack. *They live like this? Two beds, two chairs, dirt floor, not much else. Smells like stale smoked hawg, maybe with a li'l possum an' polecat throwed in. But that's a nice wahm farplace, an' that woodsmoke smells good.*

She took a chair next to the fire.

"Have some coffee er sassafras tea wid honey, Miss Aila?" offered Sally. "We jes' found some fresh honey ova yonda in dat swamp holler yesterdee."

"No thank yuh, ma'am."

"Yuh come tuh tell us somethin', Miss Aila?" asked Sally.

"Like I was tellin' Mary Jane here, Mister James said y'all don't need tuh know, but I want tuh tell y'all anyways. Our soldiers are holdin' up 'em Yankees down at Sugar Loaf, but they might be comin' this way soon if'n the line don't hold."

Sally smiled. "We done knows 'bout all dat. We ain't skeered none, on account o' dey gwaine set us free wen dey gits here. Yuh knows dere's cullud soldiers fightin' wid dem Yankees down dere?

"Yuh knows we got a Meetin' Place ova yonda whur we heared news from udda cullud folks down up an' down de road." said Sally, anticipating Aila's astonishment. "Dey done met dem cullud soldiers an' learned wat's gwaine on down dere. Ain't gwaine be long 'fo dey come up here an' set us free!"

———⌒———

Aila could hardly believe what Sally had told her. Should she tell James and Miz Ginny about the slaves' communications links? No doubt they would not believe that colored soldiers were fighting with the Yankees against the Confederates.

The assault against Confederate forces at Sugar Loaf failed on February 19, and the Union forces moved across the Cape Fear River, forcing the Confederates to abandon Fort Anderson in Brunswick County. Union control of Fort Anderson allowed Union ships to sail up the Cape Fear unobstructed and threaten Sugar Loaf from the rear.

The Confederates were sandwiched between the Union Navy northwest of Sugar Loaf and Union land forces to the south. Their only feasible option was retreat north to protect Wilmington. Federal Point Road, just east of the Sanders farm, would be their escape route. Union forces followed in pursuit.

———⌒———

Paralyzing fear shook Aila as the Yankee soldier moved toward her.

What kin I do? He got me cornered in this hawg-fattenin' pen. Ain't no way out.

The roof was so low, she could not stand upright and fell to the straw and mud floor. She pushed herself away from him, screaming and trying to kick him away. He grabbed one of her legs and pulled her out through the entrance chute into the killing stall. It was then that she saw his face in the light. It was the face of Dunbar!

He was on top of her, pushing up her dress, tearing off her underwear.

Alan suddenly appeared at the entrance to the stall.

"Mister Alan, please, he'p me!"

Alan stepped forward and with a strong thrust embedded a pack-haken timber hook into the side of the intended rapist's gut. Lifting the hook upward with amazing strength, he pulled the attacker off of Aila, spilling his intestines on the barn stall dirt floor.

Aila staggered to stand, pulled down her dress, and as discretely as she could, replaced her underwear.

"Mister Alan, yuh saved me! I knew I could depend on yuh! But now, I'm gonna have a baby an' I ain't married! Kin yuh marry me now?"

"Naw, Aila . . . I want tuh, but yuh know I a'ready got Rebecca as mah wife."

Alan bowed his head, turned, and walked out of the barn into the sunlight. Aila dropped to the barn floor and wept.

"Wake up, girl!" Ginny said, shaking Aila's shoulders. "You're moaning like you're about to die! You all right?"

"I reckin . . . I reckin so."

"Aron's downstairs on the walkway with Sally and Mary Jane. He wants to tell us all something, and he wants you to be there. Now, you get dressed and come on downstairs."

A heavy frost from the previous night still covered everything, almost like snow. James didn't ask the slaves to come in from the weather but met them with Ginny and Aila outside the kitchen door. Although she had put on her winter coat, Aila was freezing.

"Now tell us what you want tuh tell us." James ordered.

"Well, Massa James, we reckins yuh oughta knows dem Yankees is comin' up dis way from Sugar Loaf now." began Aron. "Dey likely gwaine be marchin' up Federal Road up yonda tuh Wilmin'ton."

"What the hell yuh talkin' 'bout?" demanded James. "The las' we heared our boys was holdin' the line down at Sugar Loaf. An' how the hell do *you* know 'bout all this? The Home Guard ain't told us nothin' like that!"

"It now be time fo' y'all tuh know 'bout all dis, on account o' dis world gwaine change all 'round deese nex' few days." replied Aron. "We heared 'bout de Yankees by way o' our friends on Preacha Campbell's farm. Dem Black folks down south done left dere massas an' dey leavin' an' fallerin' dem Yankees tuh Wilmin'ton. Yankees be comin' by here real soon. An' dey likely gwaine want supplies from yo' farm."

"What? 'Em slaves can't jes' leave like that!" bellowed James. "The Home Guard's gonna track 'em down an' brang 'em back!"

"Dere ain't no mo' Home Guard, Massa James. Massa Lincoln's a'ready said we be free two years back! Now dat de Yankees is here, dat be a fact now!"

James glared unbelievingly into Aron' eyes. "So I reckin y'all thankin' 'bout runnin' away like the others! Ain't that right?"

"Well now, Tootsie ain't here on account o' he ain't decided if'n he stayin' er goin' wid de Yankees. He might stay er he might go. De rest o' us gwaine stay here fo' now. But one thang's fo' sho. We ain't gwaine be slaves whureva we is!"

"Well now, yuh niggers mus' thank I'm real stupid tuh tell me lies like that!" declared James. "Y'all reckin I thank Campbell is jes' gonna let his slaves run off like that? An' y'all thank yuh gonna be free jes' 'cause yuh say yuh are? Goddamn it! Y'all mah property! Now git back over thur an' tell Tootsie he ain't goin' nowhere! I'm goin' now tuh load mah shotgun!"

The slaves were clearly surprised by James' outburst. None spoke but stared wide-eyed at each other, waiting for someone else to speak. To the surprise of everyone, diminutive Mary Jane stepped forward and stood directly in front of James, clearly in his face.

"Y'all White folks ain't tellin' us wat tuh do no mo'!" she screamed. "I's tared as I kin be o' bein' a slave, an' I ain't gwaine stand fo' dis no mo'!"

Surprised and dumfounded by Mary Jane's arrogant assertiveness, James jerked upright and stepped backward, preparing to slap the girl's face. The move triggered a flash of intense fire through his injured left hip. He screamed as he dropped to the walkway floor on both knees, wincing in pain.

Ginny rushed to his side, preventing him from collapsing on the walkway floor. Now supported by his wife, he was on his knees, his eyes raised up to the face of the Black girl, his eyes fixed on hers.

"Y'all treat us like animals. Y'all give us scraps off yo' table an' mosely jes' food y'all ain't wantin'. Y'all ain't lettin' us learn tuh read an' write! Well, yuh knows wat? I's been learnin' tuh read an' write from Aila here, an' I's he'ped learn deese udda folks here. Yuh kin't stop us no mo'!"

"Yuh been lettin' that servant girl teach 'em slaves tuh read an' write, Ginny?" moaned James.

"You been teachin' these Negroes to read, Aila?" Ginny angrily confronted Aila. "I said you can't do that! You deliberately disobeyed me!" she shouted, slapping Aila hard across her face.

"I jes' taught Mary Jane, Miz Ginny!" whimpered Aila. "I ain't been teachin' all 'em other colored folks!"

"That doesn't matter, girl! I told you not to teach any Negroes!"

Mary Jane was not deterred by the side confrontation. "An' yuh oughta know it ain't jes' Aila dat been learnin' us readin' an' writin'. We got a Meetin' Place ova yonda whur we meet wid udda Black folks an' learn from each udda!"

"Meetin' Place?" groaned James.

Glaring up into her eyes, James could do little more than listen to the girl on his hands and knees as she continued.

"Ain't y'all knowin' dat keepin' slaves is a sin in de eyes o' de Lawd! It ain't matterin' dat y'all paid money tuh buy us. Buyin' us wuz a sin in de first place . . . 'cause y'all ain't got no right tuh buy nobody!"

Everyone was now staring at Mary Jane, their eyes wide and their mouths agape.

"Yuh knows dem Yankees is comin'. Yuh knows dey gwaine set us free . . . jes' as free as y'all is. An' yuh knows dere ain't nothin' yuh kin do 'bout dat! So yuh jes' better start treatin' us like peoples . . . not animals yuh own!"

Her sermon now completed, Mary Jane spoke no further, turned her back on James, and marched back toward her shack.

"Yuh all right, Massa James?" asked Aron. "Yuh need some he'p gittin' up?"

"Yes, please help, Aron." Ginny answered for James.

Aron grabbed James under the arms from the rear and tried to lift him upright to his feet, but his legs collapsed beneath him as he cried out again in pain.

"I kin't stand . . . I kin't stand up, Ginny." he mumbled to his wife.

"Aron, can you carry my husband into the house?" pleaded Ginny.

Aron gently lifted James from the walkway floor, supporting his shoulders and legs. James cried out again and choked back tears as Aron carried him into the front room and placed him on the sofa. Ginny knelt beside him.

"What's wrong, James? Your hip?" cried Ginny.

"Seems everthang's wrong. Mah hip . . . mah whole leg . . . feels like it's gittin' teared off. The slaves is revoltin' . . . the Yankees is comin'. I kin't handle all this. Reckin' yuh better send Aila tuh fetch Doc Brooks."

Chapter 12
YANKEES EVERYWHERE
FEBRUARY 1865

N<small>OT TAKING TIME TO SADDLE</small> M<small>ARY,</small> Aila bridled the mule and mounted her bareback. Something was terribly wrong with Mister Sanders, and she needed to bring Doc Brooks back as quickly as possible.

As Mary trudged toward the sand and mud of the cart trail to Federal Point Road, Aila heard voices behind her. She turned to see Mary Jane and the other Blacks trailing her.

"What yuh doin' fallerin' me, Mary Jane? Yuh don't need tuh be out walkin', carryin' that baby in yer belly."

"I's carryin' dat boo jes' fine!" asserted Mary Jane. "We's gwaine see if'n we kin see dem culled soldiers marchin' up tuh Wilmin'ton. Ain't yuh wantin' tuh see dem?"

"Jes' men in silly uniforms. Mah job right now is tuh find Doc Brooks. Mister James is in a terrible state after yuh caused 'im tuh hurt hisself."

"Massa James deserve evathang Mary Jane say tuh 'im." declared Aron. "She a strong young woman now! She speak her mind . . . an' she tell de truth."

"Well, I'm gonna go straight tuh Doc Brooks' house now. Yuh know whurbout 'em Yankees is?"

"Naw ma'am." said Tootsie. "We jes' gwaine walk in de direction o' Federal Point Road an' see wat we kin see dere. We kin walk wid yuh tuh Doc Brooks house on de way."

After about twenty minutes, they arrived at Doc Brooks' house. His wife explained that he had gone with the Confederates toward Wilmington to help with wounded soldiers.

Aila did not want to return to the farm without someone to deal with James' hip. Aron suggested that they locate the Yankee camp and hope to find a doctor there who would be willing to help. Aila agreed, but she wasn't sure James would want to be treated by a Yankee doctor.

They soon smelled woodfires, stronger than they could expect from the few farmhouses in the area.

"Dat de Yankee campfires, fo' sho . . . dey likely right 'long Federal Point Road, I reckins." said Aron. "An' I's thankin' I kin hear some kind-ah music comin' from ova dere."

The music became louder, drums and fifes playing a marching tune, sometimes dissonant with men's voices singing a different tune:

> *The village lads and lassies say*
> *With roses they will strew the way,*
> *And we'll all feel gay*
> *When Johnny comes marching home!*

Aila's entourage arrived at the edge of the Yankee encampment, gradually comprehending the scene.

Yankees everwhur!

Hundreds, what seemed like thousands of Yankee soldiers milling about, their sharp blue uniforms clearly contrasting with gray-brown hardwood trunks and green conifer woods. Activity was everywhere, soldiers tending campsites, laughing, singing, playing instruments, tossing baseballs.

"Lord 'ave mercy!" Aila exclaimed. "I ain't never seen nothin' like this. More soldiers than I kin count!"

They stood awestruck. Mary Jane could not contain her excitement. "Look ova yonda! Deres cullud Yankee soldiers fo' sho . . . fightin' tuh free us slaves! An' look ova dere! Dere's cullud peoples, men, women, chillens, all ova de place! Dey be slaves a'ready free!"

"Dis like Judgment Day!" exclaimed Tootsie. "An' we's all gwaine be saved! De Lawd done save us all!"

A tall White soldier in a Yankee uniform approached them.

"Good mornin' folks." he greeted. "My name's Captain MacBride. Do you live here locally? What brings you here?"

"Mah name's Aila, suh, Aila MacKenzie. I come tuh see if'n I kin git a doctor tuh come see Mister James Sanders over yonder on his farm. Now, he's in real bad shape with his hip . . . ain't able tuh walk atall. I'm his servant. We went to fetch Doc Brooks over yonder, but he done went north up tuh Wilmin'ton with 'em soldiers y'all's chasin'."

"MacKenzie?" said MacBride. "Your family's from Scotland?"

"That's what mah daddy told me."

"My family too."

Aila smiled. *A Yankee from Scotland, jes' like mah daddy an' mamma's families!*

"And what about you Negroes?" asked MacBride. "Why are you here?"

"We jes' come tuh see dem cullud Yankee soldiers we heared 'bout." Aron answered.

"An' I's thankin' 'bout goin' wid y'all Yankees an' all deese udda cullud folks." said Tootsie. "Dat on account o' I reckins we's free now."

"Well, I think we might be able to arrange for a surgeon to go and see Mister Sanders." said MacBride. "We need to obtain some food products and supplies. The quartermaster, Sergeant Campbell, should accompany us. He's a local boy.

"Yes, all of you Negroes are now free as President Lincoln has proclaimed." confirmed MacBride. "But we ask you not to join the others following us. It's a dangerous march and a real burden on us. You should remain where you live until we have an absolute victory and administrative services can be set up in this area."

～⌒

As Captain MacBride approached with the Quartermaster, Aila immediately recognized Robert Campbell in a blue Yankee sergeant's uniform.

"Well, hello, Miss Aila." Robert said. "Sa'prised tuh see yuh here with all these Yankees 'round."

"You know each other?" asked MacBride.

"Yessuh." answered Robert. "Miss Aila here was one of mah neighbors. Mah daddy an' her master, James Sanders, are good friends, I reckin."

"Her 'master'?" queried MacBride. "Are you a White slave, girl?"

"I'm a indentured servant tuh Mister James. But if'n the slaves are free now, I'm hopin' I ain't a servant no more."

A puzzled look crossed MacBride's face. "I don't know about that. As far as I know, the President said nothing about indentured servants. Maybe Congress will pass a law that makes indentured servants free along with the slaves. We'll have to wait and see."

Aila's attention turned to the Quartermaster Sergeant. "How come yuh fightin' with the Yankees, Mister Robert? Yuh know yuh brother is fightin' with the Confederate boys. Y'all on opposite sides!"

"Mah daddy an' me ain't agreein' 'bout slavery . . . 'specially 'bout tearin' apart our country over it. That's jes' like treason tuh me. Daddy's a preacher, but mah readin' of the Bible tells me slavery's a sin. I do worry 'bout mah mamma, though. I was able tuh go see her the other day. It's so hard fur her tuh have her fam'ly on both sides."

The surgeon, Captain Hamilton, arrived with an enlisted soldier driving a two-horse supply wagon. Captain MacBride and Sergeant Campbell would ride horses to save room on the return route for any food and supplies they could obtain.

The former slaves had their own questions for Captain MacBride about their transition to freedom as the group all traveled toward the Sanders farm.

"The politicians are already arguing about it." MacBride explained. "Back in January, General Sherman issued special orders that promised freed slave families 40 acres from their former owners and a mule that could be borrowed from the army."

"Capt'n, yuh means we kin git free land an' a mule fo' ourself?" asked Aron. "Dat gwaine be some miracle if'n dat true!"

"That's what the orders said, and I think that's what President Lincoln wants to happen." said MacBride. "Details haven't been worked out, and the politicians will have the final say."

The more MacBride explained, the more Tootsie realized that leaving the farm now would have its own set of problems. The former slaves' labor had produced a stockpile of food crops and preserved meats to which they would lose access if they left. They had no reason to leave until their future became more predictable.

At the farm, the former slaves returned to their log shacks, and Aila escorted the soldiers to the farmhouse front door where Ginny greeted them.

"Well, Aila, seems like you went to get Doc Brooks and came back with half the Yankee army!" exclaimed Ginny. "And isn't this here Robert Campbell? In a Yankee uniform? I'll bet Reverend Campbell is not happy about that."

"Yes, ma'am. It's nice tuh see yuh aghen, Miz Sanders." Robert answered.

"Mister Sanders is right here in our front room resting on the sofa, gentlemen. Please come in."

James could barely conceal his astonishment as the group entered. His gaze was fixed on Robert, a contemptuous frown creeping across his face.

Robert explained why Doc Brooks wasn't with them and why the Yankee entourage was there. Despite James' objections, Ginny convinced him to allow Dr. Hamilton's examination to go forward.

"It's hard to know what is causing all your symptoms, Mister Sanders." Hamilton said in conclusion. "Your hip seems to be partially disintegrated, and I can feel a large mass in that area, maybe a tumor. Normally, I'd remove the leg at the hip, but that might not fix the problem for the long term."

Ginny gasped and covered her mouth. James' eyes widened at the surgeon's dire proclamation.

"I can give you morphine for the pain, and the tumor could be removed if I remove the leg. But if it's a cancer, it might have spread to the rest of your body . . . and that most likely will kill you eventually."

"Yuh ain't gonna cut off mah leg, yuh Yankee quack!" yelled James. "Yuh're lyin' jes' tryin' tuh do me harm on account I'm a Confederate!"

"No sir, I'm just trying to help you." responded Hamilton. "Let's keep politics out of it."

Ginny was tearing but managed to hide it. "Now James, this all seems terrible, but he's not trying to hurt you. Listen to what he says. Isn't there something else you can do, Doctor Hamilton?"

"He ain't cuttin' off mah leg!" screamed James.

"Not much else I can do, ma'am. Amputation might work, but it might not. If we leave it as is, it will only get worse. The morphine will help with pain, but there will come a time when it won't."

"I'll jes' take mah chances." James concluded. "I ain't got much choice 'bout nothin' nowadays."

"I'll give you some morphine now, then, and leave a small supply. But you should have your local doctor watch over you in case your condition changes."

"Now, Mister Sanders . . . if I may . . . we need food and supplies to support our soldiers." MacBride said. "We can pay for anything you have that we need."

"I ain't knowin' if'n I got anythang tuh spare, 'specially fur no Yankees." declared James.

"Mister Sanders, this war is going to be over soon, and you aren't going to be on the winning side." McBride declared. "It's best you cooperate with us now that we're in charge of this area."

James was silent.

MacBride continued. "I understand at least some of the Negroes want to stay here on your farm until they see what other opportunities they have. It would be in your best interest to work with them . . . a crop-sharing or tenant-farming agreement with them might be in order. They know the farm, and they've already put much of their sweat into making what it is."

James continued his silence as he considered MacBride's assessment.

"I ain't likin' none of this." he finally said. "This here's mah farm . . . I ain't owin' 'em nothin'."

"James, there's a lot of wisdom in what Captain MacBride says." reassured Ginny. "If the Negroes will stay an' help with the farm, shouldn't we let them? They stayed with us when the others ran away. I can't manage this place by myself with you being disabled."

"Disabled." James whispered and then fell silent.

"Settin' 'em free is like givin' away property I paid good money fur. How kin I have any agreement with 'em? That's like treatin' 'em like they're equal tuh me. This here farm jes' been gittin' by fur quite a while now. This is gonna make it worse."

"If you can share the work, make the farm a joint business with them, you can improve your chances of success." said MacBride.

"I ain't knowin' if'n I gonna be free like the colored folks, Mister James." said Aila. "But I ain't got no reason tuh thank 'bout leavin' here. I kin stay an' he'p, if'n yuh want me to. I ain't got no whur else tuh go."

Before James could respond, Ginny spoke up.

"Aila, we want you to stay! You're part of our family . . . you're almost like a daughter to us. We need you."

Aila blushed and breathed a sigh of relief.

MacBride continued. "How many acres you got here, Mister Sanders?"

"A little over a hundred." answered James. "How come you ask?"

"General Sherman has issued an order that would force you to give up 40 acres, almost half of your farm, to your former slaves. Instead of working together under a joint agreement, they would become your competitors."

"Yuh tellin' me they'd take half mah farm away an' give it to mah slaves?" James shouted. "That's crazy! How kin they do that?"

"The government can do whatever it wants, sir." declared MacBride quietly. "You're going to lose this war."

James looked at the floor, shaking his head in disbelief. "God A'mighty!" he whispered.

No one spoke for some time while James considered his situation.

"If'n they're gonna stay, I reckin we gonna need a understandin' 'bout how thangs' gonna work 'round here." he finally announced. "I reckin we kin't do that here 'less we git all the nigras involved. Aila, go fetch 'em folks an' brang 'em over here so we kin talk."

He paused. "But whatever we decide, they ain't never gonna be mah equals!" declared James. "Losin' the wah ain't gonna change that!"

While Aila went to get the former slaves, MacBride and James negotiated on supplies for the Union forces. James quoted what he considered a fair price. MacBride declined.

"That's a fair price, MacBride. Take it er leave it." James ordered.

"With all due respect, sir, we don't have to pay you anything." countered MacBride. "We could consider it the spoils of war, and just take it."

"What!" yelled James. "That's robbery!"

"Perhaps so, sir. But you don't have much choice, do you? But to be fair, I can offer you half that price."

"Lord 'ave mercy!" exclaimed James. "Yuh call that *fair?*"

"It's certainly fair, considering the alternative, sir."

"Any price is fair compared to confiscation, James." Ginny interjected. "And Captain MacBride did help by bringing Dr. Hamilton to see you."

"Then take it, goddammit!" James shouted. "An' git out of mah sight . . . all of yuh!"

The former slaves arrived as the meeting ended abruptly. MacBride thanked James for helping and wished him better health. He then addressed the entire assembly.

"Understand that your lives will continue to be turned upside down for some time, even after the war is over. Some of our soldiers will remain stationed in this area to protect you as we enter a period of reconstruction. Remember that our soldiers are no longer your enemies. They are your fellow countrymen, trying to help you transition back into the union. President Lincoln is not a vindictive man. He wants to welcome you back home into our newly united country."

To James' surprise, MacBride cordially paid him in U.S. dollars, and the Yankees dismissed themselves and left to begin collecting the supplies. James had not seen U.S. greenbacks in nearly three years.

"Well, seems like if'n y'all want tuh stay here, we need tuh talk over some sort of agreement tuhgether 'bout farmin' this place." James announced to the assembled former slaves.

"Wat kind-ah agreement yuh talkin' 'bout?" asked Aron. "It betta be somethin' betta dan wat Preacha Campbell offered tuh our friends ova dere. Thirty percent afta expenses don' make no sense."

"Well now, y'all ain't ownin' no farmin' equipment, livestock, er supplies, so I'm gonna have tuh provide that fur yuh." countered James.

"De way we's seein' dis, if'n yuh kin't offa 'nuf tuh satisfy us, we ain't gwaine stay." declared Aron. "We done heared 'bout some places offerin' 50 percent. We might jes' go ova dere."

James' face slowly turned bright red. He couldn't speak.

"Honey, don't you think it would be better for them to stay here than you trying to find another group to farm this place?" asked Ginny. "They know the farm here, and you know them. You'd have to start all over with a different group."

James shook his head in frustration, then looked out the window.

"Damn it!" he grumbled. "I ain't got no choice 'bout nothin', do I?"

"Now suh, we needs tuh know if'n yuh got any loans aghen dis place 'fo' we kin agree tuh anythang." said Tootsie.

"What the hell *you* know 'bout loans?" James asked, wide-eyed.

"We knows if'n yo' loans don' git paid off, we might be left widout no farm tuh work." replied Tootsie.

"I ain't got no loans aghen this property." confirmed James.

"Yuh sho 'bout dat, suh?" pressed Aron. "Miz Ginny, if'n you kin ax 'im, we be mo' sho he be tellin' de truth."

"If James says there aren't any loans, then there aren't any loans." Ginny confirmed.

"Den we kin go 'head an' write up our agreement, Mista James." said Aron. "At 50 percent."

Chapter 13

THE END OF WAR?

Spring 1865

U NDER PRESSURE FROM ADVANCING UNION MILITARY, Confederate General Braxton Bragg's forces retreated from Wilmington on February 22, and Union soldiers entered the city later the same day. The Confederacy's last remaining supply port was now lost.

In early March, the army commanded by William Tecumseh Sherman invaded North Carolina, taking Goldsboro on March 9 and Fayetteville on March 11. In a major battle from March 19–21 at Bentonville in Johnston County, Sherman forced Confederate General Joseph E. Johnston to retreat toward Raleigh. Bentonville would the last battle for both armies.

General Robert E. Lee surrendered his Army of Northern Virginia to Union General Ulysses S. Grant at Appomattox Court House in Virginia on April 9, 1865. For many, this event signaled the end of the war, but Union and Confederate armies were still on the move in other states, including North Carolina. On April 13, Sherman occupied Raleigh, the state capital.

On April 15, John Wilkes Booth assassinated President Abraham Lincoln as part of a conspiracy with eight other Confederate sympathizers. Twelve days later, Union soldiers cornered Booth and set afire a barn where he was hiding. He refused to surrender and was shot dead by a single Union soldier. Booth's fellow conspirators were tried and convicted. Four were sentenced to death and hanged.

With the murder of Lincoln, Vice President Andrew Johnson, a North Carolina native, became President. Johnson was a Confederate sympathizer, and his succession would have a profound effect on the South's Reconstruction and the destiny of the former slaves. Almost immediately after Lincoln's death, Johnson rescinded General Sherman's 40-acres-and-a-mule order.

After three days of negotiation, on April 26, Confederate General Joseph E. Johnston surrendered the armies under his command to General Sherman at Bennett Place on the farm of James and Nancy Bennett, near what is now Durham, North Carolina. At almost 90,000 soldiers, it was the largest single troop surrender of the war.

But the war still was not over. Skirmishes, one ending in a Confederate victory, would continue in Alabama, Texas, and Indian Territory until August 20, 1866, when President Johnson finally declared, ". . . the insurrection is at an end and . . . peace, order, tranquility, and civil authority now exist in and throughout the whole United States of America."

A Presidential proclamation may promise that the war had ended, but that conclusion would be severely tested during the period of Reconstruction that followed. Many Confederates believed that they had not fully surrendered, and they never would.

Civil War casualty estimates vary, but about 620,000 military personnel were killed or died of disease. Fully 476,000 were wounded, and 400,000 were declared missing. Perhaps as many as 100,000 civilians died from combat, disease, or starvation. Over a million horses and mules were killed. Casualty estimates do not include those who came home psychologically damaged. The war wounds of mental illness were not part of the medical and social vocabulary of the 1860s.

The war of armies was over. The war for the reunited nation's soul would continue.

We're tired of war on the old camp ground,
Many are dead and gone,
Of the brave and true who've left their homes,
Others been wounded long.

We've been fighting today on the old camp ground,
Many are lying near;
Some are dead, and some are dying,
Many are in tears.

Many are the hearts that are weary tonight,
Wishing for the war to cease;
Many are the hearts looking for the right,
To see the dawn of peace.

Dying tonight, dying tonight,
Dying on the old campground.

—Walter Kittredge, 1863

Chapter 14

BOO-BOO SANDERS

APRIL 1865

⟶

As THEY BEGAN SPRING PLANTING, the former Sanders slaves were elated at the news that the Confederate armies had surrendered. But their soaring hope was dashed by the news of President Lincoln's assassination.

"He like Moses." Tootsie declared. "He lead us slaves tuh de Promise Land o' Freedom. But he neva see it hisself."

"He done give his life tuh set us free an' save us from dem White devil massas." wept Sally. "Jes' like de Lawd Jesus died fo' our sins an' save us from the Devil!"

Aila could see the sadness that overcame the former slaves with the news of Lincoln's murder. Their optimism about their future had been crushed. They had seen the sunrise, and this one event plunged the day back into darkness. Their view of Lincoln was perhaps overly simplified, but heroes, White and Black, would be needed to inspire their arduous and dangerous journey to freedom and equality.

Before dawn on April 28, Aila was awakened by screaming from the former slaves' shacks. She arose, lit a coal oil lantern, dressed in the warmest clothes she could find, put on her coat and shoes, and stepped lightly down the stairs to the area where James, Ginny, and baby Sarah slept. She could see that the noise had awakened Ginny, but James and Sarah were still asleep.

"It's Mary Jane's baby!" Ginny answered before Aila could ask. "It's late. That's not a good sign. Heat up two buckets of water, not too hot, grab my scissors and as many clean cotton rags as you can, and meet me at her place."

By the time Aila arrived with the cotton rags and hot water, Mary Jane's screams had subsided.

"How is she?" Aila asked as she opened the door to the shack and saw Mary Jane lying on her corn-shuck tick bed, surrounded by Ginny and Sally.

"She doin' jes' fine." answered Sally. "All she need tuh do is do wat come natural. Jes' some mo' pushes now, girl. Yuh 'mose dere!"

"Aila, you got my scissors?" asked Ginny.

"Yessum."

"De baby's comin'!" Sally announced.

Within minutes, the baby was out. Sally held the baby boy and cleared out his mouth and nose with her fingers while Ginny ripped one of the cotton rags into narrow strips. When the cord stopped pumping, Sally tied two of the cotton strips around the cord inches apart and used the scissors to cut the cord between the two ties. She wiped off some of the birth fluids with a clean cotton rag, wrapped the baby in a cotton blanket, and put him belly-down on Mary Jane's belly, his head next to his mother's breast.

Aila stood motionless as she fixated on Mary Jane's newborn child feeding from his mother.

A brand-new human bein'. A new person comin' intuh this purdy an' skeery world.

"Yer baby's beautiful!" Aila said to Mary Jane.

"He a boy." sighed Mary Jane, looking into the child's eyes. "Mah daddy's gran'son."

"What yuh gonna call 'im?" asked Aila.

Mary Jane kissed the baby on his forehead. "He ain't jes' a purdy, sweet 'lil boo. I gwaine call 'im 'Boo-Boo' 'cause he gwaine be double sweet an' strong. He gwaine stand fo' his fam'ly all de way back tuh Afriky. He now be borned a free person . . . de first since we come from Afriky. I's got faith dat he gwaine be a great man . . . dat he be strong an' skeer 'way all de evil thangs in dis world."

Aila saw tears forming in Mary Jane's eyes.

"He be borned in sprang, a new beginnin' fo' dis world. Dat gwaine give 'im special power tuh make a new beginnin' an' a betta place fo' his people."

Chapter 15

WHEN JOHNNY COMES MARCHING HOME

JUNE 1865

AFTER THE FALL OF WILMINGTON IN FEBRUARY, some former slaves stayed on the farms and plantations where they lived, hoping to start new lives for themselves there. Multitudes of others were now roaming the countryside, angering farmers by covertly "foraging" livestock and crops, generally heading north toward what they thought was opportunity. Most did not know what was to be their fate. All they knew was that they were *free*, but many could not fully grasp what that meant. Freedom and the hope for a better life was sufficient to keep them moving.

They converged on Wilmington and towns farther north, looking for work and safety. In the beginning, the Union Army and the federal government were ill-prepared to manage the migration or help the former slaves adjust to their newfound freedom.

As the migrants wandered north, walking or driving mule or oxcart through the early morning muck and sand on Federal Point Road, a solitary White man trudged south. He took little notice of the migrants as they passed, ignoring their stares and occasional greetings, seemingly fixated on a targeted destination.

He appeared to have been walking all night, his eyes and face showing signs of fatigue and sleep deprivation. Virtually in rags, he carried a stuffed canvas knapsack on his back and wore a Confederate infantryman's kepi cap missing its crossed-rifles pin, heavily worn leather Brogan boots, and otherwise civilian garb. Just south of Bernard's Creek, he took the muddy wagon path to the Sanders farm.

Two-month-old Boo-Boo slept in a cotton baby sling tied to Mary Jane's back as she tended flowers and vegetables in the small garden patch allocated to the Blacks near their shacks. Looking up, she saw Aila coming across the farmyard with a milking bucket in each hand.

"Time tuh milk 'em cows. Thur bags gonna be full 'bout now." Aila called out to Mary Jane. "An' they gonna want the milk back at the house this marnin'."

"Yessum. I's ready in jes' a minute. I wants tuh jes' water mah flahers a bit."

Using a wooden bucket, Mary Jane gently poured water around the base of white and pink morning glories she had planted, now twined around tall wooden stakes.

Mary Jane finished her watering and took one of the buckets from Aila. The two walked to the milking shed and began milking the two cows. Hearing the farm's hunting dogs barking, they first noticed the man walking toward the farmhouse.

"Who dat?" asked Mary Jane.

"Don't know." replied Aila. "Looks like some kind-ah tramp."

They were accustomed to seeing "tramps" and others walk by the farmhouse from time to time. Most of them seemed to be returning veterans and did not stop at the house. Occasionally, a White man dressed in a suit would knock on the door and visit with James in private. James never revealed who the man was or the purpose of his visits.

When the tramp approached the farmhouse, Ginny opened the kitchen door to greet him. He obviously was no stranger to her. Aila and Mary Jane could overhear the kitchen door conversation as they carried the milk buckets to the well, emptied the buckets into glass jugs, and lowered the jugs into the well on linked leather straps.

"Samuel, it has been such a long time since we've seen you." they overheard Ginny say. "How are Zechariah and Cousin Nancy?"

"They ain't much of nothin' I reckin." replied Samuel. "I done had 'nuf of Daddy blamin' me fur losin' the wah an' gittin' captured. He sez soldiers what git captured ain't nothin' but cow'rds. An' he beat me with his leather strop. Said he was gonna shoot me. I ain't never goin' back home aghen! That's why I come here. I want tuh ask y'all if'n I kin stay here an' he'p on Mister James' farm."

Ginny saw Aila and Mary Jane standing by the well listening to the conversation.

"Well now, Samuel, we have to speak with Mister Sanders about that." said Ginny. "He's resting inside. You remember Aila and Mary Jane over there?"

"Yessum, I 'member 'em from a long time back." said Samuel.

"Girls, this is Samuel Price, Zechariah Price and Cousin Nancy's son." Ginny called out as the girls approached. "He's finally home from the war. Samuel was a Confederate hero at Gettysburg. Welcome him home."

Aila and Samuel nodded in greeting. Mary Jane only glared at Samuel.

⌒

The next day, Aila learned that James had asked Samuel to stay and work on the farm. If all went well, he might eventually serve to manage the sharecropper agreement.

Aila learned that with Samuel's arrival she would have to give up her sleeping area upstairs and move to one of the former slave shacks. After all, it would not be proper for Samuel and Aila both to bed down in the farmhouse sleeping area.

"An' they done kicked me out of mah bedroom tuh make room fur 'im . . . that tramp!" she complained to Mary Jane. "Miz Ginny said I was one of the fam'ly, but Mister James ain't hearin' none of that! I ain't got no choice but sleep in one of 'em shacks!"

It was then that Aila caught herself. "I ain't meanin' tuh say I'm too good fur 'em shacks, Mary Jane. But it's like I been throwed out of the Sanders fam'ly!"

"Now don' yuh fret none. If'n I had a choice, I wouldn't live in 'em shacks ne'tha. We'll take real good care o' yuh ova dere . . . an' it mo' private anyways."

Aila liked what Mary Jane said, but she still felt as if she had been moved down a notch in the farm hierarchy.

———

Aila knew the horse carriages and mule carts pulling up in front of the Sanders farmhouse meant neighbors were arriving for the meeting about building a church for the community. The structure, intended to serve both as a church meeting place and schoolhouse, would be built by the same families that helped each other build new barns and farmhouses.

The meeting went on for two hours while tasks and responsibilities were assigned, construction materials were volunteered, a schedule was laid out, and "Mount Moriah" was chosen as the church's name. Mount Moriah, revered as the place where the Jewish Temple once stood, was the place where God commanded Abraham to sacrifice his son Isaac.

James Sanders donated land for the church in a sandy section of his property not well-suited for cultivation, but close enough to his farmhouse to ease his travel.

Reverend Campbell raised the question of the former slaves' attendance at church services. "When they was our slaves, we thought we oughta learn 'em the Lord's word. The Lord's word he'ped keep 'em in line, an' that was servin' His will an' our purpose.

"Now, 'em Yankees say they ain't our property no more." Campbell continued. "The Lord's done spoke tuh me an' said they oughta go thur own way sep'rate from us. We ain't needin' 'em mixin' in with our congregation."

The assembly agreed with Reverend Campbell, especially since the Lord had spoken to him directly.

After Campbell's closing prayer and the meeting was adjourned, Gideon Campbell and Samuel Price approached Aila.

"How're yuh tuhday, Miss Aila?" said Gideon. "Yuh lookin' real fine, like a'ways. I ain't seen yuh in a long time, what with me off fightin' fur our country an' all. Maybe yuh didn't know that Samuel here was a hero in the wah."

Samuel lowered his head. "I ain't no hero, Gideon." he whispered firmly.

"Well Samuel, yuh was at Gettysburg, the biggest battle of the wah. That's a lot more than I kin say!"

Samuel said nothing and looked away as if searching for a way out of wherever he was.

"Whur's yuh brother Robert?" asked Aila. "Seems like he'd be wantin' tuh he'p with the church."

"Don't yuh know Daddy done kicked 'im out of the fam'ly fur good?" said Gideon. "We reckin he's up in Wilmin'ton somewhur. We ain't knowin' fur sure. I reckin Samuel here agrees with Daddy . . . we ain't needin' nobody 'round here what fought fur 'em Yankees."

"Yer brother fought fur the Yankees?" asked Samuel.

"Yessuh. Daddy reckins he's the enemy tuh us all now. Like I said, Daddy sez he's a traider tuh us all an' tuh our country."

"He ain't our enemy no more." countered Samuel quietly. "We both fought fur what we thought was right. Our side lost. It's over now an' time tuh bind up our wounds." Samuel paused. "We need tuh do that an' move on with our life."

Gideon searched for the words to reply. As the conversation stalled, Reverend Campbell joined the three "young'uns."

"Miss Aila, I see yuh found our two heroes. Yuh know, mah son Gideon here was at Fort Fisher an' Sugar Loaf. They held 'em Yankees off fur a long time. They sent 'em nigger soldiers aghen us, but Gideon kilt a lot of 'em single-handed."

"I ain't kilt no nigger soldiers, Daddy." said Gideon, contradicting his father. "I seen 'em thur . . . they was fightin' jes' like the rest of us."

"That's more than yer brother Robert kin say!" Campbell declared. Turning to Aila, he continued. "Yuh know, Samuel an' Gideon's heroes. They gonna be the future of our country!"

Aila could see Samuel's eyes glisten over. *Which country is he talkin' 'bout?* she thought.

"With all due respect, suh, I ain't no hero." said Samuel. "It still skeers me tuh even thank 'bout what happened tuh mah army brothers up thur. But I ain't got no hatred fur 'em Yankees . . . even after the terrible time I spent in that prison in Maryland. They fought brave, jes' like we tried tuh do."

Astonished, Campbell momentarily could find nothing to say. Then he almost shouted, "Yuh sound like a Yankee-lover tuh me, son!"

Samuel struggled to continue his thoughts. "Mose of mah soldier buddies is dead now. It oughta be me that died, not them. I ain't no future fur this country . . . I he'ped tear it apart. I ain't even knowin' if 'n thur *is* a future fur this country."

"Yeah, they say the Yankees won the wah, but we ain't done yet!" exclaimed Campbell. "Thur's more ways than a all-out wah tuh git what we want!"

Samuel tried to say more, twisting his head left and right. He seemed to be looking for a way out.

"I jes' ain't good at socializin'." Samuel explained. "Too many thangs goin' through mah head. I bes' excuse mahself." He turned abruptly and left the room, saying nothing more.

"Well, I declare!" Campbell raged. "That boy's sure messed up. Imagine sayin' he ain't no hero an' thur ain't no future fur 'im an' this country! Maybe he ain't no hero. Maybe he was nothin' but a cow'rd all along!"

"They ain't wantin' y'all tuh be part of thur church . . . er thur school ne'ther." Aila explained to the sharecroppers assembled in Sally's shack early before breakfast the next day.

Mary Jane pushed a pan of uncooked biscuits into the baking area of the fireplace. "Dat ain't no sa'prise!" she opined, returning to her corn-shuck tick bed to nurse Boo-Boo. "None o' dem wanted us 'round dem 'fo' now, cept tuh do dere work. Ain't much changed from dat."

"We kin start our own church an' school." said Tootsie. "Preacha Burkhead from Wilmin'ton done learn us some readin' an' writin' at de Meetin' Place. He say folks in town is startin' de Afriky Methodist Episcopal church like dey got now up north an' down in South Carolina. He say we oughta come tuh town an' join dem."

Realizing she would be late to make breakfast for the Sanders and Samuel, Aila excused herself and left Sally's shack for the farmhouse.

Then she saw Samuel exit the farmhouse and walk toward her. Fortunately, she didn't have to think of anything to say to him as he passed by, the remains of a biscuit in his left hand. He touched his right hand to his kepi cap, said nothing, and continued toward the shacks, where Aron and Tootsie waited outside.

"It's about time you get breakfast for us on your mind, girl!" Ginny called out as Aila started up the kitchen steps. "You made poor Samuel run off for work with just two cold biscuits and honey."

Aila said nothing as she walked past Ginny.

"I know how upset you must be about moving to the cabin, Aila." Ginny began as she started baby Sarah's basin bath. "You know I have to go along with Mister Sanders' wishes. I still think of you as a member of our family."

Aila nodded as she started the biscuit dough. "I know all that, Miz Ginny. It still hurts. An' that 'cabin' yuh talkin' 'bout is a tumbledown shack . . . ain't no 'cabin'."

"Either way . . . it's my duty as a wife to honor my husband's wishes."

Aila pondered Ginny's comment as she started the grits on the stove, then put on a pot of coffee.

"But that ain't all that's botherin' me." Aila continued. "I was thankin' the end of this wah would be the end of wah. But I hear a lot of people thank it's still goin' on. Ain't thur gonna be no peace after all that killin'?"

"It would be nice to think peace would mean no more fighting of any kind, but I'm afraid that's not how people are." Ginny answered. "Only Heaven knows why God made us that way. I suppose everybody thinks God's on their side and their cause is righteous."

Chapter 16

THE ENCOUNTER

June 1865

A<small>ILA AWOKE IN THE PREDAWN HOURS</small> to intense lightning, booming thunder, and rain torrents pounding the roof of her shack. She was warm, but she pulled the cotton sheet up over her head in a useless attempt to protect herself from the storm raging outside. She thought it would never end. Finally, the storm subsided, and she lapsed back into sleep.

The crowing of the two farmyard roosters woke her up again when the sun was just below the horizon. The air was warm and humid from the storm. She lay still in her corn-shuck tick bed, watching the dull dawn light that fell through her window on the wall above her bed. The farm's hunting dogs were not stirring yet, and she could hear a small dawn chorus of birds already chirping through her window.

The dull dawn light on her wall suddenly turned to brighter sunlight, signaling the risen sun. Time for her to rise too. She quickly changed from her sleeping gown to a light dress, slipped on her shoes, and opened the shack door. The sun's rays swept across the farmyard, making patterns of long shadows and sunrays across trees, bushes, and yard grass. The sound of running water attracted her attention to several small streams that were rippling down the farmyard incline, carrying debris collected from the yard and woods.

By the time she finished milking, the peace and quiet of the morning had vanished. Now she was not alone. From her shack, Aila could see Samuel walking slowly around the farmhouse, seemingly inspecting the structure and the large pine trees that stood next to it. He stopped next to one large pine, examining it up and down and apparently pulling dead bark near its base.

Samuel circled the house one more time before climbing the walkway steps that would take him to the rear entry to the front room. Aila waited for him to disappear into the house before she completed her walk to the house and entered the kitchen. Ginny was there waiting for her.

"Quite a storm before dawn this morning." Ginny remarked.

"Yessum. It woke me up, an' I was skeered fur a while. It made everthang seem clean an' fresh this marnin'."

Ginny stopped collecting dishes for the breakfast and looked at Aila. "I like when you look on the bright side. Sometimes, I think you worry too much about things."

"I try tuh look on the bright side, but sometimes I jes' got too many questions without no answers."

When breakfast was ready, Aila carried the fixings to the front room table where James and Samuel were waiting, while Ginny resettled Sarah in the sleeping area. As Aila took her place at the table, she purposefully took a chair as far from Samuel as she could. Still, she sensed the scent of corn liquor emanating from his area.

James asked the morning blessing and turned to Samuel.

"Did yuh look at that big pine trees next tuh the house like yuh said yuh would?" he asked.

"Yessuh. Thur's one big one right next to yer bedroom winder that's been struck by lightnin'. It ain't dead, but it's got a lot of damage, an' I ain't sure it would stand a strong storm."

"Yeah, that one was hit 'bout a year ago, the day I hurt mah hip. It caused a li'l far, but the rain put it out."

"I seen some far damage, Mister James, but thur's a crack in the trunk runnin' up the tree a fur piece. Sa'prised it's still livin'. Bes' be cut down, tuh mah mind."

"Naw. That tree's been through lots of storms a'ready, Samuel. I reckin it oughta be cut down some time, but we're in growin' season. Yuh don't need tuh take time away from farm work tuh saw it down right now."

"Yessuh. I gonna jes' finish mah breakfas' an' git goin'."

The next day the sun was so blistering hot that everyone took off early from work in the fields and concentrated on jobs inside or around the farmyard in shaded areas. Sweat, pesky gnats, and deer flies were the day's undeserved punishment. Samuel had not been seen all day, and no one knew why he didn't show up or where he was. Ginny had checked his bed but saw no evidence that he had slept there the previous night.

James had not even tried to move from his bed that morning. Throughout the day he used a handmade and hand-powered wooden paddle fan for marginal cooling comfort. To provide better air circulation, all the windows and shutters were left open.

At the supper table, conversation turned to speculative explanations of Samuel's absence.

"This ain't the first time. If'n he keeps disappearin' without no explainin', maybe I oughta ask 'im tuh leave." James speculated. "But then, who's gonna manage the farm? I kin't do it, an' I don't trust 'em sharecroppers tuh do it. I jes' don't know what's wrong with 'im."

"It's called 'Soldier's Heart'." answered Ginny. "I've heard tell that's what happens to some soldiers who get messed up by being in war."

"I ain't never heared such!" James exclaimed. "They would've throwed him out of the army if'n he behaved like that in battle!"

"It sometimes comes long after the battle is over." Ginny explained.

By the time supper was finished and Aila had washed and put away the dishes, darkness had come. Ginny insisted that Aila take one of the lanterns hanging in the walkway to light her way back to her "cabin."

Large storm clouds lit by powerful lightning flashes loomed on the horizon as Aila crossed the farmyard to her shack. Distant thunder rumblings suggested that the storm was still far away. This time of year, storms were the rule rather than the exception.

I love 'em thunderstorms. They make me feel safe in a way an' give me a sense of peace . . . like God's comin' in wrath, lightnin' an' thunda, tuh clean up the whole world an' show He's in charge.

She pushed open the door to her shack, entered, and closed it behind her. Placing the lantern on her one table, she stretched out on her bed to relax. It had been a hard day, and she was ready for some quiet rest. She dozed off, the lantern still lit beside her bed.

She awoke abruptly, sat up in bed, and looked around in a daze. *Did I hear a noise . . . a noise outside? Maybe some coon er fox?*

The door abruptly banged open, and the figure of a man stood in the lantern light before her.

"What *yuh* want, Samuel!" she shouted, covering her body with the bedsheet. "Want yuh doin' in mah house?"

He said nothing. Staggering, he looked around the dwelling and then back at Aila.

"I weren't feelin' too good, so I took a li'l walk. Did I wake yuh up?"

Aila kept quiet and glared at the man, still covering herself.

"I been out in the woods all day tryin' tuh find mahself. Took me awhile. Then I found mahself . . . I found I was lost."

"How kin yuh be lost an' found at the same time?"

"Oh, that's purdy easy fur me."

He slowly weaved to the chair next to the fireplace.

"Lookie here. I got some real good moonshine. Nice an' strong. I figgered yuh might want tuh take a li'l swig with me. I bet yuh never had no licker before, ain't that right?"

Aila's heart skipped a beat. A chill shot through her gut.

"Come on. Yuh might like it." Samuel pleaded. "It seems tuh like me a lot. Maybe if'n yuh like it, yuh'll like me too."

Aila shook her head "no."

"Suit yerself. Yer mind if'n I sip a li'l of it tuh keep me comp'ny while we talk?"

Aila shook her head "no." "I reckin yuh oughta leave now, Samuel. It ain't proper fur yuh tuh be here like this."

"Now, what harm kin come from me jes' sittin' here an' passin' the time with yuh? I really need somebody I kin talk tuh."

Aila saw sincerity in his gaze but said nothing.

"Yuh a'ready seen I ain't much at talkin' tuh folks. Well, I'm worse talkin' tuh ladies like yerself. I kin't thank of thangs I want tuh say, an' I jes' ain't knowin' how tuh say 'em noways."

"Miz Ginny sez yuh oughta say '*I jes' don't know*' . . . '*I jes' ain't knowin'* ain't the right way tuh say it." Aila corrected him.

Trying to understand and absorb what she had said, Samuel looked at Aila for a moment, then replied. "I reckin if'n Miz Ginny sez that's right, it mus' be right. I greatly admire her."

He took a long drink from his jar, swallowed, and wiped his mouth with his sleeve.

"Yessuh. I admire her too." Aila replied. "She's been like a mamma tuh me ever since mah own mamma died."

"Kin I ask yuh a question, Miss Aila?"

She paused for a moment, then replied, "I reckin so, if'n it ain't too personal."

"Yuh got a man friend?"

Caught off guard, she didn't know what to say, but then replied, "Nawsuh, nobody ever showed no int'rest in me, fur as I knowed. I ain't much tuh look at, an' I ain't got no learnin' tuh speak of."

Samuel took another long drink from his jar. "Well, I thank yuh downrite purdy, mahself. I'd be proud tuh be yer man."

Aila blushed. She didn't realize that her bedsheet had slipped down to reveal the outline of her sweaty breasts. He couldn't resist allowing his eyes to wander down to her chest.

He took another drink from his jar. "Ain't yuh 'bout ready tuh take a swaller of this here refreshment?"

"I reckin I might try it, if'n yuh thank it's all right. I ain't never dranked none before, yuh know. Nobody ever told me it ain't somethin' I oughta do."

"I ain't mindin' sharin' one bit." he said, passing the jar to her. "Jes' take a li'l swaller at first, 'til yuh git used tuh it a bit."

She put the jar to her lips and took a small sip. Shaking her head in disgust, she exclaimed "Lordy, that burns somethin' terrible. I kin feel it all the way down. How kin yuh like somethin' like that?"

"It ain't s'posed tuh taste good, girl! Yuh drank it tuh make yuh relax an' feel good. Now take 'nother small sip. It'll go down smoother this time."

It did go down a little smoother as he had promised. The liquor going down her throat warmed her whole body. He moved to sit beside her on the bed, but she barely noticed his closeness as the liquor began to go to her head.

"I'm feelin' kind-ah strange like . . . feelin' kind-ah good, like I'm startin' tuh float . . . dizzy. That the way I oughta feel?"

He took the jar and swallowed another drink. "Yes, Miss, that's 'zackly the way yuh oughta feel."

He took her hand. She pulled back a little but didn't let go. His hand rubbed her back, then her shoulders. "How's that feel?" She didn't respond.

"Did I tell yuh how purdy yuh was? I been watchin' yuh ever since I come here. How yuh walk, yer purdy eyes. Yuh been hauntin' me somethin' terrible."

She looked at his face and saw a little smile. "Ain't nobody ever said nothin' like that tuh me before. Yuh seem like a real sweet man."

"Yuh mind if'n I kiss yuh on yer lips?" he asked. "That would be real nice."

She didn't reply. He abruptly moved forward and covered her mouth with his. She felt his hand grabbing her left breast, growling, "Yuh got real nice li'l teats!"

She was completely shocked by his move but didn't push his hand away. Her body tingled all over, and somehow, it felt good and right for his hand to be where it was. He pushed her back on the bed and crawled on top of her, forcing his knee between her thighs.

What kin I do? I kin't push 'im off . . . he's too strong an' heavy. I gotta scream!

She screamed as loud as she could, over and over. But he wouldn't stop. She began begging. "Please stop . . . stop . . . STOP!"

Mary Jane and Sally burst through the door, each carrying a split fireplace log. Growling like wild animals, they both began whacking Samuel as hard as they could with the wood, over and over, his back, his head, all the while screaming, "Git off her!"

He yelled and rolled off Aila onto the dirt floor while the women continued to pound him.

Tossing the logs aside, Mary Jane and Sally grabbed Aila's hands, pulled her off the bed, and forcibly led her out through the door and into Sally's shack, leaving Samuel to writhe on the floor.

They laid Aila on Mary Jane's bed, and Mary Jane began cooling her brow with a damp rag. Sally took a hatchet from the small fireplace wood and stood by the closed and barred door. Mary Jane was the first to speak.

"Yuh all right, Miss Aila?"

"I reckin. I don't know." Aila sobbed. "Mah mind is real foggy now. He hurt me real bad. An' I thought he was a sweet an' 'umble man . . . what cared 'bout other people."

She cried out again, running her fingers forcibly through her hair and sobbing.

"Y'all all right in dere?" Aron called from outside the door.

"We all done heared screamin' an' cryin' . . . is one o' yuh hurt?" asked Tootsie.

"We's all right now." Sally lied. "Y'all ain't needin' tuh come in here right now. We needs tuh do some women talk. But y'all go see if'n Mista Samuel's in Aila's house. If'n he dere, don't let 'im go nowhur. I wants y'all to grab 'im an' tie 'im up. He done somethin' terrible tuh Miss Aila."

"Yessum." Aron replied.

"Did he put his seed inside yuh?" Sally asked.

"I . . . I don't know." Aila answered. "I don't know what that feels like. I jes' know . . . I jes' know it hurt real bad."

"We gwaine try tuh clean yuh out." Sally announced. "Dat de bes' we kin do right now."

Sally wet a cotton rag with vinegar, wrapped around a corn cob, and inserted it into Aila's vagina.

"That hurts real bad Miz Sally." moaned Aila. "Too deep . . . an' burns like far! Kin yuh please stop?"

"I reckins dat all we kin do, den." Sally concluded. "It in de Lawd's hands now. He decide wat's right."

"We ain't seein' Mista Samuel nowhere." Aron called through the door. "I reckins he done run off."

"I need tuh see Miz Ginny." pleaded Aila.

"In de marnin', Miss Aila." Sally said. "In de marnin'. Right now, yuh needs tuh rest w'ile we takes care o' yuh. Tuhmara gwaine come soon 'nuf."

Aila reclined on her bed and closed her eyes. "I reckin I oughta git some rest. I'm real tarred."

Mamma an' Daddy, I'm prayin' tuh yuh tuhnight on account of I feel so alone. I feel like I'm dyin' an' I need strength tuh carry on in this world. I thank 'bout y'all a lot, an' I miss yuh so much. I thank 'bout what it was like when yuh died. Did it feel like I feel now? Did somebody hold yer hand? Did somebody hug yuh an' tell yuh they gonna miss yuh? Did they say yuh was loved?

Aila could feel a warm hand holding her hand.

Is that yuh, Mamma?

Then she realized it was Mary Jane.

※

Aila awoke, comforted to see Mary Jane sleeping next to her with Boo-Boo on bedding she had brought from her own shack. But the terrifying memory of the assault kept running through her mind over and over. Panic and fear gripped her.

"Did he hurt me so I kin't have babies?" she moaned to Mary Jane. "Will any man want tuh marry me now? How kin I take care of a baby on mah own? Y'all warshed me, but I still feel dirdy. Will I ever feel clean aghen?"

She wept, turned in her bed, and wept again.

"Dere, dere, Honey." said Mary Jane quietly. "I knows how yuh feel. I done felt like dat mahself 'fo'. Yuh gwaine be all right. We gwaine take care o' yuh. Mamma's makin' some breakfas' fo' us."

Sally brought in warmed ham and leftover biscuits, and they ate while Mary Jane fed Boo-Boo. After eating, the three women walked to the farmhouse, Mary Jane carrying Boo-Boo in his baby sling.

Ginny was up and making coffee when they entered the kitchen. The story of the assault shocked and saddened Ginny. She hugged Aila tightly as they wept, triggering more sobs from Sally and Mary Jane.

"Where's Samuel now?" asked Ginny, clearing her throat.

"We ain't knowin' . . . de mens say dey look fo' 'im, but he wuz nowhur tuh be found." answered Sally. "Yuh thankin' o' reportin' dis tuh de law?"

"I don't even know who the law is these days." Ginny answered. "Is the sheriff still the sheriff? There's no Home Guard anymore. Are the Yankees the law now? It won't change anything if we do report it. What are they gonna do? Samuel's a war hero. If everybody knows what happened, she'll be seen as trash, not the victim of a crime. What man would want to marry her? We shouldn't be telling anybody. I won't even tell James. If he asks about Samuel, I'll say he just ran off and nobody knows where he is. If your men ask about last night, just say it's women's business, and leave it at that."

"She gwaine be called 'trash' anyways, if'n she be gittin' a boo." Sally said flatly.

"I know." Ginny replied. "But we don't know if she's really with child. We'll just have to cross that bridge when we come to it."

It was almost midmorning before Aila and the women left Ginny in the kitchen to prepare James' breakfast. Little work would be done this day, except what the men could do. For the women, it would be a day of rest, reflection, and emotional rehabilitation.

As the women crossed the farmyard toward the shacks, something unusual in the woods next to the barn caught Sally's attention.

"Lawdy, wat's dat ova dere in de woods near dat big oak tree?"

The other women strained to see what Sally was talking about. "It look like a bear done climbed up in dat dere tree. Why ain't dem dawgs barkin'?"

The women moved closer. They could see that it wasn't a bear. It was the dark figure of a man, seemingly hanging from the branches. As they approached the tree, they recognized the figure.

"Lawd 'ave mercy!" exclaimed Sally. "Dat Samuel done hung hisself!"

———

Later, on the morning the body was discovered, Ginny served James breakfast and told him the news of Samuel's death but revealed nothing about Aila's sexual assault the previous night.

James paused, then looked out his window toward the woods. "Maybe Samuel's better off now. I sure know what sufferin' is all 'bout. I ain't been much value he'pin' runnin' the farm. I reckin Aron kin take up the slack now that Samuel's gone. It sure ain't gonna be me . . . 'cause I'm useless. I might as well be dead like Samuel."

"Now, James, don't say that!" countered Ginny. "You know it doesn't bother us at all that you can't do a lot of things right now. You are the man that keeps this farm and our family going. This is your farm, and if the Negroes didn't have this place, they would probably be destitute. You should be proud you've made a home for us . . . and for them too."

"I know yuh tryin' tuh make me feel better, Ginny, but mah life like this is miserable. Mah pain kin be terrible at times. That Yankee doctor's morphine he'ps some, but it keeps me from knowin' what's goin' on mose of the time. I kin say in truth that I'm yearnin' fur Heaven. I want tuh see the Lord, mah mamma an' daddy, an' mah boys now long gone."

Ginny saw tears in James' eyes. She took James' hand and squeezed it tightly. "You're not going anywhere anytime soon, James. You're gonna stay right here and let Sarah and me love you. What would we all do without you?"

James was quiet for several minutes, staring at the floor.

"Yuh know, Honey, I been thankin'. I reckin it'd be real nice if'n I kin be laid tuh rest up whur the church's gonna be built. Since I give the land, it's part of mah farm. I'm figurin' I jes' might be the first one in the church graveyard. That'd be a real honor, I reckin."

Ginny smiled and took his hand again.

Tootsie volunteered to wagon Samuel's body to Zechariah's farm near Castle Hayne. It would take almost five hours one way, and it was near noon already. James wrote a letter to Zechariah asking that Tootsie be allowed to stay overnight. The summer heat would speed up decomposition of the body, so the men hurried to prepare the body for the trip. When all was ready, Tootsie clicked twice with his tongue, and Mary headed slowly down the path toward Federal Point Road.

"Mamma's gwaine take care o' Boo-Boo fo' a w'ile." Mary Jane said to Aila as Tootsie's wagon disappeared into the woods. "Let's us take a li'l walk."

The two women took their familiar path toward the river. The thought of seeing the river brightened Aila's spirits a little, but not enough to remove the cloud over her soul and the demons that lay hidden there.

The river in midday sun lacked its glorious aura often seen at sunset, the women's more familiar view, but it was not any less peaceful there. They did not speak. They took their familiar seats on the cypress log.

After some contemplation, Mary Jane spoke first. "Yuh knows it ain't yo' fault. I knows dat wat yuh feelin' now. I felt it afta dat devil Dunbar did it tuh me. Samuel ain't dead on account o' you . . . he dead 'cause o' 'im. His sin wuz aghen you an' aghen de Lawd."

"But I went along with 'im at the start. I reckin I made 'im thank I wanted 'im tuh do it."

"Wat yuh did ain't no sin. Yuh made it plain yuh wanted 'im tuh stop. He heared yuh clare! He's de one dat sinned, not you."

"Maybe so. But why did he go kill hisself over it? Ain't it me that cause 'im tuh do that?"

"He won't nothin' but a troubled man. Yuh kin't he'p wat messed up folks might do. It ain't yuh fault in de eyes o' de Lawd."

Except for the quiet flow of the river against its banks and the gentle breeze from the west, silence pervaded. Looking skyward, they saw the silhouette of a large bird circling high above them. Gradually descending to the top of a longleaf pine behind them, the bald eagle landed in its branches.

"I love this place." Aila confirmed. "It's so quiet an' peaceful here. Like no place else."

"Yessum. But dat world out dere ain't like dis place. It full o' trials an' tribulations. Dat why we needs tuh stay strong if'n we gwaine survive. Wid de Lawd's he'p, dat wat we gwaine do."

Chapter 17

NOAH'S CURSE & THE TOWER OF BABEL

JULY 1865

The worthy and well-disposed among you are entitled to the sympathy and encouragement of all good people. I believe you will receive it . . . [I]t is a mistake to suppose that the white people among whom you were born and raised, with whom you played when you were children . . . have all at once turned into your enemies . . . On the contrary they have known that you have simply accepted the freedom which has been given to you. They do not hate you—they are not your enemies.

I would encourage you, as a friend who desires to see you enjoy . . . happiness an' good fortune to which you can justly lay claim, to seek employment, to labor diligently and elevate your race, to abide to the laws, to educate your children, and to live in such a way as to command the respect and sympathy of your fellow men.

—Alfred M. Waddell: An Address Delivered to the Colored People, by their Request, at the Wilmington Theatre, July 26th, 1865.

IT WAS SUNDAY MORNING AND TIME FOR CHURCH. The July sun bearing down on them, Ginny drove the horse and four-person buggy through the sandy woods on a path that was barely discernable. Already, the heat and humidity seemed unbearable.

"Sure is hot out in these here woods!" Aila complained to Ginny. "Seems like the Lord might make the Lord's Day a li'l cooler fur us."

"Now, Aila, don't you go questioning the Lord's handiwork." said Ginny. "He must have a reason for making it so hot. Maybe it's because when the cool comes, it feels so much better."

"The cool ain't comin' near fas' 'nuf fur me."

Aila long had been required to attend church services at the Sanders home every third Sunday, but it was the first Sunday morning she and a congregation would fill the chairs in the new Mount Moriah Church, still under construction. The congregation hoped that services in the new building would be more frequent.

Although Aron helped James into the buggy, he and the other sharecroppers were not invited to the service on the orders of Reverend Campbell. Rumors abounded that they were having their own services at some unknown location they called "The Meetin' Place."

When the buggy arrived at the church, male members of the congregation helped James from the buggy seat into the church building. Ginny and Aila followed, doing their best to avoid sand spurs and gnats. When all were seated, Reverend Campbell began his sermon.

Aila listened for a while, but soon dropped out into daydreams. Then something Campbell said caught her attention. Something about "servants."

"The servant of Shem!" Campbell bellowed, streams of sweat pouring down the side of his face. "The Lord God told Noah tuh put a curse on a man called Canaan, sayin' 'Canaan shall be the servant of Shem'. Noah's curse made all of Canaan's descendants servants furever."

Now Campbell screamed, his face turning an angry red. "Yuh know, that man Canaan was a nigger man from Africa, an' God made 'im a slave! An' Canaan's children was black Africans, an' so was his children's children! God is tellin' us that niggers mus' be slaves furever. So makin' 'em free was a sin aghen God's will!

"In the eyes of the Lord, they're still our servants an' we're still thur masters!" Campbell yelled, striking the pulpit lectern with his gavel fist.

"And the Bible sez the Tower of Babel was all about keepin' the races sep'rate. We ain't s'posed tuh mix with people what ain't White! The Lord God made the men buildin' the tower speak diff'rent languages an' scattered 'em all over the earth. The Lord wanted tuh sep'rate the other races from his chosen people . . . us White people.

"Now we gonna sang the song of invitation." Campbell calmly announced when it was time to close the service. "Jesus wants any of y'all that ain't saved yet tuh come down tuh the front here, confess yer sins, an' ask Jesus tuh save yuh from everlastin' Hell far!

"Let the blood of Christ cleanse yer soul of all yer trials an' tribulations. Put yerself in his healin' arms an' he'll lift all that weight off yer shoulders. Everlastin' life, mah friends! Saved from death an' the fars of Hell! Livin' furever with Jesus in the Kingdom of God! Now let us sang of 'Jes' As I Am' . . . our reg'la three verses."

> *Jes' as I am, without one plea,*
> *But that Thy blood was shed fur me,*
> *An' that Thou bids me come tuh Thee,*
> *O Lamb of God, I come . . . I come!*

"This might be yer las' chance tuh git saved, mah friends." Campbell shouted. "We ain't knowin' when the Lord might take yuh. Come down now an' make sure yuh git saved before then!"

> *Jes' as I am an' waitin' not*
> *Tuh rid mah soul of one dark blot,*
> *Tuh Thee, whose blood kin cleanse each spot,*
> *O Lamb of God, I come . . . I come!*

A man and a woman Aila did not know came down to the preacher separately with tears in their eyes. They each whispered in the preacher's ear, and he whispered back. Aila knew that each had accepted Jesus as their Lord and Savior.

Jes' as I am, Thou wilt receive,
Wilt welcome, pardon, cleanse, relieve;
Because Thy promise I believe,
O Lamb of God, I come . . . I come!

Chapter 18

AND THE LORD HATH
TAKEN AWAY

AUGUST 1865

⟊

THE SUMMER HEAT WAVE CONTINUED to oppress human and beast alike as it had almost every day for the past month. In the same daily pattern, gigantic anvil-topped cumulonimbus storm clouds formed on the distant western horizon, generating intense lightning flashes.

Bending and digging Irish potatoes with the other workers in the hot sun, Aila saw the motion of billowing formations piling on top of themselves. On previous days, the clouds had moved over the area of the farm with short periods of wind and some short heavy rain showers of minor consequence. What would happen today could not be predicted.

"Lordy, Lordy! I hate gittin' all this black dirt under mah fingernails!" complained Aila. "I feel like I been standin' on mah head all day."

"We needs one o' dem mule-pulled tayda diggers like I heared dey got ova yonda on de Campbell farm." said Mary Jane.

"That would be nice." Aila agreed. "Mister James ain't ready fur none of 'em new-fangled machines, I reckin."

Baby Boo-Boo started fretting in his baby sling, causing Mary Jane to take him out, hold him to her breast, and start feeding him as she continued working with her free hand.

Aila stood upright for a short break to stretch her back and survey the landscape and sky. "Looks like it's comin' up a cloud over yonder." she observed.

"Yessum, I reckins so." agreed Sally. "Maybe we got time tuh git deese taydas all in 'fo it hit us."

The workers continued to watch the storm clouds build as they grubbed and tossed potatoes into wooden-slatted bushel baskets. Such a lightning storm could become life-threatening, especially in the open field.

The clouds and lightning came closer, and a cooling breeze began to sweep across the field. It was time to stop their work and move to less vulnerable locations. Their shacks offered the best protection, but no place would be completely safe in a lightning storm.

By the time they arrived at the shacks, the breeze had grown into a strong wind that blew pine needles and green hardwood leaves and woodland debris across the farmyard. The thickening clouds had turned the afternoon into twilight. Feeling they needed mutual support, the three women decided to hunker down in Sally's place with baby Boo-Boo.

As soon as the women had settled in, Sally turned to Aila. "How long since yuh bled, girl?"

Aila tensed up, shocked by Sally's question. "I . . . I don't know. I . . . I reckin 'bout three months. I ain't been countin'."

"Honey chile, I reckins yuh might gwaine be a mamma."

A lump rose in Aila's throat, and an intense chill came over her. "Oh, mah Lord! Are yuh sure? How kin yuh tell?"

"Yuh got a bump on yo' belly dat won' dere las' month. I saw it out dere in dat tayda patch. Yuh a skinny girl, so it 'bout time yuh start showin'."

Aila burst into tears. "What am I gonna do? No man's gonna tuh marry me if'n I got a bastard baby!"

Mary Jane moved to Aila and embraced her. "Now, now. It ain't de end o' de world. De Lawd done give yuh dat baby, jes' like he give me Boo-Boo. Ain't nothin' wrong wid dat. He ain't gwaine call yo' baby a bastard, even if'n peoples do. He ain't givin' it tuh yuh if'n he ain't wantin' yuh tuh have it."

A sudden gust of wind jolted the shack as if intending to lift it off the ground.

Sally swung open the flimsy door and scanned the threatening western sky. "Dem clouds looks full o' danger!"

"Wha . . . what kind-ah danger?" Aila stuttered. "We gonna git kilt?"

"I ain't knowin'. De Lawd know . . . not me!"

At that moment, the wind picked up dramatically into a deafening roar, violently shaking the shack as if to blow it away. The women screamed and reached out to embrace each other. Boo-Boo started crying.

"Git down on de floor an' lay flat!" Sally shouted. "Cover up dat baby wid yo' body!"

Trembling, the women huddled together with Boo-Boo on the dirt floor of the shack as the structure shook and groaned around them.

"Lawd, he'p us!" screamed Sally, as if God couldn't hear.

The wind finally subsided, and Boo-Boo stopped crying. The women embraced again.

"De Lawd done save us!" declared Sally.

A woman's distant shriek echoed outside the shack.

"What's all dat screamin'?" Mary Jane exclaimed. Departing the shack, they encountered Aron and Tootsie looking across the yard toward the farmhouse.

"Look like dat big pine tree done fell on de house!" shouted Tootsie.

The tornado had twisted the giant pine tree from its roots, just above the area damaged by lightning the previous summer, lifted it into the air, and thrust it through a window, collapsing the side of the house.

Hurrying across the yard and into the house, they heard Ginny moaning, but at first, they could not see her through the tangle of branches, twigs, and needles. Frantic, they pulled the tangle aside to reveal Ginny, cradling Sarah in her arms, with a large portion of the tree trunk resting on her lower body. Sarah was crying, but apparently unharmed. James was lying face down a short distance away, his bleeding head beneath the trunk.

Tootsie ran to retrieve the crosscut saw from the barn, and they all worked to remove the trunk, first from Ginny and then James. Ginny clearly had at least a broken leg, a section of femur protruding from her thigh. James' head was crushed. Nothing could be done to save him.

Sally attended to Ginny, the men worked to remove the trunk and James' bloody body, and Aila quickly saddled the horse and rode to fetch Doc Brooks. Despite her frantic ride, she returned with the doctor almost an hour later.

The doctor confirmed James' death and then worked to set and splint Ginny's leg. Inconsolable, she moaned, cried, and periodically screamed. Aila held and rocked Sarah and tried as best she could to verbally comfort Ginny.

What could Aila say? She had never liked James, but she found a kindred spirit in Miz Ginny and could feel her pain and sense of loss. But even more than that, she feared what would happen to her and Ginny now that James was gone.

⁓

Without James as the established patriarch, Aron stepped up and took charge of the farm for Ginny. Arrangements had to be made for James' funeral, and the crops and animals would have to be managed somehow. Aron's required work with White suppliers and customers would be difficult. Anticipating those difficulties, Ginny wrote an explanatory letter to facilitate cooperation from local businesses. The news of James Sanders' death spread quickly, and soon virtually everyone in the White community would understand the situation and agree to cooperate with Aron.

A graveside funeral was held the next day next to Mount Moriah Church, as James had requested. Aron and Tootsie carried Ginny to the gravesite, where they placed her in the rocking chair that had been her mother's. Reverend Campbell conducted the service, and several neighborhood families attended. Campbell ordered all the Blacks to stand together as a group behind and separate from the Whites.

"From the Book of Job." Campbell began. "The Lord gave, an' the Lord hath taken away; blessed be the name of the Lord. A-men."

"A-men." chanted the assembly. The preacher continued his short sermon.

"It's fittin' James Sanders be buried here, near where we're buildin' our new church on the land he give. We know y'all gonna want tuh honor 'im by finishin' this church buildin' so it kin be used fur the savin' of souls. Tuh the Lord an' his Son Jesus Christ be the glory. A-men."

"A-men!"

Campbell continued his sermon. "I reckin y'all heared 'bout Colonel Alfred Waddell's speech tuh the niggers in Wilmin'ton las' month. Now, I agree with mose of what he said. But I ain't agreein' with the part 'bout tuh nigger race elevatin' 'emselves. I wanna tell yuh right now . . . an' this is fur all yuh black folks back yonder . . . yuh ain't never gonna be equal with Whites, no matter how much yuh elevate, no matter how hard yuh work er how educated yuh git. The Lord ain't got no intention fur coloreds tuh be equal with Whites!

"An' I kin tell yuh somethang else 'bout 'em freed niggers elevatin' 'emsleves. They ain't doin' no elevatin' no way. They been set free tuh ravage the countryside, steal our livestock, murder White folks, and rape our women. There ain't no law no more in this country, an' they're jes' gonna keep comin' after us, our fam'lies, an' our property."

The former slaves looked at each other in dismay. Campbell paused to wipe his forehead with his handkerchief and continued.

"Now we all gonna miss our brother James." Campbell continued. "But we ain't sad 'bout that. No suh. We ain't sad 'cause we know death is jes' part of the Lord's great plan fur us. Resurrection an' eternal life in the Kingdom of God is waitin' fur us!"

Several White neighbors lowered James' coffin on ropes into the pre-dug grave. Tootsie and Aron gently carried Ginny to the grave where she slowly released a handful of dry black soil onto the coffin as she wept.

Aila moved to embrace Ginny and comfort her. They both were saddened by James' death, but the embrace had more to do with their bonding to face the future.

Neighbors approached Ginny with consolation, allowing her more space to speak with everyone individually. Aila separated from Ginny and patiently waited several steps away. Gideon Campbell soon approached her, smiling.

"Nice tuh see yuh aghen, Miss Aila." Gideon greeted. "Yuh lookin' fine as usual. I'm real sorry 'bout Mister James."

Aila could not look directly at the suitor. She simply said, "Thank yuh."

"Thur's somethin' I want tuh talk tuh yuh 'bout, Miss Aila, but I reckin this ain't a good time tuh do that. Kin I come visit yuh in a week's time, after thangs settle down some? I been practicin' mah fiddle, an' I kin play yuh some tunes, if'n yuh like."

What does he want tuh talk 'bout? Aila wondered. She was afraid to ask.

After the funeral guests had departed, Ginny and Aila welcomed some private time together in the kitchen. Ginny reminisced about how she and James had first met; how she was happy in the early days of their marriage, but later became disillusioned; how she learned to understand him and love him later; and how he tried to be hard on the outside but was soft on the inside.

At the last recollection Ginny began to weep and averted her eyes from Aila as if she was embarrassed to let her friend hear what she wanted to say.

"You know, your duty as a wife is to serve your husband's needs, as a woman and a best friend. Sometimes, that's real hard, but you do it anyway. I know he whipped you from time to time . . . and me too . . . but that was him just trying to be strong, like the head of the family ought to be. I'm sure he was feeling as much pain inside as we did outside."

I doubt that! Aila thought, suppressing a shudder. Both women looked away in silence. For Aila, it was time to change the subject.

"Miz Ginny, I know yuh're real sad 'bout Mister James, but kin I talk tuh yuh 'bout somethin' private. I need yer . . . yer advice."

"What is it, Honey?"

"Well, Sally reckins I got a baby in me from Samuel. It's been three months since I bled, an' it's startin' tuh show."

"I've been wondering about that myself, Aila. You are showing the signs."

"But what am I s'posed tuh do?"

"I don't see much you can do. If you're with child, you likely will bear that child. That's God's will."

"Ain't thur somethin' kin be done tuh git the baby tuh come out before it's ready? What am I gonna do with a baby without no husband?"

"You know that would be a mortal sin in God's eyes! You . . . and whoever helped you . . . would burn in everlasting Hell!"

"I heared 'bout ways that kin do that . . . make it come too early."

"That's dangerous, Aila. You could die! But good Lord, child, even if you don't die, you'll go straight to Hell for it. You have to face the fact and let nature take its course. You're gonna be a mother, whether you've got a husband or not."

"Why should I git punished fur somethin' that ain't mah fault?" Aila argued. "Why is God gonna punish me fur that? That man forced me! I screamed 'STOP!' but he forced me anyway!"

"Even if you were forced, if he put his seed in you, you make a baby if it's the Lord's plan. If the Lord didn't want you to have that baby, you wouldn't be pregnant. That's the way of the Lord. Who are we to question it?"

~~~

Two days later, Alan Smith and his wife Rebecca arrived at the Sanders farm unexpectedly with their new month-old girl, Priscilla. They had received word of James' and Samuel's deaths and had come for a few days to pay their respects, pray and mourn with Ginny, and present their newly born child.

The Smith and Sanders families shared great affection, and greetings were truly genuine. As expected, the Smiths expressed their shock and sorrow at Samuel's suicide, James' sudden death, and Ginny's injury.

Alan ran his right hand through his bushy hair, as if searching for certainty. "I was so sorry tuh hear 'bout Samuel's dyin'. I knowed 'im as a brave soldier an' a good man. But it ain't hard tuh understand how the wah kin mess a man up like that."

A chill ran through Aila. *He don't know that man an' what he did tuh me.*

"I reckin thur's a lot of questions 'bout the future of the farm." Alan continued. "I know it mus' be skeery not tuh know what's gonna happen tuh yuh. If'n we kin he'p in any way, y'all kin jes' ask."

Rebecca rose from her chair and put her arms around Ginny, then Aila. "Family he'ps fam'ly. That's the way it oughta be."

"Thank you both for offering." said Ginny. "But I think Aila and me can manage with help from our colored folks. And when I can get back on my feet, that will make things better."

Chapter 19

THE PROPOSAL

EARLY SEPTEMBER 1865

~~~~~~~

As HE HAD PROMISED, Gideon Campbell was coming to speak with Aila. Aila saw him approaching the front porch steps, dressed to the hilt, carrying his scruffy fiddle case. Even for James' funeral, he had not donned the smart suit and derby he was wearing this day. She had forgotten his promise to visit and was dressed only in her workday clothes.

"Aila, can you please answer the door?" Ginny shouted to Aila from her sofa downstairs.

"Yes, ma'am!" Aila answered from her sleeping area upstairs.

The girl tried to style her hair as best she could for what to her was a surprise visit, and then wondered why she even cared how she looked for this man. Satisfied that her appearance didn't matter that much, she descended the stairs and greeted Gideon.

"Good marnin', Mister Gideon. What brangs yuh here?"

"I promised I'd be comin' tuh visit yuh a week from Mister Sanders' funeral, Miss Aila. Don't yuh 'member? An' I brung mah fiddle tuh play a tune er two fur yuh."

"Well, of course, Gideon!" she said, lying. "Come in an' set. Yuh mind if'n Miz Ginny sets with us? Ain't it proper fur us tuh have a chaperone?"

"Marnin', Miz Ginny. I hope yuh're doin' better."

119

Ginny smiled. "Thank you, Gideon. I'm a might better."

Not seeing a hat stand, he placed his derby on a table, sat in one of the rocking chairs, and opened his fiddle case. "I learnt some ol' timey tunes from Scotland from mah Uncle John when he was still alive. Now, I kin play some fas' dance-type tunes, but I was thankin' yuh might like the slow ballads better."

Aila was embarrassed. Other than Miz Ginny's piano tunes, no one had ever sang or played an instrument for her.

Gideon began playing, Aila couldn't believe how beautiful a tune it was. Then came the words.

> *Mah Love is like a red, red rose*
> *That's newly sprung in June.*
> *O, mah Love is like a melody*
> *That's sweetly played in tune.*

> *So fair art thou, mah bonnie lass,*
> *So deep in love am I.*
> *An' I will love thee still, mah dear,*
> *'till a' the seas gang dry.*

The ballad seemed to resonate in what she felt must be the Scottish chambers of her heart. She had never heard music so sweet, gentle, and full of longing.

> *'til a' the seas gang dry, mah dear,*
> *An' the rocks melt with the sun,*
> *An' I will love thee still, mah dear,*
> *While the sands o' life shall run.*

Neither Aila nor Ginny could speak.

Ginny finally broke the silence. "That was very sweet, Gideon. We've sung together with the congregation at church, but I never knew you had such a nice singing voice, high and fine."

"Thank yuh, ma'am."

"I don't know what tuh say, Gideon." Aila admitted. "That was a purdy song. Yuh got a real nice voice. Mah daddy told me mah fam'ly a long time back was from Scotland, so I reckin that's why I liked it. Yer fiddle is real sweet too. Maybe yuh kin learn me tuh play it someday."

"I'll be glad tuh do that. An' thank yuh fur yer kind words, Miss Aila. I wanted it tuh be a special one fur yuh. Now, Miz Ginny is welcome tuh stay, but it's yerself I come tuh talk tuh, Miss Aila."

Aila nodded agreement.

"Now, Miss Aila, yuh done knowed me an' mah fam'ly fur quite a while now." began Gideon. "Yuh know I mus' like yuh on account of I a'ways talk tuh yuh when I see yuh an' tell yuh how nice yuh look. I'm here tuh ask if'n yuh'll marry me an' birth mah children."

Stunned by Gideon's proposal, both women were speechless and stared at each other in disbelief.

"Now I know this might seem sudden like, but I been thankin' 'bout it fur a long time, an' I thank yuh're the girl fur me. I'll take real good care of yuh, an' yuh'll have a good life with me."

"Gideon, kin I have time tuh talk tuh Miz Ginny 'bout all this in private?" Aila asked.

"Yes ma'am. I know y'all need tuh talk it over a bit before yuh kin agree."

"Now Gideon, Miz Ginny here kin't walk good with her broke leg. So if'n yuh don't mind, kin yuh go yonder in the kitchen fur a while so me an' her kin talk?"

"Yessum." answered Gideon. He exited the walkway door to the kitchen and closed the door behind him.

Motionless for a moment, Aila and Ginny just looked at one another, each waiting for the other to speak.

"This here is kind-ah a sa'prise fork in the path fur me." Aila said. "If'n I marry 'im, I sure ain't gonna be goin' down that path of picture drawin' an' book writin'. But this might jes' be mah only chance tuh git a husband."

"There's no way to know what'll happen in the future, Aila."

"What he's proposin' would keep us all tuhgether 'mose like it was before." Aila surmised. "How kin we git along by ourselves without no man?"

"But Aila, do you really want to marry this man? What do you know about him, really?"

"I ain't likin' his daddy much, but Gideon's a'ways been real nice tuh me. Seems tuh me most wives don't know much 'bout thur husbands before they git married. How's this so diff'rent? An' it's a way tuh keep us tuhgether an' better off than we'd be on our own."

"I don't want you to be doing this for me and Sarah. Please don't mess up your life just to help me!"

"It ain't jes' he'pin' y'all. It's he'pin' Mary Jane an' the others too. An' it's he'pin' me! It's a way fur me tuh be surer 'bout mah future, without no bunch of rabbit trails leadin' me off tuh who knows whur."

"What about your baby?"

"Maybe I don't need tuh tell 'im 'bout that right now. Maybe he'll understand an' take the baby as his own later on. Anyways, whatever happens kin't be much worse than stayin' on the path I'm on right now."

Ginny shook her head in disagreement. "I think it's a mistake, but you have to decide for yourself. If you accept, you've got to tell him about the baby now. You can't lead him on with him in the dark about it. And you should give him and yourself time to think on it."

"Yes, ma'am. Yuh're right. We need some time tuh thank. But I'm skeered tuh tell 'im 'bout the baby right now."

"If you accept his proposal, you will still have to tell him sometime. The sooner, the better."

As she brought Gideon back to the front room, Aila could sense his anxiety. Her heart was pounding. She knew she had to reveal her secret at some point, but she didn't have the courage to do it now. Clearing her throat and swallowing, she positioned herself directly in front of him, but not too close, with a clear view of Ginny's eyes.

Aila swallowed again and began. "Mister Gideon, I'm real flattered 'bout yuh proposal. Yuh seem tuh be a real nice man, an' I reckin yuh like me from the way yuh talk tuh me an' treat me so nice. Now, I'm tellin' yuh this . . . so yuh'll know. Yer proposal's a lot fur me tuh thank 'bout. I need some time. I reckin we both need tuh thank on it."

Gideon stood motionless, breathing heavily. "Yessum. Yessum. We need tuh thank on it, like yuh say. How long do we need tuh thank?"

"I got some thangs tuh work out in mah own mind. Kin we talk aghen the end of the month?"

"End of the month? That's quite a while tuh thank."

He paused, shaking his head from side to side nervously.

"I'm thankin' yuh will know some thangs by then yuh don't know right now." said Aila.

"What kind-ah thangs?"

"It's real personal, Gideon. I hope yuh kin understand. I kin't tell yuh right now."

"Well. If'n yuh say yuh need time . . . I reckin I kin wait fur yer answer. We both got tuh agree, ain't we?"

Chapter 20

HEZEKIAH WATSON

EARLY SEPTEMBER 1865

ARON AND TOOTSIE ASSUMED RESPONSIBILITY for cleaning up and repairing damage caused to the east side of the house by the fallen pine tree that took James' life. Since any cash Ginny knew about had to be tightly managed, the men agreed not to be paid for their work.

Ginny only knew about $50 in U.S. currency that James had hidden away under the flooring of the front room. Another $200 in worthless Confederate bills was kept hidden in behind the back panel of a kitchen cabinet, but they were irrelevant at this point.

Ginny had no knowledge of James' bank accounts or the farm's finances in general; expenditure planning would require extreme caution. Cash would be coming in from sales of farm products, but Ginny had no idea how much or when.

Ginny did know James had prepared a witnessed handwritten will, kept in his personal chest drawer, naming her as the sole heir of his estate. She wasn't concerned about that now. Managing the aftershock of his death and running the farm was the most immediate priority. She and Aron were learning that process together, blazing a trail forward into mostly unchartered territory.

Emotionally, dealing with James' death became more of a challenge than she expected. Her relationship with Aila proved comforting to her, and she asked the girl to move back into the farmhouse to be at her side.

Two weeks after James' funeral, a man wearing a derby, jacket, trousers, white shirt, vest, and string necktie rode his white horse to the front door of the farmhouse, dismounted, and knocked on the front door. Aila, who was watching from the upstairs window, had never seen a man so fancily attired. She descended the stairs to where Ginny reclined on the sofa and opened the front door.

The man removed his derby as Aila opened the door. "Good marnin' Miz Sanders. Mah name's Hezekiah Watson. First, let me extend mah condolences fur the passin' of yer husband."

"Thank yuh, sir, but I ain't Miz Sanders." Aila explained. "She's here in the front room. Yuh kin come on in."

Watson entered to see Ginny lying on the sofa with her splinted leg resting on a pillow.

"Good marnin' Miz Sanders." Watson repeated. "As yuh might've heared, mah name's Watson. Mah condolences fur the passin' of yer husband. I'm sorry tuh see yuh ain't farin' well."

"Thank you, sir. My leg was broke in the accident that killed my James. What brings you here?"

"I'm a banker from Wilmin'ton. Yer husband an' me did some business tuhgether."

"James never mentioned any business with a Wilmington banker . . . or any banker, for that matter."

"If yuh don't mind, it'd be bes' fur me tuh set down fur a short visit. I got a important matter tuh discuss with yuh."

"Well, please have a seat, sir. Allow me to introduce you to my friend Aila. She's helping me manage things around here. The past weeks have been hard for us all. What exactly is the important matter, Mister Watson?"

"Well, ma'am, back before the wah started in '61, yer husband borrowed 200 U.S. dollers from me with this farm an' his slaves as collateral."

"Mister Watson, when my husband made the agreement with the sharecroppers, he told them . . . and me . . . that there were no loans against this property. Now, you're saying he told us a story?"

"I'm afraid so, ma'am. But now thur's two problems. First, in '61 the farm was worth 'bout 4,300 dollers, 300 dollers fur the animals, equipment, land, house, and barns . . . an' 'nother 4,000 dollers fur the slaves. Since then two of yer slaves done run away . . . but that don't matter 'cause none of 'em is slaves no more anyways. So yer farm ain't worth more than 300 dollers now.

"An' besides that, it ain't just the original loan that's due. Thur ain't been no payments of int'rest er principal on the loan fur over a year. I've sent mah man Sellers tuh see James 'bout the delinquency at least onest ever month fur the pass year . . . warnin' 'im 'bout fore-closure . . . but I got no response from 'im. Now he's gone, an' I come tuh tell yuh I've had tuh foreclose on the property, an' I'm holdin' a auction here tuh sell it tuhmara."

"Delinquent for a year? That's about how long he couldn't get around because of his hip injury. We was hardly able to do anything during that time, Mister Watson. And I never knew about any of the notices you sent. Surely you're not expecting me to be responsible for his debt now? Especially before tomorrow!"

"That's 'zackly what I'm expectin' Miz Sanders."

"And how much do you think we owe you?"

"Tuh keep the farm, yuh got tuh give me 104 U.S. dollers an' 11 cents cash now, fur back payments an' unpaid int'rest, an' a 20 percent default penalty. That's 124 dollers an' 93 cents total."

"Lord have mercy, Mister Watson! We don't have that much cash and no way to get it right now! We might get some cash in when we sell crops, but we can't raise that much on such short notice!"

"Ma'am, this ain't short notice. I give yer husband over a year tuh settle up an' avoid foreclosure, an' he did nothin'."

"Mister Watson, surely you can understand that we want very much to settle this debt. But all this is a . . . a shocking surprise! We just need a little more time . . . time to change our spending and bring in some more cash from crops. Had we known of this debt, we would already have been trying to pay it. Surely, we deserve some sympathy and understanding for our situation."

"The document yer husband signed, ma'am, spelled out clare terms of the loan. Yuh have mah sympathy, but I got a business tuh run, an' legally, I ain't got no obligation tuh extend the terms."

"As much as it breaks my heart, sir, I have to say we can't meet that obligation."

"Then I'll jes' have tuh go ahead with the auction! I ain't in the business of givin' away money!"

———

As soon as Watson left, Aila went to fetch the sharecroppers for a meeting with Ginny. She didn't understand all the financial details, but during their walk to the farmhouse, she did her best to inform them about what was going on.

"All dis ain't soundin' like good news fo' us!" exclaimed Aron as they gathered around the dining table.

"It's not sounding good for any of us." Ginny stated matter-of-factly. "Banker Watson wants to sell the farm no matter what, so he can line his pockets. He doesn't want to make any allowances for James' sickness, my injury, or our lack of money. We could lose the farm due to no real fault of our own."

"I ain't believin' dat Mista James told yuh a story 'bout dat loan, Miz Ginny." Sally spoke up. "I knows it likely didn't matter tuh 'im if'n he did dat tuh us, but it hard tuh thank he did it tuh you."

"I reckon he thought he'd fix it all and he wouldn't have to tell me about it. I reckon he thought he wasn't gonna die and leave me with it. We sometimes forget we can die at any time."

"De Lawd kin take us anytime he want, fo' sho." Aron affirmed.

Aron shook his head. "Miz Ginny, us sharecroppas got 20 dollas 'tween us . . . our share o' de crop sale early dis summer . . . dat fo' yuh if'n it kin he'p, ma'am."

"Thank you, Aron. I appreciate your offer. But you know we're going to need a lot more than that to keep the farm."

"Sound tuh me like we ain't gwaine have no say 'bout any o' dis, so we jes' needs tuh figger out wat we gwaine do." said Tootsie.

"De man dat buy dis farm gwaine tell us wat he willin' tuh do 'bout our sharecroppa agreement." Aron said. "So we kin't decide nothin' 'til dat happen."

"I reckins we all might need tuh move if'n de farm git sold." Sally speculated.

"If'n he keep de same agreement wid us, we might be able tuh stay." said Mary Jane. "But den wat happen tuh Miz Ginny an' Aila? Dey might 'ave tuh leave anyways. We ain't wantin' dat."

For the first time, Aila fully realized the gravity of the situation. No one had a response to Mary Jane's concern.

Tootsie stroked his beard and leaned back in his chair. "I reckins all's we kin do right now is thank an' pray on all dis, wat it gwaine mean, an' wat we kin do 'bout it. I ain't got no answer right now. I knows we gwaine be jes' fine, though. De Lawd got us in de palm o' his hand."

Chapter 21

MATHEW WESTON

EARLY SEPTEMBER 1865

⌒

AILA THOUGHT IT WAS PRE-DAWN, but through her window she saw that the sun was up, lighting the farmyard. She heard James' hunting dogs barking at something, and then she saw a man she didn't recognize walking across the yard toward the barn. He opened the barn door and disappeared inside.

Throwing on her daytime clothes, she went downstairs to tell Ginny, who was already awake. Aila saw immediately that Ginny didn't seem to be her normal self.

"Miz Ginny, somethin' wrong?" she asked. "Yuh look sick."

"I'm not feeling too good, Honey." Ginny replied. "I think I got a fever."

Aila put her hand to Ginny's forehead. "Yuh're burnin' up, Miz Ginny! Let me git a wet cloth."

Aila grabbed a cotton cloth from the kitchen and dampened it with water from a jug on the kitchen shelf. Returning to Ginny's bed, she pressed the wet cloth to her friend's forehead.

"Look at my leg, Aila. It's terrible sore."

Aila lifted the sheet to reveal Ginny's red and swollen leg above and below the area of the splint.

"Miz Ginny, I gotta git Doc Brooks fur this. But first, some stranger's pokin' 'round the yard an' barn. I need tuh go see what he's up tuh. Times like this make me want tuh learn how tuh shoot Mister James' shotgun. I'm gonna go git Aron tuh he'p."

"Go. I'll be all right."

Aila ran to the shacks, trying to stay out of sight from the barn. She banged on Aron's door and told him about the stranger. They both hurried to the barn and opened the door on two men examining the mules.

Recognizing one of the men as Hezekiah Watson, she called out "Mister Watson, what y'all doin' here?"

Turning from the mules, Watson replied, "Mister Weston here bought this farm last week at the auction. I'm jes' showin' 'im 'round."

"Mister Weston, yuh kin't buy this farm without talkin' tuh Miz Ginny. She's the owner. She's cooped up over yonder in the house with a broke leg. Yuh need tuh go over thur an' talk tuh her 'bout this."

"I don't need to talk to nobody!" replied Weston in a Yankee accent. "Don't you know Watson here foreclosed on this property? You're lucky he hasn't kicked all of you out by now. He sold it to me. Didn't you see the auction last week? Do you people even know what an auction is? I own it now. And right now, I'm thinking I want you, your 'Miz Ginny' . . . and all them niggers . . . off my property!"

⁓

True to Weston's pronouncement and despite Ginny's injury and illness, Weston gave her and Aila an ultimatum to vacate the farmhouse immediately. He decided the former slaves could stay in their shacks, provided they agreed to his terms for continuing the sharecropper agreement, yet to be reassessed.

Ginny and Aila's only choice on such short notice was to move into one of the sharecropper shacks with baby Sarah. The move would be temporary. Weston saw no reason to allow them to stay on his property indefinitely.

Apparently having no family of his own, Weston occupied the farmhouse periodically, coming and going without announcement. He seemed to have little interest in preparing for and managing the upcoming harvest. Knowing the harvest would be lost if they didn't continue their work, the sharecroppers continued their farm work, despite Weston's warning against gathering crops for themselves before a new agreement could be worked out.

With Aila recording, Ginny dictated a letter to Alan Smith asking for help. Watson was supposed to mail the letter in Wilmington, but the women had no assurance that would happen. Even if Alan received the letter, how and when he might respond was uncertain.

Ginny's condition continued to worsen. Doc Brooks believed that the infection from her femur injury might have spread to other areas of her body. The doctor had few remedies to treat the infection or reduce the chances of pneumonia in Ginny's bedridden state. His only prescription was for Ginny to use Tootsie's homemade crutch and get out of bed to improve blood circulation and minimize fluid buildup in her lungs.

Were it not for the sharecroppers, Ginny and Aila's situation would have been dangerously worse. Weston's warning against gathering crops for self-consumption forced the workers to covertly collect eggs and produce under cover of night, while continuing the overall harvesting operation. Rather than deplete the supply of smoked meats, they increased their wild game trapping and hunting.

Chapter 22

GIDEON RETURNS

Late September 1865

~~~~

IT HAD BEEN ALMOST FOUR WEEKS since Gideon's last visit to the Sanders farm, which he did not know was now Mathew Weston's property. As Aila had requested, he returned at the end of the month to speak with her about marriage. He was shocked by what he saw. The farm itself seemed to be in unfamiliar disarray, and harvest appeared to be far behind schedule.

He was surprised that no one answered when he knocked at the front door of the farmhouse. Thinking the sharecroppers could provide an explanation, he went to the shacks.

As he approached, he followed the sound of a woman crying to what had previously been a vacant shack. Without knocking, he opened the door to the sight of Aila and Ginny in crowded squalor, Ginny lying on a rudimentary bed, weeping, while Aila sat in a rickety chair at her side.

"Good Lord!" he exclaimed. "What y'all doin' out here in this shack? An' what's wrong with Miz Ginny that's she's still in bed at this hour? I thought she'd be better by now."

"So much has happened since yuh left." cried Aila. "Miz Ginny's down with a fever from her broke leg. Doc Brooks kin't seem tuh he'p. We didn't know it, but Mister James had a big loan from a banker in Wilmin'ton an' didn't keep up his payments. The banker up an' sold the farm tuh some Yankee man. He kicked us out of the house, an' we don't know how long we kin even stay here."

"I'm sorry tuh see y'all like this." Gideon said quietly. "What's gonna happen tuh yuh?"

"We don't know, Gideon! An' it's beatin' us right down to the ground. We don't know what tuh do! I wrote a letter fur Miz Ginny tuh Mister James' cousin Alan in Brunswick County fur he'p, but we ain't heared back. Hadn't been fur Mary Jane an' the other colored folks here on the farm, we'd be starvin' tuh death by now."

"I'm tryin' tuh thank of how I kin he'p, but I ain't knowin'." said Gideon. "I need tuh talk tuh Daddy."

Gideon paused and looked away from Aila. He put his right hand on his forehead and slowly moved it down to cover his mouth. Looking again at Aila, he dropped his hand to speak.

"Early this month, yuh asked me tuh come back an' talk 'bout gittin' married . . . said yuh had tuh thank 'bout somethin' yuh couldn't tell me 'bout then. That's why I'm here tuhday, but I ain't knowin' if'n it's a good time fur that right now. Maybe we oughta wait."

"No, Gideon, we need tuh talk now. I been puttin' it off too long a'ready." She cleared her throat and swallowed. "Maybe yuh oughta set down before I start."

He sat on a stool beside the fireplace. She swallowed again and began.

"Yuh 'member Mister Samuel had Soldier's Heart on account of the wah? Feelin' bad 'bout hisself, drankin' licker a lot. An' he finally hung hisself in the big oak tree?"

"Yes ma'am. I felt real bad fur 'im. I knowed the wah messed 'im up somethin' terrible."

"When he kilt hisself, it won't jes' on account of the wah. He come here tuh mah place one night, drunk as a skunk, not hisself atall."

Aila's heart was racing. She stopped for a moment to gather courage. Gideon's eyes widened, staring straight into Aila's.

"He . . . he come in tuh mah place an' forced me. I . . . I tried tuh push 'im off an' screamed at 'im tuh STOP! But he was too strong. Sally an' Mary Jane drove 'im off, but it was too late."

She could see his expression change from curiosity to shock and dismay. She began to cry.

"I'm sorry!" she coughed. "So sorry I got a baby in me! But it won't mah fault!"

"What do yuh mean, it won't yer fault? How kin anythang like that *not* be yer fault?"

"She means she was forced, Gideon!" Ginny answered firmly. "She means she was violated. She means she is with child, and it's *not* her fault!"

Gideon eyes opened even wider as he struggled to respond. "Violated?" repeated Gideon. "With chile?"

"Yuh need tuh know that before yuh marry me . . . if'n yuh still want tuh marry me." said Aila. "I know this is a lot fur yuh tuh take in. Yer proposal's a lot fur me tuh thank 'bout too."

Gideon sat motionless, breathing heavily. "I thank . . . I thank I understand. I feel real sorry fur yuh, Miss Aila. I jes' need tuh thank on it . . . an' talk tuh Daddy. When's the baby comin'?"

"March, we reckon." Ginny answered.

Chapter 23

LIGHT AT THE END
OF THE TUNNEL

EARLY OCTOBER 1865

Alan and Rebecca Smith arrived at the farm with their infant daughter Priscilla the day after Gideon's visit. They recounted their surprise and shock over the news in Ginny's letter about the foreclosure. Now, they were saddened to hear of Ginny's continued bad health and the women's banishment from the farmhouse.

The conversation turned to Gideon's marriage proposal.

"Well, that's a sa'prise! Congratulations!" Alan exclaimed. "When's the weddin' day?"

"We ain't set a day yet. We decided tuh thank 'bout it fur a while. It's a real hard decision . . . an' we got 'nother big problem tuh thank 'bout too."

"What kind-ah problem?" asked Rebecca. "Y'all like each other, don't yuh? Ain't he a nice man?"

"I'm sorry. It's embarrassin' fur me tuh talk 'bout mahself. Maybe Miz Ginny . . . kin 'splain."

"It's real personal for Aila." Ginny clarified. "Nobody knows about it outside the folks here on the farm . . . and now Gideon. We want to keep it quiet."

"We ain't 'bout tellin' other people's business, Miz Ginny . . . Miss Aila." declared Alan.

"You know it's true that Samuel wasn't himself after the war." Ginny began. "Soldier's Heart. He drank a lot and felt real sorry for himself all the time. I think he suffered because he couldn't tell right from wrong anymore."

"We've heared that tuh be true." Alan said. "I knowed 'im as a good man an' a brave soldier. That wah poisoned a lot of good men."

"It's also true that Samuel came to Aila's place one night, drunk out of his mind, and attacked her."

"Lord 'ave mercy, chile!" Rebecca gasped. "Yuh poor, poor girl!"

"We all know it wasn't her fault." said Ginny. "But now, Aila is with child, and that could jeopardize her marriage to Gideon. That's one reason Gideon and Aila are taking time to think about it."

"If'n we kin do anythang . . ." started Alan.

"Thank yuh, Mister Alan." Aila interrupted. "But I don't know what yuh . . . er anybody else . . . kin do. It's kind-ah up tuh Gideon an' me tuh work out. He's comin' back sometime soon, an' we gonna talk."

At that moment, there was another knock on the door. Aila answered to find Gideon and his father at the entrance.

"We got somethin' real important tuh talk 'bout, Aila." Gideon announced.

"Come in, Gideon, Rev'rend Campbell." Aila said, not looking directly at them. "We got visitors a'ready, but y'all welcome. Mister Alan, yuh 'memba Rev'rend Campbell. An' this is his son Gideon. Gideon, this here's Mister James' cousin from Brunswick County, Mister Alan Smith, and his wife, Miz Rebecca."

"We met onest before, I reckin, Rev'rend." said Alan. Campbell nodded.

"Gideon here tells me yuh ain't farin' well, Miz Ginny." Campbell said. "Sorry tuh hear that. I want tuh stay awhile after we're finished talkin' tuh pray tuhgether with yuh."

"That would be a real comfort." Ginny replied.

"I got some news 'bout this here farm." Gideon began. "Yesterdee, we talked tuh that damn Yankee carpetbagger Weston what bought it from banker Watson.

"Now, I ain't never got no use fur Yankees, but that man Weston made me truly hate 'em all. We learnt he ain't int'rested in runnin' the farm. He jes' bought it at a low price after it was foreclosed so he could sell it at a better price. We offered 'im a price we kin afford an' give 'im a li'l profit. So now, we own the farm, Daddy an' me."

Aila and Ginny were surprised, puzzled, and speechless.

"Well, what does that mean for us?" asked Ginny. "And for the colored folks who call this home?"

"Now, I ain't mindin' if'n y'all stay here an' move back tuh the house, at least fur a while." answered Gideon. "Y'all don't belong out here in these slave shacks."

"An' what 'bout Mary Jane an' the colored folks?" Aila inquired further. "Mister James had a sharecropper agreement with 'em. What's gonna happen tuh 'em now? They gonna need tuh leave an' go tuh Wilmin'ton tuh find work?"

"I'm gonna need workers tuh make a livin' on this farm, 'specially on account of a lot of it is poor soil. I'd need fur 'em tuh stay . . . fur now."

"Reverend Campbell, folks have told me that you have been trying to make your former slaves into apprentices under the state's Black Codes." Ginny said, accusingly. "Is that true?"

"Now Miz Ginny, that ain't nothin' yuh need tuh worry yer purdy li'l head 'bout." replied Campbell. "That ain't yer business."

"Well, it certainly is our business! The Negroes here have been with us for a long time. Those apprenticeships you set up are nothing more than slavery by another name. And it's clear they're gonna be challenged by the Freedman's Bureau. Our sharecroppers are not gonna stay here under any apprenticeship arrangement!"

"The Freedman's Bureau ain't nothin' but one of 'em Yankee programs set up tuh force us tuh do thangs we ain't wantin' tuh do! We ain't gonna stand fur it!"

"Daddy, I reckin it's bes' tuh jes' keep the agreement they had with Mister James." said Gideon. "They know this farm, an' if'n I'm gonna be runnin' it, I'm gonna want 'em tuh stay.

"But that ain't all we want tuh talk 'bout tuhday." Gideon continued. "I done talked tuh Daddy 'bout me an' Aila gittin' married. An' we we now done decided."

Aila braced herself for a clarification.

"I still want tuh marry yuh." said Gideon. "But that's jes' part of it."

"How could yuh decide that considerin' I ain't no virgin no more an' I got a baby on the way?" asked Aila, averting her eyes to the dirt floor.

"Samuel seemed a li'l crazy tuh us." said Campbell. "What he did tuh yuh made 'im kill hisself. Maybe that was his atonement fur that sin of hissin.'"

"How kin 'im killin' hisself atone fur what he done tuh me?" Aila asked.

Campbell shook his head, looking for words.

"By killin' hisself, I reckin Samuel paid the price tuh the Lord fur his transgression." the reverend explained. "Maybe what happened tuh yuh weren't yer fault. Maybe the Lord sees thangs as bein' all balanced out, I ain't knowin' fur sure. I ain't never come across a situation like this one before."

"I done thought 'bout yuh birthin' somebody else's chile, Miss Aila." Gideon said. "I reckin thur's parts of it I'm willin' tuh accept, an' parts I kin't accept."

"Which parts is which?" Aila asked.

"Mah daddy an' me ain't likin' one bit 'bout yuh not bein' no virgin an' bein' with chile. But we reckin Jesus furgives yuh fur gittin' attacked an' gittin' a baby . . . an' I kin furgive yuh if'n Jesus kin."

Surprised, Aila breathed a silent sigh of relief.

"But Jesus ain't needin' me tuh raise no chile what ain't mine. When that baby's borned, yuh got tuh find a place fur it somewhur away from me. I ain't gonna spend mah money raisin' it, an' I ain't gonna be no daddy tuh it. Yuh gonna birth mah babies an' raise 'em fur me. That chile yuh got kin't be no part of mah fam'ly!"

Aila began to comprehend what Gideon was saying. She hid her face in her hands and did not speak.

"Ain't yuh got nothin' tuh say?" Gideon demanded. "We kin git married if'n yuh give that baby away. But yuh need tuh decide!"

"Yuh ain't givin' me much choice!" she cried. "Ain't much hope fur a chile an' mamma what ain't married. So I gotta throw away the chile an' keep the husband! The Lord kin't want a mamma tuh give away her baby!"

"No baby's gittin' throwed away!" exclaimed Gideon. "Somebody else jes' gonna raise it."

"We thought on this in earnest an' read the scriptures." said Campbell. "Bible sez God will furgive transgressions, but he won't clare the guilty. He'll visit the iniquities of the fathers on the children, an' on the children's children, tuh the third an' fourth generation. Yer baby's gonna carry 'em sins . . . that guilt . . . an' it kin't be part of our fam'ly."

"You mean because the father of Aila's baby sinned, God says Aila's baby sinned before it's even born?" asked Ginny.

"Yes ma'am!" Campbell asserted. "That's what the Bible tells us in Exodus an' other places. An' we know it's the Lord's will . . . we ain't abidin' no sinners!"

"But doesn't Jesus forgive our sins if we seek His forgiveness?" asked Ginny.

"The Bible don't say nothin' 'bout furgivin' no bastards." Campbell argued. "That chile's a'ways gonna be a bastard. Nothin' kin change that. An' a bastard chile carries the sins of his father. We kin't abide no bastard chile in our fam'ly."

"So what is yer decision, Aila?" demanded Gideon.

Aila calmed herself to answer.

To everyone's surprise, Alan spoke up. "Miss Aila, we'll be happy tuh take yer baby an' raise it fur yuh, if'n yuh agree."

"What?" exclaimed Aila. "Y'all would raise it fur me?"

"Yes ma'am." answered Rebecca. "We kin raise it, but yuh'll still be its real mamma furever. We'd raise it in the way of the Lord, with care an' lovin'."

"But ain't yuh gonna a'ways thank mah baby's stained with the sin of its daddy?"

"We believe in the lovin' grace of Jesus Christ tuh furgive sinners, no matter what the sin." Alan answered. "We kin raise yer chile, maybe adopt it legal like, if'n yuh want."

"I don't know 'bout yuh adoptin' it. That sounds too much like it won't be mah chile no more." Aila's eyes began tearing. "I want it tuh still be mah chile!"

"If'n that's what yuh want, Miss Aila, that's what we kin do." assured Alan. "We kin jes' be somethin' like volunteer guardians. It kin be jes' a agreement 'tween friends."

"Thank yuh." Aila whispered through her tears.

"May the love an' blessin' of our Lord an' Save-yer Jesus Christ be on yuh an' yer chile." Alan declared.

Even though her baby's future was now more secure, Aila could not ignore a feeling that she was abandoning her child. She resolved that when it was born, she would hide the pain of her baby's conception, birth, and abandonment cloistered in her heart.

Chapter 24

A HOME FOR CALUM

LATE FEBRUARY 1866

⌁

GIDEON WAS ASLEEP IN THE FRONT ROOM, and Ginny and Sarah also had retired. Aila had the night to herself for a change.

It had been a damp, cool day, not unusual for late winter. A fire in the cookstove took the edge off the weather and her somber mood. She sat alone in the kitchen by the light of a coal oil lamp on the table next to her, writing in her journal. She loved the scent of burning wood and lit kerosene lamps.

She recalled and recorded all that had happened to her since she married Gideon the previous October. Ginny had slowly recovered from her injury and illness, to be left only with a slight limp. Ginny, Mary Jane, and the other sharecroppers, everyone she loved, were happy that the Sanders farm was now the Gideon Campbell farm. Everyone's future seemed brighter.

She had endured her pregnancy as best she could, but it had not been easy. Despite the painful decision she had made to give up her baby when it came, she had found peace with herself that it would be best for the child.

Her relationship with Gideon had been surprisingly positive and supportive for the most part, despite the bitterness resulting from his rejection of her baby.

From the back pages of the journal she took out the small drawing she had made of herself and Mary Jane holding hands near the river. Smiling softly, she studied the image and recalled how she had grown closer to Mary Jane and her son Boo-Boo since her marriage to Gideon. Despite his distaste for any close relationship between Whites and Blacks, he tolerated what Aila and Mary Jane seemed to have together. The two young women still shared fond memories of their visits to the river, and they returned there together when they could.

Returning the drawing to the rear of the journal, she began writing again.

Aila, Ginny, and the sharecroppers had allowed themselves a small celebration when they had learned that the 13th Amendment to the Constitution had been ratified in December 1865.

"It's in the Constitution now!" Ginny had shouted, embracing Aila upon learning the news. "There can't be any more indentured servants or slaves now . . . now or ever!"

Eager to share the news with the former slaves, Aila had run to the shacks shouting, "Everbody's free furever now! It's in the Constitution! Everbody kin live thur own life now!"

They all had gathered outside their shacks, shouting, laughing, crying, dancing, hugging, and singing at the top of their voices.

Aila stopped writing and put down her pencil stub. Her thoughts returned to her unborn child.

Mah baby's gonna be borned soon. I know it's gonna hurt, but I gotta be strong, like Miz Ginny an' Mary Jane was. Why does God make it so hard fur us women? Makin' babies is easy fur men. They even enjoy it! I reckin God makes it hard so women kin appreciate an' love our babies that much more. It's like God's givin' us a reward fur goin' through the pain of birthin'.

Aila was awakened hours before dawn by dampness in her bed. She arose quietly to avoid waking Gideon and slowly moved toward the stairs to Ginny's room. Having heard Aila's movement, Ginny was already descending the stairs, holding a lamp.

"Water broke?" she asked. Aila nodded "yes."

"You stay right here on my bed. Sarah will be fine . . . she's asleep. I'll go heat some water."

Once she had started the fire in the cookstove, Ginny heated water and gathered a stack of cotton rags. It was Aila's first birth, so it might be awhile before the baby came. As she returned to Aila with the water and rags, Gideon unexpectantly appeared in her path.

"What's goin' on?" he demanded. "Yuh woke me up!"

"The baby's coming, but it might be awhile before it's born."

"Well, I'm goin' back tuh sleep. Ain't nothin' here fur me tuh do."

Gideon slept for another three hours before he was awakened by the baby's cries. Putting on his work clothes for the day, he didn't bother to go upstairs to see Aila or the baby. He went directly to the sharecroppers' shacks.

"Aila's baby's fine'ly borned." he announced. "Aron, carry her an' that baby over tuh the Smith place. I want yuh tuh git a ox an' cart ready tuh leave this marnin'. Yuh gonna need a ox fur 'em swamps on Eagles Island. Here's money fur the ferry tolls over an' back." Gideon turned to Mary Jane. "Yuh go with 'em tuh he'p with the baby. The rest of y'all kin git tuh work 'round here."

"Yessuh, Mista Gideon." Aron confirmed.

As Gideon departed for the farmhouse, Sally whispered to Mary Jane: "I'll take care o' Boo-Boo, don't yuh worry. I kin chew his food fo' 'im."

As he approached the farmhouse, Gideon was met by Ginny on the walkway.

"Aron's gittin' the ox an' cart ready tuh take her an' that baby tuh the Smith's." he said. "I want that bastard chile away from here this marnin'!"

"Aila needs at least a day of rest first, Gideon!" Ginny argued. "You have to understand what she's been through."

"Mah mamma was up an' workin' the same day I was borned, an' she was twenty years ol'. Aila's fifteen an' plenty strong 'nuf. All she's gonna do is lay in the back of that ox cart. It kin't be that hard."

"What if we get her out of the house and take her to Sally's place for a day or two, 'til she's stronger?"

"Ever day she's nursin' that chile is a day she ain't returnin' tuh breedin' stock. The sooner that baby ain't suckin' on her, the sooner she'll be ready tuh have mah babies."

"If she starts losing a lot of blood on that trip, she might not be alive to even have your babies, Gideon!"

"Yuh listen now, Miz Ginny. I prayed tuh God real hard las' night, an' he told me it's bes' that baby leave this house soon as it's borned. If'n it don't, this house an' everbody in it gonna git tainted with that baby's sin. That's the Lord's command tuh me. I ain't wantin' tuh go aghen the Lord's command . . . an' *you* ain't ne'ther."

Within an hour, Ginny had dressed Aila warmly with extra layers for the chill and prepared a large travel basket, stuffed with warm blankets, cotton diapers, a supply of cold ham biscuits, and jugs of water. To keep the baby safe and warm, she prepared bedding in a spare wooden-slatted bassinet she received as a gift for Sarah.

Aron had Jerry the Ox and his cart ready with pillows, extra quilts for Aila and the baby, extra hay for Jerry, and two canvas tarpaulins for at least some rain protection if needed.

Followed by the other sharecroppers coming to see the baby and give the travelers a send-off, Aron drove the cart with Mary Jane to the front porch of the house where Aila and Ginny were waiting with the baby and necessities for the trip. They could not tarry long. The trip to the Smith's would take at least four hours, and they wanted to arrive before sunset.

"Wat a purdy baby!" exclaimed Sally and Mary Jane together.

"It's a boy, jes' like I wanted!" confirmed Aila.

"He got red hair, jes' like yuh!" observed Mary Jane. "Wat yuh gwaine call 'im?"

"Calum." Aila said calmly. "Jes' like mah daddy."

"Yo' bed all right, Miz Aila?" asked Mary Jane as the cart bumped and jerked along Federal Point Road north toward Wilmington.

Aila lay on her side in the cart bed next to Mary Jane, holding and nursing baby Calum just behind Aron in the driver seat. "I'm jes' fine." she answered. "But Mary Jane, we've knowed each other fur quite a while now. Don't yuh thank it's 'bout time yuh 'jes called me 'Aila'? We're the same age. No reason atall tuh call me 'Miz'."

Mary Jane paused before answering. "I reckins dere ain't no reason, 'less yuh is thankin' dere is . . . Aila."

"I like hearin' yuh say that . . . Mary Jane." Aila reflected.

"This here bed Aron made fur me is right cozy." continued Aila. "Thank yuh, Aron."

"Yuh welcome, Miz Aila." said Aron. "I's hopin' yuh ain't gwaine mind if'n I keeps callin' yuh 'Miz Aila.' It jes' sounds mo' right tuh me. An' jes' 'cause I calls yuh 'Miz Aila' don' mean I's anythang 'cept jes' plain ol' 'Aron' tuh you.

"It might git a li'l wahm tuhday, de way it gwaine right now." Aron predicted. "Purdy wahm fo' dis time o' year, I'd say. I reckins yuh an' Calum ain't gwaine need all dem quilts an' blankets."

"It might git cooler later on if'n it come up a cloud, so we might need 'em." said Aila. "Then it might be hard keepin' 'em dry."

The cart continued to roll through muddy and sandy ruts, bobbing up and down and from side to side. No one spoke until they had traversed a shallow path through the tannin-stained water of Barnard's Creek.

"Aron, I been thankin' . . . y'all mus' be real glad now that yuh're set free furever." said Aila. "But now, I don't know what tuh 'spect next. Do you?"

"I ain't knowin' ne'tha." said Aron. "Maybe yuh kin make yo' own life now, Miz Aila, on account o' yuh White. But is all dem Whites gwaine still thank o' us like we's no-good slaves, not worth our salt? Yuh thanks dey gwaine hate us bein' as free as dey is . . . an' blame us fur all dere problems? I ain't knowin' if'n dey gwaine let us make our own life, if'n it mess up dere way o' livin'.

"We s'posed tuh be 'free' . . . but us culluds kin't even vote right now. If'n we kin't vote, how's de law gwaine git changed tuh he'p us make our own life? Right now, dere's lots o' laws dat ain't lettin' us do thangs White folks kin do. An' dey kin make mo' laws like dat wen dey wants."

"I'd vote tuh throw 'em laws out!" Aila proclaimed. "But I ain't even ol' 'nuf tuh vote, am I? I will when I'm ol' 'nuf, though."

"Naw, ma'am." said Aron. "Yuh ain't ol' 'nuf tuh vote. An' yuh kin't vote noways. De law say yuh kin't vote on account o' yuh a woman. Gwaine take lots o' good White men votin' tuh change dem laws.

"Now dat I be free, I knows one thang I gwaine do, though." Aron laughed as he continued. "If'n I kin't do nothin' else, I gwaine make some money so we kin build some wood floors in dem shacks we lives in. I thanks de time fo' dem cold dirt floors is gone!

"Yuh knows me an' Sally gwaine git married soon, Miz Aila?" continued Aron. "Tootsie gwaine git married at de same time tuh Hannah . . . yuh knows, we met her ova at de Meetin' Place. We gittin' married tuhgether in two weeks. Preacha Hunter comin' down from Wilmin'ton tuh marry us."

"No, I didn't know." said Aila. "I'm glad fur y'all. But how do you feel 'bout that, Mary Jane?"

"Well, I ain't knowin' what gwaine happen if'n mah daddy come back home." replied Mary Jane. "But Mamma say we kin cross dat bridge wen we gits dere. But I sho kin't be unhappy 'bout Mista Aron bein' Mamma's husband. He a fine, fine man tuh mah way o' thankin'."

"Why, thank yuh, Miss Mary Jane." smiled Aron. "An' yuh sho 'nuf gwaine be a fine daughter fo' me."

Aron paused. "Now, Miz Aila, we all wants yuh an' Miz Ginny tuh come tuh de weddin' . . . if'n Mista Gideon lets yuh."

"I'd be real proud tuh do that." said Aila. "An' I'm sure Ginny will too."

The route to the Smith's farm was almost 20 miles long. They would pass through Wilmington, cross the Cape Fear River, Eagles Island, and the Brunswick River. The two river crossings would require ferries rowed by former slaves.

Aron had been to Wilmington many times before to sell produce from the farm, and he had made two trips to Brunswick County. Neither Aila nor Mary Jane had ever been to Wilmington or on vessels of any sort. Brunswick County would be farther from home than either of them had ever traveled. The trip was to be more of an adventure than either could have imagined.

Soon after turning onto Federal Point Road north, Aron caught a glimpse of a Black man and an adolescent boy standing at the roadside edge of a field, waving to him.

"Dat dere's Thomas Martin an' his boy Andrew." Aron said to Aila and Mary Jane. "Back wen we wuz slaves, Thomas wuz a freedman ownin' his own farm. Dere wuz a lot o' freedmen in Wilmin'ton back den, but Thomas wuz 'bout de onlyest one out here in de country. I's gwaine stop fo' jes' a minute an' see how he's doin'."

"Hey dere, Aron!" shouted Thomas. "How's yuh doin'?"

Aron steered Jerry the Ox toward Thomas and his son. "Whoa, whoa!" Aron commanded Jerry. "Kin't complain. How yuh doin', Thomas?"

"We's doin' jes' fine, Aron." Thomas answered.

"Thomas, dis here is Miz Aila Campbell an' her new li'l boo. An' yuh 'memba Miss Mary Jane here?"

"Nice tuh meet y'all. Aron, yuh 'memba mah boy Andrew here."

"I sho do. How yuh doin', Andrew?"

"Jes' fine, suh."

"Andrew, don' yuh 'memba Mista Aron from ova yonda at de Sandas farm? I reckins he call hisself Aron Sandas now. Dat right, Aron?"

"I reckins so." Aron agreed. "'cept now yuh knows de farm's own by Mista Gideon Campbell, Preacha Campbell's son."

"Yessuh, I knows." said Thomas. "Mista Gideon bought de Sandas farm wen Mista James die. Den he marry Miz Aila here."

Thomas asked, "Wat yo' call yo' new baby, Miz Aila?"

"His name's Calum, same as mah daddy."

"Me an' Mary Jane here is carryin' dem ova tuh Brunswick County . . . tuh visit some o' Mista James Sanda's fam'ly." explained Aron.

"Miss Mary Jane, yuh look tuh be 'bout the same age as mah boy Andrew here."

Embarrassed, Mary Jane looked away.

"How's yo' fam'ly doin', Thomas?" asked Aron.

"Bessie's doin' all right." Thomas answered. "She sho is a mighty fine wife. Li'l Beth's nine now, an' Olivia's six. Mah farm here's doin' all right too, considerin' de markets dese days."

"Miz Aila, Thomas here's done real good fo' hisself. He got dat big farmhouse ova yonda, a barn, an' 'bout sixty acres."

"How did yuh become a freedman, Mister Thomas?" asked Aila. "An' how did yuh come intuh so much land?"

"Well now, Miz Aila, yuh knows not all slave ownas felt good 'bout ownin' slaves. Mah owna, Massa John Martin, inherit de farm from his daddy 'fo de wah, 'long wid me, an' mah wife Bessie. We worked fo' 'im fo' five years, an' den he decide tuh stop farmin' an' move tuh Wilmin'ton. Widout no wife er fam'ly, he reckins de city life wuz best fo' 'im.

"He wuz sho a good man, Miz Aila. He sold part o' his farm, set Bessie an' me free, an' give us de part o' his farm he didn't sell. He reckined we worked 'nuf fo' his daddy dat we earned our freedom an' a piece o' de farm tuh boot. An' wen anybody botha'd us 'bout bein' free an' ownin' dis farm, he wuz a'ways dere tuh fix it fo' us. Dat make 'im a black sheep tuh de Whites 'round here. But he ain't carin' 'bout dat."

"We got tuh move on out now, Thomas." announced Aron. "Long way tuh whur we're goin'. But it wuz sho nice tuh see yuh aghen. Tell Bessie we said 'hey.'"

"I sho will. Y'all have a nice visit ova yonda 'cross de riva."

"He's a real nice man." Aila noted as they continued their approach to Wilmington. "I never knowed some colored people was free an' owned property before the wah."

"Dere's still a lot o' dem freedmen livin' in town. Mo' dan yuh might reckins. But dey won' treated much better dan we slaves wuz. Now, dere's mo' White folks 'round dem Black folks in town dan out whur we is, an' dey git treated purdy bad."

Entering Wilmington, Aila and Mary Jane were surprised and amazed by everything they saw: the number of buildings, people, houses, carriages, wagons, horses, oxen, and mules; the contrast of wealth and poverty; and the heavy stench of uncleanliness in the air.

On the farm they could usually avoid manure piles, but in the city it was impossible. It stuck to the ox cart's two large wheels and was occasionally thrown up and into the body of the cart itself. The entire city reeked of manure. They marveled at the number of Blacks they saw, more than either of them had seen in one place before.

Approaching Market Street, they were awestruck by the emergence of St. James Episcopal Church through the trees in the distance. The only church the girls had ever seen was Mount Moriah, the small log structure where James Sanders had been buried. The magnificence of St. James was almost beyond their comprehension.

As they drew nearer, they saw scores of White federal soldiers occupying the city blocks around St. James, which had been confiscated by the Union army for use as a hospital.

"Lookie dere at dem White soldiers." said Mary Jane.

"I heared tell all dem cullud Yankee soldiers done gone from here las' fall!" said Aron.

"Colored soldiers ain't in charge o' dis city no mo'?" said Mary Jane. "Dat show our day in de sun might be gone a'ready!"

"We kin be proud dat dey wuz here, girl." Aron said. "But yuh kin be sho dese White folks in town won' likin' dat one bit! An' dese White soldiers ain't gwaine be here fo'eva. White folks ain't gwaine stand fo' dem needer!"

"Haw! Haw!" Aron shouted to Jerry, who responded with a left turn onto Market Street.

"We mus' be close tuh the river!" Aila shouted. "I kin smell it!"

The cart bumped along Market Street's cobblestones, cushioned only by the numerous piles of horse, mule, and oxen excrement. At the end of Market Street, by luck, the ferry was waiting at the dock.

The ferry was powered by two former slave oarsmen, now employed by the ferry company. After paying one of the oarsmen 18 cents, Aron drove Jerry onto the ferry. The cart movement and positioning caused the ferry to rock sporadically back and forth in the water, unnerving both Aila and Mary Jane.

Once the ferry left the dock, it floated slowly out into the Cape Fear, rocking gently with the current as the oarsmen began singing a song together to a slow rhythm matching that of the oar strokes. With help from the oars' rhythm and the oarsmen's song, Aila and Mary Jane regained their composure.

"Well, I'll swanny!" Aila exclaimed quietly. "It's real purdy from here. I ain't never been floatin' on the river before . . . never thought of the river this way. Look yonder at all 'em boats pulled up to the dock an' sailin' up an' down the current!"

"I ain't neva seen de riva in a boat floatin' on it." Mary Jane observed.

The two girls could hardly contain their excitement as they soaked up the sights, sounds, and smells of the river.

Once across the river, the ferry landed on Eagles Island, between the Cape Fear and Brunswick Rivers, where Aron disembarked the ox and cart. Plodding on the island's causeway through the muddy swampland, they passed over the barely sufficient Alligator Creek bridge to a second ferry over the Brunswick River, landing and disembarking on the other side in Brunswick County.

"Only 'bout five miles tuh go, now . . . one, maybe two hours more, dependin' on de weather." announced Aron. "Look like it comin' up a cloud ova yonda."

He clicked twice with his tongue and punched Jerry with a goad stick to signal him to move forward off the ferry and onto Georgetown Road. The road was only slightly less muddy than Eagles Island and so sandy as to make it almost impervious to civilized travel.

"Dis here wahm weather done pushed up some rain in dat cloud, looks like." Aron warned.

As Aron had forecast, the rain came after only two miles on Georgetown Road. It started as a light drizzle that prompted Mary Jane to pull one of the tarps over Aila and Calum in the back. She grabbed the other tarp an dragged it to the driver's bench, where she and Aron could use it when the rain became heavier.

Soon, the rain turned into several separate downpours. The tarp in the back of the cart kept Aila and Calum fairly dry, except for the puddles that collected in the bed of the cart. The tarp up front proved adequate, except during the heavier downpours.

The rains made the road into a muddy, sandy mess. The travel time from the ferry dock turned into almost two hours. They finally arrived at the Smith's small farm shortly before sunset. Rebecca had supper almost ready, except for biscuits and warming up previously prepared dishes.

The Smith farmhouse was smaller than Aila expected, but the same basic design as what was now her home with Gideon. There were four outbuildings, not counting the outhouse: three unoccupied former slave cabins, in better shape than the shacks on the Sanders farm and a hay barn with stables for the Smith's two mules.

Overall, the farm seemed exceptionally organized and well maintained. In the semi-lit twilight Aila noticed that the soil composition of the fields was different from the Sanders farm, more dark, rich soil and less sand, better suited for crops, she thought.

Aila, Mary Jane, and Aron were surprised that the warm welcomes included hugs among the women and handshakes between the men. The visitors had never experienced such a degree of racial inclusion. Aila had never experienced such sincerely caring and welcoming greetings.

"We know yuh mus' be sad tuh brang Calum tuh us, Aila." Rebecca said as they all took seats at the dining table. It was the first time Mary Jane and Aron had shared a sit-down meal with White folks.

"With the Lord's he'p, we promise tuh take good care of 'im an' give 'im a lovin' an' happy home." said Alan. "An' we know it's a long, difficult trip fur yuh tuh come here, but we hope yuh will be able to come an' visit us an' Calum often."

Aila's eyes were already red from weeping, but now the tears came again. "This is the las' thing in the world I want tuh do." she sobbed.

"But I don't know nobody else I want tuh leave mah baby with, 'cept y'all. I know y'all will take good care of 'im."

Rebecca rose and hugged Aila, wiping away her tears with her handkerchief. "The Lord knows yer sorrow, Honey. Trust in 'im an' he'll comfort yuh a'ways. Jesus has his plans fur Calum . . . an' fur yuh. He don't make mistakes."

Aila had her doubts but did not express them.

After supper and the dishes were washed, the group sat around the crackling fireplace, lit to add warmth to the growing evening chill.

"Fur sleepin' tuhnight, we ain't got a lot of space." said Alan. "We gonna have tuh double up a bit. We got one room upstairs with a big bed whur Aila an' Mary Jane kin sleep with Baby Calum. Aron, I hope yuh don't mind sleepin' here on the sofa. Rebecca will give yuh a pillow an' a quilt er two."

"Naw suh, I ain't mindin' one bit. Dat a lot better dan wat I's used tuh at home."

I don't know nobody what'd let a colored sleep in the same bed with a White . . . er sleep on thur livin' room sofa, ne'ther. The Smiths ain't like nobody I ever knowed.

Conversation on the promise of the 13th Amendment and the Sanders farm, now Gideon Campbell's farm, yielded to talk of the Smith family farm.

"Y'all know our farm here is small, but the soil is rich." Alan began. "I'm gonna be buyin' some more land from our neighbor, Mister Coleman. Now, a bigger farm's gonna need more farm workers on account of me an' Rebecca kin't work it jes' by ourself. An' Priscilla ain't gonna be able to he'p much fur 'nother four er five years.

"Aron, I seen how y'all work hard at the Sanders place . . . you, Sally, an' Mary Jane here." Alan continued. "An' I seen how y'all are smart as a whup. I done thought a lot 'bout it, an' I decided tuh ask if'n y'all might want tuh come here an' work with us."

Aron stroked his chin for a moment. "Wat do dat mean, Massa Alan? Y'all want us tuh be workin' fo' yuh . . . er be sharecroppas?"

"Well now, first of all, ain't no need tuh call me 'Massa'. Y'all ain't slaves no more. We're all equal here in the eyes of the Lord. If'n I'm gonna call yuh Aron, yuh oughta call me Alan, mah Christian name."

"Yessuh . . . Alan."

"Yuh kin jes' be workers if'n yuh want. But if'n yuh want tuh share in the money the farm makes, sharecroppin' oughta be yer choice . . . that is, if'n the farm makes any money. If'n it don't make money, we both share the losses."

"Wat kind-ah agreement yuh gwaine offer us? Mista Gideon Campbell done said he's gwaine give us de same as Massa James did . . . half?"

"Mose sharecroppin' I seen 'round here is 'bout that . . . er less." Alan replied. "But I kin do more than that in yer case. I kin let yuh buy mah new land parcel over six years, if'n yuh kin agree tuh four parts out of ten fur sharecroppin'."

"Well suh, I ain't knowin' fo' sho." Aron said. "We done stayed on ova dere on Mista Gideon's farm on account o' Miz Aila, Miz Ginny, an' li'l Sarah. We wants tuh make sho dey gits took good care o'."

"Aron, we'd sure miss y'all if'n yuh was here." Alia interjected. "But don't y'all wanna move here an' make a better life fur yerself?"

"Makin' a better life fur yerself." said Alan. "That's the important thang. Tuh me that means yuh oughta own yer own farmland."

"Dat all sounds mighty good tuh me, Mista Alan . . . I means, Alan. I jes' need tuh talk tuh Sally 'bout it. An' I ain't wantin' tuh do dat if'n it ain't wat Mary Jane here want."

Mary Jane turned to look at Aila. "I sho would miss Aila if'n we moves. But I reckins it'd be good tuh git our own farmland. An' if'n Mista Gideon let Aila come visit Calum, I'd still be able tuh see her now an' den."

"Gideon's gonna have tuh let me come visit mah son, if'n he knows what's good fur 'im!" asserted Aila.

Everyone chuckled.

"Well Aron, why don't yuh go ahead an' talk tuh Sally an' Mary Jane tuhgether." concluded Alan. "But let's shake hands now an' agree in principle, 'less they overrule us later on."

Chapter 25

THE REUNION

MARCH 1866

⟞⟝

Aila could feel the ferry begin to rock as they approached the Market Street landing in Wilmington. She recalled that Aron had wanted to stop for a while in town and briefly visit some friends on the way back from the Smith farm. Aron had not clarified who the friends were.

Once they had disembarked from the Wilmington ferry dock, Aron headed the ox down unfamiliar streets to neighborhoods, clearly those of impoverished Blacks. He stopped the cart at a tumbledown shack among other tumbledown shacks, tied the ox to a hitching post, and knocked on the front door.

"Who is dese folks, Aron?" asked Mary Jane. "I hopes yuh ain't plannin' tuh stay long."

"Yuh find out real soon, girl. Yuh gwaine know dem from some time back."

The door opened revealing a Black man in the doorframe shadow that both Mary Jane and Aila recognized but could not immediately place.

"Lawd 'av mercy!" Mary Jane then exclaimed to Aila. "Dat dere is Isaiah . . . he run away from de farm wid Nat afta Dunbar got kilt!"

Aron and Isaiah shook hands and embraced. "Brotha, good tuh see yuh!" said Isaiah.

"Brotha, it done been a long time!" said Aron. "Y'all knows Mary Jane an' Miz Aila here from de Sandas farm?"

"We sho 'nuf do. How yuh is, Miss Aila?" said Isaiah. "Yuh still looks mighty fine, Miss Mary Jane. It so good tuh see yuh doin' all right."

Aila and Mary Jane smiled and nodded greetings.

"Y'all come on in quick." invited Isaiah. "We ain't wantin' fo' no White folks tuh see Miss Aila 'round here."

The interior of the shack resembled the Sanders farm shacks, except the floor was wooden, not dirt. Mary Jane and Aila then saw another man seated on a ragged sofa. He arose and walked to greet the visitors.

As the man approached, Mary Jane realized who he was and suddenly ran across the room shouting "Daddy!" She and her father embraced.

"Mah li'l girl!" Joshua exclaimed, scooping up Mary Jane into his arms.

"Daddy, Daddy, Daddy!" Mary Jane cried.

Aila stood in silence watching Mary Jane crying and hugging her father, Joshua. Aila suppressed the urge to shed a tear.

"I done missed yuh so-o-o much, Daddy!"

"I's missed yuh, too, Boo." Joshua said. "Mah, mah, mah. Yuh sho done growed up. I ain't hardly knowed who yuh wuz."

"Whur yuh been all dese years, Daddy?"

"James Sandas sold me off tuh a farmer up yonda in Castle Hayne, but den I heared tell dat Yankees done took ova New Bern an' slaves wuz runnin' away to James City. Dat wen I run away tuh James City mahself. An' dat whur I run intuh Isaiah an' Nat up dere."

"Yessum, Miss Mary Jane." Isaiah said. "Wen we run off from de Sandas place, me an' Nat went all de way tuh James City, whur we found Joshua an' his new wife, Ruby."

"Yuh married, Daddy?" asked Mary Jane, surprised. "I wuz full o' hope dat yuh someday come back an' marry Mamma."

"Boo, I neva thought I'd be comin' back tuh anywhur near Sandas' place, since I wuz a runaway from dere. Den me an' Ruby jes' fell in love an' got married."

"Aron, how come yuh didn't tell me an' Mamma dat mah Daddy wuz here in Wilmin'ton?" Mary Jane asked.

"I won' knowin' he wuz here an' married." answered Aron. "I got word dat Isaiah wuz here, but right now's de first time I knowed Joshua wuz here. I's jes' as sa'prised as y'all is. All dis time, I's worried dat he wuz gwaine come back an' steal yo' mamma away from me."

"Aron, yuh ain't gwaine need tuh worry 'bout dat." said Joshua. "Me an' Ruby's as happy as kin be. An' we's got our own baby boy now."

Mary Jane shook her head. "Yuh means I got a baby brotha?"

"His name Abraham . . . fo' President Lincoln."

Mary Jane paused. "I reckins I kin abide wid all dis, if'n yuh an' Ruby is happy tuhgetha. But I's worried dat Mamma's gwaine be mad."

"Yuh ain't needin' tuh worry 'bout dat!" said Aron. "Sally an' me love each udda, an' we gwaine get married ourself. She gwaine be glad if'n all o' y'all . . . includin' Joshua an' Ruby . . . come tuh our weddin'!"

"I reckins we be proud tuh come." said Joshua. "A lot o' wadda unda de bridge, now. We ain't needin' tuh hold no grudges. De Lawd ain't wantin' us tuh do none o' dat."

Aila then realized one of the former slaves was unaccounted for. "Is Nat still in James City?"

For a moment there was silence.

Shaking his head, Isaiah finally explained. "Nat wuz kilt up yonda near James City, Miz Aila. Some White woman said he look at her de wrong way, an' dey drug 'im off an' lynched 'im south o' town. He likely won' lookin' at her any way, much less de way she said. Dey likely hang 'im anyways, even wid no excuse like dat!"

"I thought the Yankees controlled that area." Aila said. "Ain't they protectin' folks up thur?"

"They ain't doin' no good job protectin' the Black folks, dat fo' sho." answered Isaiah. "Sometime, dey be de ones dat doin' de harrassin' . . . an' even de murderin'!"

Aila couldn't believe what she was hearing.

"How all dem White soldiers here in Wilmin'ton treatin' y'all, Isaiah?" asked Aron. "Mus' be all changed since de cullud soldiers left."

"Times unda dem cullud soldiers won' so easy ne'tha." Isaiah said. "White folks 'round here wuz mad as hornets dat Black soldiers wuz here, an' dey took it out on us. Las' summa, a cullud soldier wuz kilt an' dumped in de riva. Shot in de face wid buckshot . . . dey said nobody couldn't even recognize 'im at first. An' we ain't knowin' 'bout why he shot fo' sho. De Whites 'rested six Black men fo' it. Yuh knows as well as me, ain't no Black men kill no Black soldier. Dem six men mose likely dead by now, I reckins."

"An' dem White soldiers in town ain't carin' nothin' 'bout us." Joshua spoke up. "Any Whites dat wants kin scare us in our homes an' whup us, men an' women, in public fo' jes' 'bout anythang dey want . . . lookin' dem in de eye, walkin' too close tuh dem on de street, de tone o' our voice! Don' matter. If'n yuh wearin' a hat, yuh better tip it tuh dem on de way by. Dey jes' showin' us dey ain't on de bottom by losin' dat wah. It 'mose worse dan wen we wuz slaves!"

"It jes' ain't dat." added Isaiah. "Dem White soldiers 'mose as bad as de White folks in town. Dey cuss us an' spit on us, jes' like de udda White folks."

"But ain't de Freedmen's Bureau he'pin' y'all out none?" asked Aron.

"It ain't de Freedmen's job tuh keep de Whites from hatin' us." answered Joshua. "Dey mosely try tuh he'p wid how de boss man treat cullud workas. Sometimes dey he'p cullud folks in court. But I's kin't say dey do a real good job wid ne'tha one o' dem."

"De Freedmen's Bureau do he'p wid feedin' an' clothin' some Black folks dat is hard up er sick." added Isaiah. "An' dey work wid some Yankee churches tuh set up some schools. An' dey he'ped me an' Joshua git work in Mista Robert Campbell's mule stable up yonda in Brooklyn. We sellin' mules an' all kind-ah farmin' tools an' equipment. Robert's learnin' us de business. He say we might be able tuh take it ova someday."

Aila was surprised to hear Robert's name. "Yuh mean Gideon Campbell's brother?"

"Yessum." answered Isaiah.

"Miz Aila is married tuh Mista Robert's brotha, Gideon, now." explained Aron.

"Whur's 'Brooklyn'?" Aila asked. "We didn't even know fur sure whur Robert was."

"Brooklyn's up whur mose o' de colored folks live in town." explained Joshua. "Mista Robert a real fine man."

"Yessum." agreed Isaiah. "All dem freed slaves from de country's been comin' intuh Wilmin'ton lookin' fo' work an' ain't findin' nothin'. We's real lucky Robert's he'pin' us out. An' most udda Whites ain't likin' 'im doin' dat one bit! 'Specially afta he done fought on de Yankee side."

Chapter 26

MARRYING TIME

APRIL 1866

GIDEON HAD RELUCTANTLY GIVEN PERMISSION for Aron and Tootsie to have their weddings on his farm property on the condition that no liquor be involved.

Word of the weddings got out to neighboring farms and as far away as Wilmington. The weather was fair and quite suitable for outdoor ceremonies.

Sally was aware that Mary Jane's father Joshua, his wife Ruby, and their baby, Abraham, would be attending, and she had prepared herself to receive them hospitably. As soon as Joshua and Ruby arrived from Wilmington with Isaiah, she approached her former lover and his family even before she greeted Isaiah.

"I's so happy tuh meet yuh, Miz Ruby." she said to Joshua's wife as they embraced. Nodding to Joshua, she continued. "Look tuh me like dis ol' friend Joshua here done made one good choice fo' a wife. An' wat a purdy baby y'all got!"

"Thank yuh, Miss Sally." replied Ruby. "I's real glad tuh meet yuh too. I thanks yuh fo' welcomin' us tuh yo' weddin' day."

The men then greeted each other with handshakes. Tootsie introduced Hannah to Joshua, Ruby, and Isaiah.

"I ain't hardly recognizin' yuh wid dat beard." said Tootsie to Isaiah. "But I reckins' yuh gotta be careful 'bout showin' yo' face 'round 'bout here. Dem wiskas he'p wid dat fo' sho."

The other guests, most of whom knew each other from the Meetin' Place and Aron's trips to Wilmington, began arriving in early afternoon. Reverend Samuel Hunter, a former slave who served as chaplain to U.S. Colored Troops, arrived with a small entourage from Wilmington to conduct the ceremonies.

"Lawd, yuh done give us such a nice aftanoon fo' dis weddin' git tuhgetha here!" Hunter announced to the heavens as he arrived. "We all's prayin' fo' mo' o' de same de rest o' dis day! A-men!"

Watching from the farmhouse, Aila realized, having accepted Aron and Tootsie's wedding invitations, she had not yet asked Gideon for permission to attend. Not knowing what his response would be, she approached him in the front room with some apprehension.

"Husband, some time back our colored folks invited me tuh thur weddin' party, but I furgot tuh ask yuh 'bout it before now. Is it all right fur me tuh go over thur fur a while?"

"Yuh know I ain't likin' yuh socializin' with 'em darkies. I kin work 'side 'em, but they ain't never gonna be no friends of mine! Daddy sez they ain't never gonna be equal with us Whites, an' I agree with 'im on that."

"I know how yuh an' yer daddy feel 'bout 'em. But they never did me any wrong, an' they a'ways been as he'pful as they kin be, tuh me an' Miz Ginny. So kin I go er not?"

"I reckin so." said Gideon. "But yuh gotta be careful thur ain't no White folks sees yuh."

"I reckin I kin sneak out through the woods if'n I see any White folks comin' 'round."

"But yuh gotta take Ginny with yuh. Ain't no tellin' what 'em nigras might do with jes' one White woman thur by herself. Ginny gonna have tuh take Sarah with y'all. I ain't doin' no baby settin'!"

Aila and Ginny quickly changed into their homemade Sunday frocks, straight full-length calico print dresses covered with a self-knitted woolen shawl, and button-up black leather boots. Normally, they would wear a small bonnet with their Sunday outfit, but they felt that would be overdressing for the occasion. They dressed Sarah in her favorite ensemble, a pink dress with white pinafore, white stockings, and brown leather shoes.

By the time they had finished dressing and reached the area near the shacks where the weddings were to be held, all of the other wedding guests had arrived.

"I'm a li'l skeered 'bout all this." Aila whispered to Ginny. "I ain't been 'round this many colored folks all at onest before. I don't know what tuh say tuh all those folks I don't even know."

"Well, we both know Mary Jane and Sally and the others who live here." said Ginny. "No reason for us to be scared of them."

"I reckin not." Aila replied.

Reverend Hunter was the only person wearing a suit and necktie. Everyone else, including the couples to be married, were wearing everyday clothing. The brides' singular decoration were colorful traditional headwraps.

"I'm glad we didn't wear our bonnets." commented Ginny. "Seeing the rest of these folks, our dress seems a little too fancy."

"I's wantin' tuh introduce y'all tuh Miz Ginny an' Miz Aila." Aron called out when the two White women approached. "An' dat dere's Sarah, Miz Ginny's chile wid dem. I's wantin' y'all tuh give dem a real wahm welcome now."

Aila and Ginny were surprised as guests and Reverend Hunter lined up to greet them and introduce themselves.

"How we gonna 'member all these names?" Aila whispered to Ginny."

"I don't know." answered Ginny. "But it's nice of them to welcome us like that."

"Y'all gatha 'round me here now fo' de marriage o' dese fine folks here!" Reverend Hunter shouted. "It now time fo' the ceremony!"

"First, let us pray . . . Lawd, we all gatha here now tuh join dese folks in holy matrimony. We ask dat yuh bless dese folks as dey start dere new life tuhgetha. In de name o' Jesus Christ, our Lawd an' Save-ya, A-men."

"A-men!" responded the guests.

"Now, y'all needs tuh hear wat de Good Book say 'bout gittin' married." said the Reverend, opening his Bible and beginning to read from pre-marked scriptures.

"An' de rib, which de Lawd God had taken from man, made he a woman, an' brought her unto de man. Derefo' shall a man leave his father an' his mother, an' shall cleave to his wife, an' dey shall be one flesh.

"Wives, submit yuh selves unto yo' husbands, as unto de Lawd. Fo' de husband is de head o' de wife, even as Christ is de head o' de church. Wat derefo' God hath joined tuhgetha, let not man put asunda."

The Reverend closed his Bible and shouted to the grooms "Does y'all want dese women tuh be yo' wives?"

"Yessuh, we do!" shouted the grooms together.

"Do y'all want dese boys in marriage?" he shouted to the brides.

"Yessuh, we do!" shouted the brides together.

"Den brang in de broom!" he shouted. Two male guests came forward with a broom and held it horizontal to about six inches above the ground.

As each couple came forward in turn and jumped over the broom, the Reverend shouted, "Dat yo' husband an' dat yo' wife!

"Let de dancin' begin!" declared the Reverend.

Music and rhythm floated over the crowd as three Black friends of the grooms started playing banjo, fiddle, and rhythm sticks. The sticks were replacements for drums, which had been banned by slave owners before emancipation because they were thought to incite slave uprisings.

Guests began a juba walkaround to the music, clapping hands, slapping legs and arms, turning, and singing.

"'Em folks sure kin dance an' sing!" remarked Aila as she and Ginny watched from afar. "I never seen that kind-ah thang before."

The White women were so absorbed in the dance, they failed to notice a lone White man riding his horse up to the farmhouse and dismounting. He paused for a moment to watch the festivities and then entered the kitchen.

"What in the name of God is goin' out thur, Gideon?" Reverend Campbell asked, entering the kitchen. "An' why is yer wife an' Ginny out thur with 'em niggers?"

"Two of our colored boys is gittin' married out thur, an' I said mah wife an' her could go." said Gideon. "I ain't seein' no harm in it."

"We gotta protect our White women aghen 'em Black bucks, Son!" shouted the preacher. "They're a'ready goin' wild an' threatenin' our women up near Wilmin'ton. I heared tell one of 'em raped a White woman up thur jes' las' week, after he done stole from thur smokehouse! We kin't let that happen down here er anywhur else!"

"I ain't heared 'bout nothin' like that. Anyways, Aila an' Ginny knows 'em coloreds purdy good, so they'll be safe, Daddy. Both of 'em work with our coloreds ever day, jes' 'bout, an' we ain't had no problems."

"Well, that ain't never gonna set right with me . . . mixin' like that. An' 'em Yankees gonna force all kind-ah other thangs on us we ain't wantin' . . . makin' 'em coloreds citizens an' givin' 'em the vote, givin' 'em power they ain't never had before. Thur's talk of organizin' a group like the ol' Home Guard tuh protect our women an' fight aghen 'em Yankee's changes bein' forced on us."

"Daddy, that sounds jes' like we gonna keep the fight aghen the Yankees goin' after the wah done been lost."

"That's 'xactly right, Son! 'Em Yankees thank they won the war an' kin tell us what tuh do, but they got 'nother thang comin'.

"An' 'nother thang, Son. If'n yuh gonna let 'em mix like that, thur's gonna be consequences. Some men 'round here ain't gonna put up with that. Yuh better git ready fur it . . . 'cause it's comin'!"

Campbell exited and slammed the kitchen door behind him. Gideon followed him out of the kitchen. Both watched the wedding guests in the distance, dancing what seemed to be a combination of square dance and African steps.

"That's some kind-ah square dance over thur?" said the preacher. "That's some gall fur 'em tuh be doin' a White people's dance an' playin' White people's music!"

"Now, that music an' dancin' don't belong jes' tuh us, Daddy. I heared tell . . . an' I seen it happen mahself . . . we barra from niggers an' niggers barra from us. 'Em tunes are jes' 'bout as much colored as they's White."

Ginny and Aila couldn't resist keeping time with their feet as they watched the dancers.

"You want to try a step or two, Aila?" Ginny asked. "I think I can help you learn."

"Miz Ginny, I feel like I want tuh join in, but I don't know nothin' 'bout dancin'."

"I'll teach you! All you got to do is listen to that man calling the figures, watch the other dancers, and follow my lead."

Aila resisted, but Ginny pulled her into the dance figure, and before long, they both were dancing like the others, laughing and singing:

Sugar in de gourd,
Sugar in de gourd,
If'n yuh wan' tuh git de sugar out
Den yuh gotta shake dat gourd about!

Chapter 27

RETRIBUTION

APRIL 1866

⟜⟞

Aron lay on his bed remembering the wedding celebrations two days earlier. Sally slept beside him. He heard the gentle spring rain outside and wondered why it hadn't already lulled him to sleep. Perhaps it was the excitement of the occasion, the happiest day of his life, that had not yet worn off. Perhaps it was the expectations of the life that lay out before him and his new family. Perhaps it was both that gave him a profound sense of peace and hope for the future.

He recalled the joyous reunion with his friends, Isaiah and Joshua, as a celebration of how far they, and all the other Blacks, had come since slavery. The gathering had become not only a wedding celebration, but a celebration of their future lives as free people. With that memory, he drifted into sleep.

⟜⟞

Aron awoke to sounds of horses' hooves in mud outside the shack. As he arose, the door was kicked open and three White men, bandanas covering their faces, entered, grabbed him, and shoved him out through the entry onto the ground, to his surprise, on top of Tootsie. There, he realized that there were five White men with covered faces.

"Wat y'all want?" Aron shouted. "Wat dis all 'bout?"

"Yuh stupid nigger!" shouted one White man whose voice Aron did not recognize. "Yuh know what it's all 'bout! It's aghen God's law fur yuh to mix with White women!"

"We gonna learn yuh a special lesson!" yelled another man.

By now, Mary Jane and the sharecropper wives had emerged from the shacks.

"Wat's gwaine on here?" screamed Sally.

"Ain't none of yer business, bitch!" yelled one of the White men.

With that, the White men started lashing Aron and Tootsie with bullwhips mercilessly. Mary Jane ran to one of the White men, grabbed his arm, and struggled to pull the whip from his grasp. He pushed her away and struck her in the face with his fist, knocking her to the ground.

For a moment, she was dazed by the blow, but then pulled herself to her knees. She saw Boo-Boo standing in the doorway to her shack, crying. She launched herself toward the door, grabbed him in her arms, and carried him inside, shielding him from the violent scene.

Aila awoke to the cries coming from the shacks. Seeing that Gideon was still asleep, she slipped quietly out of bed and wrapped herself in a raincoat and started toward the door.

"Whur're yuh goin' at this hour?" Gideon slurred, now awake.

"Somethin's goin' on out at the coloreds' place. Some kind of commotion. I'm goin' tuh see."

"Naw, yuh ain't, woman! Yuh better not git involved in what might be goin' on out thur. It likely ain't none of yer business!"

Ignoring his orders, she continued her rush out of the house. "They might be in danger!"

"God A'mighty!" he cursed.

Rushing out the kitchen door, in the distance she could see the movement of several horses and people, but she couldn't make out what was going on. As she drew closer, she could see three White men kicking three Black men on the ground and beating them with lashes.

"Stop it! Stop it!" she yelled at the White men as she approached. "What yuh doin' tuh these people?"

"Learnin' 'em a lesson!" one of the men shot back at her. "An pro-tectin' yuh from 'em black bastards! Yuh oughta be glad we doin' this!"

The men abruptly stopped kicking and whipping the Black men moaning on the ground.

"What yuh talkin' 'bout?" cried Aila.

"We know 'bout yuh an' Miz Ginny dancin' with 'em niggers! Maybe we oughta be whuppin' *you* while we're at it!"

"Who are *you!* Who are *you* that yuh gotta hide behind 'em masks? Yuh ain't nothin' but a bunch of cow'rds! Show yer faces! Tell me who yuh are! Er git out of here! Git off our property now!"

Having finished with the Black men, the assailants ambled toward their horses. As they passed Aila, one suddenly turned and hit her hard in the face with his fist, knocking her to the ground.

"Yuh're on our list now, woman!" he screamed, as the masked men rode away.

Aila slowly pulled herself from the ground and tried to stand upright. Stumbling, she felt herself being caught by Mary Jane who had rushed to her aid.

"Yuh all right, Aila?" asked Mary Jane.

Dazed, Aila couldn't answer directly. "I . . . I need tuh sit down."

"What the hell is goin' on here!" Gideon demanded as he approached with Ginny.

"Dem White men come ridin' in here, pulled our men out of dere sleep, whupped 'em wid cowhide, an' beat an' kicked 'em in the mud!" explained Sally.

"I need tuh sit down." said Aila weakly. "I'm feelin' sick."

Supporting Aila by one arm, Mary Jane started leading Aila into her shed when Gideon stopped them both.

"If'n she needs he'p, me an' Miz Ginny'll take her back tuh the house." barked Gideon. "She ain't needin' no more he'p from niggers. She done had 'nuf he'p from yuh a'ready! Goddammit, Aila, I told yuh not tuh socialize with these people. Now they done brought this on thur heads an' on *you!* I told yuh this would happen!"

"We ain't brought dis on her, Mista Gideon." said Mary Jane. "We ain't neva wanted her tuh git hurt!"

"Well, you all did cause it!" accused Ginny. "You asked us to come to those weddings when you knew something like this would happen. You knew she would feel obligated to come, and you had to know it would come to this! Now it has, and you all are to blame!"

The sharecroppers stood utterly dumbfounded.

"Now, y'all need tuh all calm down!" Sally intervened. "Evabody's on edge. Thangs bein' said we ain't meanin'."

"I need tuh go tuh bed." said Aila. "Somebody please take me home."

Chapter 28

THE CONSTITUTIONAL
CONVENTION

APRIL 1868

THE SHARECROPPERS GATHERED in the farmhouse kitchen at Aila's invitation for a taste of Sally's chess pie.

"Dat is some mighty good pie, Sally." praised Tootsie. "Jes' 'bout sweet as you is."

"Thank yuh, Tootsie." said Sally.

"When did Gideon say he was coming back from his daddy's place, Aila?" Ginny asked.

Aila wiped bits of residual custard from her lips. "Late this evenin'. Now, while we got some time tuh talk, I want tuh know more 'bout what went on at that . . . what do yuh call it? . . . that *convention* I heared 'bout in Raleigh."

"They called that convention because North Carolina didn't approve changes to the federal Constitution that would give Negroes equal protection under the law." Ginny explained.

"I know all that from what Gideon told me." replied Aila. "I reckin that, along with the Black Codes, made Congress real mad."

Ginny continued. "So Congress threw out our state government, put the state under military law, and wouldn't let North Carolina back into the union 'til we approved changes to the federal Constitution. They said folks here couldn't vote unless they took a loyalty oath and swore they hadn't helped the Confederacy. That meant a lot of White folks couldn't vote and a lot of coloreds could."

"I heared dere wuz a lot o' cullud folks elected tuh dat state convention in Raleigh." Aron added.

"That's what I want tuh know." Aila said. "What did that state convention do?"

"Dey did evathang Congress wanted!" exclaimed Aron. "No mo' Black Codes, an' we kin vote!"

"The convention's state constitution proposal was approved by the voters just this month." Ginny confirmed.

"But ain't that gonna make White folks 'round here mad as they kin be?" surmised Aila. "Ain't they gonna blame y'all coloreds for what Congress an' the convention did?"

"White folks' hearts ain't gwaine git changed jes' 'cause dey lost dat wah, Miz Aila." Aron answered. "It jes' make a lot o' dem even madder now. An' dey sho 'nuf gwaine take it out on us cullud folks."

Chapter 29

A VISIT WITH CALUM

September 1868

~~~~~~~

AILA ROCKED ON THE FRONT PORCH of the Smith farmhouse, her twins Jacob and Elizabeth playing at her feet. Amused by their antics, she watched Calum, Boo-Boo, and Priscilla playing in the black muck left by the afternoon thunderstorm. Water vapor rose like steam from the trees and plants surrounding the house, evaporated by the increasingly intense rays of sunshine piercing the mist.

But for the children's giggles, morning birdsongs, and the gentle clock-like rocking of her chair, all was quiet. She picked up Elizabeth and gently positioned the girl in her arms at her breast. Perhaps it was the serenity of the scene, the gratification of watching Calum and Boo-Boo at play, the emotional release of the war's end three years before, or now the motherly emotion toward Elizabeth, but she now felt a long-lost sense of tranquility come over her.

A squeal from Calum distracted her from her reflections. "Ooh, Mamma! Look unda da house! Da rivas, da rivas, da opples, da opples!" he announced with awe from the edge of the porch.

She arose, descended the porch steps still cradling Elizabeth, and peered under the open two-to-three-feet high storm flood crawl space under the house. This morning storm had blown dozens of pears and several pools of rainwater under the house from the fruit tree next to the porch. She suppressed a quiet chuckle, realizing that the "rivas" were pools of rainwater and the "opples" actually were pears.

"Yuh're such a smart li'l boy!" she said as she hugged him with one arm while holding her baby girl with the other. "Why don't you an' Boo-Boo git a basket from the kitchen an' gether up some of 'em 'opples' an' we'll make a pie later on?"

The children ran to get the basket, scurrying past Mary Jane and Rebecca coming onto the porch from the house. Aila climbed the porch steps to meet the two women.

"Looks like we gonna have some 'opple' pie fur supper." said Aila. "Calum an' Boo-Boo done decided."

"That sounds good tuh me!" Rebecca replied, chuckling as she squeezed back into the house past the exiting children. "I'll go git the fixin's ready."

The children frantically began collecting the pears as if the fruit would somehow escape their grasp if they didn't entrap them as quickly as possible.

Aila and Mary Jane chuckled quietly. "Yuh reckin they gonna let any of 'em pears git away?" asked Aila.

"I's sho doubtin' dat." laughed Mary Jane, taking a seat in the porch swing as Aila took a seat in one of the rocking chairs.

Aila rocked quietly for a time. "I love comin' here tuh see Calum an' visit y'all an' the Smiths. It's real peaceful here. I been meanin' tuh ask yuh, how's it workin' out with Aron, Sally, an' you livin' here an' workin' with the Smiths?"

"Jes' fine . . . jes' fine. De Smiths go out o' dere way tuh make us feel welcome. Dey's tryin' dere bes' tuh make farmin' here work out fo' us. But I do miss yuh an' de uddas back at yo' home place."

"I miss y'all too. It's good tuh see yuh now."

Aila continued rocking and absorbing the peace and quiet.

"It's nice Gideon lets me come over here tuh visit Calum." Aila continued. "I jes' don't trust 'im sometimes . . . like after Aron an' Tootsie's weddin's a couple of years back when 'em men come an' beat us? I kind-ah thank Gideon might've had somethin' tuh do with that. I'm purdy sure his daddy did."

"Now yuh listen here, Aila. Mista Gideon's yo' husband. Yuh married tuh 'im an' I reckins yuh gwaine 'ave tuh put up wid 'im."

"I reckin so. If'n I brang it up, he'll deny it. But I sure don't trust 'im sometimes."

"I tell yuh now, I ain't neva trusted Mista Gideon. But I a'ways liked Miz Ginny . . . 'til dat time wen she blame us fo' dem men comin' an' beatin' us. How kin she blame us?"

"Maybe she was right. Y'all should've knowed 'em men would come if'n yuh had us at tuh weddin's."

"Wat yuh talkin' 'bout, woman? Yuh sayin' it wuz our fault dey come an' beat us? We kin say it wuz yo' fault 'cause yuh knowed yuh oughta not come!"

"Well, I don't know. Maybe I'm wrong. These are confusin' times. It jes' seems we oughta try tuh take care of each other these days."

"I thought we wuz takin' care o' each udda all 'long. Den yuh bring up somethin' like dis. I's beginin' tuh wunder how much I kin trust *you!*"

"I'm sorry. Maybe I need tuh thank 'bout this some more."

"I thank so!" grumbled Mary Jane. "I's gwaine back out tuh de field an' he'p pull dem peanuts before suppa. Oughta been back workin' a hour ago!"

Rebecca and Aila finished making supper about the time the sun disappeared behind the stand of loblolly pines to the west of the Smith farmhouse.

"Yuh kin put the biscuits in the stove now, Miz Rebecca." Aila announced. "I'll go rang the bell."

Aila went to the kitchen window and grabbed the rope attached to the cast iron bell on a cedar post outside the window, ringing it six times. "They oughta be here direckly." she said to Rebecca. "I'll set the table.

"I'm glad Calum is livin' here with y'all." said Aila as she set dishes on the table. "He ain't been no trouble?"

"No ma'am, no trouble atall. He's still that happy, sweet li'l boy yuh 'member. I know he misses yuh an' a'ways looks far'erd tuh yer visits."

"It's real nice of yuh tuh teach 'im tuh call me 'Mamma'. I don't know if'n he understands why yuh're called 'Aunt Rebecca' an' I'm called 'Mamma,' but I sure like the sound of it."

"I thank it's good he knows yuh as 'Mamma'. An' I kind-ah like bein' his Aunt Rebecca."

The sound of footsteps on the porch announced the arrival of the field workers.

"Y'all come on in." Rebecca welcomed Aron, Sally, Mary Jane, and Alan.

"We's jes' waitin' fur Boo-Boo on the porch." answered Mary Jane. "Y'all send 'im on out, an' we'll go on ova tuh our cabins fo' suppa."

"Ain't they stayin'?" Rebecca asked. "Me an' Aila done fixed supper fur 'em. Y'all comin' in an' havin' supper with us, ain't yuh?"

"Now, Miz Rebecca, we ain't wantin' tuh make trouble fo' y'all." said Aron. "Yuh knows dem militia mens gwaine pay y'all a visit if'n dey find out we in yo' house eatin' wid y'all. Ain't no tellin' wat dey might do tuh us . . . an' tuh y'all too."

"I know the folks 'round 'bout here." said Alan. "They're Christians an' go tuh church with us. I kin't believe any of 'em would do anythang tuh hurt y'all . . . er us."

"Well, maybe yuh is right." said Aron. "But we's hearin' all 'bout dem militia mens skeerin' folks in Wilmin'ton an' right here in Brunswick County."

"Y'all go on back tuh yer place now, like normal." said Alan. "When it's dark 'nuf nobody kin see yuh, leave a lamp burnin' in yer house, then come 'round tuh our back door, outta site from the road. Rebecca will keep supper wahm 'til y'all come back."

"If'n yuh say so, suh, an' y'all thankin' it all right."

Chapter 30

A SIGN FROM GOD

AUGUST 1869

～⌒～

AILA STOOD FROM HER BENDING POSITION, wiped sweat from her forehead, and gazed down the seemingly endless row of okra before her. The sun had been blazing down on her and her fellow workers most of the day. Now, it was lower in the sky, but the air was still warm and humid. The heat was made worse by the long sleeves and stockings she had to wear to protect herself from the itchy plant.

Now a year old, Aila's daughter Elizabeth slept in a sling tied to Aila's back while her twin brother Jacob wiggled in a similar sling on Ginny's back. Aila and Ginny bent down again and again, using secateurs to cut the furry okra pods from the plant and toss them into the bushel basket the women drug behind them.

Aila stood upright again and surveyed their two co-workers, Tootsie and Hannah, harvesting sweet potatoes, butterbeans, cabbage, carrots, and snap beans. Ginny's five-year-old daughter Sarah also tried to do her part in the carrot row.

"Li'l Sarah workin' jes' like de grown-ups!" laughed Tootsie from several rows over. "She be startin' early. 'Nudda three years an' she be ready tuh work jes' like a growed up person."

"Yes sir!" called back Ginny. "Eight is plenty old enough to do grownup work." Sarah smiled and tossed her harvested carrot into the carrot basket.

"I'm sweatin' like a mule, an' mah back's killin' me!" complained Aila. "I sure hope we kin git a good price fur all this tuhmara in Wilmin'ton."

"How come Mista Gideon ain't out here wid us?" asked Tootsie. "Somethin' 'bout fixin' de house?"

"He said some dry rot an' shingles need replacin' tuhday." answered Aila.

The twins awoke from their naps about the same time and started fussing to be put down. Aila and Ginny took the babies out of the slings and let them play in the field dirt on their own.

"That eclipse of the sun is supposed to happen sometime before sundown today." Ginny said to Sarah. "Remember, you can't look direct at the sun, except real quick and only when I tell you. It can hurt your eyes real bad."

"Yessum." agreed Sarah.

"I know yuh told me 'bout that, Miz Ginny." said Aila. "But I don't understand much 'bout it."

"I've never seen one myself. But it's when the moon blocks out the sun for a short time, and everything gets a little dark . . . not as dark as night, but kind of like twilight."

"But how come the moon blocks out the sun? Ain't that some kind-ah miracle?"

"I don't understand it all. You know how the sun moves across the sky every day, and the moon moves across at night . . . sometimes in the day when you can see it? Well, I reckon sometimes the moon catches up with the sun and blocks it out."

Aila thought for a moment. "Don't that mean the moon's closer tuh us than the sun? I never thought much 'bout which one is closer. Can the sun ever block out the moon?"

"Maybe . . . I've never heard about it." Ginny answered. "I never thought about the moon being closer, either. But I don't know if it's always closer. Maybe just while the eclipse is happening."

Aila continued her work until she sensed increased darkness around her. Glancing up, she could see a dark shadow beginning to cross the sun.

"Looks like it's startin' now!" she shouted. "But y'all jes' glance . . . don't stare, jes' like Miz Ginny told yuh!"

Aila and Ginny were quick to shade the twins' eyes. They all glanced up to see what was happening, then returned to their work.

As the light grew dimmer and dimmer, Aila continued to periodically glance up.

"De sun's goin' 'way!" shouted Tootsie. "Maybe it ain't gwaine come back! Wat we gwaine do widout de sun?"

"It will get darker for a while and then it'll come back." explained Ginny. "It's not gonna go away forever!"

"I ain't so sho 'bout dat!" exclaimed Tootsie. "Is dis de Lawd's work er de Devil's?"

Gradually, daylight became obscured by premature darkness, the temperature dropped, and a chill swept over them.

"Look dere!" screamed Hannah. "Dem wild birds an' guineas done gwaine tuh roost in dem trees, like de night comin'!"

Even Ginny felt some apprehension overcoming her. "Look now! The sun's completely covered! Look at that red circle around the sun and the golden rays shooting out!"

"It like fire shootin' out!" gasped Hannah. "De sun gwaine blow up? We oughta git inside de house right now!"

"There's nothing to be afraid of." shouted Ginny. "This is all God's handiwork! Just don't stare at it!"

"The sun's all covered up!" shouted Aila. "The sun an' moon mus' be 'bout the same size! Look at the stars! Stars are comin' out!"

The group was speechless as they tried to comprehend the magnificent display above and around them. Awe, wonder, fear, curiosity, and delight were all merged into feelings they could not express.

"The moon's moving and the sun is coming back now!" Ginny observed.

When full daylight returned, it was late afternoon and time to carry the harvested produce back to the barn and finish other routine tasks in preparation for supper.

"Y'all gatha up yo' baskets, w'ile I go git Mary de Mule an' a cart." said Tootsie.

The workers collected and carried the full baskets to the end of the rows to await the mule and cart. Within a few minutes, Tootsie returned, and they stacked the baskets in the cart. As Tootsie drove the cart back to the barn, the group followed alongside.

"Y'all remember back in '59 when we had them northern lights?" asked Ginny. "I was in Pennsylvania then, but James told me y'all saw it down here. That was a glorious wonder, wasn't it? I felt like it could be some kind of message from God."

"I 'member it." said Aila. "I was only 'bout eight, but it's still stuck in mah mind. It was the first time I realized God sure did give us a wunderful world an' beautiful heavens 'bove it."

"It *wuz* a sign from de Lawd!" declared Tootsie. "All o' us knowed He wuz tellin' us our freedom wuz comin'. An' den de wah come an' made us free, jes' like He promise wid dem northern lights!"

"It might have been a sign from God." agreed Ginny. "But we really didn't know what it meant."

"Us Black folks knowed wat it mean!" said Tootsie. "It mean we wuz gwaine be free! Now, we *is* free! An' dis here eclipse is 'nudda sign dat de Lawd gwaine take care o' us. He gwaine take 'way all de hate dem White folks got fo' us an' make dem do 'way wid dem laws aghen us!"

"Yuh right, husband." concurred Hannah. "Dis mean he gwaine make dem White folks treat us right, jes' like all o' God's chillens! Maybe Jesus hisself come back tuh he'p make it all happen!"

⸻

The sun had not yet arisen when Aila rose from the bed she and Gideon shared. Babies Elizabeth and Jacob and the others were still sound asleep. She crept from the sleeping area through the door to the kitchen walkway and into the kitchen, where she lit a lamp on the kitchen table. Retrieving her journal from its secret place on the space behind the cupboard, she sat at the table and recalled the eclipse from the previous day. It had been an even more profound experience than the aurora borealis of 1859.

I see the way God works. He don't git involved in our lives, like Rev'rend Campbell sez. He inspires us with this beautiful, wunderful world tuh try an' do better fur ourself an' other people. We make mistakes, but he wants us tuh a'ways try tuh do better . . . tuh he'p other folks an' spread kindness. Our prayers ain't so much us askin' fur he'p as they are our way of strengthenin' ourself tuh do what we know we oughta do.

As she began writing her thoughts on the page, she could hear footsteps approaching from the main house. She closed her journal, dashed to the cupboard, replaced it in its hiding place, and started stacking kindling in the woodstove.

"What yuh doin' in here before the crack of dawn?" asked Gideon, opening the kitchen door.

"I woke up early an' jes' couldn't git back tuh sleep. I thought I'd git the stove far started tuh fix breakfas'. I know yer daddy's comin' here this marnin' tuh go with yuh tuh Wilmin'ton. Y'all gonna need a early breakfas'."

"Well, now that I'm up, I reckin that's a good thang yuh oughta be doin'. He wants tuh carry crops an' produce in with us tuhday."

Aila went about preparing breakfast, but soon heard Elizabeth and Jacob fussing in the main house. Soon the fussing stopped, signaling that Ginny had come to the babies' rescue, with help from Sarah.

"I need tuh go feed the babies now." Aila said. "I'll send Miz Ginny over tuh finish fixin' breakfas'."

Ginny and Sarah entered the kitchen shortly after Aila left. "It may be crowded in here with Reverend Campbell joining us." Ginny said to Gideon. "You want to move to the big table in the front room?"

"No, I reckin it'll be fine here. Yuh an' Sarah kin set over yonder at that side table."

Not wanting to be too close to the preacher, Ginny silently agreed.

"Yuh know it's out of the kindness of mah heart that I let yuh stay here like yuh was fam'ly." said Gideon, watching Ginny as she moved to prepare breakfast. "An' I kind-ah like havin' two women 'round tuh take care of me an' mah children. Yuh ain't still mad at me fur me bein' sweet with yuh when Aila was in Brunswick, are yuh?"

"That's water under the bridge, now. But you can't do that ever again."

"Yuh ain't told Aila 'bout that, have yuh?"

"No. But you can't ever do that again. It's good of you to let me stay here with Sarah, but what you wanted then isn't part of that. I do my fair share of work here, and I owe you nothing more."

"But yuh is a mighty fine woman. Yuh oughta be flattered I done took a likin' tuh yuh."

"Hear me straight, Gideon! You are never to come near me again! I will do my work in exchange for my room and board, but I have no further obligation to you!"

Gideon stood up from his chair and looked out through the open kitchen window to see Reverend Campbell approaching with his mule and cart.

"Un-huh. We'll jes' see 'bout that."

"Yuh see that thur eclipse yesterdee, Son?" asked Campbell, noisily slurping his black coffee. "That was a mighty display of the Lord God's power!"

"Yessuh, I sure did. I was on the roof here, fixin' shingles. Mighty wundrous, it was. I still got some blind spots from it in mah eyes."

"Miz Ginny sez yuh kin hurt yer eyes from starin' at the sun!" exclaimed Aila. "Yuh reckin that's what happened?"

"No! I ain't never heared that! Ginny don't know what she's talkin' 'bout!" snarled Gideon.

Aila and Ginny's eyes met. Ginny shook her head in disgust.

Gideon slurped his coffee. "I looked at the sun before yesterday, an' I ain't never hurt mah eyes. Thur's spots fur a while sometimes, but they go 'way after a bit."

"Jes' on account of she's a Yankee, she reckin she knows more than us ig'rant Southerners." Campbell pronounced, ignoring Ginny's presence.

The women said nothing.

"That thur eclipse is a sign from the Lord." continued Campbell. "The Lord ain't gonna hurt mah son's eyes with His signs."

Campbell continued chewing his smoked sausage as he elaborated.

"It's a sign the Lord's gonna end this terrible situation we got with 'em damn Republicans in Congress an' here local. They sent all 'em nigger troops 'way, but they put us under 'em White troops an' forced us tuh accept that amendment tuh give the niggers equal rights!"

The boom of Campbell's voice now had the focus of everyone in the room, even the children.

"Nineteen niggers was in the state legislature when they approved that amendment! That got that Yankee army fine'ly moved out, thank the Lord. But they set up statewide schools fur coloreds . . . tuh be paid fur by our taxes. Kin yuh tell me how 'em niggers oughta git free education paid fur by taxes on me?"

No one in the room spoke. Campbell continued his tirade.

"So that eclipse is the Lord's sign that all this mess has got tuh change! An' He's gonna step in an' change it with White Anglo-Saxon Protestants . . . His chosen race . . . as His soldiers!"

───────

"Gideon's sleeping late this morning." Ginny said as she put Aila's twins on the kitchen floor to play with Sarah. "Was he up late last night?"

"No, he was in bed early tuh satisfy hisself in me." Aila replied. "I reckin he's still sleepin' from that."

"I'll stir the grits and start the ham." said Ginny. "You want me to go call Gideon?"

"If'n yuh don't mind. I'll start rollin' out the biscuits."

Aila finished hand rolling, pinching off, and placing the biscuit dough in a baking pan. She shoved the pan into the oven as Ginny retuned from Gideon's wakeup call.

"He said he was coming." announced Ginny, as she started re-tending the grits and ham.

"I feel purdy sure I'm gonna have 'nother baby 'bout Febwary." announced Aila, rinsing flour from her hands over the sink. "I feel all the signs, an' I'm beginnin' tuh show some."

"Well, congratulations!" said Ginny. "How do you feel about that?"

"I ain't lookin' far'erd tuh it. Gideon wants one 'bout ever year, an' ain't much I kin say 'bout it. He sez he needs a brood tuh work the farm, if'n Tootsie don't work out. He's figurin' he's gonna need 'em when his daddy passes an' he inherits that farm. Plannin' fur the future, he sez."

"You know it's a wife's duty to meet her husband's needs and bear his children."

"Yessum. Yuh told me that more than onest. But yuh ain't married an' yuh ain't got tuh lay with no husband er bear his children no more. Yuh don't carry that burden."

"It's not a burden if you love your husband."

The two women were quiet for a moment.

"I loved James, Aila. Despite his rough edges, he was the love of my life. I doubt if I will ever marry another."

"If'n Gideon decides he don't want yuh tuh stay here, how yuh gonna support yerself without no husband?"

"I'm hoping that won't happen. But if it does, I'll find a way to take care of myself. It won't be easy, but I'll find a way."

"I'll do what I kin tuh make sure yuh kin stay here. Maybe Gideon will decide he needs yuh."

The conversation ended as Gideon opened the kitchen door and entered. Without speaking, he took a seat at the table and waited to be served.

"Whur's mah coffee? I need mah coffee!" he demanded.

"I got it right here." answered Aila. "An' I got yer plate ready right here too."

The women joined him at the table with their breakfast plates. They all immediately bowed their heads and closed their eyes for Gideon's blessing.

Afterward, no one spoke for several minutes while they fed themselves.

"I still kin't see right." Gideon almost whispered. "I got a blind spot right in the middle of mah eyes an' everthang's kind-ah blurry 'round it. I ain't seein' colors that good, ne'ther."

Startled by his admission, both women stopped eating and stared at each other.

"Yuh better go see Doc Brooks soon as we finish breakfas'." said Aila. "That don't sound right."

"Yuh might need tuh go with me, Aila. I ain't knowin' if'n I kin see the way good 'nuf.

Chapter 31

THE REDEEMERS

AUGUST 1870

⟶

Curly locks, curly locks, wilt thou be mine?
Thou shall not warsh dishes, nor yet feed swine,
But set on a cushion an' sew a fine seam,
An' feed upon strawberries, sugar, an' cream.

Rᴇʙᴇᴄᴄᴀ Sᴍɪᴛʜ ꜱᴀɴɢ ɢᴇɴᴛʟʏ ᴛᴏ Cᴀʟᴜᴍ as he lay in his feather-bed, his eyes drooping into slumber.

"Good night, mah sweet one." she whispered. "Sleep well."

She rose from his bedside, kissed her daughter Priscilla on the cheek, put out the lamp, and tiptoed out of the bedroom, gently closing the door behind her.

"They both asleep?" asked Alan. "They mus' be real tared of playin' with Boo-Boo all afternoon."

"They're sound asleep." said Rebecca.

"Like I said, Alan, I hain't aghen 'em li'l ones playin' with 'em nigger children." Zechariah declared. "I played with li'l niggers when I was a boy. But y'all hain't s'posed tuh be socializin' with 'em growed up niggers. Y'all gonna git in trouble if'n y'all keep that up. Yuh know who I'm talkin' 'bout. 'Em people ain't playin' games!"

"Now, Zechariah, I know who might be Klansmen 'round here." said Alan. "Ain't none of 'em ever said a bad word tuh me 'bout it."

"Yuh know they lynched that Wyatt Outlaw nigger politician up in Alamance County las' May." argued Zechariah. "An' most folks thank they kilt that Freedman's Bureau agent John Stevens what was organizin' niggers up thur in Caswell County. He was kilt right in the County Courthouse an' found in the woodpile the next day."

"We go tuh Galilee Church with some of 'em." said Rebecca. "A couple of 'em is deacons with Alan."

"Do y'all a'ways have tuh carry on 'bout politics?" Nancy dipped her finger into her snuff tin and placed a pinch between her jaw and gum. "That was a mighty fine oyster roast y'all had fur us tuhday. Oysters dipped in hot peppa vineger! An' hushpuppies on top of that! Um, um, um!"

"Thank yuh, Miz Price." said Rebecca. "I'll git the spittoon fur yuh."

"Who y'all votin' fur in the election this week?" asked Zechariah, ignoring Nancy's comment. "We need tuh git rid of 'em scalawag an' carpetbagger Republicans in office now. That goes double fur 'em stupid niggers. Why ought they count the same as Whites if'n they don't pay property taxes like we do?"

"I know colored folks ain't got much experience in gover'ment." said Alan. "But they're learnin'. Black folks need somebody tuh represent 'em. Yeah, thur's been some corruption an' other bad thangs goin' on with the Republicans. But they did approve public schools in '68. That was a good thang. An' I reckin thur reconstruction plans in Congress is good overall. Colored folks done been through a lot, an' we need tuh he'p git 'em back on thur feet after slavery."

"But they git tuh vote without payin' no property taxes!" shouted Zechariah.

"Yuh're furgittin' coloreds pay rent 'cause they can't git loans from White bankers tuh buy property." Alan continued. "The rents they pay a'ready got taxes rolled up in 'em. It ain't right tuh say the coloreds ain't payin' thur share."

"Yuh sound like a damn scalawag, Alan!" yelled Zechariah. "Hit's real simple. All we want is tuh make our way in this life an' do what's best fur us an' our families. We need tuh redeem our country, our Southern way of life! Yeah, we lost that damn wah, but it was a noble cause. We still got a noble cause, one that the Lord smiles on. What we need is redemption! An' the way I see it, Democrats is the Redeemers!"

"Some folks reckin freein' the slaves, makin' 'em full citizens, an' givin' 'em the vote was a noble cause." countered Alan.

Anger and frustration flared in Zechariah's face. "God sez in the Bible He's on our side on this! Hit's jes' common sense! White people is jes' better than niggers. That's why the Lord made us diff'rent. If'n yuh kin't see that, yuh're jes' blind!"

A sudden loud boom outside the farmhouse startled the group. "What the hell was that?!" exclaimed Zechariah. "A shotgun?"

They all rushed to the front door. Alan opened it to reveal a crowd of men on horseback dressed in robes of various colors, some wearing bull-horned masks, others donning open-faced cone-shaped hoods, but all with Christian crosses prominently displayed. In front of them stood a nine-foot-high blazing wooden Christian cross.

To his left, Alan could see a second burning cross and similarly attired group of men on horseback in front of Aron and Sally's cabin.

"What yuh want here?" Alan shouted. He recognized some of the men's faces as fellow church members. The shotgun had awakened Priscilla and Calum, who now were clinging to the corners of Rebecca's dress.

"We got a message fur yuh!" yelled one of the men from behind his mask. "We ain't takin' too kindly tuh nigger lovers. We're warnin' yuh not tuh vote fur 'em goddamn Republicans! This time, we come with a warnin'! Next time, ain't gonna be no warnin'!"

A woman's scream penetrated the night air from the direction of the sharecroppers' cabin. Sally was screaming from the porch, Mary Jane and Boo-Boo at her side, while three Klansmen dragged Aron into the yard, kicking and beating him as they went.

Alan started down the porch steps as Rebecca grabbed his arm.

"Alan, yuh kin't he'p Aron now!" she screamed. "Thur's too many of 'em!"

"They gonna kill 'im!" yelled Alan. "I kin't jes' stand here an' watch!"

"Alan, they said this was jes' a warnin'! Thank of me an' the children! We need yuh tuh stay alive! We promised tuh keep Calum safe, 'member?"

They stood transfixed on the violent scene unfolding before them. The Klansmen repeatedly lashed Aron with a bullwhip as he lay defenseless on the ground.

As suddenly as they had come, the Klansmen at the Smith farmhouse withdrew and joined those at the sharecroppers' cabin. As Aron's whipping finally ceased, Sally vaulted to embrace his bleeding body, weeping. Two of the men spat on the couple before mounting their horses and riding into the night.

"Yuh hain't goin' over thur, is yuh?" asked Zechariah.

"We gotta go see if'n we kin he'p!" replied Alan. "Kin y'all stay with the children?"

"Well, we sure hain't goin' with *you!*" declared Zechariah.

As Alan and Rebecca approached the cabin, Sally and Mary Jane helped Aron struggle to his feet.

"Go git a wet rag an' bucket o' wadda from de kitchen, Honey." Sally instructed Mary Jane. "An' dat jar o' turt-n-tine."

"How bad yuh hurt, Aron?" asked Alan.

"No worse dan gittin' a slave whuppin'." mumbled Aron, blood dripping from his nose and corners of his mouth.

"What'd they say tuh yuh? What'd they do this fur?"

"Somethin' 'bout mixin' wid Whites an' votin' fo' Republicans dis week. I reckins dey ain't wantin' me tuh do needer one."

Mary Jane retuned with the wet rag and bucket of water Sally had asked for. Sally sponged blood from Aron's face and body, causing him to sporadically wince as she cleaned and applied turpentine to his wounds.

"They jes' tryin' tuh skeer yuh, Aron." said Alan. "An' us too. Jes' like they did when yuh was tryin' tuh register tuh vote."

"I knows dat. I wuz borned a slave, an' I's spent 'mose mah whole life a slave. I took a lot o' beatin's den, an' I kin take mo' now. Dat on account o' I's a freedman now, tryin' tuh make mah way in dis life an' do wat's best fur me an' mah fam'ly. An' dere ain't no 'mount o' skeerin's gwaine stop me from dat. Dey gwaine have tuh kill me tuh stop me now!"

———

As smoke filled the front room of Gideon's farmhouse, the women arrived from putting the children to bed and their clean-up duties in the kitchen.

"Yuh jes' set right thur while I build up more smoke in the far-place with that green wood I brung in tuh keep the 'skeetas away." said Reverend Campbell.

"I kin close the winders." said Aila.

"Keep 'em open!" barked Campbell. "It's still too hot tuh close the winders."

"We gonna be able tuh breathe with all that smoke?" wondered Aila, taking a seat on the sofa with Ginny and Martha Campbell.

"It's better than gittin' eat up by 'skeetas!" answered Gideon. "When it's cooler outside, we kin crack the windows an' let the smoke out a bit."

"I'm so sorry tuh hear yer eyesite ain't no better, Gideon." Martha said. "But yuh seem tuh git 'round some better, ain't yuh?"

"No, Mamma, it ain't no better." said Gideon. "I still kin't see good 'nuf tuh do hardly nothin'. Doc Brooks reckin it ain't gonna git no better. It might git worse."

"It's good the women is here tuh he'p take care of yuh." said Campbell. "But yuh need a White man here tuh run this farm an' keep 'em sharecroppers in line. They gonna be stealin' from yuh if'n yuh kin't see what they up tuh."

"Yuh know how bad thangs is right now, Daddy. It was all I could do tuh keep this farm goin' even before mah eyes got messed up. Yer farm ain't doin' no better. Everbody else is hurtin' too. I kin't afford tuh hire nobody tuh oversee the sharecroppers."

"Truth be known, I kin't ne'ther." confessed Campbell. "I kin't hardly manage mah own farm with mah arthritis."

"Maybe Robert kin come an' he'p out." said Aila, without thinking.

"Listen here, young lady!" roared Campbell. "Yuh ain't got no right talkin' 'bout that traider comin' back intuh this fam'ly!"

"Daddy, Aila don't mean no harm!" countered Gideon. "She's jes' tryin' tuh he'p."

"Ig'rant female!" grumbled Campbell through his teeth.

"Daddy, these is hard times." Gideon said. "I know Robert was in the Yankee army, but he's still mah brother an' I need he'p. It's somethin' tuh thank 'bout."

"It sure would be nice tuh see mah boy." whispered Martha. "I heared tell he's somewhur in Wilmin'ton now. I do miss 'im so."

Everybody was quiet for a time, watching the green wood smoldering in the fireplace.

"Martha, reckin' yuh oughta fetch some of that milder lye soap, wadder, an' a basin?" Campbell said in a more relaxed tone.

Aila and Ginny eyed each other questioningly as Martha left the room.

"Yuh know that nigger Thomas Martin up yonder's been campaignin' fur 'em niggers, scalawags, carpetbaggers, an' Republicans in the election this week." said Campbell.

"That don't sa'prised me none, Daddy. Yuh didn't thank he's be workin' fur the Democrats, did yuh?"

"Don't yuh be sarcastic with yer Daddy, Son! Yuh know I'm fur the Redeemers!"

Martha returned with the basin, water, towel, and lye soap. Without speaking, she knelt at her husband's feet and began to lather and massage his feet.

Aila and Ginny were astonished at the display of wifely subservience.

"Does Martha do that ever night, Rev'rend Campbell?" Aila asked.

"She knows what her duties is." replied Campbell.

Campbell paused and shook his head. "That there Thomas Martin sticks in mah craw! Yuh ain't gonna vote fur 'em niggers an' Republicans, are yuh Son?"

"Nawsuh." answered Gideon. "Republicans has sure made a mess of thangs. But what's that got tuh do with Thomas Martin? He kin vote fur who he wants, kin't he?"

"Not if'n I got somethang tuh say 'bout it!" said Campbell. "It's time tuh put a end tuh this mess an' git on with Redemption!"

A knock on the rear door of the front room awakened Aila. She glanced at the wall clock. It was midnight.

Without waking Gideon, she put on a robe and opened the door to see Tootsie's anxiety-ridden face.

"Miz Aila, look like dere a big fire ova on Federal Point Road!" Tootsie whispered, to avoid waking the others. "I kin see de sky's all red! It might be Thomas' place! We needs tuh run ova dere an' see if'n we kin he'p!"

Ginny also had been awakened and was now standing behind Aila.

"Miz Ginny," said Aila, "kin yuh stay here an' watch over the children? I want tuh go with Tootsie an' see if'n I kin he'p!"

Ginny nodded "yes."

"We got de mules ready outside." said Tootsie. "Yuh kin ride on Mary's back wid me."

"Miz Aila, somethin' strange 'bout de barn. We ain't seein' Preacha Campbell's mule out dere. His cart is dere in de barn, but de mule is gone."

By the time they arrived at the Martin farm they could see that the main house was almost totally burned to the ground.

"Wat's dat smell?" wondered Tootsie. "Dere's de smell o' burnin' wood . . . I knows dat smell. But dere's some smell on top o' dat."

"I smell it." said Aila. "A kind-ah sweet smell like a roastin' hawg."

Sobbing and screaming, Thomas' wife Bessie ran to meet them some distance from the burning farmhouse, but the heat of the fire could still be felt.

"Yuh all right, ma'am?" cried out Tootsie as Bessie came nearer. "Whur's Mista Thomas an' de chillens?"

"Oh mah Lawd . . . oh mah Lawd!" Bessie wailed, coughed, and screamed through her tears as she threw herself into Tootsie's arms. "De Klan done beat an' cut mah Thomas, drug 'im tuh dat live oak tree, set 'im on fire, hung 'im up, an' cut open his belly like a slaughtered hawg. He's hangin' ova yonda now in dat tree!"

"Dem men hurt yuh, Bessie?" Tootsie asked nervously. "Whur's de chillens?"

"Dem men done forced demself on me, four o' dem, I reckins!" Bessie sobbed. "Dey beat me an' forced me naked right in front o' mah chillens! Andrew an' Beth took Olivia an' run off tuh de woods. I ain't knowin' whur dey is! If'n dey stayed, dey likely be dead now too!"

Aila could resist no longer and pulled Bessie from Tootsie's embrace into her own. In the distance, he could barely see Thomas' body, lit by the fire and dangling from the oak tree. Not only had he been disemboweled, but she could see his genital area had been gutted.

She struggled to find the words to comfort the widow, but none came. What can be said to someone who has just lost her husband as she watched his body being mutilated and hung from a tree limb, been sexually assaulted herself by a White mob, and left with no idea where her children were? She tried her best to search for the right words to comfort Bessie, but those that came seemed grossly inadequate.

"The Lord knows yer pain." Aila whispered into Bessie's ear. "We all here's gonna he'p take care of yuh and yer family We gonna find yer children, we gonna care fur yuh and keep yuh safe. Yuh gonna be safe now!"

Aila wasn't sure she believed what she was saying, but she knew she had to say it.

Bessie suddenly released Aila's embrace and collapsed weakly to the ground, continuing to weep, howl, and moan in tones Aila would never forget.

By now, several Black men and women from the community had arrived, and they, too, tried to console Bessie.

As timbers collapsed, giant waves of sparks flew into the night sky, lighting Bessie's agonized face and tears. A haze of smoke hung over the area and a strong scent of burnt wood filled the air.

The house disappeared in flame and smoke while Bessie stared helplessly from her prone position on the ground, looked up at her friends and neighbors, and sadly shook her head.

"We loss jes' 'bout evathang. I ain't knowin' wat we gwaine do now." she cried.

"Ain't lookin' like dere's much we kin do tuh he'p right now, but don' yuh worry none, Miz Bessie." consoled Tootsie. "We gwaine take care o' y'all de bes' we kin. Y'all kin come home wid us tuhnight, an' yuh kin stay wid us a long as yuh needs tuh. We kin git tuhgetha wid de neighbors tuhmara an' plan out how we gwaine build yuh a new house."

"We a'ready talkin' 'bout dat." said a man from the neighborhood Aila didn't recognize. "We meetin' tuhmara marnin' 'bout eight o'clock tuh start plannin' if'n y'all wants tuh he'p."

"We be here den." Tootsie said. "An' we brang some food fo' y'all wen we comes."

"Miz Bessie, we all knows Thomas wuz he'pin' wid Abraham Galloway's election an' supportin' udda cullud candidates." continued Tootsie. "I reckins we knows who want tuh do dis tuh 'im an' his family!"

―――――

Ginny was already making breakfast when Aila came into the kitchen.

"I'm not gonna say 'good morning'." greeted Ginny. "It's real hard to think of this as a good morning after what happened to the Martins last night."

"Yuh know it ain't gonna do no good fur us tuh try an' git the law tuh do somethin'." Aila said. "I got a purdy good idee 'bout at least one man what done it."

"No, the law won't do anything." sighed Ginny. "Some of them likely were part of it. And if we did try, they'd might come after us too."

"It jes' makes me so mad!" Aila almost shouted. "After what all 'em colored folks went through with slavery, be set free, an' now have tuh go through all this . . . this torment an' sufferin' jes' fur tryin' tuh make a life fur 'emselves! They jes' git beat down ever time they try tuh git up. An' the harder they try, the more they git beat down. It jes' makes me sick!"

"It doesn't surprise me." Ginny admitted. "Not a bit."

"Mary Jane a'ways said yuh gotta be strong, stay strong, no matter what happens. Yuh kin't give up! Jes' stay strong, an' it'll come 'round fur yuh. It sure ain't lookin' like that tuh me. They try tuh be strong, but tuh some folks, bein' strong is the same thang as bein' uppidy. Stay strong, an' they come back an' beat yuh down some more."

"You better not let Gideon or Reverend Campbell hear you talk like that!" cautioned Ginny.

"I was wrong." confessed Aila. "Back when 'em men come an' beat us after Aron an' Tootsie's weddin's, yuh said it was Mary Jane an' the other colored folks' fault we got beat. *You* was wrong, but I believed yuh. It won't thur fault. It was the fault of 'em White men what beat us. It was thur hate that was at fault!"

"I know, Aila." replied Ginny. "I was wrong, and I'm so sorry."

"We both oughta be sorry." Aila admitted firmly. "But I oughta be even more sorry 'cause I told Mary Jane it was the colored folks' fault. How could I accuse 'em of somethin' like that?"

"What's all this yackin' 'bout?" Gideon said, feeling his way through the kitchen entrance with a jar half-full of a clear liquid.

"We're just talking about what happened at the Martins' house last night." Ginny said.

"I went over thur with Tootsie after they saw the far light up the sky." explained Aila. "Yuh was still asleep. Some White men came, set far tuh the Martin's house, attacked Miz Bessie, an' killed Mister Thomas. The children ran off intuh the woods, but Tootsie found 'em this marnin'. Miz Bessie an' the children's gonna be stayin' with Tootsie an' Hannah fur a while."

"They likely deserved it." grumbled Gideon, taking a drink from his jar. "Ain't I told yuh tuh stop doin' thangs with 'em coloreds! Yuh goin' over thur's like yuh takin' thur side. Yuh gonna git us all in trouble!"

Neither Aila nor Ginny spoke.

"Daddy an' Mamma's comin' down fur breakfas'." announced Gideon. "Ain't it 'bout ready?"

"We'll brang it tuh the big table direckly." replied Aila. "Yuh go back an' keep 'em comp'ny."

Aila and Ginny brought in the breakfast and arranged a small side table for Aila's twins and Sarah. The adults sat down around the big table for the morning meal. Without being asked, Campbell bowed his head and asked the blessing.

"Pass the biscuits!" he commanded as soon as he pronounced "A-men!"

The toddler twins fussed for some more crumpled biscuit and blackberry jelly. Aila complied, then returned to her place setting, sat, and stared directly at Campbell.

"Yuh see that far over at Thomas Martin's place las' night?" she probed.

Ginny stopped chewing and stared at Aila, wide-eyed.

"What yuh talkin' 'bout, girl?" Campbell asked. "I ain't seen no far! Why would I see a far?"

Ginny began to shake her head, fixing a stare at her plate.

"Tootsie an' me saw it." said Aila. "Lit up the whole sky over that way. We went over tuh see if'n we could he'p."

"Yuh went over thur with yer niggers tuh he'p 'em other niggers?" shouted Campbell. "Ain't yuh been warned 'bout socializin' with 'em?"

"Now Rev'rend, how'd yuh know 'bout that warnin'?" asked Aila. "Yuh won't thur when I got that warnin' from 'em White men what beat us after Tootsie an' Aron's weddin's, was yuh?"

"I heared 'bout it!" answered Campbell. "Yuh know how word gits 'round."

"No sir. I kin't say I do know how word gits 'round." Aila responded. "Maybe yuh kin 'splain it tuh me?"

Campbell didn't reply.

"Tootsie said yer mule was gone from the barn las' night. Yer cart was thur, but yer mule was gone. Now whur might yuh be goin' that late at night, Rev'rend Campbell?"

"Well now, that jes' ain't none of yer business, woman!" Campbell yelled.

Terrified of the commotion, the twins and Sarah started crying. Aila and Ginny rose from their chairs and moved to console the children.

"It's 'bout time we went home, wife!" Campbell shouted to Martha. "I done had 'nuf of this woman's disrespect!"

"Daddy!" Gideon shouted. "What's this all 'bout? Set down an' finish yer breakfas'! Aila ain't knowin' what she's talkin' 'bout! She ain't got no business questionin' yuh 'bout whur yuh go er do!"

Campbell stayed in his chair with his wife beside him

"Aila, yuh stop questionin' Daddy 'bout somethin' that's none of yer business. What's wrong with yuh? Now, jes' shut up!"

"Redeemers!" Aila screamed.

Everyone continued their breakfast and spoke no further.

Chapter 32

THE SCREAM

AUGUST 1870

⁓

For years, Aila had dreaded the late summer harvest season, not so much the hard work, but the oppressive heat and humidity that comes with that season. As she grew older, though, she came to feel a real sense of responsibility to bring in the harvest. What she had seen as hard work now gave her a feeling of accomplishment and completeness. Hard work had become a virtue, a reward in its own right.

Nonetheless, pulling feed corn in the hot August sun was a physical challenge.

"I kind-ah feel sorry fur Gideon settin' back yonder in the house in the shade." she only half joked to Ginny. "He don't know what he's missin'!"

"I think he knows exactly what he's missing." replied Ginny.

"He kin't do much of anythang on account of his eyes. He ain't good fur much, 'cept fatherin' babies. He don't need tuh see tuh do that!" Aila chuckled.

The children were now old enough to play on their own in the shade of a white oak tree at the end of the corn rows. Sarah, who had started doing her small part in the fields at age five, now served as a kind of playmate and babysitter for Aila's twins, age three. The children were happy when the grownups took their water breaks with them in the shade of the oak, but otherwise they were content to play with their homemade dolls by themselves.

"Mamma!" squealed the twins, seeing their mother coming for a break, and ran to Aila's arms.

"Hey thur, mah babies!" cooed Aila, hugging her children. "Yuh miss yer mamma?"

"Yes ma'am!" answered Elizabeth. "Yuh out dere pickin' corn fur us?"

"I sure am pickin' corn, all right, Miss Elizabeth!" replied Aila. "But it ain't fur us people tuh eat. It's fur the farm animals tuh fatten 'em up. Yuh got some wadder fur yer mamma, Elizabeth? I sure am thirsty!"

"I mose surely do, Mamma!"

"Yuh mose surely do'? Sounds like Miz Ginny's been teachin' yuh how tuh talk, Miss Smarty!"

"Ant Ginny told me I am a real Miss Smarty." Elizabeth agreed. "I don't even need hippins no more!"

Jacob, remembering that he was still wearing diapers, remained quiet.

Ginny handed Elizabeth the dipper from the water bucket. The girl held it to her mother's lips for a drink.

"Thank yuh, Miss Elizabeth! That's mighty fine wadder!"

"Yuh're most welcome!" Elizabeth giggled.

After her sip of water, Aila returned to pulling corn ears. "Tootsie, I been meanin' tuh ask yuh how's Miz Bessie gonna manage the farm all by herself, now that Mister Thomas is gone?"

"Well now, me an' some o' de neighbors is gwaine he'p her and Andrew out 'til dey kin git on dere feet. Yuh knows Andrew's ol' 'nuf tuh carry his own load, an' fo' too long, he kin take ova hisself."

"Yuh say 'neighbors' but don't yuh mean jes' *colored* neighbors?"

"Yessum. Dat right. Yuh knows no White folks gwaine he'p Black folks, even if'n dey wanted tuh. Dey might git burnt out jes' like the Martins."

It had been a long, hard, hot day in the corn fields, but Aila wanted to take Elizabeth and Jacob down to the river before supper.

"They ain't seen it before." Aila explained to Ginny. "I reckin' they's ol' 'nuf tuh appreciate it some. We won't be long. I'll be up tuh he'p fix supper direckly."

"Now Elizabeth an' Jacob, this here river is a special place fur me." Aila told the twins as they followed the path to her "secret place." "I used tuh come here with Miss Mary Jane when we was young."

Elizabeth had trouble dealing with the path, soggy in places, but the promise of a special "secret place" kept her going. Jacob had no trouble, almost sprinting down the incline.

The canopy of trees overhanging the path finally opened, and the opening to the view of the river came into view. The twins' eyes and mouths opened in awe. The view revealed more sky than they had ever seen.

"The 'secret place'!" Elizabeth squealed.

"Look! The river!" Jacob shouted.

Aila's heart leaped at the twins' excitement as they sat on the familiar cypress log and gazed out across the river.

"I do love this place." Aila whispered.

"I love this place too, Mamma." said Elizabeth.

"This is gonna be our secret place too!" announced Jacob.

What a wunderful feelin' tuh be here in this place with mah children, tuh share the mem'ry of this place with 'em. Ain't that what it's all 'bout? Passin' on important thangs tuh yer children . . . the beauty of this world, love an' carin' fur each other, how important simple kindness is.

She felt herself tearing.

This world is mah home. This world, the natural world, is so wunderful! Life . . . trees, plants, an' animals pass the life inside 'em from parents tuh children, jes' like us people do. If'n I could, I'd spend eternity right here in this world, not carin' much 'bout goin' tuh Heaven, somewhur way in the sky . . . somewhur I ain't even been before.

Neither Aila nor Ginny wanted to spend much time making supper. Gideon had to have his freshly-baked biscuits at every meal, but the women didn't want to make much more than that from scratch. Some fried ham slices with the biscuits, butter beans cooked with fatback, and boiled Irish potatoes sufficed.

In the relative privacy of the kitchen after supper, the two women took turns basin-washing the dried sweat and itchy corn residue from themselves and playground dirt from their children with soap and washcloths. Gideon and the girls then scampered to the front room to play and listen to Gideon play his fiddle.

Aila couldn't help but think about what happened to the Martins and how Blacks were being treated.

"I heared tell, if'n they win the election 'em Republicans is gonna make thangs better fur the colored people." she said to Ginny. "They gonna make us Whites treat 'em fair an' equal?"

"Aila, it will be a miracle if the Republicans win this election." Ginny said. "Democrats are doing everything they can to keep the colored people from voting. What happened at the Martin farm is just one example. And from what I've heard, the same thing has been going on all over the county, the state . . . the whole South."

Aila sighed. "Has the whole world gone hateful?"

There was a knock on the kitchen door. "Who is that at this hour?" Ginny wondered.

Opening the door, Ginny saw Tootsie standing on the walkway, his sweaty work hat in his hand.

"Miz Ginny, I jes' wanted yuh tuh know some folks from Wilmin'ton come by an' say de Democrats done won de election an' dey's in control o' de gov'ment. Y'all knows wat dat mean fo' us culluds?"

"You can bet they're not gonna help y'all." answered Ginny. "With all this intimidation we've seen from the Redeemers and the corruption we've seen from Republicans, it's no wonder the election turned out the way it did."

"Thank yuh fur lettin' us know, Tootsie." said Aila. "Now y'all gonna have tuh do the best yuh kin . . . an' we will too."

Closing the door after Tootsie left, Aila returned to finish cleaning up with Ginny. Afterward, they joined Gideon in the front room where he had been playing slow airs on his fiddle for the girls. He struck up a jig and the girls danced and giggled around the room as Aila and Ginny clapped to the beat.

When the jig ended, the three children rushed to their corner of the front room to play with their homemade toys and listen to another of Gideon's airs, two of their favorite activities. Ginny got comfortable on the sofa, where Aila joined her, and began to work on her knitting.

"I reckin it's 'bout time fur yuh tuh start teachin' me the fiddle, husband." said Aila. "Maybe we kin start in the evenin's next week?"

"That'd be jes' fine with me." Gideon agreed.

"I'm lookin' far'erd tuh the time when me an' Miz Ginny kin play tuhgether . . . her on the pianer an' me on the fiddle."

Ginny smiled warmly.

"Now, I'm gittin' a li'l tired." continued Aila. "Y'all mind if'n I go tuh bed?"

"Yuh go on." permitted Gideon. "I'll come direckly."

Aila reclined onto the bed across the room from the children's corner, retrieved her journal, now hidden underneath the bed, and began writing. She knew that Ginny would not interrupt her, and Gideon would be unable to see what she was doing. She felt a special need to record her thoughts in private after the long day.

⁓

She was awakened by a piercing scream cutting through the relative quiet, startling her and causing her to jump upright in bed.

"What was that?!" Gideon and Ginny shouted almost in unison.

Aila saw Ginny hurrying toward the screams coming from the area where Elizabeth slept. Rolling out of bed, she joined Ginny at Elizabeth's bedside. Both women were shocked wide-eyed to see that Elizabeth's tiny body had drawn up into a fetal position, her hands clutched like claws and pressed with her knees against her chest.

Aila tried to take her in her arms, but her body had drawn rigid as it collapsed and rocked back and forth on the wooden floor.

"She's burnin' up with fever!" Aila yelled as she finally was able to embrace the child. "Look at her eyes! They rolled back into the sockets like she's lookin fur her brain!"

"I'll get a cool cloth!" exclaimed Ginny, dashing away to the kitchen.

Aila held Elizabeth tight as she could and started crying as the girl continued to scream. She then realized Gideon was standing over them and Ginny had returned from the kitchen.

"I'll hold her while yuh try an' cool her far'ed!" Aila directed Ginny.

Ginny's hands and body shook as she pressed the wet cloth against the girl's forehead, trying to calm her.

"Why the hell is she screamin'?" Gideon demanded.

"There's something terrible wrong with her!" answered Ginny. "She's burning up with fever and all drawn up into a ball, like she's trying to get back into her mamma's womb!"

Elizabeth projectile vomited all over Aila and up into the air, and then lay silent.

"She's still breathin'!" announced Aila. "But she's burnin' up!"

"Let me clean up the mess." said Ginny.

"No. It's still light. Yuh need tuh go git Tootsie an' ask if he kin ride tuh git Doc Brooks. Thur's somethin' serious wrong with mah baby. I'm skeered she's gonna die!"

<hr />

It had been two days since the scream. Elizabeth simply lay on the bed, her fever gone, but her eyes closed and her body motionless. She seemed to be asleep, but never awoke from that sleep. Doc Brooks had said she was in a coma, but he didn't know what caused it. Maybe it was the result of an infection that settled in her brain. Measles had been going around, but he didn't think anything as benign as childhood measles could have caused it. Now, she just lay still on the bed, unresponsive.

"Doc don't know how long she might be like this." Aila explained to the sharecroppers assembled in the front room around the little girl's bed. "An' he don't know if'n she will ever wake up. He reckins thur ain't nothin' we kin do fur her, 'cept watch an' wait."

"Now Miz Aila, yuh jes' got tuh pray tuh the Lawd dat she git better." proclaimed Tootsie. "I reckins He answer our prayers if'n we pray hard 'nuf an' believe real strong."

"We all been prayin' real hard." said Gideon. "An' Daddy come an' prayed fur her too. He sez the Lord don't answer prayers fur some folks, but I ain't believin' the Lord's got somethin' aghen me."

"Look!" gasped Ginny. "Her eyes are open!"

"Oh, mah Lord!" cried Aila. "She woke up!"

Aila embraced her daughter and lifted her off the bed, turning toward Ginny. "She's like a rag doll!"

As Aila held her, she could feel Elizabeth's body stiffening and returning to the fetal form it had assumed two days earlier.

Aila wept. "She's windin' back intuh that ball she was in! Somethin's still wrong with her!"

"Put her back on the bed." suggested Ginny. "Maybe she just needs to stretch out."

The girl grunted and moaned as Aila returned her to the bed, her hands drawn up into fists against her chest. Her eyes seemed to search for something over her shoulder. Gaped open, her mouth emitted a throaty howl from deep within her throat. Tears streamed down her cheeks.

"She's tryin' tuh cry!" Aila moaned, beginning to weep herself. "An' she's peein' in the bed! Maybe we oughta put a hippin on her. We ain't even thought 'bout it before now. First time she's peed fur over two days!"

Chapter 33
SWEET ELIZABETH
MAY 1871

⁓⫶

GIDEON WAS NOW TOTALLY BLIND and unable to provide even basic help to run the farm. In addition to her normal farm work, Aila now had to care for her invalid daughter Elizabeth and her five-month-old son Gideon Jr. She and Ginny had become increasingly responsible for finding ways to feed the family, with help from the sharecroppers, who also had to feed their own families.

The hardship was not limited to the Gideon Campbell farm. The war and resulting economic collapse had left many small farmers, both White and Black, almost destitute. The financial health of larger farms and plantations having been further diminished by the loss of their slave property.

Aila, Ginny, and Ginny's daughter Sarah worked together as a team, helping in the fields and managing livestock, as well as maintaining the farmhouse and making meals for Gideon and the children. Because of Elizabeth's condition, Aila had to cut her meal into small pieces and thoroughly chew it before feeding it to her helpless child. Any state other than mush could trigger what seemed to be dangerous choking and coughing.

Caring for Elizabeth was time-consuming and left little time for Aila to do anything else, much less fully attend to the needs of her sons Jacob and Gideon Jr. Gideon couldn't and wouldn't help, his own needs requiring even more of Aila's time.

When supper was finished, the dishes done, and the children were all in bed, Aila, Gideon, and Ginny sat together in the front room and breathed sighs of relief that the day was finally over. Elizabeth was quiet. Aila doubted that she was asleep.

"Our Elizabeth's such a sweet chile!" Aila said to Gideon. "She kin't talk tuh complain, but she could make a fuss an' fret 'bout thangs if'n she wanted. But she don't do that much. I thank she knows we do the best we kin fur her. I kin see it in her eyes. I kin tell she wants so much tuh talk. She tries tuh tell me thangs with her grunts an' groans an' shakin' her head."

Gideon frowned. "She might be a sweet chile inside, but she's a real burden on us."

"Now, how's she a burden tuh yuh? Yuh don't do nothin' fur her."

"She keeps yuh from attendin' tuh mah needs."

"I do the best I kin, husband. I cook fur yuh an' he'p yuh eat it, I warsh yer body, I shave yuh face, I he'p yuh use the pot, I keep yuh comp'ny. I do 'mose as much fur yuh as I do fur poor Elizabeth. An' yuh want me tuh lay with yuh whenever yuh want on top of all that."

"I'm yer husband. I kin't see, but I kin still give yuh a good beatin' if'n I've a mind tuh. That'll be comin' if'n yuh ain't meetin' yer obligation tuh attend tuh mah needs!"

"An' here I am with chile aghen, three months along. So let me add baby-birthin' tuh that list!"

No one spoke for some time before Ginny broke the silence.

"I've seen it too. You might think Elizabeth can't understand what's goin on, but she does. And she wants to talk. But with her, it has to be a guessing game. You guess what she wants to say, and she shakes her head 'no' or looks up and blinks her eyes to say 'yes'."

"It takes a long time that way, but it's tuh only way we kin do it." Aila explained. "I feel bad I ain't got 'nuf time fur Gideon er even our two sons. Ain't 'nuf time in the day."

"Huh!" Gideon snorted.

"You are a dedicated and loving mother." said Ginny. "I'm just glad that you and Gideon let us live here. I want to do as much as I can to help."

Aila smiled. "I couldn't do it without yuh, Miz Ginny. I don't know how good a mamma I am. Sometimes, it takes more strength than I got. I never 'spected mah life tuh turn out like this. I'm lucky I had you an' Mary Jane tuh he'p me git through all the bumps."

"Aila, we never know what the future will bring." Ginny replied. "We have to understand that life's gonna have its surprises, some good, some bad. We need to take them head-on as best we can."

Chapter 34

HELP FOR THE WEARY

JUNE 1871

AILA ROCKED ON THE FRONT PORCH next to Ginny, resting for a few minutes after a hectic morning of chores and tending to Gideon, Elizabeth, and the other children. She watched a busy army of ants scurrying in, out, and around an ant mound by the porch steps.

"Ain't the way life works wunderful?" she asked Ginny. "Look at 'em ants workin' their little hearts out tuh build a home fur each other an' their babies. All workin' tuhgether tuh he'p each other an' pass life on tuh the next generation."

"That's one interesting thing about you, Aila." Ginny replied. "You notice little things about the world around you that most people don't even think about."

"God made such a wunderful world."

"It's about time for us to get back to work, if that garden's gonna get weeded." Ginny urged.

Aila clearly heard Ginny, but she didn't show any effort to get up from her rocker. "I thank maybe we need tuh git some more folks tuh he'p out 'round here."

"What do you have in mind, Honey?"

"I wish Mary Jane was back here, 'stead of over yonder at the Smiths' place."

"Maybe there's a way we could get her to come and help out here. Your baby's coming in November. Maybe she can come back and help before the baby comes. I think Isaiah usually sees Aron when he goes to Wilmington. Tootsie can get a message to Isaiah next time he's there, and Isaiah can get the word to Aron."

Gideon stepped into the front room doorway to the porch. "I ain't sure I want that nigra livin' in mah house. Ain't she got that boy she'd brang with her?"

"I'm sure she'd want tuh brang Boo-Boo with her." Aila answered. "What's wrong with that? They both kin he'p out. An' we need tuh git Robert tuh come back an' he'p manage the farm too."

Gideon felt his way to sit in an empty rocker. "We done talked tuh Daddy before 'bout this. He owns part of this farm, an' he ain't gonna want Robert back here. I ain't sure 'bout havin' 'im back, ne'ther."

"But yuh know an' yer daddy knows we need more he'p. Maybe yuh kin change his mind."

"I ain't knowin' if'n Robert would come back here anyways, knowin' how Daddy feels. We ain't even knowin' whur Robert is."

"It won't hurt tuh try." countered Aila. "Maybe if'n yuh jes' talk tuh yer daddy aghen."

Gideon thought for a moment, twisting his head in uncertainty.

Ginny sensed Gideon's uncertainty. "I know it's hard for you to travel. But you know your daddy's a proud man and might be more likely to listen if you go to him and ask. I can take you over there tomorrow."

"I reckin Miz Ginny's right 'bout that." agreed Aila.

"All right, all right!" Gideon finally agreed. "We'll ride over thur in the marnin'."

⁓

Several hours had passed since Ginny and Gideon had departed to speak with the Reverend. Now, Aila could see Ginny through the kitchen window, riding Mary back alone across the farmyard. Ginny stabled Mary and met Aila at the kitchen door.

"Whur's Gideon? How come yuh rode back by yerself? Did Rev'rend Campbell agree tuh let Robert come back?"

"I'm sad to say . . . Rev'rend Campbell died in his sleep last night. Gideon stayed to be with his mother. She's pretty upset right now."

"Lord 'ave mercy!" exclaimed Aila. "Was he sick?"

"Martha said he felt odd before he went to bed last night, but that's all she knows. Sounds like it might've been a heart attack."

"We never know when we will be taken." Aila thought out loud. "He was a mean man, even if'n he was a preacher. I thank he hated everbody what won't like 'im er didn't see everthang the way he did. Yuh thank all his sermons 'bout bein' saved from Hell gonna work out fur a man like 'im?"

"I don't know." Ginny replied. "He had his own way of reading the Bible."

"He did pick an' choose what parts of the Bible he wanted an' furgot 'bout the rest." agreed Aila.

"I'm sure Robert will be coming out here to be with his mother when he hears about his daddy's passing." said Ginny. "That will give Gideon a chance to talk with him about managing the farm."

"An' Miz Martha's gonna be over there all by herself now." observed Aila. "Thur's ever reason in the world fur Robert tuh come out here an' he'p manage thangs now."

<hr />

Reverend Campbell's funeral service was held at Mount Moriah Church, which he had helped found and where he served as its first pastor. Because some time would be required to gather the expected large number of mourners, burial had taken place a week before the funeral, attended only by his wife and two sons.

The small church could hold only about twenty-four people, requiring another sixteen to stand outside. None of the sharecroppers from either of the Campbell farms attended. The attendees largely ignored Robert, only nodding and expressing abbreviated condolences to the former Yankee soldier.

Circuit rider Donald Flowers presided over the funeral. After a regular short sermon, Flowers focused on Reverend Campbell's service to the failed noble Southern cause.

"He won't jes' a true servant of God . . . he was a servant tuh our homeland. It's fittin' tuh call 'im one of the great peacemakers in our country. Mah mem'ry of 'im reminds me of that wunderful poem by Miz Mary Ware, 'Song of Our Glorious Southland'."

> *Oh, sing of our glorious Southland,*
> *The pride of the gol'en sun!*
> *'Tis the fairest land of flahers*
> *The eye e'er looked upon.*
>
> *Sing of the noble nation*
> *Fierce strugglin' tuh be free.*
> *Sing of the brave who bartered*
> *Thur lives fur liberty!*
>
> *Weep fur the maid an' matron*
> *Who mourn thur loved ones slain.*
> *Sigh fur the light departed,*
> *Never tuh shine aghen.*
>
> *A smoulderin' far is burnin'*
> *The Southern heart is steeled.*
> *Perhaps 'twill break in dyin'*
> *But never will it yield!*

Aila, seated on the front row beside Gideon, Robert, and Martha, could see tears in the eyes of many in the congregation as Flowers recited the ode to their homeland and the Great Cause lost, but not forsaken.

Aila already had seated herself in one of the remaining rocking chairs on the front porch of the farmhouse. Gideon paced back and forth, felt his way to the rocking chair next to his mother, and took a seat. His brother Robert continued to stand.

"What yuh want tuh talk 'bout, Gideon?"

"Yuh know, Robert, 'bout the las' thang I want is fur yuh tuh be part of Daddy's fam'ly aghen. Yuh turned yer back on yer fam'ly an' yer country . . . yuh was a traider tuh us an' the country of yer birth!"

"I ain't here now 'cause yuh want me back. I'm here on account of Mamma."

"Daddy kicked yuh out fur good cause. Yuh got no reason tuh be mad 'bout 'im cuttin' yuh out of his will an' givin' this farm tuh me, along with the ol' home place over yonder with Mamma."

"I ain't wantin' any part of e'ther farm noways. I got mah own business in town."

"I reckin yuh hate us on account of we fought fur The Great Cause. An' yuh thank we hate yuh on account of yuh went the other way."

"I ain't got no hate fur yuh er nobody else. I hated slavery an' what y'all did . . . that y'all tried tuh destroy our country. I'd fight tuh keep e'ther one from hap'nin' aghen. But Jesus told us tuh furgive 'em that sin aghen us an' love 'em that hate us. An' that's what I try tuh do."

"Yuh ain't needin' tuh furgive us. What we did was right! We fought fur our freedom an' tuh protect our homeland an' our way of life. Ain't nothin' wrong with that! Our men give thur life an' the South gave all she had fur liberty an' state sovereignty."

"Thur ain't no rightness in tryin' tuh tear this country apart . . . only treason!" Robert countered. "An' it's real hard as a Christian tuh understand the hate an' disrespect y'all direct at the colored people. I reckin' I'll never be able tuh abide with that."

"We ain't never agree on this, Robert, so we might as well accept that an' move on."

"Then what is it we kin talk 'bout, Gideon?"

"Truth is, Robert, I ain't wantin' yuh back. But we need yer he'p with this farm an' Daddy's ol' home place over yonder. Without mah eyes I kin't run this farm an' Mamma kin't manage the ol' home place by herself. An' somebody needs tuh oversee the sharecroppers."

"Comin' back out here tuh he'p? That would mean me givin' up mah business in town."

"I reckin so."

"Robert, it means yuh got tuh give up everthang yuh got now an' start a whole new life." interjected Martha. "But we need yuh out here. Thur ain't no way we kin manage these two farms without yuh."

Robert didn't respond immediately as he visually surveyed the farmyard.

"Mamma, if'n yuh need me tuh come an' h'ep run these farms, I'd be honored tuh do it."

Aila had just finished Elizabeth's basin bath and dressed her when she heard the hunting hounds barking at someone at the front door. After carrying Elizabeth to her resting place on the reclined chair that Isaiah had made for her, Aila approached the door, anticipating a knock. Opening the door, she was surprised to see Mary Jane, Boo-Boo, and Aron approaching the entrance.

"Y'all got mah invite from Isaiah in Wilmin'ton!" Aila shouted with excitement. "We didn't thank y'all would be able tuh come."

Aila and Mary Jane rushed into each other's arms, hugging and dancing in circles.

"I'm so happy tuh see y'all!" exclaimed Aila.

Mary Jane giggled. "We glad tuh see yuh too, Aila!"

"An' jes' look at Boo-Boo! He's growed so much . . . I kin't hardly recognize 'im! Thank yuh so much, Aron, fur brangin' Mary Jane an' Boo-Boo over!"

"Yessum, yo' welcome, Miz Aila." replied Aron. "I be gwaine back tuhmara early, so I ain't no burden on yuh."

"Boo-Boo here gwaine miss Calum." Mary Jane explained. "But he all right wid comin' ova here tuh he'p y'all out, ain't dat right Boo-Boo?"

"Yessum, Miz Aila. Mamma sez we ain't gwaine stay too long, so dat all right."

"Jes' a few months, that's all, an' then yuh kin go back tuh 'im in time fur Christmas." explained Aila.

Mary Jane moved to Elizabeth's taut body lying motionless on the sofa. She knelt on her knees at Elizabeth's eye level and whispered.

"Elizabeth, mah name's Mary Jane. Yuh don' 'member me on account o' yuh wuz jes' a li'l baby de las' time we met. Me an' yo' mamma knows each udda from a long time back, 'fo yuh wuz borned."

Elizabeth lay still and listened, her mouth agape and slobbering, her eyes intensely focused on Mary Jane's face. Her lips formed into what seemed to be a smile.

"Me an' mah boy Boo-Boo here is gwaine stay wid yo' mamma fur a w'ile tuh try an' he'p take care o' yuh. I's lookin' far'erd tuh gittin' tuh know yuh better an' lovin' yuh as much as she do."

Chapter 35

THANKSGIVING

November 1871

"Robert, I ain't sure I like what we're doin'." Gideon complained. "Daddy would roll over in his grave if'n he knowed we was honorin' a Yankee abolitionist holiday, birthed in Yankeeland, an' declared by Lincoln."

"Now Gideon, some folks 'round here been havin' Thanksgivin' fur some time." countered Robert. "Anyways, I thank it's a good time tuh offer praise fur the harvest an' git tuhgether with all the fam'ly. We oughta invite the sharecroppers here too. Mary Jane an' Boo-Boo's gonna be with us anyways. An' yuh know Mamma agrees."

"Now that Daddy's gone, I thank Mamma done turned Yankee 'long with yuh."

Aila seemed worried. "Robert, ain't yuh skeered the Klan might come here an' do us harm 'cause we gether with the coloreds? Some crazy White men come here before an' beat us on account of we went tuh Aron an' Tootsie's weddin's. They said I was on thur list."

"I hear President Grant's enforcin' that KKK Act passed by Congress." reassured Robert. "He arrested a crowd of 'em an' put 'em on trial here in North Carolina an' sent troops down tuh South Carolina tuh arrest hundreds of 'em. They say tuh Klan's layin' low now."

"Well, it's mighty good tuh hear we might git some law an' order fur a change." said Aila. "It was gittin' like 'nother Civil Wah, with all 'em Klansmen an' other White folks attackin' the colored folks an' anybody what tries tuh he'p 'em."

———

Fortunately, the weather was crisp and clear since Robert wanted to hold the Thanksgiving gathering outside. Tootsie had fashioned tables and benches from pine boards to accommodate the celebrants, Aila's family, Robert, Martha, as well as Tootsie and Hannah's family, which now included three girls.

Robert rose to speak. "It's so good tuh have us all here tuhgether tuh give thanks tuh the Lord fur the bounty of His blessin's an' fur the fellowship of fam'ly an' friends."

Then Robert offered a prayer:

"Lord in Heaven, we ask yer blessin' on all us here tuhday. We ask yer blessin' on innocent li'l Elizabeth here. She ain't never sinned, Lord, so we ask yuh tuh send yer healin' power an' make her whole aghen. An' bless Miz Aila here an' her baby what's gonna be borned sometime soon. We 'umbly pray in the name of our Lord an' Save-yer, Jesus Christ. A-men."

"A-men!" pronounced the assembly, save Gideon.

Following the Thanksgiving meal, Robert approached Aila alone while the others were cleaning up. "I know Gideon's got that shotgun in the closet inside the house." Robert whispered. "Now that gun works jes' fine, but I'm thankin' . . . with 'im not bein' able tuh see, yuh're gonna need some personal protection that's easier an' quicker than that shotgun."

"It is hard tuh manage." agreed Aila.

"I brung mah Colt revolver with me tuhday. I ain't used it since the wah. I want yuh tuh take it fur yer protection. No tellin' what kind of tramps an' marauders might come by yer place. But I don't want Gideon tuh know 'bout it. He's a proud man. I don't want 'im tuh thank yuh need he'p from me fur protection."

———

Thanksgiving afternoon, Andrew Martin turned his mule and cart south on Federal Point Road, heading toward the Campbell farm, his younger sister Beth seated beside him. The air was cool, pleasant, and refreshing. Andrew enjoyed the contrast of some still colorful hardwoods against the background of dark green conifers and the open fields of bright sun-lit golden broomstraw waving in the gentle breeze.

"I's kind-ah skeered 'bout tryin' tuh ketch Mista Gideon's roosta." admitted Beth. "Dem roostas skeer me tuh death!"

"Wen I wuz li'l, one red roosta chased me all 'round de yard." Andrew reminisced. "I wuz hollerin' an' cryin' all at de same time. He skeered me so bad I fell in dat stinky, muddy drainin' ditch 'hind de house. Smelled like a outhouse! . . . But I kin show dem roostas who's de boss now!"

"I sho hope yuh kin show dis one who de boss!" Beth said.

When they arrived at Gideon and Aila's farmhouse, Aila greeted them at the front door.

"Mister Andrew . . . Miss Beth. Good Thanksgivin' tuh y'all. What brangs yuh down here?"

"We jes' come down tuh buy some more hens an' barra yer red roosta fo' a w'ile." Andrew explained. "Mista Robert said we could come down dere dis aftanoon."

"Mister Robert's right here inside. Y'all come on in an' meet everbody."

Robert greeted them as they entered the front room. "How y'all doin'?"

"We doin' jes' fine tuhday." answered Andrew. "I reckins' y'all knows mah li'l sister Beth here."

"Yessuh, we sure do." replied Aila. "Now, Beth, I got a li'l girl called Elizabeth. I reckin that's whur yer name comes from, ain't that right?"

"Yessum. But I likes tuh be called Beth."

Aila led them all into the front room where Gideon, Ginny, Mary Jane, and Boo-Boo were waiting. Elizabeth lay asleep on her reclined chair and Jacob played in the corner of the room.

"Mister Andrew an' Beth, this here is Miz Ginny, Miss Mary Jane, an' Boo-Boo, Miss Mary Jane's boy. An' that's mah little girl Elizabeth over there. That's Jacob, Elizabeth's twin brother, over thur in the corner."

"Mister Andrew, I thank yuh a'ready met Mary Jane." Aila remembered. "Yuh met her some time back when Aron wuz carryin' us over tuh Brunswick County."

"I do 'member Miss Mary Jane real good." confirmed Andrew.

Embarrassed, Mary Jane forced a smile and looked away. "I 'member yuh too, Mista Andrew."

Long awkward silence.

Elizabeth awoke, twisted and turned in apparent discomfort, and began to grunt and moan. Beth was repulsed by what she saw. "She all crooked an' knotted up. Somethin' wrong wid her? She hurtin'?"

"Honey, she had a sickness we don't understand." Aila answered. "The doctor don't know what's wrong with her. But we reckin she ain't hurtin' none now."

"Is I gwaine ketch it?"

"Naw, Honey. The doctor sez what she had is gone now. It jes' left her like this."

Beth stared intently at the freakish features of the girl whose name she shared. "How ol' she is?"

"Jes' a li'l over four an' a half. She's been like this fur li'l over a year. I'm sorry, Beth. She mus' skeer yuh."

"Wat dat stink, Miz Aila?"

"I'm sorry. I need tuh change her hippin. I'll do that when y'all go tuh ketch the chickens."

"What's a 'hippin'?" Beth asked. "Yuh mean 'diaper'? She still wear diapers?"

"She kin't go by herself, I'm sorry tuh say." Aila explained. "She kin't hardly do nothin' fur herself."

No one spoke.

Robert finally moved the conversation forward. "Well then . . . I reckin y'all kin go ketch 'em hens an' that mean ol' roosta. Y'all got a chicken wire pen on that mule cart tuh put 'em in?"

"Yessuh!" answered Andrew. "Let's go ketch some chickens!"

———

"I reckin everthang turned out real good." Aila said to Mary Jane and Ginny as they washed the Thanksgiving dishes. "We all et our fill."

"Dat wuz 'bout de best meal I eva et!" critiqued Mary Jane. "Evabody seem tuh git 'long an' have a good time. An' I wuz kind-ah glad tuh see Andrew wen dey come fur de chickens."

"Ha, ha!" laughed Aila. "I was purdy sure yuh liked Andrew! He's a fine-lookin' young man."

"Now, don' yuh go doin' no match-makin' fo' me, Miz Aila! I kin pick out mah own man, thank yuh!"

"Now Mary Jane, some time back, we agreed yuh ain't needin' tuh call me 'Miz Aila'." said Aila.

"And how about you drop 'Miz' in front of my name too?" declared Ginny. "Both of you. I'm not much older than either one of you."

The three women laughed, hugged, and danced a little jig together.

"Uh oh!" exclaimed Aila. "All this dancin' 'round done caused mah wadder tuh break!"

"We need tuh git yuh tuh yo' bed!" Mary Jane squealed. "No tellin' how quick dem babies gwaine come!"

———

The end of November brought an unexpected change in the weather. The autumn air was still crisp and clear, but the chill earlier in the week had been replaced by balmy, sun-drenched days that seemed more like late summer than late fall.

Mary Jane and six-year-old Boo-Boo rocked on Gideon Campbell's farmhouse porch, soaking up the warm air while shaded from the hot sun by the porch roof. Chickens roamed the yard, now almost devoid of grass that had long since been removed by the hens and one rooster scratching and pecking the dirt for insects. The constant clucking and cooing of the hens added to the tranquility of the afternoon.

Boo-Boo stopped rocking for a moment. "I likes de sound dem chickens make. 'Mose put me tuh sleep. An' I likes dat nice soft smell dey make wen dey all cuddle up."

Mary Jane agreed. "I knows wat yuh mean, Boo. Dey still kind-ah smell like li'l biddies afta dey first hatch an' dry out . . . but yuh kin't hardly walk 'round widout steppin' in dat chicken poop all ova de yard. Not too bad tuhday, but wen it all muddy, it a mess!"

"Mamma, wen is we gwaine back home?" Boo-Boo asked after a moment of quiet. "I miss Calum."

"Maybe 'fo Christmas, Boo . . . but yuh knows, me an' Andrew's thankin' 'bout gittin' married."

"Yessum. I kin tell by de way y'all look at each udda an' talk tuh each udda. I likes Andrew a lot, so dat be all right wid me, I reckins."

"But yuh knows wen me an' Andrew git married, yuh an' me's gwaine move ova tuh his place up de road from here. Yuh ain't gwaine be seein' Calum much afta dat . . . maybe jes' wen he come tuh visit his mamma."

"I's sad 'bout dat, Mamma. Calum an' me is like brothas."

"I's sad 'bout it too, Boo."

"But I wants yuh tuh be happy, Mamma."

"Dere ain't no reason why you, Andrew, an' me kin't be happy tuhgetha, Boo."

"Mamma, if'n yuh gwaine marry Andrew, ain't he gwaine be mah daddy? I been wantin' a daddy fo' a long time now."

"He gwaine be a real fine daddy too. His fam'ly gwaine be yo' fam'ly now, so yuh oughta know 'bout dem. Wen we wuz slaves, Andrew wuz a free man on account o' his daddy wuz free a'ready. Dey won' many cullud folks what wuz free back den."

Boo-Boo turned his mother's words over and over in his mind, trying to understand.

"Now, yuh oughta be real proud o' dat! He gwaine be yo' daddy, an' yuh gwaine be part o' his fam'ly line o' *free* men. Don' yuh pay no attention tuh wat White folks say 'bout yuh. Jes' 'memba wat yuh is! Yuh is a free Black boy . . . the son o' a free Black man, jes' as free an' equal as any White man."

Chapter 36

THE COMPROMISE

1877

PRESIDENT LINCOLN'S INTENT after the Civil War had been to pursue reconciliation with the former rebel states, reconstruction of the South's destroyed infrastructure and economy, and a transition to freedom for the former slaves. Whether he could have succeeded had he not been assassinated is debatable.

Many Republicans in Congress felt the South should be punished for its treason and favored harsh policies that alienated the former secessionist states. Despite resistance from President Johnson and Southern state governments, prior to 1876 Republican policies for Southern Reconstruction had been moderately successful.

Constitutional Amendments had been ratified to abolish slavery, and for the former slaves, grant citizenship and equal protection under the law. The right to vote also was granted to former *male* slaves.

The reforms initially led to the election of a significant number of former slaves to federal, state, and local government positions. Some previously freed men and former slaves became political and governmental leaders and achieved a degree of economic success, especially in Wilmington. But for the most part, the former slaves remained dominated by White society and were obstructed from fully realizing many of their newly-granted rights.

Attempts by Blacks to realize their rights were vehemently and often violently undermined by groups like the Ku Klux Klan and the so-called "Redeemers." In effect, these groups sought to continue a kind of Civil War using intimidation, guerrilla violence, and suppressive politics.

Under the Ku Klux Klan Act of 1871, President Grant initiated federal military action in some Southern states to curtail Klan violence. The Act temporarily neutralized the Klan itself, but other groups continued racial intimidation and violence, and in 1882 the Supreme Court declared the Act unconstitutional.

Grant's second term was marred by corruption allegations that compromised his political support. That loss of support and concern over continued violence in the South led to a distaste for Reconstruction policies among northern and southern Republicans alike.

Neither Republicans nor Democrats wanted a continuing political Civil War. A *laissez faire* attitude toward the Southern states emerged in the federal government, and many officials, Northern and Southern, concluded that enough had been done for the former slaves already.

The hotly disputed presidential election of 1876 precipitated an informal agreement in Congress referred to as "The Compromise of 1877." The agreement awarded the Presidency to Republican Rutherford B. Hayes over Democrat Samuel J. Tilden and withdrew all remaining federal troops from the South. It reconfirmed state sovereignty and allowed states to enact laws and adopt a culture that limited the freedoms and rights of African Americans.

The Compromise, culminating in the inauguration of Hayes on March 5, 1877, effectively ended the promise of Reconstruction and the hope for complete freedom and equality for former slaves and freedmen.

Chapter 37

SHE WEEPS IN HER HEART

October 1880

⁓

A COOL EARLY-MORNING FOG HUNG over Federal Point Road where it crossed Barnard's Creek near the Andrew Martin farm. Boo-Boo Sanders sat in the porch swing of the Martin farmhouse watching the farm's confusion of guinea fowl cross the yard onto the sandy roadway in excited, discordant chorus.

He discerned the cause of the excitement: an oxen-drawn lumber wagon swaying back and forth as it was pulled south through the shallow creek crossing. He knew it would be the last of four loads of lumber that Robert was transporting from J. W. Taylor's steam sawmill in Wilmington to Gideon Campbell's farm.

Boo-Boo waved to Robert as he passed and started back to the farmhouse of his adoptive father, Andrew Martin. It was time for him, Andrew, and his mother to help with construction projects at the Campbell farm, farmhouse additions, upgrades to sharecroppers' cabins, and erection of a small flue-cured tobacco barn.

The birth of Aila's second set of twins, Martha and Davis, in 1871, her daughter Virginia in 1873, and her son Timothy in 1876, had tested the capacity of Gideon's farmhouse. If Gideon had his way, there likely would be even more babies in the future. Tootsie and Hannah also had an additional three children to feed and bed in the sharecropper shacks.

Labor would be provided by Mary Jane, Boo-Boo, and Andrew from the Martin farm, Aila's son Calum Smith from Brunswick County, Robert, and the Campbell household and sharecroppers. The work would require several days.

Aila welcomed Mary Jane, Boo-Boo, and Andrew at the kitchen door upon their arrival. It had been several months since they had visited, and Aila was excited to see that Mary Jane was about three months along with her pregnancy.

"What yuh want? Boy er girl?" asked Aila.

"E'tha one fine wid me. If'n it a boy, I gwaine name 'im Joshua, like mah daddy. If'n it a girl, her name gwaine be Aila."

Aila blushed at Mary Jane's announcement of her possible namesake.

"Now, Mary Jane . . . it's a 'onor that yuh name yer girl chile fur me. Yuh know, I wanted tuh name Elizabeth fur you. Gideon wouldn't have none of that."

"I knows dat. But it all right. I knows Mista Gideon don' want his girl named fo' no cullud person."

"Yuh know Calum's gonna be here tuh he'p later on, Boo-Boo?" said Aila. "I know he's gonna want tuh see yuh."

"Yessum, I sho do wants tuh see 'im too. It been a real long time since I seen 'im, seem like."

Shortly after the workers from the Martin farm arrived, Robert gathered them, along with Ginny, Sarah, and the sharecroppers and organized them into work teams. Sawing and hammering began outside while Aila left to take care of Elizabeth and Gideon in the farmhouse.

Aila basin-bathed Elizabeth on her cot with a damp soaped cloth, singing a quiet song to soothe the girl.

> *The wadder is wide, I kin't cross o'er,*
> *An' ne'ther have I wings tuh fly.*
> *Build me a boat that kin carry two,*
> *An' we both shall row, mah boo an' I.*

Aila gently caressed Elizabeth's skin with the cloth as she sought to catch her daughter's eyes, now strained toward the ceiling. Elizabeth struggled to look directly into her mother's face, reinforcing the loving bond between them. Aila wiped tears away with the back of her hand and continued to hum the tune.

"She's breathin' heavy tuhday." Gideon observed from his chair. "She's been coughin' an' wheezing' fur over a week, an' she seems tuh be gittin' worse."

Aila nodded agreement. "Doc Brooks said ain't much we kin do 'bout that. Muscles don't work right . . . causes her tuh be so drawed up an' bent over hunchback like that. Sometimes, that makes food go down the wrong way an' makes her cough."

"What we gonna do with her when she gits older?" mumbled Gideon. "She's twelve now an' a woman. She's jes' gonna be more of a burden the older she gits. Yuh ain't gonna be able tuh carry her 'round like yuh do now. Tuh tell the truth, she's a'ready a worthless burden on yuh an' the rest of us. She takes time away from yer farm an' housework."

"Gideon, *you* take time away from mah farm an' housework too. Yuh kin't he'p with the work 'round here, ne'ther, but that don't make yuh worthless! Yuh mah husband . . . she's our daughter. Both of yuh got value in our family! Sometimes . . . I wunder whur yer heart is."

"Listen woman!" Gideon yelled. "Yuh ain't got no understandin' of what mah life is like! Yuh need tuh choose 'tween me an' that female vegetable thur . . . which one is more important? She ain't never gonna have no life. Jes' a burden on all of us an' 'nother mouth tuh feed!"

Aila didn't respond to Gideon's tirade. It would just lead to more argument and probably a beating from her husband.

Finishing the bath, Aila lifted Elizabeth from her cot while wrapping her in a towel to dry and cover her body. She temporarily placed the young woman in a wooden chair next to the warm fireplace.

"How 'bout yer purdy flaher frock tuhday, Angel?" asked Aila. "Yuh'll look real nice in that fur the comp'ny what's comin'."

Aila finished slipping on Elizabeth's fresh undergarments and dress when she heard a knock at the front door.

Opening the door, she squealed and shouted, "Calum!"

"Mamma, I'm so glad to see yuh." Calum replied as they hugged.

"I knowed yuh was comin' tuh he'p with the buildin', but I was thankin' it would be tuhmara. What a nice sa'prise!"

"Mister Alan said he won't be needin' me to stay thur, an' I kin leave fur here right away. I figgered the sooner I start, the more time I'll have tuh visit."

"Let me look at yuh, Son! It's been a year since yuh was here las', ain't that right?"

"'Bout a year, I reckin. Seems longer. But I'm bein' rude, here. Good marnin' tuh yuh, Mister Gideon. Good tuh see yuh."

"I kin't say the same 'bout you." grumbled Gideon.

"Ain't changed much, has he Mamma?"

"I ain't needin' tuh be reminded whur yuh come from, boy." Gideon complained. "Even if'n yuh came out of mah wife's body, yuh ain't none of mine."

Aila ignored Gideon's comment. "Boo-Boo's here with part of his family, Calum. I know he wants tuh see yuh."

"Yes ma'am. I saw 'im outside workin' on the house, an' we talked a li'l bit. I hope we git time tuh ketch up on thangs."

"An' how's mah darlin' sister?" Calum continued, striding over to Elizabeth's cot. "What a angel yuh are, so purdy in yer bright flaher dress!" He placed his hand gently on her forehead. "A angel with broke wings."

"Sounds like she's havin' trouble breathin', Mamma. She all right?"

"Doc Brooks reckins we kin't do much 'bout it."

"She won't like this las' time. She sounds purdy sick tuh me."

—⁓—

A full moon rose over the farmyard, negating the need for lamplight. Wrapped in her woolen shawl to take the edge off the nippy October night air, Aila sat on the front porch with Calum and gently hummed a hymn.

"Ain't that 'Abide with Me,' Mamma? Ain't that a funeral song?"

"It's sung at funerals a lot. But I jes' like the tune . . . an' some of the words is 'bout evenin' time . . . like right now."

The music of crickets and katydids had faded since an unexpected frost a week before, and the evening was tranquil, but for distant hoots of a great horned owl floating through the chilled evening air.

"That ol' owl out thur reminds me of the drawin' I made of one las' week."

"Yuh draw thangs, Mamma?"

"Yessir. I draw animals, plants, thangs on the farm and in the woods, people. An' I keep a journal too. That's whur I keep mah private thoughts an' mem'ries. Yuh oughta keep one fur yerself."

"Kin I read it sometime?"

"Well, thur's more than one now. I started a long time back. I was thankin' it was fur mah children an' grandchildren after I'm gone. But maybe I'll let yuh see 'em someday before then."

Calum reflected on what seemed a beautiful idea of a journal, preserving your private feelings and memories for yourself and your descendants. A kind of life story.

"It's so peaceful here, Mamma. It's a beautiful world we live in."

"I never cease tuh wunder at it all, Son. Ever day I'm thankful fur everthang God's made fur us. That beautiful river, the peace of this place, the livin' thangs all 'round us, the smell of flahers an' new plowed earth in the sprang, the friends an' family we hold dear ever day."

"But ain't it been a hard life fur yuh, Mamma?"

Aila looked straight at Calum. "It seems real hard at times, but it's kind-ah what we learned tuh expect. Yuh move far'erd an' git knocked down, an' yuh git up an' git knocked down aghen. Then yuh jes' git up aghen."

Aila paused for a moment. "Mary Jane taught me 'bout all that. Lord knows, if'n anybody gits knocked down over an' over, it's the colored folks like her. The worse part is they ain't allowed tuh git back up. They've had worse times than me . . . an' more of 'em."

"But didn't Jesus say we oughta he'p other folks what need us? Why kin't us White folks he'p the colored folks?" asked Calum.

"I hear a lot 'bout what Jesus said from a lot of people, an' jes' 'bout ever fourth one is different." Aila replied. "Whatever he said, I think we oughta he'p folks what need he'p as much as we kin. But Tootsie said tuh me one time, 'White folks kin help, but thur ain't 'nuf White folks tuh raise us up. Black folks gotta raise 'emselves up."

"But, Calum, the problem is, Black folks kin't raise 'emselves up 'cause thur's too many White folks keepin' 'em down. An' they been doin' that fur a long, long time . . . since the first slave stumbled off that boat from Afriky."

Calum looked up at the lustrous moon, now partially obscured by strands of silvery hair-like clouds. He was quiet for several minutes.

"Mister Alan an' Miz Rebecca talk tuh me a lot 'bout the Lord Jesus Christ, Mamma. Gethsemane Church's got a service ever second Sunday. They all talk 'bout believin' in Jesus an' bein' saved, but I ain't sure what all that means."

"I don't understand all of it ne'ther, Son. We go tuh every church service we kin, an' I do feel renewed ever time I go. But thur's a lot 'bout it I kin't quite figger out. I go 'long with it mosely tuh satisfy Gideon an' git along with the neighbors, but it leaves me with a bushel of questions. I kin't answer all 'em questions, but I thank it's all 'bout faith . . . faith tuh accept an' believe, even if it don't make sense sometimes."

"But ain't it purdy simple? If'n yuh believe in Jesus, yuh go tuh Heaven when yuh die. If'n yuh don't, yuh go tuh Hell."

"I know that's what they say. In the Bible I read whur Jesus talked 'bout the comin' of the 'Kingdom of God' an' the 'Kingdom of Heaven'. I reckin they both mean the same thang. He said don't look fur the comin' of the Kingdom somewhur else . . . 'cause the Kingdom is *within you*. I thank that means if'n we faller Jesus' teachin's, His Kingdom is inside each of us a'ready.

"An' I kind-ah thank 'bout this world in the same way, Calum. God's spirit is inside everthang in this world. In us, an' in ever livin' thang. An' in thangs that ain't livin' too. Like the sun an' moon an' stars, the river an' the ocean, the trees an' soil of the earth. Ever person an' ever thang is sacred 'cause God made 'em that way."

Calum looked puzzled. "What yuh sayin' . . . it's all kind-ah confusin'. I ain't never heared nothin' like that in church. If'n we're faithful tuh Jesus' teachin's, we got Him in us, I reckin. But how we s'posed tuh be faithful?"

"A lot of what Jesus said was 'bout lovin' other folks . . . carin' fur other folks . . . he'pin' the needy an' bein' kind tuh each other. It ain't so much 'bout ourself an' what *we* need er want, but what other folks need.

"Jesus said 'love thy neighbor'. I thank Jesus believed we're all neighbors tuh each other, even folks we don't even know. As far as I kin tell, Jesus never said we oughta hate other people, Calum, even if'n they're different from us."

"Mamma, some of what yuh're sayin' don't seem like what a lot of people 'round here believe. Ain't that causin' problems fur yuh?"

"I keep it tuh mahself. Anyways, I ain't really carin' much 'bout what people 'round here believe . . . er thank. I got tuh be true tuh mahself."

Anticipating that Aila needed help making dinner for the work crew, Ginny and Sarah stopped their work on the farmhouse and entered the kitchen to help prepare the meal. Aila's terrified face met them at the kitchen door.

"Somethin's terrible wrong with Elizabeth!" she screamed. "She's chokin' an' kin't stop coughin' . . . an' she's burnin' up with fever!"

The three women hurried to Elizabeth's side to see her coughing up blood uncontrollably and moaning, her frail, fevered body convulsing in a discharge of her own vomit.

"Look, her lips are blue!" cried Aila. "She kin't breathe!"

"Kin't yuh quiet her down!" shouted Gideon. "I ain't never heared such a commotion!"

The women stared at Gideon in disbelief.

"Yer daughter is terrible sick, husband!" cried Aila. "She kin't he'p herself! If'n yuh kin't stand it, why don't yuh jes' go outside!"

"Huh!" grunted Gideon. "I'll do jes' that!"

With that, he felt his way out of the room through the kitchen door, passing Robert and Calum on the way in.

"What's goin' on?" questioned Robert. "What's wrong with Elizabeth?"

"We don't know!" answered Alia. "Somebody needs tuh go fetch Doc Brooks!"

"I know whur his place is!" declared Calum. "I'll git mah mule an' go right now!"

"Hurry, Son!" sobbed Aila. "I thank she's dyin'. . . . She's dyin'!"

⁓

By late October, the farmhouse additions, the new tobacco barn, and improvements in the sharecroppers' cabins had been completed. Now, it was time to return to the fall harvest. Despite their wishes and prayers, Gideon and Aila's lives had not approached normalcy or stability.

Gideon had lost the great and glorious cause in 1865, and had lost his eyesight in 1869, which to his mind had rendered him useless. The loss of his father and his inability to actively manage his own farm had further diminished his self-esteem. From his perspective, the death of Elizabeth after more than ten years of incapacity and suffering lifted a burden from his shoulders, but that was not sufficient to relieve his melancholy. All that was left was a depressed shell of a man, longing for what was, but could never be again.

Aila suffered despair from the tragic, horrifying, and sorrowful events of her earlier life, and she hopelessly lamented for her difficult and loveless marriage to Gideon. Over time she had overcome at least some of the pain, defiantly struggling toward a brighter future. But the death of her beloved Elizabeth emotionally devastated her.

The prospect of bearing another child—or more than one—in February did little to improve her optimism and deepened her sense of loss. Often, bouts of depression overcame her, housekeeping chores were left undone, and her remaining children lacked her attention. Even her occasional pilgrimages to her beloved river seemed to help little.

She no longer cried openly as she had for some time after her sweet Elizabeth's death.

"She weeps in her heart." whispered Ginny.

Chapter 38

THE CYCLONE

SEPTEMBER 1881

$\sim$

Eᴀʀʟɪᴇʀ ᴛʜᴀᴛ ᴍᴏʀɴɪɴɢ, ᴛʜᴇ ʀᴀɪɴ ʜᴀᴅ ꜱᴜʙꜱɪᴅᴇᴅ to an intermittent light drizzle, but the wind had picked up briskly. The weather did not interfere significantly, so the farm workers returned to their normal tasks. Although Jacob had routine jobs assigned to him, he was concerned about the disappearance of one open-range cow the previous day. He approached Gideon with his concern.

"Daddy, yuh know that ol' cow 'bout tuh git down an' have a calf . . . the one I been stayin' behind out thur in the woods?"

Gideon nodded.

"Well, she's real ol', an' I didn't see her yesterdee. I'm kind-ah worried 'bout her."

"Well, go look fur her—an' watch fur buzzards."

Jacob grabbed a rope lasso and halter from the barn and started his search for the cow, trudging through the woods toward the swampy area where he had seen the herd the previous day.

From a distance, he saw buzzards circling over the swamp and headed in that direction. As he approached the edge of a wetland marsh, a baby calf ran into the marsh grass. The mother cow was lying dead, her body partially submerged in a pool at the edge of the wetland. Two of her teats were under water, where half of her udder seemed swollen tight with milk. The other two teats were above water, where her udder seemed limp and depleted, as if the calf had been nursing only from them.

He was able to lasso the calf and put the halter on her for the trip back to the farm, where he put her in a stall in the barn with a milking cow.

"I found the ol' cow." Jacob told his father. "She had her calf an' died in the swamp. I ketched the calf, brought her tuh the barn, an' put her in with a milkin' cow."

"Yuh did good, boy. I reckin yuh kin keep the calf an' raise it like yer own. When it's growed up, yuh kin sell it an' keep the money yerself."

Hearing his father's promise, Jacob was filled with pride and ambition. After all, maybe he could make something of himself one day.

"Thank yuh, Daddy. I'll take real good care of her."

<hr />

By mid-afternoon the weather had intensified with stronger wind gusts and sporadically heavier bands of rain. Worried that the storm might become more dangerous, Robert departed for his mother's farm to comfort her and supervise the workers there.

The worsening weather provoked the field workers to finally quit about an hour before supper. The wind and rain showed no signs of diminishing, and it was time for the evening meal anyway.

"I'm thankin' we might be in fur a nor'easter!" Aila announced to her family. "Thur's no way tuh tell fur sure, but Robert sez we need tuh shutter the winders."

Gideon, awakened by Aila from his armchair slouch, sat up, his head noticeably bobbing up and down.

"Yuh sleepin' Gideon?" inquired Aila.

"Ain't sleepin' no more *now*." he slurred. "Whur the hell yuh been?"

"Finishin' up work. Tryin' tuh git ready fur the storm."

"What storm?"

"Looks like a nor'easter comin'."

Gideon swayed his head tenuously side to side. "Whur's mah supper? That's all I care 'bout right now."

Aila could tell that Gideon was arriving from a different place. He tried to stand, but first staggered and then collapsed to the floor with a thud. He slowly pushed himself upright and sat slumped over, his head bobbing.

"Gideon, that's licker I smell on yuh."

"Yuh kin't say nothin' 'bout what I do!" yelled Gideon. "Yuh don't know nothin' 'bout what I'm goin' through!"

"Licker ain't gonna brang yer sight back. An' it's gonna send yuh straight tuh Hell! An' yuh're gonna take the rest of us with yuh!"

"Nothin'! Ain't nothin' gonna brang back mah sight! That drank he'ps me git through the day. It ain't gonna make me no more useless than I am a'ready!"

<hr />

The storm grew stronger as the night progressed, whistling, howling, blowing tree limbs onto the roof, and periodically waking everybody except Gideon. It continued to intensify into the morning.

Alia awoke to see Gideon continuing to sip from the mason jar he had stowed behind his favorite armchair.

"Yuh reckin we oughta hide that jar from 'im?" Aila asked Ginny. "An' whur did he git it from in the first place? Where'd he git the money?"

"Maybe we ought to indulge him in this one sin." Ginny replied. "It must be hard going through life blind."

The morning light revealed heavy debris, small and large tree limbs and shingles from the house and barn, scattered throughout the farmyard. The wind and rain had stopped, and the sun began breaking through the overcast. Leaks had appeared in several areas of the roof during the storm, and rainwater had dripped onto the front room furniture and the children's beds.

"Looks like that storm's over, thank God." Aila observed. "We got some cleanup tuh do."

The women began mopping up the puddles created by leaks from blown shingles, while Sarah, Jacob, and the other children began clearing some of the debris in the farmyard.

The clear-weather sky was not to last. Jacob was the first of the outdoor crew to notice dark storm clouds moving rapidly up from the southeast.

"'Nother storm is comin'!" he shouted to Aila.

They continued to work until a wall of strong wind and torrents of rain swept across the farmyard, driving them into the house. As soon as they closed the kitchen door, the children screamed as the farmhouse shook when suddenly hit by the oncoming gale.

Screaming and crying, the children sought refuge with the adults, huddling in the corners of the front room. Despite the closed exterior shutters, glass exploded across the room as the windows were blown in, allowing sheets of rain to penetrate whatever security remained of their hiding place.

They ventured out after the "two storms" had passed but were concerned that another storm would surprise and force them to take shelter again. Fortunately, none of the large pines near the house had been affected, but about ten pines and oaks around the perimeter of the yard lay on the ground, their root systems exposed to the open air. The house exterior appeared to be intact, save the multitude of missing shingles and broken windowpanes.

The torrents of rain had carved a large gully across the incline of the farmyard. A large pine had crashed through the side of the barn, but none of the animals had escaped. The barn roof had lost numerous shingles. Undoubtedly, much of the hay stored in the barn would be saturated with rainwater, requiring removal all together or attempts to somehow dry it out.

Several dead chickens lay flung across the farmyard. Still chained to its post, one of the hunting dogs lay motionless on the muddy ground, covered by a massive oak limb, the obvious instrument of its demise.

Aila and Ginny, seeing Tootsie and his family surveying the damage to their cabins, tramped across the mud field to join them.

"Y'all all right?" asked Aila.

"We's all right, ma'am." Tootsie answered. "Thought fo' sho de Lawd wuz comin' fo' us, but He spared us dis time. Jes' a li'l damage tuh de cabins. But I reckins a lot o' de crops ain't doin' too good. Might mess up de harvest dis year."

While they conversed, Robert appeared, riding on his mule across the farmyard and surveying the damage as he approached.

"Yuh git much damage?" asked Aila. "Is Miz Martha all right?"

"We fared purdy good, an' Mamma is jes' fine." Robert reported. "But Jake Stewart an' his family, Lemuel Wilkins' tenants next tuh us, ain't doin' too good. Lot of damage tuh thur house an' crops. His daughter Edna got a bad cut on her head from a pine branch that got blowed through the winder.

"I went by the Wilkins' place tuh tell 'im 'bout the Stewarts' situation, but he don't seem tuh care. I come tuh ask if'n y'all could come in a day er so tuh he'p git Jake back on his feet."

"We kin he'p, soon as we git some shingles on the cabins an' fix the winders an' roof on Mista Gideon's house." Tootsie said. "We kin do dat tuhmara an' come tuh Mista Jake's place a day er two afta."

"Me an' Ginny kin come tuhmara with some food." Aila said. "Then we kin come aghen later tuh he'p fix up thur place, when Tootsie's ready."

"Much obliged." Robert smiled. "The Stewarts is gonna appreciate yer he'p."

Chapter 39

JANE EYRE

Spring 1884

⟿

In 1867, Alan Smith had sold part of his Brunswick County farm to Aron Sanders under a mortgage payoff agreement. In 1884, he consummated a similar sale with Calum MacKenzie Smith. Alan, Aron, and Calum now owned a total of thirty sheep on their three farms.

Roaming free, the sheep grazed on stargrass in the woods in the winter. When the sheep's winter coats were fully grown in the spring, they were driven from the woods into a large pen, sheared, and released back into the woods until the next spring.

The 1884 spring sheep shearing involved Aron Sanders' family, Alan and Rebecca Smith, their daughter Priscilla, Calum, and Aila, who was visiting Calum.

The long shearing day now ended, Aron's family bid *good evenin'* and returned to their cabin. Aila gathered with the Smith family around the Smith's table for supper. After Calum said the blessing, Aila was the first to speak.

"Calum, I'm so happy 'bout you an' Jeanette gittin' married next month." smiled Aila. "Yuh said yuh met her at Gethsemane Church?"

"Yessum." chuckled Calum. "An' we went tuh a peanut shellin' an' a wood sawin' tuhgether . . . then thur was that corn shuckin' when I found the red ear of corn, an' I got tuh kiss her fur the first time."

"She lives with folks that ain't her mamma an' daddy, ain't that right?" Aila asked.

"Yessum. Her daddy died of malaria in the wah." Calum explained. "Her mamma died of typhoid a few years after that. The MacIntyres took her in 'cause thur won't nobody else."

"I'm so lookin' far'erd tuh comin' back fur the weddin'." beamed Aila. "I reckin she's a Christian girl, seein' as y'all met in church."

"She is. I'm so glad yuh kin come."

"I heared Pastor Hicks at Gethsemane died las' week, ain't that right?" asked Aila. "Ain't a lot of preachers 'round this way tuh take his place, is thur?"

"Thur scarce as hen's teeth." Alan answered. "But I'm a elder at the church, an' we done took care of that. We asked our Calum here tuh take over as pastor."

"After prayer an' layin' on of hands, the elders called me tuh administer Christ's ordinances." Calum declared. "God has called me tuh be pastor an' tuh brang many souls tuh the Lord Jesus Christ."

"Well, I'll swanny!" exclaimed Aila. "That's a honor, Calum! Yuh mus' been studyin' yer Bible real good."

"I been readin' an' studyin' the Bible since I was ten, Mamma. Yuh know I was saved and baptized when I was twelve. I been teachin' Sunday School at Gethsemane since I was fifteen, an' Pastor Hicks got me tuh lead the Sunday service a lot of times."

"The congregation done voted Calum in. He's gonna make a fine pastor." confirmed Alan.

⌒

Aila stared at the pine planks of the Smith farmhouse ceiling above her bed. She had awakened in the middle of the night and couldn't go back to sleep. Too much on her mind. Everyone else appeared to be asleep.

Lying on her bed wide awake in the middle of the night seemed a waste of time. She slipped out of bed, wrapped herself in a cotton robe Rebecca had lent her, pulled on her slippers, and crept quietly out of the house onto the front porch.

The night was unexpectedly pleasant, and the near-full moon lit the serene nightscape, glowing pale ivory in the dim light. The sound of the front door opening abruptly startled her.

"Lovely evenin', ain't it?" a male voice asked.

She turned to see Alan stepping onto the porch beside her. Her heart jumped.

"Yes . . . lovely, Mister Alan."

"Yuh ain't able tuh sleep ne'ther?"

"No, suh. Too much on mah mind, I reckin."

"Now, what could be on yer mind, Miz Aila?"

"Lots of thangs. I still miss mah sweet Elizabeth. She had a short . . . a hard life . . . but that didn't make her any less sweet."

"She was a sweet girl. An' you was a lovin' mamma tuh her. Yuh lived fur her . . . yuh give her yer life . . . an' yuh never complained. I greatly admire yuh fur that."

"I been thankin' 'bout life." she continued. "Thur's a lot 'bout mah life I'd change, if'n I could."

"Why on earth would yuh want tuh change yer life? Seems tuh me yuh got a good life. Yuh got a fam'ly . . . a husband an' children. We all love yuh. Yuh're a fine . . . a good woman."

"Ginny give me one of her books tuh read las' fall. It was the first real book I ever read all the way tuh the end."

"What book was that?"

She could feel her heart pounding in her chest.

"It's called *Jane Eyre* . . . I felt so sorry fur her. She had a real hard life. But she kept goin' an' never give up. She was in love with a man . . . with a man what was married. He wanted her tuh marry 'im. But she couldn't brang herself tuh do that . . . 'cause he was married a'ready. I felt so sorry fur her."

"Well, I thank she did the right thang. It ain't right fur a woman tuh want 'nother woman's husband. An' it ain't right fur a man tuh want 'nother man's wife."

Alan's lightning words struck her soul.

"Why would yuh feel sorry fur her, Miz Aila? She decided not tuh do somethin' that was wrong. She oughta be admired."

"But what 'bout her happiness? Ain't she got the right tuh be happy? Our life passes so quick. Don't ever one of us deserve happiness? What's wrong with that?"

"We kin't git happiness if'n it hurts other people, Miz Aila."

Aila looked away, moved to the front of the porch, and stared up at the moon.

"Excuse me . . . Mister Alan. I ain't feelin' so good right now. I . . . I reckin I oughta go back tuh bed now."

Without good night wishes, she quickly exited the porch, gently pushing the door closed behind her. She held on for as long as she could before bursting into quiet tears and throwing herself onto her bed.

———

"Good marnin', Miz Aila." said Rebecca as Aila entered the kitchen. "I hope yuh're feelin' all right this marnin."

"Good marnin'." Aila nodded, but otherwise didn't speak.

"I saw yuh out thur on the porch las' night. I thought yuh might be havin' trouble sleepin' 'cause yuh won't feelin' good."

"No ma'am, I'm feelin' all right. I jes' had trouble sleepin'. Had a lot on mah mind."

Rebecca stared directly into Aila's eyes in a way that seemed to touch Aila's very soul.

"I know, Honey . . . I know how yuh feel." Rebecca whispered. "I feel the same way sometimes. I try not tuh worry 'bout thangs I kin't do nothin' 'bout. But it's hard sometimes. I gotta 'member I need tuh jes' thank on 'em thangs I *kin* do somethin' 'bout."

———

Later that day, Aron and Calum walked toward the edge of the Green Swamp where they suspected Calum's cattle were feeding. They each picked up a dead four-foot cow-driving tree limb as they went.

"I been thankin' 'bout how times is real hard right now." said Aron. "Small farmas like us is gittin' hit real hard . . . po' crop prices, cost o' farmin' goin' up . . . high borrowin' rates. Wat go fo' White folks go double fo' us culluds."

"I agree, Aron. I heared it called a 'depression'. Everbody's hurtin' . . . 'specially small farmers like us. We need somethin' like the Farmers' Alliance. Yuh heared 'bout 'em?"

"Nawsuh. Wat dey?"

"Farmers like us organize tuhgether tuh change laws, set up exchanges fur supplies at lower prices, an' even work tuh git lower borrowin' rates. I'm thankin' folks like us oughta join up."

"Now Calum, I reckins dey ain't gwaine let me er no udda cullud man join up."

"Nawsuh, they ain't lettin' no coloreds in. But I heared thur's a Colored Farmers' Alliance doin' purdy much the same thangs. They thank coloreds oughta lift 'emselves up."

"I sho kin agree wid all dat. Onlyest way we gwaine betta ourself is work hard, stick tuh wat we want, an' git mo' education. We needs tuh do it ourself on account o' nobody else gwaine do it fo' us!"

Chapter 40

THE DRUNKARD

Late October 1888

A CHILLY HOWLING WIND PUSHED A MULTITUDE of individual cumulus clouds across the sky as Aila stood on the kitchen walkway. Her three-year-old son, Johnny, held his mother's dress skirt, watched the clouds pass over, and marveled at the pattern of cloud shadows that sped over the farmyard and into the woods beyond.

Gideon was already suffering from a severe cold, and Aila realized that it was time to prepare poultice bibs to protect the children from the coming foul weather. The bibs were unpleasant, and the older children were likely to refuse them. None would be given a choice.

Ginny joined Aila to walk to a cast iron pot suspended over a small burning firepit in the farmyard. Jacob had killed two polecats and carefully removed their musk glands before skinning and delivering their carcasses to Aila. Aila put the carcasses into the pot of boiling water to boil out the polecat grease. Then they waited.

"I think I know why these poultices can keep colds away, Aila."

"Why's that?"

"Nobody wants to get near the children when they're wearing polecat bibs."

Both women chuckled at Ginny's analysis.

"Ginny, I was thankin'. It's been twenty-one years since Mister James passed. Yuh ever thank 'bout marryin' aghen?"

"No, Honey. Like I said before, he was the love of my life. I've never had the urge to marry again."

"What 'bout Robert? He's 'bout the sweetest man 'round here."

"Robert is a real nice. If I was inclined to marry, he'd be at the top of my list. But you know, Aila, I'm pretty sure he doesn't want to bed any woman."

"What yuh mean? Don't all men want tuh bed women?"

"No, not every man. Some men like Robert care for women but don't want to be intimate with them."

"I never heared such a thang! Yuh mean they don't do *it* with women?"

"Maybe. You'd have to ask each one. Of course, that's not something you should ever do. It's a real personal question."

Aila watched the polecats boil in the pot, trying to sort out what Ginny had told her.

"But I love Robert. Next tuh Alan, he's the sweetest, kindest, mose carin' man I know."

"And I'm sure he loves you. Just not in the same way a husband loves a wife."

Aila scooped grease from the pot and emptied it into a wooden bucket. When the bucket was full, they emptied the water from the pot and returned it to the fire. Ginny scooped the grease back into the pot to cook and turn it into tallow. They scooped out the tallow and mixed it with turpentine into four poultices, each made cotton cloth layers, and attached to two rawhide strings.

The poultices would be tied around the children's necks and worn throughout the winter months to prevent colds. If by chance, anyone caught a cold, the patient would be given a teaspoon of turpentine spirits twice a day. Gideon was already taking this dosage, along with sips of corn liquor, to "cure" his cold.

⌒

"But Daddy, yuh promised me!" Jacob exclaimed. "I found her after her mamma died an' raised it up mahself! Yuh told me she would be mine if'n I raised her!"

Gideon grimaced, shaking his head. "That won't no promise I had tuh keep. This here is mah farm, an' yuh ain't got no say 'bout me sellin' livestock that was borned here. That calf was mah property jes' as much as its mamma was."

"Gideon, yuh told 'im she would be hissin!" objected Aila. "This jes' ain't fair!"

"She would've died, but I saved her." Jacob argued. "Fed her an' took care of her. An' yuh ain't done nothin' tuh he'p me raise her. Now, yuh done stole her from me!"

"Yuh callin' me a thief? Don't yuh disrespect yer daddy like that! Yuh're eighteen an' I'm blind, but I kin still wear yuh out with that rawhide strop over yonder! Naw . . . I done got 'nuf of yer sassin' me. I'm gonna go git mah shotgun!"

"Yuh gonna have tuh ketch me first, an' yuh kin't see me tuh do that noways!"

"What are yuh doin'!" shrieked Aila.

Gideon almost sprinted to the closet, feeling his way as he went. Opening the closet door, he grabbed his shotgun.

"Lucky I keep it loaded now fur times like this!"

"Aaaah!" Jacob screamed and ran through the front room door toward the farmyard.

Aila yelled after him as he bounded down the porch steps. "He's gone plum crazy!"

"He's gonna shoot me!" screamed Jacob.

"How's he gonna shoot yuh if'n he kin't see you?"

"I ain't takin' no chances! He kin hear me whur I run! I'm goin' tuh find Uncle Robert!"

Gideon appeared behind Alia on the porch, shotgun to his shoulder, and fired one barrel, then the other in the direction of Jacob's footsteps, now about thirty yards away and headed for Federal Point Road.

"AAGH!" Jacob shrieked, stumbled as he ran, and continued running, disappearing into the woods.

"Yuh hit 'im!" yelled Aila. Yuh gone crazy! What is wrong with yuh! Yuh drunk aghen?"

"Damn 'im tuh Hell!" cursed Gideon. Throwing the shotgun to the floor, he screamed up to the heavens as if cursing to God. "Who the hell he thank he is?"

Aila could see Robert through her kitchen window, riding his horse up to the kitchen walkway. She and Ginny stopped washing the dinner dishes and rushed out onto the walkway to learn news of Jacob's condition.

"Is Jacob all right?" asked Aila. "Gideon went crazy an' skeered us all half tuh death!"

Robert dismounted and tied his horse to the walkway handrail. "He ain't hurt bad. He got hit in the back by two buckshots, but they didn't do a lot of harm. Mamma was able tuh dig 'em out with a butcher knife. Rubbed some turt-n-tine spirits in the holes an' wrapped 'em up. He's restin' over at our place right now."

"Thank God!" said Ginny, with a sigh of relief. "I reckon he won't be coming back over here for a while."

"Naw." Robert said. "He's plum skeered out of his wits. I tried tuh calm 'im down. I don't thank I did much good. But I come tuh let y'all know how he was . . . an' talk tuh Gideon."

Gideon was sitting in his armchair, holding his liquor jar as the three entered the front room. He spoke before they could say anything. "I heared y'all outside. If'n yuh come tuh talk 'bout that idiot former son of mine, yuh're wastin' yer time!"

"Former is right." confirmed Robert. "He don't want nothin' tuh do with yuh. He wants the sheriff tuh put yuh in jail. An' I kin't disagree."

"He disrespected me! 'Im an' all the rest of yuh gotta know I'm the head of this house. I kin't let that go with no punishment!"

Robert glared at his brother. "None of us kin respect yuh if'n yuh don't respect 'im . . . if'n yuh kin't keep yer word."

Gideon thought for a moment, then took a sip from his jar.

"An' that licker ain't he'pin'." admonished Robert. "Yuh turned intuh a drunkard. Yuh kin't be the master of this place when that jar is master of yuh. An' how did yuh git money tuh buy that licker anyways?"

"Y'all so damn stupid! Kin't yuh figger out I got it from sellin' that calf. I paid Jeremiah Wilkins tuh sneak it over here from that still of hissin over yonder. He come by when y'all ain't 'round, an' we work it all out."

Aila lashed back. "So yuh stole that calf from Jacob. An' yuh sold it tuh stay drunk all the time. Yuh drive 'im off an' try tuh kill 'im as he goes. Truth be knowed, yuh ain't much of a daddy!"

Jacob and Robert stood next to the giant longleaf as the autumn sunset flamed the now copper-toned cypress trees, rendering an almost spiritual vista of the silently flowing Cape Fear River. A gentle breeze bore the scent of saltwater and marshy inlets, reminding them of their numerous floundering and oystering ventures together.

It was time to return to the farmhouse. Martha would have supper ready by the time they got there, but they both needed to absorb more of the tranquility.

The sound of hooves sloshing through the mud surprised them. Turning, they were further surprised to see Aila riding Meg the Mule bareback.

"Mamma, how come yuh comin' down here this late in the day?" asked Jacob.

Aila dismounted, tied Meg to a drooping branch of a young black gum tree, and approached Jacob, looking straight into his eyes.

"I got some real bad news, Jacob. Tootsie found yer daddy layin' out in the hay pile in the barn. I'm sorry tuh say . . . Jacob . . . yer daddy's dead."

Jacob could not speak.

"Dead?" asked Robert. "What happened?"

"We don't know fur sure." Aila answered. "Busted vein in his head maybe. Died holdin' his licker jar. Won't no reason tuh git Doc Brooks. He was stone dead when Tootsie found 'im."

Jacob bowed and wagged his head from side to side, slowly comprehending the news. "I 'member 'im long time back bein' nice tuh me." he whispered. "That all changed fur some reason. I reckin I oughta feel sad 'bout 'im, but . . . but yuh know . . . right now, I ain't feelin' nothin'."

Aila thought out loud. "I reckin we'll bury 'im next tuh his daddy at the church tuhmara. We kin have the funeral next week so Calum, Jeanette, an' the Smiths kin come over from Brunswick if'n they want."

The mention of Calum's family caused Aila to pause. "Yuh know, I ain't seen Calum an' Jeanette in quite a spell. Er thur baby girl Joanna. I reckin she's three years ol' a'ready."

They all paused to absorb the moment.

"I reckin both farms'll be comin' tuh me now." Jacob reflected. "Uncle Robert, seems tuh me Daddy a'ways treated yuh like a outcast. But I a'ways had a lot of respect fur yuh. Yuh been like a daddy tuh me, much more than mah real daddy was. The way I reckin it, the place whur yuh an' Grandma Martha live . . . oughta be yers. We need tuh talk 'bout that when the time's right."

Chapter 41

THE FUSIONISTS

LATE SUMMER 1894

⌒

NINE-YEAR-OLD JOHNNY CAMPBELL swatted the gnats away from his sweaty head, trying to keep them from flying up his nose and into his ears. Meg the Mule, pulling the sled of wooden frame and burlap seed-bag sides, stopped in mid-stride, to first take a gigantic waterfall piss that trenched a small well and flooded the tobacco row dirt.

Meg knew when to stop to allow the "croppers"—Jacob, Robert, Jake Stewart, Tootsie, and Benny Campbell, the Black tenant farmer on Robert's farm—to dump their bundles of stripped tobacco leaves into the sled. When the sled was full, Johnny tapped the reins on her rump to get her started toward the tobacco barn. Meg knew the way and only would stop when she arrived at the barn. There, the all-female crew strung the leaves onto wooden tobacco sticks.

As the women and girls emptied the last sled and strung the leaves onto sticks, the croppers returned to the barn and began hanging the leaf-laden sticks in the curing barn.

Robert called out to the hangers as they worked. "Now, y'all remember, I want yuh tuh git tuhgether over at Miz Aila's house fur a spell after work."

"Reckins I kin be dere." said Tootsie. The other croppers nodded in agreement.

⌒

The day's work was completed earlier than usual, and the assembly Robert had requested started well before sunset and suppertime.

Jacob arrived as Aila and Ginny started making supper. "Mamma, I spent a li'l time talkin' tuh Miss Edna, Mister Jake Stewart's girl, before she went home from stringin' tuhbaccer tuhday."

"Yuh a li'l sweet on her, Son? Yuh ain't told me 'bout that. She sure is purdy."

"No, Mamma. I won't sure 'bout her before now. But she is real sweet, smart as a whup . . . an' real purdy. I'm thankin' 'bout askin' her tuh marry me. I'm twenty-six now. Ain't it 'bout time I got married?"

"Now, Son, ain't no special age fur yuh tuh git married. It's a li'l diff'rent fur girls. They gotta thank 'bout havin' babies while they're young."

"I know, Mamma. The main thang is how yuh feel 'bout each other. I got a real strong feelin' fur Edna, an' I know she feels the same."

"Then I'm happy fur yuh both, Jacob. I hope y'all don't make the same mistakes I did."

Jacob knew what his mother meant, but he said nothing.

At the agreed-upon time, Robert arrived at the farmhouse to meet with Jacob, Tootsie, and tenant farmers Jake Stewart and Benny Campbell. They took their seats as Robert spoke.

"I been talkin' tuh a lot of local small farmers, colored an' White, 'bout how 'em politicians ain't doin' much tuh he'p us small farmers. We need tuh git organized tuh git anythang done.

"Now, I don't know if'n y'all heared 'bout the People's Party. Some folks call 'em 'Populists'. They come from the Farmers' Alliance what worked tuh he'p us small farmers before. I joined up with 'em two years back, jes' tuh see what they was all 'bout. We run candidates in the '92 election, an' they done purdy good.

"This year, we been talkin' tuh Republicans 'bout how tuh work tuhgether fur the election this November. We call it a 'fusion' of the two parties. We gonna split our ticket with 'em so we ain't competin' with 'em head-on. Our candidates gonna run fur some of the offices, an' Republicans gonna run fur the others.

"Now, I'm tellin' y'all this so yuh know who yuh oughta vote fur in November . . . an' tuh ask y'all to join in with us. This close tuh the election, I ain't seein' how we kin he'p that much. But thur's gonna be more elections after this one. Might make more difference next time."

"Yer 'fusion' idee got some holes in it, Uncle Robert." said Jacob. "One thang is, mose of 'em Populists is White, but there's a lot of coloreds in with the Republicans. How yuh gonna git the Populists tuh take in colored folks?"

"We a'ready got mose of 'em tuh agree on that." Robert answered. "We gotta git it worked out somehow. Everbody agrees it's better tuh work tuhgether."

"Dat sound good tuh me." said Tootsie. "Dat's 'bout de onliest way we gwaine change thangs."

"I thank it's a good idee." Jake said. "But I thank we need tuh talk 'bout it some more. Maybe we could set up some more meetin's tuh do that."

Chapter 42

SECRETS

SPRING 1897

⟞⟝

Rocking alone on the porch of Calum and Jeanette's new farmhouse, Aila enjoyed the spring rainstorm that had just blown in from the west.

She breathed in the earthy-sweet scent of the spring rain falling on Calum's plowed fields and the open front yard of his home, immersing herself in the comforting sounds of the falling rain and gentle thunder.

She watched the now-streaming flows channel over the black earth in front of the porch, how it first pooled, then meandered around obstacles on its path to the small creek near the dirt roadway.

'Em li'l rain wadder creeks is kind-ah like us trav'lin' through life. We run smooth 'til we git tuh somethin' in our way, then if'n we push through, try hard 'nuf, we go over er 'round it, makin' our own channel. If'n we don't push far'erd, we jes' pool up whur we got stopped an' don't go nowhur.

"What yuh thankin' 'bout Mamma?" Calum asked, grabbing the screen door behind him to keep it from slamming.

"Don't yuh like the smell of fresh rain, Son?" Aila replied.

"Yessum. I do indeed."

"Yuh know, Calum . . . I been thankin'. We all gonna die someday. Dyin' is jes' as much 'bout livin' as . . . as livin' is. Yuh borned, yuh live, an' yuh die."

"I reckin so, Mamma. But how yuh live . . . the good thangs yuh try tuh do in yer life . . . matters tuh yer family an' the folks 'round yuh. It matters tuh yer children an' thur children, if'n yuh got 'em. An' at least in some way, it matters tuh all the folks what come after yuh."

"I reckin so . . . I reckin so." Aila agreed, then fell quiet for several minutes.

"I miss Mary Jane, Calum. Ain't seen her fur quite a while. Too much goin' on, I reckin. I need tuh go see her . . . an' her sweet li'l girl Aila . . . when I git back home."

"I thank it's real nice that Miz Mary Jane named her girl after yuh, Mamma. She mus' be 'bout fifteen now, ain't that right?"

"Yuh know, I feel bad that Gideon wouldn't let me name any of mah girls after Mary Jane . . . 'cause she was colored."

"Mamma, I been thankin'. Back when mah girl Joanna was li'l, yuh asked me tuh call yuh 'Ant Aila' when she was 'round. Yuh thought she was too young tuh understand why she was yer granddaughter an' not yer niece. She's twelve now . . . 'most thirteen . . . an' she's still askin' 'bout who everbody is. I had tuh tell her what yuh wanted her tuh hear, but I don't like doin' that. I thank she oughta know the truth."

"Part of me . . . what happened tuh me . . . still hurts . . . hurts me tuh the core. I still don't want tuh talk 'bout it. I need tuh keep what happened sep'rate an' apart from me an' you . . . an' Joanna."

"But Mamma, fam'ly secrets kin't be kept furever."

"I know . . . I know, Son. But I've tried . . . an' I kin't let that go yet. Thur's still too much hurt. Maybe I'll git the nerve tuh tell her mahself someday . . . but . . ."

Chapter 43

THE KINGDOM OF GOD

SPRING 1897

"Y'ALL COME ON AN' GIT IN THE BACK OF THE WAGON. We gonna be late fur church!" Calum shouted.

Jeanette took Joanna by the hand and climbed into the wheatstraw-filled Weber harvest wagon bed with Aila and Rebecca. Alan and Calum sat together on the wagon seat, and with Alan driving and two mules pulling, they headed down Georgetown Road toward Gethsemane Church for Sunday services.

"Now, Joanna, I want yuh tuh behave an' make Aunt Aila real proud of yuh tuhday in church." Calum said. "No gigglin' 'round with yer friends on that thur back row!"

"Yessuh." promised Joanna.

Passing by Aron and Sally Sanders' farmhouse, they waved to the couple and their six children as they prepared to make their own pilgrimage to Emanuel AME Church.

"Aron' a fine man." Alan said to Aila. "Did you know he was with the Republicans what joined with us Populists three years back in the Fusionists movement. We beat 'em Democrats that year. An' we was able tuh keep control of the legislature an' elect Republican Daniel Russell gov'ner las' year."

"I used tuh care 'bout all that, but I done lost mah interest in politics." Aila proclaimed. "But Jacob told me they got thur own Fusionist group goin' over in New Hanover County. I never thought I'd see the day when White an' Negro politicians would work tuhgether."

"We're glad tuh fine'ly git some laws that favors us small farmers, White an' colored." said Calum. "New votin' laws . . . colored judges, deputy sheriffs, po-licemen appointed . . . we're glad tuh see so many coloreds holdin' important jobs in Wilmin'ton now: doctors, lawyers, businessmen . . . a lot of progress. An' that *Daily Record* run by Alex Manly is the onlyest colored newspaper in the state . . . maybe the whole country."

"Jacob told me 'bout what's goin' on in town." Aila said. "I never thought all that would come tuh be."

"Most Whites is mad 'bout it." Calum added. "Jes' 'bout ever member of mah congregation is mad 'bout it. They thank the coloreds is takin' over everthang. I worry we gonna have some kind-ah White uprisin' before long."

"Lord, I hope not!" exclaimed Alan. "Ain't we seen 'nuf hate an' violence? Lord he'p us all!"

———

"Whoa!" Alan commanded the mules as they arrived at the church. "Let me tie 'em up first, then y'all kin git out an' go take a seat."

Alan secured the mule reins to the church hitching post while everyone piled out of the wagon and entered the church. A small pine log structure, the single-room sanctuary contained an assortment of wooden chairs for sixteen seated congregates. Overflow arrivals had to stand for the duration of services.

A cast iron stove and woodpile occupied an area to the right of a centered pine speaker's podium, which during church services was designated as a pulpit. The pinewood floor, walls, and ceiling discharged a sharp, yet comforting, scent of pine sap.

As Calum explained the order of service to Aila, a White couple entered the church and approached.

"Mister an' Miz West." Calum said in greeting, walking to the couple to shake the husband's hand. "Good tuh see y'all. Have a seat here 'side mah family."

The couple nodded to Calum's family and took seats next tuh Aila, since she was the only member of Calum's family they didn't recognize.

"Mah name's Manroe . . . Manroe West." the husband said to Aila. "An' this here is mah wife, Christine."

"Good marnin' on this fine Lord's Day, ma'am." said Christine.

"Good Sabbath. Mah name's Aila Campbell." replied Aila.

"We ain't seen yuh here before." said Manroe. "Yuh mus' be one of Rev'rend Smith's aunts?"

Aila smiled but did not answer. Several more families came in and took their seats.

"We simply love our Rev'rend Smith." Christine gushed. "He's a real 'umble man . . . a true servant of our Lord Jesus Christ."

Manroe leaned over to whisper. "Now, some folks from some other churches bad-mouth 'im sometimes. They say they ain't never gonna go tuh any church whur he's the pastor. Yuh know, fur a while he also was pastor over at Mount Tabor, but they run 'im off."

"Why would they bad-mouth 'im an' run 'im off?" Aila wondered out loud.

"Well, thur's rumors he was borned out of wedlock." whispered Christine in answer. "An' they reckin he's a . . . a . . . ah. Well, I ain't gonna say it, but yuh know what I mean. He got a mamma somewhur over near Wilmin'ton. Nobody knows who his daddy is, though. But all that ain't no fault of hissin. All I know is he's a good Christian man an' a good preacher . . . an' he kin sang real good . . . an' loud!"

Aila remained silent. Alan, sitting next to her, whispered in her ear. "Mister West is one of the leaders in our Fusionist group. An' he was on the pulpit committee that called Calum tuh preach here."

Aila nodded, understanding.

As Calum took a stance behind the pulpit, several other families and one couple arrived.

"Welcome y'all!" Calum said, enthusiastically. "Welcome tuh Gethsemane! Come, set down. I'm jes' gittin' started. Now, if'n y'all will stand, let's all sang 'The Tie That Binds.' Now, if'n yuh don't know it, yuh kin listen tuh me an' yer neighbors 'round yuh. I'll call out the line each time, then y'all kin sing it after me."

Blest be the tie that binds
Our hearts in Christian love,
The fellowship of kindred minds
Is like tuh that above.

From sorrow, toil, an' pain,
An' sin we will be free,
An' perfect love an' friendship reign,
Through all eternity.

The hymn finished, Calum raised both hands into the air, smiling and proclaiming: "Now, let us pray!"

He assumed a position on his knees, lifted his face toward Heaven, and cupped his hands just below his chin.

"Heave'ly Father, we pray fur yer mercy on us, fur we all have sinned. Guide us, oh Lord, on the straight an' narrow path in these hard times. Teach us tuh turn hate intuh love, vanity intuh 'umbleness, envy intuh compassion . . . an' lead us tuh yer Kingdom. We pray in the name of Jesus Christ, our Lord an' Save-yer. A-men."

"A-men!" responded the congregation.

"Friends, y'all know 'bout the turmoil all 'round us. White aghen colored, Republican aghen Democrat, city folks aghen country folks. Let me tell yuh . . . it's the Devil causin' it! He wants us tuh fight with each other. Mah friends, it's time tuh throw the Devil aside an' cling tuh Jesus!"

"A-men!" shouted the congregation.

"Jesus wants us tuh be kind tuh each other. Jesus wants us tuh respect each other, in spite of our differences, tuh work tuhgether t'ward makin' everbody's life better. That's what the Kingdom of God is all 'bout!"

The congregation was quiet.

"But jes' what is the 'Kingdom of God'?"

Calum, having previously inserted torn strips of paper as book-marks in his Bible, turned to his first marked passage.

"In mah Father's house thur's many mansions. I go tuh prepare a place fur yuh. An' I will come again an' receive yuh tuh mahself, that whur I am, thur yuh may be also.

"Now, yuh might thank that means Christ is preparin' a place in Heaven fur us tuh go when we die. But I thank the 'Father's house' John's talkin' 'bout ain't somewhur up in the sky. It's the Kingdom God wants us to make right here in this world."

Several in the congregation began shaking their heads in dismay.

"Revelations sez 'The kingdoms of *this world* are become the Kingdoms of our Lord, an' of His Christ'. Thessalonians sez 'Fur the Lord 'imself shall *descend from heaven* with a shout . . . an' the dead in Christ shall rise first: Then we which are alive shall be caught up tuhgether in the clouds, tuh meet the Lord in the air: an' so shall we ever be with the Lord.'

"Them clouds don't mean the clouds is in Heaven . . . it's jes' whur we meet the Lord. Heaven is up higher than the clouds. We don't go tuh Heaven . . . the Lord descends *from* Heaven."

He means the Lord will brang Heaven down tuh this world. thought Aila. *Jes' like 'em lightnin' bugs down by the river.*

"The clouds is jes' a meetin' place!" Calum shouted. "They ain't in Heaven! An' it don't mean we stay with 'em in the clouds, 'cause in other places the Bible sez Jesus brangs his Kingdom tuh this earth!

"In Revelations aghen, John writes 'I saw the holy city comin' *down from God out of Heaven* an' I heared a great voice out of Heaven sayin' *Behold the tabernacle of God is with men, an' He will dwell with 'em . . . an' God 'imself shall be with 'em.'* That means the Lord will come an' dwell with us. We don't go tuh dwell with Him!"

Now, the preacher raised his voice even more and began to *preach!*

"Luke writes we don't need tuh look fur the comin' of the Kingdom somewhur else. He sez yuh kin't *look here* er *look thur* fur the Kingdom. He sez that's 'cause *the Kingdom of God is within you!*"

Calum's face now had turned a bright red, the rhythm and melody of his voice intoning "Glory! Hal-le-LU-yuh!"

"A-men!" chorused the congregation.

"*The Kingdom of God is within you!* It ain't somewhur else! An' it ain't jes' sometime in the future! If'n we believe in the Lord Jesus an' faller his teachin's, it's inside yuh right now!

"What do we gotta do tuh be saved intuh His Kingdom? In Mathew, Jesus said God's first commandment is tuh love the Lord God with all our heart, all our soul, an' all our mind. An' he said the second commandment is we oughta love our neighbor as much as we love ourself.

"But who is yer neighbor? Y'all remember the Good Samaritan? A Jew got attacked, beat, robbed, an' left tuh die on the roadside. A Samaritan man passed by and had mercy on the Jew.

"In 'em days Jews an' Samaritans was enemies. But the Samaritan he'ped the Jew an' took care of 'im. Jesus said the Samaritan saw the Jew as his 'neighbor'. An' he commanded us tuh 'Go an' do thou likewise.'"

"If'n we faller his teachin's, we will love our neighbors, even 'em what are a diff'rent from us . . . even a diff'rent color er religion . . . even our enemies.

"The trumpet will sound on Judgment Day, an' Christ will return tuh this world an' brang the Kingdom with 'im! Jesus will raise up the dead, an' they'll be judged along with the livin'. 'Em what's rejected, will be cast into Hell tuh burn furever. 'Em what He accepts will be taken into His Kingdom on earth an' live with Him fur eternity.

"An' why is it important that His Kingdom be here on this earth?" he whispered just loud enough for the small congregation to hear. "Because this world is our home, mah friends . . . *the only home we will ever know.*"

With a loud bang and a collective gasp from the congregation, the church door flew open as a man stepped in. A black bandana mask and wide-brim hat covered his face and shadowed his eyes. In his right hand, he raised a Colt 1851 Navy revolver and fired three rounds at Manroe West. The rounds narrowly whizzed past West's head and rammed into the wall behind, splintering an explosion of pinewood fragments into the air.

Chaos and frantic screams erupted as the man took aim directly at Calum, who froze and stared wide-eyed at the revolver muzzle. The man tilted the barrel up and down as if to say, "Remember this!"

The man turned, and as quickly as he came, exited the church door, slamming it with a crash behind him.

The congregation broke into shouts of terror and questioning.

"Are yuh all right, Miz Aila?" exclaimed Manroe.

"The question is, are yuh all right, Mister West? Looked like he was aimin' right fur *you!*"

"I'm all right . . . I . . . I'm all right." West breathed. "I . . . I don't know what that was all 'bout!"

"Seems tuh me . . . seems tuh me that was a warnin." Aila said quietly. "Yuh . . . an' Calum . . . mus' be on somebody's list!"

Chapter 44
COUP D'ÉTAT
NOVEMBER 1898

⁓

When there is not enough religion in the pulpit to organize a crusade against sin; nor justice in the court house to promptly punish crime; nor manhood enough in the nation to put a sheltering arm about innocence and virtue—if it needs lynching to protect woman's dearest possession from the ravening human beasts—then I say lynch, a thousand times a week if necessary.

— *Mrs. W.H. Felton, August 11, 1898*

Every negro lynched is called a "big, burly, black brute" when in fact many of those who have thus been dealt with had white men for their fathers and were not only not "black and burly" but were sufficiently attractive for white girls of culture and refinement to fall in love with them as is well known to all.

— *Editorial,* The Daily Record *[Wilmington, NC], August 18, 1898*

⁓

THE SIZE OF AILA'S FAMILY HAD DIMINISHED BY 1898. Her son Gideon Jr. had died of yellow fever in 1897. Her daughter Martha had been stillborn in 1871, and Martha's twin brother Davis had died of typhoid in 1874. Her daughter Virginia had married Silas Flowers and relocated to his farm in Masonboro. Her one-year-old son Timothy had died of "the hoopin' cough" in 1877.

Her son Johnny, now thirteen, still lived with her and Ginny in the farmhouse, but Jacob had married Edna Stewart and moved with their twin girls about 100 yards away in a newly built smaller home.

Early on the morning of November 10th, Aila and Ginny stopped making breakfast to welcome Jacob's wife Edna to the kitchen.

"Marnin' Miz Edna." Aila said. "We're makin' breakfas' fur yuh . . . an' Jacob and Robert before Jacob heads off tuh town."

Edna nervously rubbed her hands together to warm them from the morning chill. "I need tuh talk tuh y'all before Jacob an' Robert gits here. I'm real worried 'bout Jacob goin' tuh town tuhday."

"Worried about what, Edna?" asked Ginny.

"Robert told me he heared 'bout that meetin' of Democrats yesterdee at the courthouse." Edna said. "They said the colored man ain't allowed tuh run Wilmin'ton no more. An' they voted tuh somehow git rid of that Fusion party Jacob's in. I'm skeered he might git hurt er kilt."

Aila was puzzled. "We heared Democrats ain't happy 'bout thangs, but I ain't heared nothin' 'bout 'em killin' folks."

"I expect they're mad about Manly's *Daily Record* editorial about Negro men and White women." said Ginny.

"They gonna run 'em an' Manly out of town." said Edna. "An' it sounds like they gonna jes' shoot colored folks all over the place. I ain't wantin' Jacob in the middle of all that."

"I'm worried 'bout Calum too." Aila said. "He's a Fusion man over in Brunswick County. That man what come in shootin' over at Calum's church skeered the Devil outta us."

"What y'all talkin' 'bout?" asked Jacob as he entered the kitchen.

"I reckin' we're all a li'l worried 'bout yuh goin' intuh town tuhday . . . what with all 'em Democrats sayin' they gonna take over the town." Aila explained.

"Me an' Boo-Boo's jes' goin' up tuh Isaiah an' Joshua's farm supply up in Brooklyn." Jacob explained. "I need tuh pick up a gang plow, an' Boo-Boo needs tuh git a ox they been holdin' fur 'im. We ain't gonna do nothin' tuh rile up Democrats, Mamma. They mosely mad 'bout Manly an' his newspaper."

"But Robert sez the Democrats is gonna take over the town." Edna argued. "They gonna shoot coloreds an' run the mayor an' po-lice chief off. We're worried 'bout yuh gittin' in the middle of all that."

"Mayor Wright an' Chief Melton's been duly elected tuh thur jobs." Jacob countered. "The Democrats kin't jes' kick 'em out without a election. That's aghen the law."

"Boo-Boo's going with you." said Ginny. "Who knows what they might do to him and the colored folks in town?"

"Yuh know 'em Democrats is all 'bout bluffin'." declared Jacob. "They try tuh skeer folks . . . jes' like they did on election day. I don't thank y'all need tuh worry 'bout me an' Boo-Boo."

With Boo-Boo beside him on the driver's bench, Jacob drove his one-mule wagon into town that Thursday after election day. An off-and-on chilly drizzle fell from a gray overcast, but they figured the two canvas tarps packed behind them in the wagon would help keep things dry.

Entering town, they traveled north on Third Street. Approaching Market Street, they saw a crowd of about 500 armed White men and boys milling around in front of the Light Infantry Armory. Eight or nine men were standing next to a large machine gun mounted on a one-horse wagon.

Jacob yelled out to one of the men, asking him to come over.

"What's goin' on here?" Two other White men joined him.

"We gotta git rid of 'em niggers runnin' this town!" answered the man. "An' all 'em rich uppidy niggers makin' money on us, an' 'em goddamn Republicans an' Fusionists what's he'p 'em!"

"Colonel Waddell's in charge now!" shouted a second man, raising a rifle over his head. "He swears we gonna choke the Cape Fear with carcasses an' 'redeem North Carolina from Negro domination'.

We gonna kick that Republican mayor out an' put Colonel Waddell in, long with all 'em other Republicans an' Fusionists!"

"It's time tuh take action!" screamed a third man.

Jacob stared at the three men. "What kind-ah action yuh talkin' 'bout?"

"We gonna find that nigger Manly, burn his newspaper buildin' down, an' strang 'im up tuh the nearest tree." declared the first man. "Then we gonna kill ever damn nigger in sight . . . throw 'em in the river 'til it runs red with thur blood! We kin start right here an' now with that nigger sittin' up thur beside yuh!"

"Well sur, I ain't got no quarrel wid y'all tuhday." Boo-Boo replied to the man. "I ain't neva done yuh no harm . . . er any udda White man fo' dat matta. I done seen what yuh an' yo' kind's done tuh mah kind 'fore, but we ain't got no reason tuh fight tuhday. We all brothas in de eyes o' de Lawd. An' de Constitution give me equal protection unda de law."

"What the hell yuh talkin' 'bout, yuh uppidy nigger!" shrieked the man. "Yuh ain't no brother of mine, asshole! An' we make the law here!"

"Now sur, no reason tuh let 'im rile yuh up." said Jacob, attempting to defuse the confrontation. "This here Black man ain't even from Wilmin'ton. Him an' me's from way out in the country, south of town. He's here tuh he'p me pick up a plow an' ox from the farm supply."

"Then I reckin yuh better git that nigger the hell out of here now, if'n yuh want tuh git 'im back tuh the country alive!"

"Yessuh!" yelled Jacob, slapping the mule's rump with his reins and turning back south down Third Street.

"Jacob, my mamma a'ways told me tuh be strong." asserted Boo-Boo. "She say tuh stand up tuh all de evil thangs in dis world."

"I know how yuh mus' feel, Boo-Boo, but yuh kin't stand up if'n yuh're floatin' face down in that river. We all need tuh stand up tuhgether tuh fight evil without dyin' in the street."

"We be leavin' town now, Jacob? . . . Like some kind o' cow'rds?"

"Nawsuh." Jacob responded. "I ain't gonna let 'em mo-rons keep us from finishin' our business. They gonna be goin' down tuh the *Daily Record* building on Church Street. We kin go down two blocks on Third tuh Dock Street, then over tuh Front Street an' then drive north tuh Brooklyn. They won't see us that way."

"Ain't they gwaine up tuh Brooklyn tuh shoot niggers? Ain't we gwaine run intuh dem up dere?"

"Naw, they gonna be lookin' fur Manly down on Church. If'n they even go up tuh the Brooklyn district, we'll likely be gone before they git up thur."

With Waddell inciting them, the large mob of armed Red Shirts and other vigilantes marched to Alexander Manly's newspaper office. They were unable to find and lynch Manly, who had made his escape the previous night. Instead, they vandalized and tossed the printing equipment into the street and set the building afire, rendering it unsalvageable. Then they headed for the Brooklyn district.

Arriving at the farm supply exchange in Brooklyn, Jacob and Boo-Boo were surprised to encounter Calum and Aron conversing with Isaiah and Joshua in the stable. Boo-Boo and Calum immediately embraced.

"Good tuh see yuh, Boo-Boo!" said Calum.

"Good tuh see you too." replied Boo-Boo. "Y'all pickin' up some equipment?"

Aron said, "I's gittin' a harrow, an' Calum's buyin' a mule."

"Now, y'all listen. Mista Jacob might reckins I's ova-reactin' here, but we run intuh some crazy White folks down yonda at de Armory." Boo-Boo reported. "Dey say dey gwaine kill ever nigger in town an' throw 'em in de riva 'til it runs red wid blood!"

"Dey been talkin' like dat fo' weeks." added Isaiah. "White folks done gone crazy! Dey got a damn machine gun on a wagon! Lot o' our neighbors done got dere guns ready . . . some shootin' a'ready gwaine on 'round here."

Jacob was dumbfounded by what he was hearing. "I didn't take all that talk serious." he confessed. "I'm skeered I got Boo-Boo an' me in some deep shit."

"We better git our business here done an' git out of town quick as we kin." said Calum.

"Y'all betta git yo' guns ready er git da hell outta here!" yelled a Black man running up the street. "Dey burnin' houses an' stores all ova de place . . . shootin' folks in the streets! De gov'na done call out de state militia, but dey jes' shootin' evabody!"

"Reckin we oughta brung some guns tuh town!" exclaimed Calum. "Let's git the wagons loaded!"

With the wagons loaded and the animals secured, Calum and Aron and Boo-Boo and Jacob hurriedly began their retreat from the city. Reasoning that taking Third Street south would be more likely to expose them to the mobs, they took Dock Street. They were unaware that no route south would be safe.

After four blocks, they encountered the remnants of about twenty drunken White marauders shouting and sporadically discharging their shotguns, pistols, and rifles into the damp air. Seeing a Black man on board each of the two wagons, they crowed together to block the wagons' passage.

"What the hell yuh niggers doin' ridin' with White men?" the leader demanded. "An' what the hell yuh White men lettin' 'em niggers ride up thur with yuh? Don't yuh know we's runnin' niggers out of town tuhday?"

"We jes' leavin' town fur home." Calum explained. "These here men is jes' he'pin' us out . . . pickin' up these here animals an' equipment fur our farms."

"Whur is yuh farms? An' who are yuh?"

"Well, I'm Calum MacKenzie Smith, an' mah farm is over yonder in Brunswick County."

"An' what 'bout yuh, nigger lover?" the leader asked Jacob.

"Jacob Campbell . . . down Federal Point Road, out in the county."

"Yuh niggers belong tuh these here White men." the leader demanded.

"Mista Calum be mah boss man." Aron lied. "I work fo' 'im on dat farm o' hissin."

"An' you?" the leader asked Boo-Boo. "That man beside yuh yer boss?"

Boo-Boo thought in silence for a moment, then answered. "Nawsuh. Me an' mah daddy work our own farm. Mah granddaddy wuz free an' equal wid Whites 'fo de wah, an' mah daddy afta 'im. We's a long line o' free men!"

"Well, what the fuck!" the leader shouted. "Yuh lying' through yer teeth! Niggers ain't never been free an' equal tuh Whites . . . an' they never gonna be! Yuh under the White man, an' that's whur yuh gonna stay!"

"Well suh, now. De law an' de Constitution say we's free an' de law give us equal protection." Boo-Boo countered. "Dat means yuh ain't ova us, an' we's equal wid eva one o' y'all!"

Several men in the mob laughed out loud. Aron and Jacob looked away from Boo-Boo and kept quiet.

But Calum spoke up. "Now, y'all know what Jesus said 'bout lovin' yer neighbors. I reckin y'all don't thank of these men as yer neighbors. But Jesus said we're all neighbors an' all Children of God."

"What the hell yuh talkin' 'bout?" yelled the leader.

"Y'all Christians, ain't yuh?" Calum continued. "Jesus said yuh oughta love yer neighbor. These Black men is yer neighbors, jes' like any White men."

"Well men, looks like we got us a nigger-lovin' preacherman right here!" shouted the leader. "An' we got this here shit-mouth uppidy nigger too! Y'all know what we do with uppidy niggers, right?"

The mob yelled in agreement. Someone screamed, "Lynch his black ass!"

Calum stood erect and shouted over the crowd noise. "Now . . . now . . . I'm pastor over at Gethsemane Church, an' I've knowed this colored man since we was boys!"

"We don't care if'n yuh is a damn apostle . . . yuh still a nigger lover!"

Calum climbed down from the wagon and raised his hands before the mob. "He don't mean no harm! He ain't got no argument with y'all!"

Two men grabbed Boo-Boo's legs and forcibly pulled him off the driver's bench into the muddy, manure-infused street. Calum rushed to help him stand but was hit in his face with the butt of a shotgun, knocking him down in the mud.

Dazed, Calum regained his balance, stood, and tried to pull Boo-Boo out of the mob's grasp, only to be struck again with a gun butt, this time in the groin. Doubled over, he lost balance again and fell back into the muck.

Two men lifted Boo-Boo upright, then shoved him back down on his knees. Another man stepped forward with a shotgun and fired buck shot into the back of Boo-Boo's head and neck, exploding his skull, severing both carotid arteries, and splattering blood and bits of brain tissue over Calum's contrite body.

"No! . . . No! . . . No!" screamed Calum, over and over, as he crawled to Boo-Boo's convulsing body.

Tears streaming down his face, Calum embraced his now motionless friend with both arms, as if to protect him from further assault. Calum's embrace could do nothing to constrain the gush of blood from the back of Boo-Boo's neck into the mud-manure street.

"Git off 'im, yuh crybaby!" demanded the leader. "We need tuh dump 'im in the river, along with 'em others. Gotta keep the streets clean, yuh know!"

"No . . . no need fur that." Jacob stammered. "He come intuh . . . intuh town with me. His family lives right up the road from my farm. The Christian thang tuh do now is let us take 'im home tuh his family."

The leader took a visual survey of faces in the White mob, then announced: "A'ready dumped enough niggers in the river fur one day, I reckin. Ain't that right?"

The mob seemed to approve of his conclusion. But one man yelled out: "We oughta git rid of that White crybaby nigger-lover rootin' in the mud while we're at it!"

The mob yelled its approval.

"No . . . no, please, suhs." shouted Jacob, standing up from the wagon driver's bench. "Yuh know, mah daddy was Gideon Campbell. He fought fur the Confederacy down at Fort Fisher."

The mob drew quiet, listening to Jacob's proclamation.

"An' mah granddaddy was Rev'rend Jacob Campbell . . . head of the county Home Guard in the wah! Now, Rev'rend Smith, here . . . he's a fine Christian man, respected by all 'em what knows 'im. Y'all need tuh thank long an' hard 'bout killin' a man like 'im, loved by God an' man alike."

The leader smiled and turned to face the mob.

"I reckin we'll let this nigger-lover be this time. Killin' White men ain't gonna look good in the newspaper. Maybe we kin git 'im next time, when ain't no witnesses 'round."

Chapter 45

AFTERMATH

NOVEMBER 1898

⤙⤚

W<small>RAPPED IN A CANVAS TARP</small> next to Jacob's gang plow, Boo-Boo's bloody corpse jolted about in the rear of Jacob's wagon as it bumped along Federal Point Road. Tied to the rear of the wagon, the ox that Boo-Boo had picked up from the farm exchange calmly followed behind. Calum, feeling that he should accompany his dead friend home, quietly rode Aron's mule bareback beside Jacob's wagon. Aron, who had taken Calum's mule and wagon, had returned to his Brunswick County farm with Calum's harrow.

Calum and Jacob did not speak. Too much had happened to be completely absorbed by either man. Their thoughts were smothered with sadness, remorse, and anger. What could they say to Mary Jane and Andrew?

"I caused Boo-Boo's murder." Jacob confessed to Calum. "An' I didn't do nothin' tuh try an' save his life. At least *you* tried! This is gonna haunt me tuh the end of mah days."

In shock, his clothes stained with Boo-Boo's blood and covered with mud, Calum could say little in response. His boyhood friend and companion, a man he loved as a brother, was murdered simply because he was Black and proud of his heritage.

"How kin Christians be filled with such hate?" Calum asked. "How kin they murder? . . . How kin they? . . . How kin they?"

Calum's anguished reflections were interrupted by the sight of a score of Black men, women, and children walking south on Federal Point Road in the continuing drizzle. As he overtook the first group, he whoaed the mule to ask where they were going.

"We's tryin' tuh git out o' town fas' as we kin!" answered one man. "Dey is done drivin' hundreds o' us out o' town . . . screamin' dey gwaine shoot us er lynch us! We's jes' tryin' tuh find a place tuh hide . . . in de woods, swamps . . . anywhur out o' town."

"This is like the Children of Israel runnin' from the Pharaoh out of Egypt." Jacob thought out loud.

"'Cept thur ain't no Promised Land waitin' fur 'em this time." Calum whispered.

The road was now filled with Blacks carrying what little they could on their heads and backs, now refugees driven from their homes and livelihoods.

At the Martin farm, Mary Jane's family had been watching the refugees' flight on the road for some time and already knew what was happening. Mary Jane, Andrew, and Little Aila were watching from the front porch as Jacob and Calum forged the shallow creek just north of the farmhouse.

"Calum, I's sa'prise tuh see yuh!" called out Andrew. "Jacob . . . I see yuh got yo' gang plow an' mah ox . . . whur's Boo-Boo?"

Neither Jacob nor Calum answered. Pulling up to the front steps, Jacob climbed down from the wagon and tied his mule to the hitching post as Calum dismounted from Aron's mule. Walking slowly up the steps and onto the porch, both men removed their hats before speaking.

"We got some real bad news." Jacob started.

"Whur's mah Boo?" Mary Jane asked apprehensively wide-eyed.

Jacob bowed his head toward the porch floor and spoke without looking up.

"I'm so sorry tuh say . . . Boo-Boo's gone, Miz Mary Jane." Jacob revealed. "I'm so sorry . . ."

"Wat yuh means? He's gone? Gone whur?" demanded Mary Jane.

"Miz Mary Jane . . . he was kilt by that White mob in town." answered Calum.

Mary Jane screamed and dropped to her knees. Andrew knelt to his knees to comfort her as she sobbed and moaned.

"Wat happen'?" Andrew asked.

"They was shootin' Black people left an' right . . . throwin' 'em in the river." Jacob explained. "We went down a side street tryin' tuh git 'round 'em, but thur was a group thur what saw Boo-Boo an' Aron. They stopped us in the street . . . Boo-Boo stood up tuh 'em, real proud-like . . . Calum tried tuh stop 'em . . . but they knocked 'im down an' shot Boo-Boo."

Mary Jane continued to gasp, weep, and moan uncontrollably. Little Aila cried out and stooped to her side and wrapped her arms around her mother and father.

"I'm sorry." repeated Jacob. "It's mah fault. Mamma, Miz Ginny, an' Edna tried tuh stop us from goin' intuh town tuhday on account of the rumors 'bout 'em Democrats riotin'. I didn't listen tuh 'em. An' now Boo-Boo's gone 'cause of that."

"Whur . . . whur's mah Boo, now?" asked Mary Jane, wiping tears from her cheeks.

"Wrapped up in a tarp in back of the wagon." Jacob answered. "Miz Mary Jane . . . ah . . . I thank it bes' . . . it's bes' yuh don't see 'im like he is right now."

Mary Jane lifted her face toward Jacob. "Now, yuh listen. I birthed dat boy out o' mah body in love, an' we done went through hell on earth tuhgetha eva since. He mah boy! An' dere ain't nothin' in Heaven er earth gwaine keep dat dead body from his mamma now!"

Though the weather was still chilly after Jacob and Calum left Boo-Boo's body at Andrew's farm, the drizzle had subsided by the time they arrived at Jacob's farm and gathered with Aila, Ginny, young Johnny, and Robert in the farmhouse front room. The story they told of the events of the day devastated everyone.

Aila labored to speak. "Mary Jane's heart mus' be broke tuh pieces." Aila said flatly under her breath. She stared off into space.

"Your heart must be breaking too, Aila." said Ginny, consolingly.

Aila buried her face into her hands and sighed. "Sometimes . . . I thank it jes' ain't fair." she murmured. "Life jes' ain't fair. How kin the Lord let this happen?"

"Yuh all right, Mamma?" asked Johnny.

"I'll be all right, Son." Aila sobbed. "But not now."

They all stared at the floor. All were quiet. Ginny moved to Aila's side and embraced her. "You know as much as I do that the Lord doesn't make any promises that life will be fair. It is what it is. What matters is how we deal with unfairness and hardship. You know that. And so does Mary Jane."

"I know . . . I know." Aila agreed. "But sometimes, it's jes' so hard. I want tuh go over tuhmara an' pray an' mourn with mah poor, poor Mary Jane."

"How come they kilt Boo-Boo?" asked Johnny. "He was a'ways nice an' kind tuh me."

"That's a real hard question to answer." Ginny said. "We've been trying to answer questions like that for a long time."

"A lot of White people jes' want tuh keep Black folks on the bottom." Robert tried to answer.

"I know that, Uncle Robert. But what did the Black folks do this time tuh deserve that?"

"They didn't do nothin' but try tuh make a good life fur 'emselves an' thur families." answered Aila. "They didn't need tuh do much more than that. Jes' bein' Black was 'nuf by itself."

A knock on the kitchen door interrupted the mourning. The open door revealed Tootsie, Joshua, and Isaiah on the walkway.

"Joshua an' Isaiah wuz chased out o' town by dem crazy Democrats, an' dey come here wid dere families tuh stay wid us." Tootsie explained.

"Y'all come in." invited Aila.

"We come here tuh find out if'n Aron, Calum, Jacob, an' Boo-Boo got out o' town all right. I see Jacob an' Calum right here . . . whur Boo-Boo an' Aron?"

"Boo-Boo's dead." said Calum. "He got shot dead by that mob. The rest of us was lucky tuh git out alive. We brought 'im back home tuh tell Miz Mary Jane . . . then come here tuh tell Mamma."

"Lawd 'ave mercy!" Joshua cried. "Miz Mary Jane mus' be sorrowful sick!"

"Dem white bastards!" screamed Isaiah. "Wat 'bout Aron?"

"Aron took mah mule an' wagon back tuh Brunswick with mah harrow an' his mule." explained Calum. "He's home safe, far as we know."

"What happened tuh y'all after we left?" Jacob asked. "Y'all run intuh that mob?"

"Dey come all right . . . jes' aft . . . afta y'all left." stuttered Joshua. "We seen dem comin' up de street an' took off, sneakin' 'round back alleyways. Dat damn militia wuz settin' fire tuh houses . . . murderin' an' dumpin' wat look like hundreds o' Black bodies in de riva. We heared womens an' chillens screamin'! We seen White preachas wid guns huntin' fo' culluds.

"Now, dere wuz some culluds shootin' back at dat mob. But dey wuz defendin' dere homes. Dere won' no cullud mob roamin' de streets shootin' eva White man in site, dat fo' sho."

"We seen cullud folks cryin' an' wrangin' dere hands in de street!" Isaiah explained wide-eyed. "Cullud mens won' gwaine nowhur near dere house . . . 'cause dat whur dere womens an' chillens wuz hidin'. I heared one man cryin an' screamin', *Wat has we done? Wat has we done?*"

Mary Jane fell into Aila's arms as the two friends met, sobbing, on the Martins' front porch.

"I'm so sorry 'bout Boo-Boo." consoled Aila. "What right did 'em crazy men have tuh take yer son from yuh?"

"No . . . no right!" Mary Jane whispered. "But dat ain't neva stop dem from killin' Black men 'fo'. An' I reckins dis ain't gwaine be de las' time ne'tha."

"Thank yuh fo' comin' . . . both o' yuh." Mary Jane continued, turning to hug Ginny.

"We all are so sorry." Ginny said. "He's in the Lord's arms now."

"Y'all ladies come on inside whur it's wahmer." said Andrew, opening the front door to invite the women in.

They entered the farmhouse and took seats around the warming fireplace.

"I heared yo' Calum tried his best tuh save my Boo-Boo." Mary Jane said. "I reckins dey wuz friends tuh de end."

"Yessum." sighed Aila. "That's what I heared. He did what he could . . . but that mob was crazy. They run the legal elected gov'ment out of town. Ain't nobody done nothin' 'bout it . . . the gov'ner, the president . . . nobody! Now, I'm skeered what they might do tuh mah Calum."

"All dis is tearin' mah heart out." wept Mary Jane. "I thank back on all de happy times we had tuhgetha. I had faith he'd be a great man . . . dat he'd be strong an' make a betta place fo' his people. But now, dat ain't gwaine neva be."

"I lost more than one chile, mahself, so I know what it's like fur a chile tuh be took away." Aila tried to console. "Children ain't s'posed tuh die before thur mammas an' daddies."

"I knows, Aila. Two udda fam'lies down de road los' dere daddies in dat riot . . . dey neva come home. We reckins dey got throwed in de riva like de udda Black folks. Yuh knows, down de road dere's a mamma an' six chillens in one fam'ly . . . an' a mamma an' fo' chillens in de otha. I's thankin' we gwaine need tuh work tuhgetha an' share tuh he'p dem out."

"Maybe we kin he'p make sure they git 'nuf tuh eat . . . an' he'p 'em with the farm work." Aila proposed. "Maybe we kin git some folks from the church tuh he'p."

"Aila, you know a lot of people in the church think colored folks shouldn't get help." Ginny said.

"I reckin yuh're right." Aila admitted. "So we'll jes' do it ourself an' keep it quiet."

Chapter 46

THE FIRE

DECEMBER 1898

"Daddy, my friend Amy's been talking about how much fun they had over at the beach last summer." said Joanna. "Could you take us to the beach this spring or summer?"

"Well, Honey, I'll thank on it." Calum answered. "Her daddy's a member of our church. Barham Walters is a good Christian man, an' he's done a good job takin' care of Amy after his wife died las' year."

"They moved here from Delaware two years ago." Joanna said.

"We knew they was from up north." said Jeanette. "Yuh kin tell by the way they talked. An' it sounds like yuh're startin' tuh talk like that, Honey."

"Well, I've been practicing. Amy's been my best friend for two years now. I feel real close to her. She says Carolina Beach is a real nice place to visit."

"We'll see." said Calum.

Joanna waited to ask her next question, allowing enough for her to gather sufficient courage to ask it.

"Daddy, you never seem to want talk about your family. Why is that? All I know is Cousin Alan an' his wife Rebecca raised you."

Calum searched for words to respond. "Yuh need tuh understand that some folks in our family suffered great pain in the past. They want tuh put that hurt behind 'em. Don't yuh thank we oughta respect their wishes?"

"I reckon so, Daddy, if you think it's the right thing to do."

Joanna's dream about Carolina Beach was interrupted by the smell of woodsmoke. At first, she thought it was coming from the fireplace downstairs, but then realized it was in her room. The air, clogged with smoke, burned her eyes and lungs. She felt her way to her bedroom door and threw it open, only to be blasted with a wave of searing heat.

"Mamma! Daddy!" she screamed, realizing a massive fire had engulfed the north side of the farmhouse where her parents slept.

The wall of fire prevented her from venturing further, and she slammed her bedroom door and scrambled toward her window. Raising the window and throwing open the shutters, she jumped through the open space, landing on her mother's thorny rose bushes and onto the frigid ground of the farmyard. She ran to the edge of the yard, then looked back to see the entire north end of the farmhouse engulfed in smoke and flame.

She strained to look for her parents through the smoke, the heat of the fire scorching her face. She saw three dark figures mounting horses, riding away from the raging inferno.

Not her parents! Three White men! Running!

Terrified, she bolted toward Alan Smith's farmhouse, sobbing as she ran.

"Mister Alan!" she screamed, pounding on the Smith's door, then pushing it open to enter the front room. "Our house is on fire! Mamma an' Daddy's in there! I can't get to them! The fire is too hot!"

Alan appeared in an instant, panic on his face, Rebecca behind him, both in sleepwear.

"They still in the house?" Alan yelled.

"I don't know . . . I don't know! I don't know where they are! I was burning! I had to get out! I don't know where they are!"

"Yer face an' hands!" screamed Rebecca. "They're red as far!"

"Don't worry about me! We've got to go get Daddy and Mamma out!"

Alan threw on shoes and a coat over his nightclothes and dashed into the darkness with Joanna, their pathway lit by the blaze from Joanna's home.

By the time he and Joanna got to the burning farmhouse, Alan knew there was nothing that could be done.

"It's too far gone, Joannie! Thur ain't nothin' we kin do! We need tuh look fur 'em outside the house . . . maybe they was able tuh git out somehow!"

Joanna sat crying on the sofa with Rebecca while Alan spoke with Sheriff Taylor in the front room. Alan handed her his handkerchief to dry her eyes.

"Now, I know Joanna sez she seen what she thinks was three men leavin' the scene, Alan, but she won't able tuh see thur faces. I ain't sayin' she made that up, but she was half asleep an' skeered . . . her eyes was burnin' from the smoke. Sometimes, folks thank they see thangs what ain't really thur."

"I ain't believin' she made all that up, Sheriff." countered Alan.

Joanna stiffened.

"Well, I ain't sayin' she made it up. But folks' don't a'ways thank real good in cases like that. But even if'n she saw 'em men, she don't know who they was. I don't know how we kin find 'em."

"But yuh gotta try, Sheriff. It left Joannie here without no mamma an' daddy. An' she's only thirteen."

"We're gonna try, Alan. But I kin't make no promises. I'll go now an' git workin' on it."

The sheriff turned to Joanna. "I'm real sorry 'bout yer daddy an' mamma, Miss Joanna. We gonna do the best we kin tuh find 'em men yuh thank yuh saw."

"Thank you, Sheriff." said Joanna. "I know . . . I hope you will."

"I gotta leave yuh now. Y'all have a good afternoon." Taylor turned and opened the front door.

"Thank yuh, Sheriff." Alan said as Taylor exited.

"Where will I live now, Mister Alan?" Joanna asked after the sheriff was gone. "I love Aunt Aila, and I reckon I could go live with her, but I got my friends here, and I love y'all too. Can I come live with y'all?"

"Of course, Honey!" exclaimed Alan. "We'd love tuh have yuh."

Rebecca nodded in agreement.

Joanna looked out the window toward the blackened remains of what had been her family home in the distance. She dried her eyes once again.

"Mister Alan, last night was the last time I ever talked to Daddy. I asked him to tell me about my family. He said it all was some kind of family secret that would hurt some folks in the family if we talked about it. He asked me to respect that."

"I understand." Alan said. "An' yuh want me tuh tell yuh what I know . . . is that right?"

"I was hoping you would."

"Joannie, I thank the time will come when yuh will know 'bout all 'em thangs. But outta respect fur folks, I don't feel I'm the person tuh tell yuh fam'ly secrets. But I thank yuh will know in due time."

Even though her questions went unanswered by Alan and her father, Joanna now believed that the root of the secret centered on one person.

Chapter 47
CAROLINA BEACH
JUNE 1902

⌒⌐

JOANNA COULD HARDLY WAIT to get to the beach with her friend Amy. The 20-cent round-trip steamer fare from Wilmington to Carolina Beach was well worth the cost. Having been to the seaside resort only once before, memories of her last trip ran through her mind as the Cape Fear River steamship *Wilmington* approached the dock at the New Hanover Transit Company pier near Doctor's Point.

The trip had already taken almost three hours since Amy's father, Barham Walters, had picked up Alan and Joanna at Alan's farm with his mule wagon. Besides Joanna, Alan, Amy, and Barham, the beach entourage included Barham's nephew, Richard Walters, who was visiting from Chapel Hill.

Joanna had not met Richard before, but the long trip from Brunswick County allowed some time for them to become acquainted. A native of Maryland, he was a handsome man, nine years senior to seventeen-year-old Joanna. A graduate of the Wharton School of Finance and Economy in Philadelphia, he was now an instructor in the newly-created economics department at the University of North Carolina in Chapel Hill.

Initially awed by his background and appearance, especially his stylish pencil-thin mustache, Joanna soon discovered that Richard was not the arrogant man she had expected.

"Can you tell me about Carolina Beach?" asked Richard. "This is my first trip here."

"Well, after we dock at Doctor's Point, we take a little noisy train through the woods over to the beach. The beach is real pretty, and there's a pavilion for dances and band concerts. Do you dance?"

"I know some steps, but it depends on the dance. I can do a waltz and I have been known to square dance."

"The beach is long and wide, covered with the finest sand." continued Joanna. "I love the sound of waves breaking on the beach . . . it's so restful."

"I brough a bathing suit." Richard said. "Do you swim?"

"We just splash around in the shallows and don't get too close to the waves. Those waves scare me a little . . . sometimes, the undertow can be dangerous.

"There's a boardwalk, and last time I was there, there was a bowling alley, a grocery store, and a billiard hall. But I don't play billiards. My daddy never thought billiards was ladylike. He doesn't mind dancing, though, like a lot of preachers do."

The steamer docked at the Transit Company pier, the passengers disembarked and climbed into the open-sided cars of the small steam train Joanna had described, and the train chugged off toward the beach on the east side of the Cape Fear headland.

"I figured out the last time I was here why they call this the Shoo-Fly Train." laughed Joanna as the train continued through the longleaf pine and turkey oak woods. "These swarms of biting sand flies an' mosquitos are about to carry me away!"

"They need to eat, too!" joked Richard. "They're not bothering me, though. You just must be too sweet."

Joanna blushed as Amy giggled. Alan and Barham remained stoic.

"If you're quick, you can grab 'em in the cup of your hand." Amy advised. "Then you can pull their little wings off and toss 'em aside. Each one means one less to pester you!"

"You're terrible, Amy!" declared Joanna.

They all laughed.

Arriving at the beach pavilion, the group grabbed their carpet bags and exited onto a wooden ramp to the beach and the changing rooms. Serving primarily as chaperones for the females, Alan and Barham waited patiently for their return.

Soon, the girls were on the beach, looking like twins with their open pale-blue parasols, matching straw boaters with pale-blue silk bands, and navy-blue woolen and cotton bathing dresses with white trim.

Richard returned from the changing room clad in his white-belted, white-trimmed navy-blue woolen bathing suit bottom with coordinated shirt, and a dapper straw boater with a red-and-black striped band.

"What a wonderful day for the beach!" Richard called out as he approached the girls. "This is a beautiful place! I've never seen anything quite like it!"

"It's lovely, isn't it?" replied Joanna. "And the clouds seem to be breaking a little. We might even get some sunshine today."

"Are you going to take a splash in the water, girls? It looks irresistible to me."

"Perhaps . . . in a little while." Amy answered. "We're just enjoying sitting here in the sand right now."

"Well, all right. But here I go!"

Richard sprinted toward the waves and soon was splashing in the surf like a boy ten years his junior.

"He seems to be enjoying himself." remarked Joanna. "Looks like a boy at play!"

"Looks like a *man* to me!" countered Amy.

The girls broke out giggling together.

Hearing the laughter, Richard jogged back up to where they were sitting.

"What's so funny?"

"Oh . . . nothing." Joanna answered. "Fine day, isn't it?"

Richard looked puzzled. "Yes. A fine day, indeed."

Joanna and Amy couldn't find a way to look directly at Richard.

"A fine day for a nice walk on the beach, Joanna . . . don't you agree?" asked Richard, after an uncertain pause. "I've heard a great deal about your father, and I'd like to know more about him. Will you walk with me?"

Joanna was surprised at his invitation, partly because it came out of the blue and partly because she was surprised by his interest in her father.

"I . . . I would be happy to." was her reply.

They walked slowly north along the beach, the sun now peeking in and out of the clouds, making cloud shadows on the undulating ocean. White squawking gulls soared overhead, hoping for some form of edible handout. Pelican formations skimmed the ocean surface behind the relatively small breakers, searching for fish near the surface. A gentle breeze pushed her long auburn hair away from her face and over her shoulders as they sauntered forward in bare feet, the music of the waves breaking gently on the shore.

They stopped for a moment to watch the ocean.

"Look, Joanna. Look how the cloud shadows float across the water. Water in the shadows is gray, but in the sunshine the water reflects the beautiful blue of the sky. What a wonderful pattern in motion!

"Cloudy skies make the ocean dark and a little gloomy. Sunny skies make it bright and uplifting. But the changing patterns seem more interesting and inspiring . . . and in a way, more beautiful than constant bright sunny skies alone."

They walked on.

"I understand your father was a remarkable man." he said. "A White man with empathy for the Black man. A peacemaker."

"I knew him only as a loving father . . . and my mother as a loving mother. I didn't know much about his politics."

"As I see it, it wasn't politics that drove him. He wanted everyone to be treated honorably, with fairness, respect, and dignity. I understand he gave his life . . . and your mother's life . . . for that."

"Fairness . . . fairness? Fairness in this world is fantasy! My father and mother were stolen from me. Where is the *fairness* in that? I saw them burned to death! I saw the men who burned them, but never their faces! I want to see their faces . . . the faces of men who hate enough to murder those who never did them any wrong. They have never been found or punished for what they did to my father, the Black man he tried to save, my mother . . . and to me!"

Richard paused. "I doubt I ever could fully understand the intensity of your sorrow, Joanna. I can only imagine. But I do believe that you can be proud to be the daughter of your parents. They wanted a better world. Doubtless, his parents must have similarly influenced him, and that heritage is passed on to you."

"His parents?" Joanna said. "I don't even know who his parents were. I know Mister Alan and his wife Missus Rebecca raised him, but neither they nor Daddy ever wanted to talk about the details. Aunt Aila must know, but she won't talk about it either."

Her eyes searched the distant offing.

"What is her story?" questioned Joanna. "I really don't know her story either."

Chapter 48
JOANNA'S WEDDING
EARLY SUMMER 1903

⌁

THE OCCASION OF JOANNA'S JUNE MARRIAGE to Richard Walters would be a bittersweet gathering for everyone. The sadness of Rebecca Smith's death the previous year from typhoid fever still darkened the mood of Joanna's extended family and friends. Joanna felt a special connection to Rebecca as the woman who raised her father and served as a mother to Joanna herself.

The all-White guest list for the marriage ceremony at Gethsemane Church had been accepted by Manroe West, now the church's pastor. Joanna and Richard agreed to avoid offending church members by asking the "colored folks" staying at Aron and Sally's farmhouse not to attend the ceremony.

Instead, the bride and groom invited the Blacks to attend the wedding breakfast, since it was to be held at Alan Smith's farmhouse and not the church.

Alan's daughter Priscilla, and her husband James West, the reverend's son, did attend, along with Richard's Uncle Barham Walters and his daughter Amy, Joanna's close friend.

Joanna's family and friends, White and Black, gathered at the Smith farmhouse for the wedding breakfast after the wedding ceremony concluded at 11:30 a.m.

A traditional breakfast of bacon, fried and scrambled eggs, smoked link sausage, grits, sausage gravy, and buttermilk biscuits had been prepared by Aila and Ginny. A large vase of fragrant red roses graced the dining table. A Loblolly Bay flower adorned Joanna's auburn hair.

"That thur Sweet Bay flaher in yer hair sure is purdy." Aila told Joanna. "I 'member puttin' 'em mah hair too when I was young."

"Dat Sweet Bay sho brangs back good ol' mem'ries." agreed Mary Jane.

"Y'all need tuh come sit down, now!" announced Aila. "We need tuh bless this here food."

The guests cut short their conversations and eagerly took seats at the crowded dinner table and two smaller side tables.

"Before we git started, I want tuh say a few words 'bout Miz Rebecca." said Aila. "That woman . . . Alan's sweet wife . . . was one of the kindest, mose understandin' an' carin' Christian ladies I ever knowed. Fur Alan an' Miz Priscilla, she was the best wife an' mother anybody could ever hope for."

"She sho wuz." agreed Mary Jane.

"And we all miss her terribly." Ginny added.

Alan lowered his head, perhaps to conceal a tear.

"Thank y'all so much fur sayin' what's in yer hearts." expressed Priscilla. "We all loved her an' miss her now."

"Richard, yuh the head of this here getherin'." Priscilla continued. "Only fittin' yuh say the blessin'."

Surprised and unprepared for Priscilla's request, Richard had to think fast. He had heard blessings before at the Smith's home, but he had never been asked to give one himself.

"Let us pray." he said after some thought, bowing his head and closing his eyes. "Heavenly Father, we are thankful today for these blessings and all others received in thy name . . . Ah . . . we . . . we remember Missus Rebecca Smith today, Lord, and how much she meant to my lovely bride . . . and to Mister Alan Smith and Priscilla. Bless us on this special day in our lives . . . and bless all our friends and family here with us today . . . We ask these things in Jesus' name. Amen."

"A-men!" said everyone.

⌒

Following the meal, conversations broke out within the assembly. Richard had been waiting for an opportunity to converse with Aron, Andrew, and their wives. Having grown up in Maryland and now a resident of Chapel Hill, he didn't have a good sense of racial relations in the Cape Fear Region, especially considering the Wilmington riot of 1898.

"Well suh, we's been mo' skeered dan usual afta all dat riot happen." Aron explained. "We been worried dey gwaine come out here in de country an' go afta us all."

"We thought Reconstruction wuz gwaine he'p us, but den the gov'ment up north jes' kind-ah fo'got 'bout us." Andrew interrupted.

"Now dem Democrats took ova de gov'ment down here." added Aron. "An' dey's passin' all dem crazy votin' laws."

"The state constitution was changed tuh add a literacy test an' a poll tax." explained Alan.

"Yessuh." agreed Aron. "Now, all dat made votin' fo' culluds real hard. But it made votin' fo' poor White folks real hard too. But dey won' carin' nothin' fo' dem Whites ne'tha. All dey wanted wuz tuh keep the culluds from votin'."

"But it ain't jes' votin' rights we talkin 'bout." Andrew added. "We use tuh call 'em Black Codes . . . now, dey's *Jim Crow* laws. Dey keep us sep'rate from White folks, sep'rate from dere schools an' udda places. Schools is de big thang. Dey say 'sep'rate but equal' . . . but we all knows dey might be sep'rate, but dey sho ain't equal."

"Politics ain't got nothin' tuh do with a weddin'!" pronounced Priscilla, entering with a piping-hot coffee pot. "Anybody want coffee?"

Priscilla filled all the waiting cups and sought to steer the conversation toward happier topics. "Miz Aila, I know yuh're a talented fiddle player. We'd love tuh hear a tune er two from yuh."

"Oh, thank yuh, Miz Priscilla." Aila said, embarrassed. "But I never kin play in front of a crowd like this."

"You and Missus Ginny . . . and Missus Mary Jane . . . are all special ladies." Richard said. "I can well understand why you have been friends for so long."

"You all are remarkable ladies." agreed Joanna. "Daddy told me how special you all are, especially you, Aunt Aila. I've been wanting to ask you about your life and how you all became friends."

"Ain't much tuh know." replied Aila. "An' some of it . . . don't deserve tuh be told."

"I respect that, ma'am. Tell me what you can. What hardships did you face? I'd like to learn from you."

"Hardships? Don't know what yuh might thank is 'hard'. None of mah life . . . er none of the White folks here . . . ever had a life hard as Mary Jane an' the other colored folks had . . . an' still have."

"You're the only White person I know who has colored friends." said Joanna. "Most Whites think coloreds are beneath them."

"That jes' shows how ig'rant they are. All they see is thur black skins, thur diff'rent way of talkin', an' the way they was onest slaves under the White people. They kin't look inside an' see the goodness an' kindness thur."

"But how did you come to know that?"

"Well, Honey, back before that wah ended, we all stayed tuhgether on the farm Ginny's husband owned before he died. I was a indentured servant an' Mary Jane was one of his slaves. In the beginnin', I was skeered of her. I'd been told all kind-ah bad thangs 'bout slaves. But I got tuh know her an' learned she weren't much diff'rent from me."

"Yuh wuz skeered o' me?" asked Mary Jane. "Truth be knowed, I wuz skeered o' you. If'n I messed up an' said de wrong thang tuh yuh, I wuz sho tuh git twenty lashes."

"Yuh skeered me 'cause I didn't know no Black people." Aila admitted. "Y'all was a myst'ry tuh me. Thur was a time when I thought it was yer fault 'em crazy White men come an' beat us."

"Yuh still thank it wuz mah fault?"

"I don't know why I ever thought that." Aila replied. "I'm so sorry I did . . . an' I'm sorry I waited so long tuh say I'm sorry."

"'Bout time!" said Mary Jane. "It all kind-ah strange how we come tuh be friends, ain't it?"

"Friends?" replied Aila. "I thank that's the first time we've used that word fur each other. But it's true, an' it's past time we use it."

"What rich, bittersweet memories, Aunt Aila." said Joanna. "You really ought to write your memories down. I'd love to read them and pass them on to my children."

"Well, Honey, that does sound like a real good idea." said Aila.

Aila and Mary Jane sat in rockers on the front porch, immersing themselves in the sight and sound of rain softly falling on the Smiths' farmyard in the late afternoon.

"'Em footprints we left in the mud tuhday is done warshed away." observed Aila. "Kind-ah like us after we done passed on."

"Naw, ma'am." objected Mary Jane. "We ain't fo'got afta we gone. De Lawd 'memba us, fo' sho. Our fam'ly an' friends 'memba us."

"But what 'bout when they're gone too?" argued Aila. "I kin't 'member mah granddaddy an' grandma. I don't even know who they was."

"I ain't worried none 'bout dat." Mary Jane countered. "We all gwaine be tuhgatha in Heaven. I reckins Jesus gwaine need tuh intraduce evabody. Some o' dem might done gone tuh Hell, but it still gwaine be crowded up dere, afta all dem thousands o' years o' dead folks keep comin'. All dat intraducin' might jes' take fo'eva! An' dey gwaine need some kind-ah big outhouse too!"

Both women chuckled at Mary Jane's insights as Alan came out the front door onto the porch.

"What's so funny, ladies?" Alan asked.

"Oh, just women's talk." explained Aila. "Yuh know how silly we kin be! Come an' join us, Alan."

"I jes' want tuh thank yuh all fur sayin' all 'em good thangs 'bout Rebecca." said Alan, still standing. "It a'ways makes me feel better tuh hear yuh cared so much fur her."

Aila fixed her eyes on Alan, gathering courage to ask the questions that had been surging inside her since she learned of Rebecca's death.

"What yuh plannin' tuh do now, Alan?" she asked, trying to appear innocent.

"Well now." he began. "I ain't sure. I'm sixty-eight now. Maybe let Priscilla an' James take over the farm. Er maybe Aron might want tuh buy it. It's clear I'm gonna be real lonesome here by mahself."

"I 'spect yuh *will* be lonesome." Aila agreed. "Now, yuh jes' 'member . . . yuh're a'ways welcome tuh come visit us at Jacob's farm."

Aila and Mary Jane looked at each other in silence, as if to mutually agree that Aila needed to be alone with Alan. Mary Jane conveyed her goodnight wishes as she departed for Aron and Sally's farmhouse.

Aila and Alan fell silent, glancing at each other to see who would speak first.

"I been . . . I been wantin' tuh talk tuh yuh fur some time now 'bout somethin' real important." Alan finally said. "But the courage won't in me."

Aila suppressed a gasp. "An' what is that, Mister Alan?"

"Kin I . . . kin I sit, ma'am?" Alan shuddered. "That thur rockin' chair looks mighty relaxin'."

Aila nodded approval.

"Yuh know, Miz Aila, it's been 'bout a year since Rebecca passed. Mah health ain't been so good, an' I'm gittin' 'mose too ol' tuh run mah farm. I thank it's time fur me tuh stop an' take it easy."

Alan paused. Aila waited.

"I ain't got much more time on this here earth, but I want tuh ask if'n we . . . yuh an' me . . . kin spend it tuhgether."

"Yuh mean . . . live tuhgether, Alan?"

"I mean git married. I ain't gonna be livin' in sin. Now, I know it's real late in life fur it, but we might as well be happy, if'n we kin be.

"Aila, yuh been in mah heart fur a long time, even when Rebecca was alive, but thur won't no way I would be unfaithful tuh her. But a man kin love more than one person in his life. Rebecca knew that. She knew yuh cared fur me, but she never resented it. She understood. I'm hopin' yuh still care fur me . . . 'cause I still care fur yuh."

"Good heavens, Alan! I've loved yuh ever since that first mule ride we took tuhgether tuh ol' Preacher Campbell's place back when I was fourteen. I been waitin' all mah life tuh show mah love fur yuh!"

The two arose from their chairs and embraced as if the promise of their lives had been fulfilled.

"Of course, we kin marry. That'd make me the happiest woman alive!"

Chapter 49
THE EPIDEMIC
October 1919

Wɪᴛʜ ɪᴛs sɪɢɴᴀᴛᴜʀᴇ ᴄʟɪᴄᴋɪᴛʏ-ᴄʟᴀᴄᴋ, the train rocked and bumped along its tracks. The boy adjusted the gauze mask covering his nose and mouth and stared vacantly out the open passenger car window at the vast tan-and-brown soybean fields awaiting harvest.

"Dad, I'm so tired of wearing this silly mask." the boy complained to the man seated next to him. "I see a lot of people who aren't wearing them."

"It's better to be safe, Owen." Richard Walters answered. "Some people just don't like to be told what to do, even when it's in their best interest and the best interest of society."

Joanna Walters was seated across the aisle from her husband and son. "Listen to your father, Owen. This is a dangerous time. Remember Cousin Amy? She died from the Spanish Flu last year. And we don't need you to be your contrary self on this trip."

"I'm not contrary on purpose, Mother. I just have to see value in things I'm told to do."

"You're fifteen now, Owen. I want to make certain you understand that you have to act grown up and be nice to my family while we're down east."

"I never figured out who everybody was when we were down there for Cousin Amy's funeral. Am I going to see a whole new group of strangers this time? Those people seemed really primitive to me.

There was no electricity or telephones . . . water came from a bucket in a well. Those outhouses were repulsive."

"We're going to a different farm . . . Aunt Aila's place south of Wilmington . . . but it won't be much different from Cousin Alan's old farm in Brunswick. *Primitive* is much too strong a term. They do have simpler lives than folks in Chapel Hill, but they have many redeeming qualities . . . strong family ties, neighbors help neighbors, integrity, strong religious values."

Owen frowned. "I don't understand their religion. It makes me *really* uncomfortable."

"You have to be more understanding and tolerant, Owen." declared Richard. "Their culture is different from your experience, but that doesn't mean you shouldn't respect them . . . their customs and beliefs."

The train slowed, and one short blast of the whistle sounded, indicating an approach to a station. A dense, boiling gray cloud of coal smoke erupted from the engine stack as the train came to a hissing stop at the station platform.

Owen stared through the window at what seemed a mere cross-roads apparently named "Selma." "Seems as if we stop every half hour for some little town."

"We change to the Atlantic Coast Line at Goldsboro, the next stop, in about twenty miles." explained Richard.

Owen groaned. "We're never going to get there! How much longer?"

Richard frowned. "I'd say another six hours or so. That's sure better than two days by horse and carriage or a day and a half by Model T."

"Criminy!" the boy bellowed. "It'll be after dark before we get there!"

"Watch your language!" admonished his mother.

⁓

Alan greeted the travelers at the new Wilmington Union Station in light rain with his covered two-horse surrey. More than a few people wore the gauze masks Owen despised. Richard helped Alan with the suitcases, while the rest of the group took seats in the surrey. Alan and Richard took the driver's bench.

Two quick tongue clicks and a firm slap of the reins on the two horses' rumps started the surrey wheels bumping down the brick street pavement.

Owen was surprised to see electric and telephone lines paralleling the streets and impressive homes and public buildings lining Third and Market Streets. Considering the general elegance of the architecture, he also was surprised to see numerous privies partially concealed behind hedgerows.

Leaving the town behind them, they headed down Federal Point Road. Other vehicles busily passed by on the road, some Model Ts, farm trucks, mule- and horse-drawn wagons and carriages, faster-moving traffic than Owen expected.

"What's that awful smell?" Owen asked.

"A petroleum coating they spread to keep the dust down and help hold the gravel in place." explained Richard.

Intrigued, Owen watched the cotton fields pass by, filled with teams of Black men, women, and children picking cotton from the bolls and stuffing it into burlap bags strapped over their shoulders. Bright-white cotton bolls carpeted the landscape into the distance, like a fantasy of snow on the black soil.

Alan turned the surrey from the gravel surface onto a dirt path, barely wide enough for two vehicles to pass, winding through thick pine and oak woods and occasionally fording shallow-running creek beds.

As they rounded a curve, a farmhouse and several smaller outlying houses and cabins came into view. It seemed to be a small village of dwellings, separated by a large farmyard.

Alan stopped the surrey in front of the largest house.

Lit by lamplight, Alan started a small fireplace blaze to help take off the evening chill as Robert, Mary Jane and Andrew Martin, and

Joanna's family found seats in the front room of Aila's farmhouse. Soon, the conversation turned toward the epidemic.

Joanna shook her head in bewilderment. "So many people sick and dying. I read it killed over 100 people in Wilmington. Thirty or more in Brunswick County."

"I heard 10,000 or more have died across the state." Richard added. "In Chapel Hill, we've had a lot of people get seriously ill. The president of the university died from it, and so did his successor."

"I heared before it's over, 'cross the country it might kill as many as the Civil Wah did." added Robert.

"Hospitals have been swamped." said Richard. "The government banned public gatherings and quarantined the sick, but neither could be enforced. People ought to be wearing masks, but not many are."

"Dat mus' be de hand o' God at work." Mary Jane observed.

Owen could not withhold comment. "You really think God is interested in our daily lives and punishes some people with death, while letting other people live because He likes them?"

Richard glared at his son. "Don't be disrespectful of someone's religion, Owen."

Joanna added her rebuke. "You'll have to forgive my son, Mary Jane. We've miserably failed in our vigorous attempts to educate him in traditions of civility."

"Dere's a burnin' cross an' a mob o' men out dere in white robes an' hoods!" Mary Jane screamed as she stared wide-eyed through the kitchen window. "Look like dey roped an' draggin' Tootsie in de dirt! Good Lawd! Dey gwaine lynch 'im!"

Aila, Alan, and Robert rushed to the window.

"Everbody jes' stay here inside!" shouted Alan. "An' stay away from the winders. I'm goin' tuh talk some sense intuh 'em!" Without pause, he and Robert dashed through the kitchen and out the walkway door to confront the men.

Owen couldn't believe his eyes. "What's going on, Mother?"

"Those are Klansmen!" Joanna answered. "Looks like they've come to punish Tootsie for some reason!"

"You mean the KKK? I didn't know this kind of thing really happened! Are they after us too?"

"They might be." answered Aila. "They're likely mad 'bout us Whites mixin' with coloreds. Won't be the first time. Right now they're goin' fur Tootsie, but they might be comin' fur us too!"

Owen couldn't contain himself. "I can't believe it's happening! What did Tootsie do to deserve this?"

"It's happened too many times before!" Joanna cried. "Listen, Owen, don't you go anywhere near the windows!"

"What in hell yuh thank yuh're doin' tuh that man?" Robert demanded, challenging the Klansmen with Alan at his side.

"Well, if it ain't that that faggot nigger lover!" yelled one of the Klansmen from behind his hood. "An' that nigger-lovin' preacher from Brunswick County we heared so much 'bout. We kin jes' add 'em both tuh the stew we're cookin' up. A li'l extrie seas'nin'!"

"Untie that man!" ordered Alan, marching into the fray. "He ain't done nothin' tuh you."

"What yuh gonna do?" laughed a second Klansman. "They's jes' two of you, an' they's six of us. Good odds, I'd say."

Two other Klansmen lunged at Alan, grabbing his arms and shoving him to the ground. One pushed Alan's head into the dirt with his foot, drew his revolver, and pressed it against Alan's skull.

Robert bolted to help but was knocked to the ground from behind with a baseball bat.

"Git up, faggot!" ordered the man. "Git over thur with 'em niggers!"

They jerked Robert off the ground, the pistol jammed into his side, and pushed him and Alan to stand with Tootsie. Another Klansman grabbed a whip from his horse's saddlebag and began whipping the three captives, while a third began fashioning two rope nooses to complement the one already at hand.

A thunderous pistol blast struck the revolver-holding Klansman in the rear of his right leg, toppling him to the ground with a scream, abruptly ending the whipping. Aila stood alone, still aiming the vintage Colt revolver Robert had given her almost fifty years earlier.

She waved the Colt back and forth from one white-hooded vigilante to another. "Who's next?" None moved, as the one wounded man lay moaning on the ground.

"Nobody? Then git 'im up an' git the hell off mah farm! Now!"

The men pulled their wounded comrade up and placed him on his horse, where he lurched forward and vomited into the animal's mane. Following suit, the other terrorists mounted their horses and rode into the darkness.

Contrary to Alan's orders, Owen stared out the farmhouse window, fixated on the scene that had unfolded before him, now etched in his memory.

Chapter 50

THE AWAKENING

CHRISTMAS 1919

⌒

Wʜɪᴛᴇ-ᴄᴇᴅᴀʀ ᴡʀᴇᴀᴛʜs ɢʀᴇᴇᴛᴇᴅ ᴠɪsɪᴛᴏʀs to Aila's home on exterior doors, and the front room was decorated with a red-cedar Christmas tree, cut from the woods on the farm and decorated with handmade ornaments and wax candles. White and red cedar branches, red-berried American holly, and mistletoe sprigs adorned doorways and windows. The blazing fireplace warmed the winter chill.

"Merry Christmas! Y'all come in!" Aila answered the front door knock and welcomed Mary Jane, Andrew, Tootsie, and Hannah. "Y'all a'ready know Robert here, and mose of yuh know Joanna, Richard, an' Owen here from Chapel Hill. We're happy tuh have everbody join us fur Christmas."

As Aila finished those introductions, the door creaked open again. "An' here's Jacob, Edna, an' thur twin girls, Verna an' Cleo."

"Happy Christmas, everbody!" Jacob chuckled.

Aila gave welcome hugs to Jacob and each member of his family. "Y'all jes' in time tuh sit down fur Christmas dinner."

The group clustered and took their seats around the table, chattering all the while, until Aila announced the call to prayer. "Now, let's all bow our heads while Robert sez grace."

Robert arose from his chair, closed his eyes, and began the blessing. At a loss for protocol, Owen lowered his chin slightly and glanced around the room to see what others were doing.

His prayer completed, Robert continued the celebration. "Now, y'all what been here before know we got a tradition of sangin' the first verse of 'Silent Night' before we start the meal." Robert continued. "I'm askin' Miz Ginny if'n she'll start it out fur us."

Ginny started the first line softly, then the others joined in. Owen marveled at the quite reverence and comforting harmony of the singing, the first time he has ever hear the carol sung so *silently*, so sincerely.

Owen was both amazed and repulsed by the quantity and variety of food laid out by Aila and Ginny on the Christmas table. Hog head cheese and pickled pigs' feet; venison hash; smoked ham; breaded fried chicken and quail; baked sweet potatoes; mashed Irish potatoes; fatback-seasoned collards and black-eyed peas; buttermilk lard biscuits and cornbread.

As instructed, everyone lined up to fill their plates, all the while engaged in buzzing conversation, punctuated with sporadic laughter.

The meal finished, the table cleared, and the dishes washed and put away, the group gathered around the fireplace for Christmas music on fiddle, banjo, and piano by Aila, Tootsie, and Ginny. After the holiday music, Robert and Jacob rearranged the furniture for dancing. Foot-tappin' string band and do-si-doin' barn dance tunes filled the room. A few couples squeezed into the small space in front of the fireplace to tread a measure.

After a while, even Owen smiled and clapped in time.

The Christmas afternoon festivities finished, the larger group of family and friends departed for their homes, and only Aila, Alan, Ginny, Robert, Mary Jane, Andrew, Joanna, Richard, and Owen remained by the fire.

"Missus Martin . . . Mary Jane . . . I think it's so sweet that you named little Aila for Aunt Aila. You two must go way back."

"Yessum, way back 'fo dat dere Civil Wah ended. We all stayed tuhgetha on dis here farm what Ginny's husband owned. Miz Aila wuz one o' dem indenture servants an' Tootsie, Aron, mah mamma an' daddy, an' me wuz slaves, 'long wid some udda Black folks."

"I heared all sorts of bad thangs 'bout Black folks." explained Aila. "But I learned she won't much diff'rent from me. We liked a lot of the same thangs, an' we both had some bad thangs happen tuh us. But she was much stronger than me, an' I learned tuh look up tuh her. We become close, but we had tuh be careful 'bout bein' close, 'cause it was dangerous."

Owen's curiosity was aroused. "Dangerous? Why was it dangerous?"

"On account o' Black folks an' White folks might git beat up er lynched fo' mixin' tuhgetha." Mary Jane answered for Aila. "Yuh seen some o' dat wen yuh wuz down here back las' fall. An' dey even kin git burned alive. Dat how mah Andrew here lose his daddy."

"I'm so sorry for you, Andrew." said Joanna in sympathy. "My daddy and mamma were burned alive in the same way."

"Your parents were burned in a fire, Mother?" asked Owen. "Was it arson? Was it the Klan?"

"They was called 'Red Shirts' back then." Robert clarified. "We all knowed they murdered Joanna's parents. But the law never did nothin' 'bout it."

"That was the worst experience of my life." said Joanna, drying her eyes. "I felt so helpless . . . I saw the men who did it . . . I saw them burn my parents alive . . . and I could do nothing to stop it."

Aila came to Joanna's side and held her hands tightly. No one could speak. Owen suppressed the urge to weep.

"That must have been a really sad time, Mother." Owen said with a sincerity that surprised Joanna.

"It was deeply sad for all of us." Joanna explained. "But I know Aunt Aila, Mary Jane . . . and just about everyone here has experienced a lot of real sadness and hard times."

"Oh . . . thur was many sad, hard times. Too many tuh name 'em all." Aila's voice trailed off as she realized she shouldn't name them all.

"Who owned this farm back then . . . when you all lived here?" asked Owen.

Staring directly at Owen, Ginny tried to answer. "James Sanders owned it. He was my husband, don't you see? Ah . . . what is your name again, young man? Are we related?"

"Well . . . my name is Owen, Missus Sanders . . . Miz Ginny. I'm not sure we're related."

"Then why are you here? Why are you in my house?"

Aila tried to clarify. "Ginny, Owen is Joanna's son . . . yuh 'member Joanna, mah niece, don't yuh?"

"Well now, Aila. You know as well as I do . . . you don't have a niece. You don't have a brother or a sister, so how could you have a niece?"

"Ginny, let's try not tuh confuse these folks." asked Aila gently. "Yuh know how lately yuh git confused an' kin't 'member thangs sometimes."

Aila maneuvered back to the former subject. "He was a good man, James was. But he beat me at times, an' . . . "

"He wasn't that good." Ginny objected, now alert. "He beat me too, Aila . . . an' the slaves, even when they did nothing wrong. I still see his red, angry face. I'll never marry him . . . or anybody else . . . ever again."

Aila allowed some reflective silence before continuing. "A lot of sad times. When Gideon went blind . . . drunk all the time . . . beat me an' mah children. When mah sweet Elizabeth got sick . . . an' when she died. When Boo-Boo was murdered in that Wilmin'ton riot. When mah sweet Calum an' Joanna's mamma was kilt in that far."

Joanna dried tears again. "So, Daddy . . . Calum . . . was your nephew?" she tried to clarify.

"Yuh kin thank of 'im like that, if'n yuh want." Aila evaded the question, then continued.

"An' when I birthed an' lost all 'em children . . . had tuh watch 'em die, he'pless. But the hardest was mah sweet Elizabeth . . . she suffered so much . . . she died . . . in mah arms."

The room was quiet as Aila wept. "I miss Calum so much."

"Maybe it's time to move on and ask about your happiest times." proposed Joanna.

"Happy times?" Aila reflected. "Ever time me an' Mary Jane went down tuh the river tuh watch the sunset. When I found that Sweet Bay flaher down thur. When Ginny played her pianer . . . that moonlight song. Ever time Calum come tuh visit er I went tuh visit him. Ever time Elizabeth smiled . . . lot of happy times fur one life."

"You are a beautiful human being, Aunt Aila." Joanna whispered. "I hope and pray that I can be as special as you."

"I jes' try mah best tuh do the right thang. I ain't no more special than any other woman an' mother what tries tuh do the right thang."

"As I've said before, you really ought to write down your memories. I'd love to read them and pass them on to my children."

"That's one of mah secrets, Joanna. I been keepin' a journal fur over fifty years now. An' I make drawin's too. I'm plannin' tuh pass mah journal an' mah drawin's on tuh yuh someday . . . on account of yuh're . . . yuh're the chile of . . . of mah fave-rit nephew."

Owen was perplexed. "Your favorite nephew? How many brothers and sisters did you have, Aunt Aila? How many children?"

"Eight. I birthed eight children. Four of 'em died at birth er before they was growed up. One was kilt when he was a man."

"And who was he?" Joanna asked. "And how many brothers and sisters did you have?"

The weight of her painful memories bore down on her. She could no longer keep that secret either.

"I ain't never had no brothers er sisters." she spoke just above a whisper. "Ginny was right. I ain't got no nephews er nieces. The truth is . . . yer daddy . . . Calum was mah first baby."

Silence. Aila stared at the floor, then the blazing fireplace.

"Then I'm your granddaughter, not your niece." Joanna exclaimed. "And Owen is your great-grandson. Why . . . why didn't you want us to know that?"

"On account o' she felt . . . shamed." Mary Jane explained. "She love her son, but dere wuz too much pain tuh 'member whur he come from . . . an' how she had tuh give 'im up."

"What do you mean?" Owen asked. "What pain . . . what shame? Why did she have to give him up?"

"She won't married wen the seed dat made Calum wuz put in her belly, don' yuh undastand?" was Mary Jane's firm reply. "She wuz attacked by a man wat won' her husband, forced aghen her will. Gideon made her tuh give her baby tuh Alan an' Rebecca tuh raise."

All eyes were on Aila. No one spoke.

"I *was* ashamed, Joanna . . . *ashamed* of what happened tuh me an' whur he come from. There was too much pain there. An' when Calum was kilt, somethin' died in me. I kept mah story inside tuh protect the memory of 'im . . . tuh protect me from people's ridicule an' pity . . . tuh protect his children from that awful story."

"You didn't need to protect us." Joanna declared. "What we needed was . . . and still is . . . to know and treasure your story. It is our treasure now."

Ginny awoke from her daze. "I remember now. I remember . . . Samuel was messed up in his head . . . soldier's heart . . . a drunkard. He came home and attacked Aila. Gideon made Aila send baby Calum away to be raised by Alan and Rebecca."

"But we treated each other like mother an' son, anyways." Aila reflected. "Mah heart ached fur 'im. I wrote all this down in mah journal, Johanna. Someday, that journal's gonna be yers tuh read . . . read, know, an' 'member."

———

Chapter 51

RECONCILIATION

Late December 1919

⤳

THE TWO TRAMPED THROUGH THE FROZEN MUD of the conifer and deciduous woods in the cold air of the late afternoon, their faces red from the cold and randomly scratched by the briar and bramble overhanging the narrow pathway.

"How far did she say it was?" Owen asked. "Seems as if nobody has been on this path for ages."

"She didn't say." Joanna answered.

The pathway widened and opened into a view of the sun over the river in the western sky, partially hidden by scattered clouds.

"I don't see that cypress log she was talking about." Owen said. "Maybe that's what's left of it . . . there, almost covered with mud. And there's the old pine tree still standing. I've never seen one that big!"

"It *is* a beautiful view of the river." confirmed Joanna.

"This place could be made into a nice little park."

"I think she probably likes it just the way it is, Owen."

"She's so hard to understand, Mother. I still have unanswered questions. Hard to imagine the life she's lived. I always thought the simple people down here lived simple lives."

"Owen, that just shows how wrong you are to stereotype. You can be such an elitist at times."

The sun continued its slow path toward the horizon, casting brilliant rays and shades of red, yellow, and purple on the sky, water, and scattered clouds. Aila, Ginny, and Mary Jane emerged from the pathway, pausing at the opening to absorb the scene.

"That cypress log we used tuh sit on has done worked its way intuh the ground." observed Aila.

"But dat dere big pine tree's still standin'." Mary Jane added. "Thangs done changed. But in a lot o' ways it still de same."

"I just so glad we've been able to spend time with you and everyone." Joanna said. "It's been like a family homecoming."

"It's real nice tuh have everbody here this Christmas." agreed Aila. "Fam'lies kin be God's gift tuh us, if'n we let 'em."

"Sometimes, we don' see how much fam'ly means." Mary Jane said. "We don' a'ways see how much we learn from folks dat's close tuh us."

Aila nodded in agreement. "I learned so much from you, Mary Jane. It took us a long time fur us tuh call each other 'friends'. But truth be knowed, we was more like sisters most of our life. I'm so sorry White folks has made it so hard on yuh, yer family, an' all Black folks. I wish I done more tuh change all that."

Mary Jane embraced her "sister." "Dey's only so much one person kin do, Aila. Yuh done he'p me as much as yuh kin . . . an' yuh made mah life so bright."

"Yuh made mah life bright too, Mary Jane . . . An' *you* was mah guidin' light, Ginny. Yuh taught me tuh read a' write. An' yuh taught me so much 'bout life . . . he'ped me better understand folks."

"You're like a daughter to me." said Ginny.

The three women group-hugged as Joanna watched, tears in her eyes.

"I knows y'all's heart is in de right place." Mary Jane added. "Dem otha White folks won' let yuh do much mo' dan yuh did."

Aila nodded with sadness. "We fought that damn wah . . . all yer people was set free . . . y'all tried tuh make a life fur yerself as free people. Then they took it all back, pushed y'all back down an' kept yuh there."

"But what can be done to stop it?" asked Owen. "Are some White people ever going to stop hating Black people? Are they ever going to let them to be as free and equal as White people?"

"Too many folks want tuh drive us all apart tuh serve thur own selfish purpose." Aila said reflectively. "But that ain't right. We need tuh brang ourselves all tuhgether. Our Black sisters an' brothers done come a long way from slavery, but there's still a long way tuh go. We gotta work tuhgether tuh git there."

"We kin see clare what the world is now. The Kingdom of God is . . . what this world can be. The lives we all live will make that Kingdom come . . . not up in the sky somewhur, but right here on this world. The only thangs what really matters is the life we live here in this world an' what we pass on tuh future generations.

"We're put on this earth tuh he'p each other . . . tuh share goodness an' kindness. We kin't furgit the sins of our fathers, but we kin learn from 'em an' pass that wisdom down tuh our children . . . jes' like life gits passed down tuh new life when the seed is planted. The planted seed, nourished an' protected, will yield a bountiful harvest.

"Why else are we on this here earth fur anyways?"

No one could speak. They looked away from Aila to view the sky and the river, still aflame in color. The tranquil breeze that had been rustling the bushes and fallen leaves around them slowly faded to reveal the sound of horse hooves in the mud behind them.

Turning, they saw six masked Klansmen on horseback, aiming an assortment of rifles, shotguns, and pistols directly at them.

"No! . . . No!" Aila screamed, her voice choking off as she ran out of breath. She knew she should have brought Robert's Colt revolver.

The End

ABOUT THE AUTHOR

CHARLES M. CLEMMONS was born at home in the countryside near Clayton, North Carolina, on what is now an educational state forest. Growing up in the American South, working on his father's farm, and exploring 300 acres of forest accompanied solely by his faithful dog Snowball, proved to be formative life experiences.

He received an engineering degree from NC State University in 1966; an MBA from the University of Connecticut in 1976; and an AAS degree in Film & Video Technology from North Lake College in Irving, Texas, in 1994.

Retiring from a corporate career in telecommunications in 1994 at age fifty, he refocused on his real passions: documentary filmmaking, photography, and discovering the history and lifeways of his parents' families in Brunswick County, North Carolina.

In 2004, he was awarded two Boston/New England Emmys® (writing and production) for the American Public Television documentary, *Mystic Voices: The Story of the Pequot War*. After forty years in Connecticut, Charles returned to his roots in North Carolina in 2016.

His inspiration for *Aila's Journal* came from his own experiences and aspirations growing up in the American South, his own family's oral history, and his historical research of the Civil War and Southern Reconstruction. *Aila's Journal* is his first novel.

For further information, visit www.wiltonwood.com.

Printed in the USA
CPSIA information can be obtained
at www.ICGtesting.com
LVHW052134270723
753705LV00015B/61/J